M. A. Hunter has been a huge fan of crime fiction series since a young age and always fancied the idea of trying to write one. That dream became a reality when One More Chapter signed The Missing Children Case Files.

Born in Darlington in the north-east of England, Hunter grew up in West London, and moved to Southampton to study law at university. It's here that Hunter fell in love and has been married for fifteen years. They are now raising their two children on the border of The New Forest where they enjoy going for walks amongst the wildlife. They regularly holiday across England, but have a particular affinity for the south coast, which formed the setting for the series, spanning from Devon to Brighton, and with a particular focus on Weymouth, one of their favourite towns.

When not writing, Hunter can be found binge-watching favourite shows or buried in the latest story from Angela Marsons, Simon Kernick, or Ann Cleeves.

twitter.com/Writer_MAHunter

Also by M. A. Hunter

The Missing Children Case Files

Isolated

Trafficked

Discarded

Repressed

Exposed

RANSOMED

The Missing Children Case Files

M. A. HUNTER

One More Chapter
a division of HarperCollins*Publishers* Ltd
1 London Bridge Street
London SE1 9GF
www.harpercollins.co.uk

This paperback edition 2020

First published in Great Britain in ebook format
by HarperCollins*Publishers* 2020

A catalogue record of this book
is available from the British Library

ISBN: 978-0-00-844328-3

Printed and bound in Great Britain by
CPI Group (UK) Ltd, Croydon CR0 4YY

Dedicated to all the key workers who kept the world ticking during Lockdown 2020

There I walked, and there I raged;
The spiritual savage caged
Within my skeleton, raged afresh
To feel, behind a carnal mesh,
The clean bones crying in the flesh.

– *Full Moon*, Elinor Wylie

Chapter One

THEN

Rickmansworth, Hertfordshire

'I can't find Cassie Hilliard,' Gerry Connors declared, his Belfast accent betraying the rising panic in his voice as he stepped through the patio door.

Penny finished counting the party bags on the kitchen counter, trying to prove to herself that she hadn't underestimated how many were needed. 'What do you mean you can't find her? She must be outside somewhere.'

Gerry turned and stared back out across the vast expanse of lawn, where the fully inflated castle wobbled as a dozen or so princesses and pirates threw themselves about inside. From here it was difficult to see the wild and overgrown end of the garden where Sean loved to while away the summer holidays building dens out of fallen branches and plant pots he had managed to scavenge from his mother's greenhouse.

'She's not with the other children,' Gerry repeated, his eyes dancing over the faces of those inside the castle, searching for six-year-old Cassie.

Frustrated with the interruption, Penny Connors joined her husband at the patio door, staring out into the garden. 'Have you asked Sean where she is? Or any of the others? Maybe she's talking to a friend behind the castle.'

Gerry stepped out into the garden, the late September sun warm enough that coats weren't required, but not warm enough to worry about sun lotion. He'd opted for tailored shorts and the Avengers T-shirt Sean had given him for his birthday the month before. 'I'll go and have another look,' he said, moving forward into the garden, his mind already wandering to the potential repercussions of explaining to Richard Hilliard that he'd lost his daughter.

'Okay, well I'll double-check she hasn't come inside,' Penny said affirmatively, less troubled than her husband. 'She's probably just in the toilet or something.'

Penny took a final glance at the party bags before moving through into the dining room where the spread of sausage rolls, finger sandwiches, crisps, pizzas, and chocolates looked good enough for a king to consume. Sean's seventh birthday party had been months in the planning, and after much debate with Gerry, they'd finally settled on hosting a gathering for all of Sean's class at their house. Certainly cheaper than hiring a venue or taking them all bowling as Sean had requested.

'Money is tight,' Gerry had reminded her every day since he had been made redundant from the factory, and she couldn't help but feel proud of what she'd achieved on such a tight budget. She hadn't told Gerry that she'd borrowed an extra hundred pounds from her sister to buy Sean the handheld console he'd desperately been craving.

No sign of Cassie in this room, and although they'd told their guests that they weren't to come into the dining room until feeding time, she could see a hand-shaped gap in one of the crisp bowls; she ducked to look beneath the table. Penny closed the door as she left, and stepped into the living room. The mountain of brightly wrapped gifts the party guests had brought stood beneath the bay window, and to the right of that was the large black rubbish sack they'd started filling as Sean had torn into his gifts from them first thing this morning. With the sofas flush against the walls, there really wasn't any place to hide, so Penny left the room, closing the door behind her again, and proceeded up the stairs of their three-bed semi-detached house.

Spotting the door to the bathroom closed, Penny moved across to it, and gently knocked. 'Cassie? Is that you in there?'

There was no answer, but Penny could hear the tearing of toilet paper, and waited patiently. This was followed by the flushing of water, taps turned on, taps turned off, and fumbling with the towel at the radiator. A moment later, the bathroom door opened, and a startled boy emerged.

'Oh, Jason, it's you,' Penny said, disappointment dripping from every word. 'You haven't seen Cassie Hilliard recently, have you?'

The boy stared back at her wide-eyed, slowly shaking his head, before hurrying past her and back down the stairs.

Such an odd boy, Penny thought to herself. Had she been able to, she wouldn't have sent an invitation to Jason Knightwood, but Sean had wanted practically everyone else to come over so it had felt harsh to single out those he didn't interact with as much. Of course, none of the children really interacted with Jason. Penny didn't know for sure whether there was a reason why he rarely spoke but there was more to it than that. Although she'd just heard him washing his hands, the pong emanating from his body hadn't escaped her. Jason's mother was just as difficult to engage with, arriving at the school in a ratty headscarf and moth-bitten cardigan every day, always staring at her feet, and making no effort at small talk with the other parents.

Penny continued her search of the upstairs, but with their own bedroom locked, it didn't take long to complete a circuit of Sean's messy room – resembling the aftermath of a burglary as it always did – and the spare room which was still filled with boxes they'd yet to go through following their move nearly two years ago. Heading back down the stairs, Penny made her way back through the kitchen and out into the garden. Gerry was nowhere in sight, and she could only assume he'd found Cassie.

Excited squeals echoed off the bouncy castle, almost drowning out the incessant hum of the machine keeping it inflated. It was nearly four o'clock, and the afternoon sun was already hanging low in the sky beyond the wild trees and fence at the foot of the garden. Gerry's head appeared from behind a tree, and she waved, but he didn't seem to notice her as he bent and stooped, and Penny's heart skipped a beat as she realised he was still searching for Cassie.

Upping her pace, Penny darted to the bouncy castle, her eyes scanning the faces and costumes inside as she tried to recall exactly what Cassie had been wearing. Picturing the moment when Elizabeth Hilliard had arrived, carrying a parasol for the short trip from the chauffeur-driven Range Rover to the front door, Penny couldn't forget the involuntary urge she'd felt to curtsy. It was silly really; it wasn't like

Elizabeth Hilliard was *actual* royalty, although rumour had it she was some distant cousin of the Earl of Wessex. Wearing an expensive-looking cerise-coloured coat, she'd pulled a face when she'd offered to stay and help supervise the crowd of children. Penny hadn't wanted to disappoint, and had waved away the offer, telling her that some of the other parents were already inside helping, even though the two mums who had offered to help had cried off at the last minute.

Cassie had been hiding bashfully behind her mum's perfectly tanned legs until Penny had crouched and told her how pretty she looked in her luminescent green dress and cherry-red wig.

Penny snapped her fingers together: Cassie had come dressed as Ariel, the little mermaid from the film of the same name, not the eccentric Shakespearean spirit. Of course she had!

Staring back towards the pirates and princesses dashing from one side of the castle to the other, some tumbling as they howled with laughter, there was no sign of a red wig.

'Has anyone seen Cassie?' Penny called into the group.

Either nobody heard her, or they chose not to listen.

'Sean?' she tried again. 'Sean, have you seen Cassie?'

Her son stopped and stared at her with the one eye not covered by a black eye patch, the bandana soaked through with sweat, before shrugging and running again.

'Sophia?' Penny called next, catching sight of the Moana-inspired outfit. 'Do you know where Cassie Hilliard is?'

Sophia bounced to the edge of the castle, before dismounting and landing on the soft mat where the shoes were scattered. 'What did you say?'

'I'm looking for Cassie Hilliard,' Penny said, her voice

tightening as the first pangs of paranoia took hold. 'Do you know where she is?'

Sophia wiped the wet fringe clinging to her forehead. 'She *was* here. I don't know. She said she wanted to go to the toilet.'

Penny's brow furrowed as she looked back at the house, certain she hadn't missed any obvious hiding places. She couldn't remember anyone passing through the kitchen, but then, she'd been focused on setting up the party bags, placing an equal number of sweets, stickers, toys, and party poppers in each. In fact, she hadn't noticed Jason Knightwood move past her and upstairs, so would she really have noticed Cassie Hilliard?

'Is everything okay?' Sophia asked, snapping Penny's attention back to the garden.

Penny forced a reassuring smile. 'Everything will be okay, sweetheart. Can you let Sean know we'll be going in for food in the next ten minutes or so?'

Sophia nodded, all concern wiped from her face, leaping back onto the castle, and re-joining the madness.

The wild side of their garden loomed beyond the castle and its pump. They'd planned to clear out the section and build a small summer house where they could unwind on a long summer's day. But problems with planning permission and then Gerry's redundancy meant the plans had been shelved, and so the throng of weeds and wild grasses towered above the freshly mown green lawn it bordered. Gerry was still moving about, lifting fallen branches, and rising and stooping as he went.

'She's not in the house,' Penny said nervously, as she joined him in the tall grass.

Gerry paused momentarily, out of breath, a fresh sheen

clinging to his cheeks. 'I've checked the fence and there are no holes she could have squeezed through to get out, and it's too high for a six-year-old to scale. I've been calling her name, but there's no response. Most of the ground here is uneven, and there are so many branches that it's impossible to see whether she might have fallen and bashed her head.'

Penny hadn't even considered that Cassie could be lying hurt somewhere. 'I think we need to get all the children together and ask them whether they know where she went.'

Gerry surveyed the rest of the wilderness, and slowly nodded. 'I'll keep checking out here just in case. It's not like anyone has come in and snatched her from under our noses!'

Penny reached for her husband's hand and squeezed tightly; he reflected her concern with an assured nod. 'She'll turn up. She has to.'

Returning to the castle, Penny hollered at the group of children and told them it was time to eat. One by one, they stopped rushing about, slowly disembarked and began the hunt for their shoes. After nineteen pairs had been located and pulled on, the panting group remained on the mat waiting for their next instruction.

'Cassie's wearing her shoes,' Penny whispered to Gerry as he joined her, pointing down at the mat. 'Whenever she left the castle, she put on her shoes.'

'Can anyone tell me where Cassie Hilliard is?' Gerry said, staring at each of the faces, looking for any sign of recognition. 'We can't go in for food until we've got everyone together. Has anyone seen Cassie?'

The faces remained blank, with the odd shrug of shoulders.

'Everyone just wait here a minute,' Penny said, putting on a brave face, before leading Gerry away from the group. 'What are we going to do? Should we phone the police?'

'It's a bit premature for that,' he replied. 'She must be here somewhere; if not in the garden then in the house—'

'I checked the house, Gerry,' Penny interrupted with a low growl. 'She is not in the house, and she is *not* in the garden. What if…' But she couldn't bring herself to finish the sentence.

'What if what?' Gerry began, before connecting the dots. 'You think someone's come in and taken her? Don't be ridiculous! We've both been here all day, and there hasn't been a spot of trouble. Besides, we would have seen someone.'

Penny eventually let out a frustrated sigh, knowing Gerry was trying to remain pragmatic. 'Well, if she is here, where the hell is she hiding?'

Wrapping a large arm around her shoulders, he pulled her closer to him, and kissed the top of her head. 'I don't know, but someone must. Get the other children inside and I'll check the security camera footage for the last hour and see if it caught her.' He paused. 'We'll find her. We *have* to find her. There's more than just her future at stake here.'

Chapter Two

NOW

Blackfriars, London

A champagne cork fires somewhere behind me and I start at the sudden eruption of cheering that accompanies the fizz as it explodes from the bottle.

'Can you pass me a glass, Emma?' my agent Maddie asks, stretching out her hand as if it's one of those claw-grabbing devices that children use to try and win impossibly angled stuffed toys at amusement arcades.

There's a pyramid of plastic flutes stacked on the cloth-covered shelving unit. It is a lame attempt to add a touch of class to the occasion and to make it appear that the room, surrounded by books, looks less like Maddie's cramped office and more like a privately hired venue fit for a celebration. There are three times more glasses than people gathered in the room, and I can't be certain if that's because Maddie overcompensated or because she was expecting more guests at the impromptu gathering. I reach for the flute atop the pyramid and hand it to her crab-like claw; she immediately places it beneath the rim of the bottle to intercept the out-of-control liquid.

'Here you go,' Maddie says, handing the half-full flute back to me. 'You should have the first taste, as you're the reason we're all gathered here today.'

I understand why she's so excited, but I'd rather be anywhere else than at a small party thrown in my honour. Being the centre of attention has always made my skin crawl. Even as a child, I would dread that moment every birthday when family and friends would gather to watch and sing as I attempted to blow out the candles on my birthday cake. At least that level of celebration stopped after my seventh birthday – every cloud and all that.

I understand that book launches and parties are a necessary evil of what we do as writers, but that doesn't make me any more comfortable with the practice. Maybe I wouldn't be as on edge if all we were here to do was sign some books.

Maddie moves to where I'm standing and ushers me over towards the television she's set up in the tight corner of the office, just in front of the landscape window with a view of the Shard, Tower Bridge, and the London Eye in the distance. She proceeds to take and fill one flute at a time, before distributing them to the handful of people crammed into the small office space.

'Be a love and switch it on,' Maddie encourages. 'It'll be live in a minute.'

Maddie is one of my favourite people in the entire world. As my agent and closest confidante, I speak to her more than my own mother, but I wouldn't call Maddie a friend. Don't get me wrong, I love her to bits, and I wouldn't be where I am now without her passion, patience, and editorial eye but ultimately, she is by my side because the royalties I earn pay her wages. I don't see how an employee of sorts can be counted as a friend. If my next book sucks, I can't be certain she'll still be there shouting my name at anyone who will listen. It's an odd dynamic that we have. But I wouldn't change her for the world.

Reaching for the remote control on her jumbled desk, I am amazed at how she doesn't get her clients' manuscripts confused. As well as her laptop, there is a printer and at least four bound manuscripts on the desk. I struggle to read more than a few thousand words in a day, let alone ninety thousand words per manuscript. I guess that's just one of the differences between us.

Although Maddie is only twenty years older than me, you'd have guessed the gap was larger. While I'm still struggling to make ends meet, and wearing the same cardigans and jeans I did at university, Maddie's professional approach to life is more than just a leap away. Even now, as she fills glasses and chats enthusiastically with each of the invited guests, her business suit is perfectly pressed, her mop of chestnut curls carefully sculpted into an off-the-shoulder number. She looks pristine, her skin fresher even than mine. I know she hits the gym five nights a week, and swears by her vegan diet, but I'm certain it takes more than that to look so alert all day.

Flattening the khaki cardigan that I managed to rescue from the laundry basket this morning, I wish I'd made more of an effort with my own appearance, but then again, donning a cocktail dress and perfectly straightened hair doesn't feel right for this occasion either. Fumbling with the remote, I succeed in switching on the set, and flick to BBC One where the news is just starting. The bald newscaster reads out the headlines: more bad news about climate change; yet another established high-street name going into administration; and finally that a verdict has been reached in the High Court case against three men standing trial for historic abuses at a former children's home.

My heart aches as I see the faces of the victims' families, people I have met and spoken to on too many occasions to recall, people I've cried with, people I've hugged, people whose lives were tortured by those who should have been protecting them.

I lower the volume of the television before sipping from my flute, the champagne suddenly tasting bitter.

'Has everyone got a drink now?' Maddie calls out. 'Good. Emma, can I have a quick word outside please?'

She's already heading for the open door before I've had a chance to respond. I follow her into the corridor, and when she closes the door behind us I already know what she's going to say.

'Is everything okay?' she asks quietly, leading me further along the corridor so that nobody inside the room will hear us.

'I'm fine,' I say, delivering my usual response. But I'm chewing the sleeve of my cardigan, an involuntary habit I've had since school.

'You should be buzzing,' she chirps cheerfully. 'Today's verdict is bound to see a spike in sales over the coming days and weeks. That *Sunday Times* number-one bestseller slot will likely be yours again this weekend.'

I turn away from her, not because I'm annoyed, but because I don't want to see her disappointed face when I speak. 'It just feels... wrong... profiting from such evil inflicted on helpless children.'

She spins me back around, waving a finger of warning in my face. 'How many times do we have to go through this, Emma? You weren't the one who abused those children. You weren't the one who left those children in the care of that home, nor were you the one who ignored the mountain of complaints made against that disgusting ring of paedophiles. You weren't even alive when the first abuses started! It is *because* of you that those victims are receiving the justice they deserve today. If it weren't for your investigation, and subsequent publication of one of the most powerful books ever to come across my desk, they would still be burying those nightmares beneath years of torment.'

It's easy for her to say; she didn't have to hear them recount their anguished stories. When I was first approached by Freddie Mitchell, and he told me about what had happened to him at the St Francis Home for Wayward Boys, I knew it was my duty to help him fight for justice, to pursue the men who still walked the streets, free from punishment. I never expected to uncover so many other victims, nor that they'd all be so willing to go on the record. What started as an honest piece of journalism, something to finally get the police authorities to pay attention, had snowballed into something far bigger. There were moments when I had considered giving up the story, such was the emotional toll it took, but I couldn't turn my back on Freddie and the others.

'It was your exposé that led to the police investigation,' Maddie continues. 'It was *your* candid interviews with the victims and staff linked to the home that uncovered the ringleaders, and brought the law to their doors. Don't feel bad that all those long days and nights are now being rewarded.'

This isn't the first time she's delivered this impassioned speech, and I doubt it will be the last time I hear it. I fix her with a strained smile. 'I know you're just looking out for me, but I feel like I'm taking advantage. Every time my name is used in conjunction with their story, it's as if I've put myself forward as their spokesperson when that was the last thing on my agenda. I wanted to give *them* a voice, rather than speak for them.'

'And your words have done exactly that. You're thinking about this far too much. Look at how you live; it's not like you're high-rolling at their expense. You're still holed up in the same one-bedroom apartment in Weymouth; still using the same tatty Oyster card to travel up here when required, rather than investing in a car of your own; and still wearing moth-eaten clothes. In fact, on that note, you and I seriously need to go and expand your wardrobe! I can't have my number-one bestselling author turning up for interviews and events looking like an impostor.'

What an appropriate word; an *impostor* is exactly what I am.

'You're appearing at the Harrogate Literary Festival and Crimefest in Bristol next year, and we definitely need you looking your best at those.'

'Those are festivals for fiction writers, Maddie. I'm just a journalist who wrote a piece of non-fiction. Nobody in their right mind wants to hear from me.'

'That's what you think. What if I told you tickets for your panels are already fully subscribed? Face it, lady, your star is on the rise and it's about time you got used to it.'

Oh great, I don't add, *rooms full of people hanging on my every word is just what I need.*

The door to Maddie's office opens and one of the in-house editorial assistants at my publisher pokes her head out. 'I think it's about to come on.'

There's a twinkle in Maddie's eyes as she beams and claps her hands together. Grabbing my hand, she practically yanks me back into the room, just as the picture on the screen cuts to a grey-haired reporter standing outside the High Court only a few miles from where we're standing now.

'It took just three hours for today's verdict to be reached. Lord Eagleton chose to speak directly to the victims and their families, telling them how sorry he was that this miscarriage of justice was allowed to continue for as long as it did. He thanked them for their bravery, and advised that the verdicts and sentences would reflect the severity of the offences under review. He then turned and addressed the three defendants directly, speaking of his utter disdain for their nefarious activities. Arthur Turgood, who had overall oversight of the home, was not present at court today, owing to a deterioration in his health overnight, but the sentence was passed in his absence. Turgood will serve three fifteen-year custodial sentences concurrently and, owing to his recent medical diagnosis, is unlikely to live past that term. His two co-defendants – Geoffrey Arnsgill and Timothy MacDonald – will each serve concurrent six-year sentences for their part in a scandal which has shocked the nation. Today's verdict follows a rigorous investigation by officers in the Metropolitan Police's specialist Yewtree team, and as a result of *Monsters Under the Bed,* the bestselling exposé written by investigative journalist Emma Hunter.'

Maddie whoops at the mention of my name and book, while I simply cringe and hunch my shoulders. The phone ringing on Maddie's desk couldn't have come at a better time.

Maddie grabs it while downing the rest of her champagne, but her neck muscles tighten and her eyes widen in shock as she stares directly at me. 'There are police in reception, Emma, and they want to speak to you.'

Chapter Three

NOW

Blackfriars, London

There are butterflies in my stomach as the lift doors close and the carriage begins its descent to the ground floor. I rack my brains for what might have happened to warrant the police turning up at my agent's office demanding to speak to me. Is it as a result of today's verdict? Are they angry that my book exposed their lack of investigation years earlier? Has a relative been fatally injured, and they're here to break the news? I'm a law-abiding citizen so there is no reason for me to feel this tense at the prospect of meeting with the police. I left that past behind me a long time ago. But the look of shock in Maddie's eyes has me on edge now.

I've never so much as pinched a bag of sweets, let alone anything to cause the police to come looking for me. Not for *me*. It has to be related to today's verdict. *It has to be.*

Another woman gets in on the floor below wearing a blue tabard and wielding a trolley filled with two mops, a vacuum cleaner, and a variety of disinfectant sprays dangling from the rim. Her hair is the bright black of the sea at night, a frown creasing her brow in seemingly deep thought as she fiddles with the impression of a thin band on the ring finger of her left hand.

I shift to the right to further accommodate the trolley and her eyes flicker up, before narrowing in suspicion. I try to look away but I can feel the burn of her stare as it burrows into the back of my head. I can see her reflection in the shiny brass plate on the wall in front of me, and for the briefest of moments our eyes meet, until I bend my gaze away.

Then her hand is on my arm and the tension in my shoulders cranks up another notch. 'Excuse me,' she says, her accent unfamiliar. 'You're her, aren't you?'

The knot in my stomach tightens as I turn and try to offer a smile to placate her. I'm not yet used to strangers recognising me when I'm out and about, let alone being so willing to strike up conversation. That's one of the bugbears of having your book selling so many copies. Suddenly you become a commodity for anyone to use however they see fit. I was against putting my picture on the website Maddie insisted I create to advertise the book. That same picture has now been replicated countless times in the press as word of my book and investigation spread like wildfire. Not that I'm ungrateful that the book – the victims' stories – are now common knowledge; a wrong was done that required fixing, and thankfully today's verdict is a giant stride towards that. The punishments handed out by the judge will do little to redress the years of torment and nightmares suffered by Freddie Mitchell and the others, but hopefully when they seek civil remuneration, their pain will be somewhat alleviated.

I extend my hand to the woman. 'I'm Emma Hunter.'

She wipes both sides of her hand on the already stained tabard, before shaking mine. 'You wrote that book. Um… what's it called… um…?'

'*Monsters Under the Bed*,' I confirm for her.

'Yes, that's it. I can't believe what those poor boys went through. It is criminal to forget there are people out there capable of such… perversion.'

Her grasp of English belies her thick accent, and I can feel my cheeks starting to warm. 'If you'd like me to sign your copy of the book, I'd be happy to. My agent, Maddie Travers, has an office on the sixth floor. If you drop your copy by, she can get me to sign it next time I'm here.'

I feel quite pleased with myself that I haven't hidden my light behind my usual bushel, and have made an extroverted gesture – though why anyone would want *my* autograph is beyond me. Still, Maddie tells me it's all part of the marketing game these days.

'Oh, I haven't read your book,' she says matter-of-factly, as if my mere suggestion that she has is offensive. 'My daughter has, and told me all about it.'

An awkward silence descends, as I've no idea how to rescue us both from the faux pas.

'Oh well,' I eventually say, conscious that the lift is slowing as it reaches the ground floor, 'if you want me to sign your daughter's copy, just drop it off with Maddie.' The lift doors open with a ping, and I'm relieved. 'It was nice to have met you,' I offer as I dart out as quickly as I can without running.

At least the exchange distracted me from the purpose of my lift journey. Maddie's agency occupies half of floor six in this ten-storey building; the other floors are occupied by a variety of other small businesses – including two other literary agencies – who can't afford to let an entire building in London without support. I've been here enough times now but the lobby always takes my breath away, the overhead lights reflecting off the shiny marble walls, the floor buffed to within an inch of its life. Strangers hustle about either side of me, all here for one purpose or another, their faces gone in the blink of an eye. I've often thought that working in the heart of London must be quite isolating. Millions of people commute through this city every day; how many ever actually stop to acknowledge their shared experience? It makes me glad I get to work out of my tiny flat in Weymouth, although I do occasionally pack up my laptop and head to the local café or library when I'm bored of staring at the same four walls.

As I approach the front desk, there is no obvious sign of a police officer. I'm about to interrogate the handsome hulk of a receptionist when I spot my best friend, Rachel Leeming, chuckling mischievously and waving at me just beyond the security barrier.

'I should have known it would be you.' I smile as I swipe through the barrier and hug her. 'What are you doing here?' I ask, pleased by the surprise visit.

'I was at the High Court when the verdict was read out and wanted to congratulate you. I remembered you saying you'd be watching from your agent's office, so here I am.'

This is so typical of Rachel; anyone else would have phoned or sent a message, but despite her reliance on technology for her job, she prefers the personal touch in her private life. It's why I love her to bits, and am thankful we got lumped together in halls of residence at university.

'You could have come up, you know,' I say, nodding back towards the bank of elevators.

Rachel pulls a face. 'Thanks, but I know what Maddie really thinks of me, and I'm not her biggest fan either. That's why I couldn't tell that gorgeous receptionist who I really was, or Maddie wouldn't have let you come down.'

'You make her sound like a monster! She's really sweet.'

'You only think that because she mothers you. I know people who knew her before she became a literary agent, and some of their stories would put your hair on end.'

She must see I'm hurt that the two most important women in my life are in adversity.

'I'm sorry,' Rachel offers, 'I know people can change, and I'm glad she's clearly taking such good care of you. If that ever changes though, you can tell her from me that I'll be coming for her. Nobody takes advantage of my best friend. Not on my watch.'

I've never been able to stay angry with Rachel; she's always had my back, and I don't doubt that she'd make a beeline for Maddie if she ever crossed a line.

'Here, you should have seen how those rotters squirmed when the judge read out their sentences; pity the worst one wasn't there too, but they've put an armed guard outside Turgood's room, ready to escort him to a Cat-B facility as soon as he's fit enough. You must be thrilled!'

'I'm pleased those men have finally got the justice they deserve,' I say, choosing my words carefully.

'Well that probably wouldn't have happened if it wasn't for you. You should be proud of yourself! I'm proud of you. It's okay to be happy with the verdict.'

I close my eyes and nod my head, allowing a short sigh to

escape. I know she's right; I know Maddie is right too. I need to get this chip off my shoulder and accept the repercussions of my investigation. I wrote that book because I felt compelled to tell their story in the most factually accurate way possible. Better that than allowing some tabloid to sensationalise a tragedy.

'My editor was asking me about you again today,' Rachel says, wiggling her eyebrows suggestively. 'Wants to know how much it would cost to convince you to join our paper. I told him he'd have to pay top dollar, but he said he didn't care and asked me to bring you in for a chat.'

I back away slightly, no longer enjoying this surprise visit.

'We've talked about this before, Rachel,' I begin, as calmly as I can. I don't want to upset her. 'You know it just isn't practical.'

She closes the gap. 'Why not? Think about it: you could dust the sand from your shoes once and for all and move to London. You could move in with me if you wanted and it would be just like the good old days of university: Rach and Em putting the world to rights and breaking the biggest news stories.'

The thought of moving to London fills me with dread; I'm not ready to turn my back on the only town where I've ever felt comfortable in my own skin. Too many memories – good and bad – to simply move away. She doesn't understand what really keeps me in Weymouth, and how I don't ever see myself leaving.

'Your flat is tiny,' I say, opting for logic over honesty.

Rachel reluctantly nods. 'Fine, we'd get a new place for the two of us to share. You must be making a fortune in royalties anyway, which would supplement any money the newspaper would pay. We'd make a formidable team.'

Of that I have no doubt, and if the job was in Weymouth or any of the neighbouring towns within Dorset, I'd genuinely consider it, but London is too noisy, too polluted, and too crowded for my liking.

'I'll think about it,' I lie, but she looks crestfallen.

'Of course you will,' she says despondently, before brightening. 'What are you doing to celebrate tonight? How about I see if that gorgeous receptionist fancies taking out two of the UK's deadliest bachelorettes?'

I glance back over my shoulder at the blonde man, but I can't see why he'd have any interest in someone like me, and the last thing I want is to be at the mercy of Rachel's matchmaking.

'I have plans already,' I lie. 'Sorry.'

Rachel raises her eyebrow questioningly. 'Just tell me you're not planning to spend all night sitting at your laptop on that missing people site again? I don't mean to be insensitive, but I'm your best friend, and I can see how much it takes out of you.'

If she knew the real reason I hunch over the screen at night, she wouldn't think to question it. But I can't tell her; not now, after all these years. I don't want it to muddy her view of me.

'Actually, I'm giving a talk at the library tonight for the WI,' I say, as assertively as the deceit will allow. 'It's been planned for months.'

Her eyes don't leave mine as she attempts to smoke out the lie, but eventually she gives up, her gaze dropping. 'Okay, well if you do find yourself at a loose end in the next few weeks, you really ought to come and stay with me. It would do you some good to get away from the coast, and they do say that change is as good as a rest. Why don't you come for a long weekend? Then I can show you what it's really like to live in our nation's capital, and you'll see it's not as scary as you think.'

I'm about to argue that it isn't fear keeping me from moving when a gravelly voice calls out over my shoulder. 'Excuse me, excuse me!'

We both turn to look, coming face to face with an older gentleman I feel like I vaguely recognise.

'Ah, good, it *is* you,' he says, with a smile that doesn't reach his eyes. 'I thought it was. May I have a moment of your time, Miss Hunter?'

He has the whitest head of hair I think I've ever seen and beneath the thick beard is a weathered face, yet there's a glint in his bespectacled eyes. The cane hanging from his arm is gilded and well-cared for, and the tweed suit has been tailored to fit his ample body shape. Later in the year and dressed in red, I'd almost think I was speaking to a Lapland local. Something tells me he hasn't interrupted us for an autograph.

Rachel opens her mouth to speak but the older man bangs the end of his cane on the hard floor. 'It's about my granddaughter, you see,' he says firmly, evidently not a man used to being ignored. 'One year ago today, she was abducted, and I want you to find out what happened to her.'

Chapter Four

THEN

Rickmansworth, Hertfordshire

Penny Connors stepped back from the table and watched as small hands on spindly arms shot out and quickly emptied the bowls of crisps, pizzas, and sausage rolls. The plate of crustless sandwiches remained untouched, but she wasn't surprised Sean's class had all opted for the less healthy snacks first. That was precisely why she had yet to bring the large platter of cakes to the free-for-all, and why it was hidden in a draw of pans in the kitchen.

'If anyone needs anything, Mr Connors and I will be just outside in the garden. Sean, can I borrow you for a minute?'

Sean pulled a face as he met his mother's gaze, but didn't challenge her request, sliding off his chair, and sullenly following her out of the room and into the kitchen.

'Cheer up, sweetheart,' Penny said warmly, keen not to spoil his day, but desperate to know the answer to her next question. 'I just need to ask you something, and I wanted to do it away from all the others. When is the last time you remember seeing Cassie Hilliard? Only, your dad and I have checked the house and the garden, and we can't seem to find her.'

Sean didn't seem concerned by her absence. 'I don't know. Are you sure she's even here?'

The image of Elizabeth Hilliard with that parasol filled Penny's vision again. 'Yes, she was definitely here. Do you remember? She was dressed as Ariel from *The Little Mermaid*, and gave you a present wrapped in silver and gold glitter paper.'

She knew this last detail would refresh his memory as he'd told her it looked really girly, whereas all the gifts from the rest of his class had come in wrapping paper adorned with superheroes and footballers.

'Oh yeah,' he said, twisting his mouth awkwardly, as he tried to recall any other details about the missing girl. 'She was on the bouncy castle with the others. I remember that because she bashed into Jason, and they both fell over. They banged their heads I think.'

Penny widened her eyes. 'Was she hurt?'

'She didn't cry,' Sean confirmed, 'but I don't know where she went after that. Sorry, Mum. Can I go back to the food now?' He began to move away.

'Just a second,' she said, reaching for his arm and gently pulling him back. 'Did she say anything after she bumped her head? Was there any blood? Did she seem in pain?'

Sean shrugged, as he always did when he didn't know how to answer a question. 'No idea. We were all bouncing and laughing, and I don't know what happened after. I don't think she was bleeding.'

Penny nodded, knowing there was little further detail she'd be able to extract from her son's fragile memory. 'Okay, thank you. Listen, I'm going to go and join your dad searching in the garden. If anything happens in there,' she indicated towards the dining room, 'I want you to come and get one of us. Okay? If anything gets spilled, anyone needs anything else to eat or drink, or there are any arguments, *come and get one of us*.'

'Sure,' Sean replied, his mind already back on the plate of food waiting for him.

He hurried away and Penny took one final look in the dining room. She spotted Jason Knightwood at the end of the table, head low, nibbling on a sausage roll much like a squirrel might. Despite the raucous chatter from everyone else, he was sitting in silence. *Odd boy*, Penny thought again. Satisfied that all nineteen children seemed happy enough, and not in need of her attention, she made her way back through the kitchen and out onto the patio. Gerry was halfway up the garden, raising each side of the castle systematically, before stooping and looking beneath it.

'Find anything?' Penny asked as she joined him.

'No,' he sighed gruffly. 'I just wondered whether she might have wandered behind the castle, and somehow got sucked under it.' He shrugged his shoulders in the same way his son did. 'Silly, but I just can't work out where else she could be. I've tried looking at the rough end of the garden again, but there's no obvious sign that any of them have been up there. You did tell them they weren't to go beyond the castle or they'd get no cake, so I'd be surprised if any of them had.'

'Was there anything on the security camera?'

'No,' he bristled. 'She definitely didn't leave via the front door.'

'Sean said she bumped heads with one of the other children. What if she's got a concussion, or is unconscious somewhere?'

'I'd have found her by now if she was passed out somewhere in the garden. I'm telling you, Pen, she's not out here. She must be inside.'

Penny could see the concern growing in her husband's mocha-coloured eyes, and his thick, dark, bushy beard glistened with sweat. 'I think we need to phone the police,' Penny repeated. 'I know it sounds ridiculous, but we don't know where she is. There's no way she could have got out, but what if someone did come in when we weren't looking and took her? Can you, hand on heart, say you were watching all of the children the entire time? I can't. I was so busy preparing the food and answering the door as new children arrived that I couldn't tell you when she was even last seen by any of the children. For all we know, she could have been missing for nearly an hour.'

'But who would want to abduct a six-year-old child from a classmate's birthday party?'

'You know as well as I do that the Hilliards are from good money. Her dad made the Forbes rich list two years ago. People with that kind of wealth attract enemies.'

'But who even knew she was here apart from her parents? And who would have the audacity to snatch her from a stranger's house? It's too risky if you ask me. They'd have to know the whole layout of the building, all the entry and exit points, and that there wouldn't be a houseful of parents watching. Even we thought there'd be at least another two adults here until this morning.'

Penny couldn't answer. She felt sick to her stomach that

they now found themselves in a situation where they might have to phone the authorities.

Gerry pivoted to scan the top end of the garden again before sighing heavily. 'Okay, okay. Listen, we'll do another check of the house, and if we still can't find her, then we'll phone the police.'

Penny followed him back to the house and they were about to head upstairs when Sean called out to them. 'I'll go,' Penny said, as Gerry's foot landed on the first step. 'What is it?' she asked Sean as he emerged from the dining room.

He was grinning like a Cheshire cat. 'Look who I found.' He turned back towards the dining room and as he did, Penny's gaze immediately focused on a girl in a luminescent green dress with a wave of flowing cherry-red hair.

'Cassie!' Penny gasped.

Cassie Hilliard looked up at the call of her name and smiled as she pushed a Pringle into her mouth.

'Gerry,' Penny shouted over her shoulder as relief flooded her body. 'It's okay, she's here. You can come back down.'

'Do I get a reward for finding her?' Sean asked, a cheeky glint in his eye.

Penny found herself chuckling and pulled her son into her arms, smothering the top of his head in kisses until he squirmed away, embarrassed in front of his friends, none of whom seemed to have noticed the onslaught of affection.

'Cassie, can you come and speak to me in the kitchen please? It won't take a minute,' Penny asked.

Cassie lowered the next Pringle to her plate and made her way around the table, following Penny into the kitchen and waiting patiently until she was spoken to.

'You gave us quite a scare there, young lady,' Penny said,

not wanting to chastise someone else's child, but also keen to stress the worry that had built up almost to breaking point in the last fifteen minutes. 'We thought you'd gone missing. Where have you been?'

Cassie lowered her eyes but didn't respond.

'It's all right, sweetheart, you're not in any trouble. I just want to understand where you went and what made you disappear.'

Her head remained bowed. 'I got scared.'

Penny crouched, forcing eye contact. 'What scared you? Was it because you bumped into Jason?'

The little girl shook her head. 'I-I-I thought I heard a gun.'

Penny blinked several times as she tried to process this statement. 'A gun?'

Cassie raised her head slightly. 'Daddy told me that if I ever hear a gun I'm to run and hide, so that's what I did.'

Gerry entered the kitchen, hanging back to allow the conversation to continue, but Penny couldn't conceal her alarm at what Cassie had just told her. What kind of parent warned their child about what to do in a gun-related situation? Why would there ever be such a need? Although Sean had probably seen guns in use in some of the superhero films he'd watched, as far as he was concerned – based on the consistent message she and Gerry had delivered – that was just something that happened in the movies; people didn't carry guns in the real world.

'There are no guns here, sweetheart,' Penny resumed. 'Okay? Guns are what you see in films.'

Cassie pulled a disbelieving face. 'No, Daddy said that there are bad men in the world who might want to hurt us, and they have guns. So, if I ever hear or see one, I'm to run and hide.'

Penny looked up at her husband, exasperated.

'What made you think you'd heard a gun?' Gerry asked from where he was leaning against the counter top.

'There was a loud bang,' she protested. 'Didn't you hear it?'

Gerry thought back before snapping his fingers. 'A car backfired,' he said, glancing at Penny. 'I remember now. One of the neighbours' cars I presume. Around twenty to thirty minutes ago. That must have been what you heard, Cassie. Just a car backfiring. Mrs Connors is right; there are no guns here.'

Penny couldn't recall hearing any car backfiring, but the radio had been on in the kitchen when she'd been cutting the crusts off the sandwiches. 'Where did you go when you heard the bang, sweetheart?'

'I was in the toilet when I heard it so I hid in your bedroom, under the bed.'

Penny frowned. 'Our bedroom? But the door was locked.' She turned back to Gerry. 'I never checked that room because I remember locking it this morning before the first children arrived. There was no way she could have been in there.'

Gerry pulled a face. 'Shoot! That may be my fault. I went up to change my shirt and I don't remember locking the door again. I'm sorry.'

Penny turned back to Cassie. 'Well, there's no harm done. I'm sorry that the backfiring car scared you, Cassie. I wish you'd come and spoken to me or Mr Connors and we would have assured you that it wasn't the sound of a gun.'

'Can I go and eat now, please?'

Penny nodded, offering a reassuring smile. 'Of course you can. Run along.'

The cherry-red wig swished as she skipped back to the dining room, leaving Penny searching her husband's eyes for reassurance before he looked away.

'Come along, Cassie,' Elizabeth Hilliard said as she waited impatiently by the front door, not wishing to enter in case any of the other children caught her new cashmere coat with their grubby fingers. The sun was close to setting, and she was bloody freezing.

'Can I have a word?' Penny asked, as she handed Cassie a cheap-looking party bag. 'There was an incident earlier when Cassie got scared by a neighbour's car backfiring.'

Elizabeth raised an eyebrow, feigning interest, but hoping not to be held up much longer. They were already running late for her next appointment and she didn't have time to pander to some woman's irrational concerns.

'Anyway, I told her that guns aren't something a six-year-old should be worrying about in this country,' Penny continued, with no obvious let-up in sight.

'Thank you,' Elizabeth interrupted, 'but we really must be on our way. Come along, Cassie. And say thank you to Mrs Connors.'

Cassie did as she was told and soon fell in step behind her mother, climbing up into the Range Rover and fastening her seatbelt. Elizabeth signalled to the driver they were ready, the engine started, and they pulled away.

'Did you have fun at the party?' Elizabeth asked her daughter.

'Yes, thank you. They had a bouncy castle, and we ate pizza

and crisps and cake for supper. It was fab!'

Elizabeth tried not to turn up her nose, instead reaching for her phone, unlocking the screen, and opening her emails. 'Well, at least you enjoyed yourself, I suppose. I'll have Rosa draw you a bath when we get in and get you cleaned up.'

The Range Rover picked up speed as they joined the narrow A-road that would eventually return them to more clement surroundings. In Elizabeth's periphery, the large hedgerows streamed by the window in a blur and the air conditioning hummed as it maintained the cool climate.

An explosion shattered the silence.

The rear end of the car swung round as the driver lost control and Elizabeth's world slowed as it rose and dipped, her beaded necklace flying past her eyes, fragments of the shattered window floating through the air like powder in a snow globe, the phone falling from her grip.

The ringing in her ears wouldn't stop as the Range Rover landed on its side.

Cassie was suspended just above her by her seatbelt. It felt like a dream. No, a *nightmare*. She was paralysed by fear, unable to comprehend what had just happened.

Had they hit something? Was that it? But what on earth could have been large enough to flip a car this size?

A muffled scream wrenched her attention back to the vehicle, and she looked up in horror as a gloved hand reached in through the broken window and hoisted Cassie back out through it in one seamless movement, the seatbelt hanging uselessly in her wake.

Elizabeth reached up in desperation but barely brushed the edge of her daughter's cherry-red wig before she disappeared into the darkness.

Chapter Five

NOW

Blackfriars, London

'My name is Templeton, Lord Fitzhume,' the man with the cane begins once we're seated in the lobby. 'Forgive me for intruding on your day, but you are a difficult woman to get hold of.'

I never used to be. Rachel has gone, excusing herself with traitorous mutterings of deadlines, so I try to fix an earnest and encouraging expression on my face.

Fitzhume removes a red silk handkerchief from inside his tweed jacket and wipes his forehead, pausing to regain his composure. I'd probably place him in his mid-seventies on account of how much he's panting from just the movement to the seat. Something tells me that despite the polished exterior, things are not quite right beneath the surface; his reliance on that cane is further evidence of a man in pain.

'Have we met before?' I ask, unable to quite place the familiarity of his face.

He smiles and returns the handkerchief to his jacket pocket. 'I, like you, am not immune to having my picture captured for one periodical or another. Alas for me, mine is more to do with my family's wealth rather than noble deeds such as bringing a ring of monsters to justice.'

'I was just an instrument; the victims are the real heroes for coming forward. You said you've been trying to contact me. What is it exactly that you think I can do for you?'

'Cassie Hilliard is my granddaughter. Does that name mean anything to you?'

I can't say I recognise the name but the way he's looking at me, his eyes glowing with expectant hope, his lips slightly parted, as if he is willing me to say I know exactly who his granddaughter is, makes me want to tell him I do.

'I'm sorry, it doesn't,' I tell him as gently as I can, expecting to see the despondency return, but he bangs his cane on the floor once again, the sound echoing off the marbled wall closest to the leather bench we're propped up on.

'The car carrying Cassie and her mother – my daughter, Elizabeth – was driven off the road twelve months ago, and that was the last time any of us saw six-year-old Cassie. She was extracted from the car by a pair of masked invaders, leaving my barely conscious daughter in a state of shock. The family chauffeur was able to confirm to police that he witnessed two masked bandits in dark jeans and leather jackets, but they were gone before he could release himself from the upturned vehicle. It's a story which would have made all of the newspapers had I not paid to have it kept out of the public eye. It doesn't surprise me that you are not aware of what happened because only a dozen or so people in the entire world know that my granddaughter was so cruelly taken from us.'

As he speaks, I'm desperately trying to recall any stories from the past year that match any of the detail he has provided, but I soon draw a blank. He could have just as easily invented the whole thing and I would be none the wiser. But the way he speaks, with such authority and more than a hint of remorse, I find myself believing every word.

'I'm so sorry to hear about your loss,' I offer, but I know better than anyone that my words mean nothing to someone who has lived through those events. 'I don't wish to be blunt, Lord Fitzhume, but why is it you're telling *me* about this?'

The twinkle is back in his eyes and he straightens slightly, taking in the vast lobby. 'Do you have children, Miss Hunter?'

I shake my head.

'Any brothers or sisters?'

'A sister,' I say, picturing her sweet face. 'Well, I did… I mean…' I can't finish the sentence. He doesn't need to hear about the baggage I carry with me every day.

'They say having children changes you as a person,' he continues. 'It changes your priorities and expectations in life. Most will learn to settle for what they have and wave goodbye to any long-term dreams they had. Don't misunderstand me, Miss Hunter; becoming a parent doesn't force you to give up on hope and ambition – if anything, it focuses that hope towards your infant – but we all make a conscious choice to put the best interests of our child ahead of our own. Granted, that's not true for every parent, but most do experience some kind of shift in their moral compass.'

He wipes his forehead again and sighs. 'I wasn't as involved in Elizabeth's life as I wish I had been. My own stupid fault chasing after one foreign adventure or another and I didn't realise the error of my ways until it was too late. And that is why, you see, when Cassie was born, I was determined to make amends. She became my reason for living. If becoming a parent changes you as a person, then becoming a *grandparent* changes you even more. Every day since that angel arrived in our lives has been a blessing, and when she was taken it was the saddest day I can ever recall.'

'I'm sorry for your loss,' I offer, still uncertain why he has approached me… and today of all days.

'My granddaughter hasn't been seen since the day she was abducted, Miss Hunter, but I am certain she is still alive out there somewhere and I want your help to find her.'

I don't speak for what feels like an eternity. 'With respect, Lord Fitzhume, I'm not sure I'm the right person for this. I'm a journalist, not a private investigator. Presumably, you've made the police aware that your granddaughter was abducted?'

The bang of the cane echoes off the wall again. 'Of course we did!' The relaxed smile has gone, and he is once again leaning heavily on the handle of the cane, as if he might crumple if it were swiped away. 'They were the first people we called, and they did what they could – even caught up with one of the abductors – but they never brought Cassie home. As far as they're concerned, she died in their company and so the case is closed.'

My phone is buzzing in my pocket and, as I look at the screen, I can see it is Maddie, probably wondering how much longer I plan to be away from her small office party.

I reject the call and fix Fitzhume with my sincerest smile. 'If the police have reason to believe that Cassie died after she was taken, what makes you think they are wrong?'

He reaches for the handkerchief again, this time wiping the small pool of spit gathered at the corner of his mouth. 'It is too easy a conclusion to assume that they killed her. With everything that happened after that awful day, it is the easy way out. It's more convenient to say she died than continue to search. I offered them a king's ransom to continue searching but they refused. That's why I need *you*, Miss Hunter. I need the help of someone who doesn't take no for an answer, someone who knows what it takes to separate the lies from the half-truths. Without your help, Arthur Turgood and that ring of monsters would never have faced justice. I'm willing to pay whatever it takes to secure your time, Miss Hunter. I need your investigative skills.'

I can just picture the pound signs in Maddie's eyes, but he really has approached the wrong person. 'I'm sorry, Lord Fitzhume, but I think you have the wrong idea about me. I am not some investigator for hire. My role in the St Francis Home case came about because I felt passionately about helping those in need of a voice. With all due respect, I'm not what you need. I appreciate that my name is being bandied about because of the High Court case, but I'm not a resource that you can add to your payroll. There must be hundreds of qualified, professional investigators who'd be prepared to take on your case. I'm just a writer. I'm sorry, but the last thing I want to do is lead you down the garden path. You need more than I can offer.'

I'm half expecting to hear the sound of the cane reverberating again but instead he sticks a hand back into his jacket and withdraws a card, handing it towards me. 'I appreciate your honesty, Miss Hunter, and thank you for your time. Please take my number in case you change your mind.'

I accept the card out of politeness but have no intention of ever using the contact details on it. We both stand and I wish him good luck with finding his missing granddaughter. I'll admit I feel guilty as hell as I watch him struggle through the revolving door and out into the warm, late-summer sunshine.

Swiping my pass at the security barrier, I head back towards the bank of lifts and wait to board and return to the sixth floor. Only Maddie remains in her office as I enter.

'Oh, there you are,' she coos from behind her desk, four half-empty champagne flutes standing on the periphery of the mess. 'I was beginning to think they'd carted you off for some devious offence I had no idea about. I told the others you're probably some top-secret agent needed to defuse a diplomatic incident or secretly leading a double life as a porn star.'

I raise my eyebrows at this last remark but she waves away my concern.

'Only kidding. Shall I get the others back? I didn't know how long you'd be so I told them to go back to work, but if you're ready to get the celebration going again, I can—'

'Do you mind if we don't?' I interrupt, realising I'm once again chewing the sleeve of my cardigan.

She fixes me with a sympathetic look, but doesn't oppose. 'I had a phone call from Freddie Mitchell. He wanted you to know how grateful he is and said they'll be throwing a small wake in honour of those voices silenced before today's verdict, if you wanted to go along. He says they'll be holding it in The Black Horse on the waterfront but that you'd know where that was.'

The place where Freddie first opened up about his history; I know it well. I don't think I really want to intrude on what is sure to be an emotional night for all involved. I'll give Freddie a call later and make my excuses.

'Thanks for letting me know,' I tell Maddie.

'We should probably book some time in to discuss your next project. Have you had any thoughts yet on how you want to follow up on *Monsters Under the Bed*?'

I'm glad she's raised this question as we've been skirting around it for the last couple of weeks, but with all the hoo-ha of the trial, neither of us has been brave enough to take the first step.

'I want to write about my sister,' I say in the same voice in which I've rehearsed it in front of the mirror. 'I think, given my personal interest in the story, I can give it a unique spin. I still think there are people out there who know more about what happened than they've previously shared with—'

'I know how passionate you are,' she interrupts, 'but I just don't think there's a market for it now. If you had a fresh source who could shed some light on the story then fine, but all you've got is hearsay based on your hours of research when the rest of us are receiving a healthy dose of sleep. I admire your determination to discover the truth about what happened, but I just don't think it has the legs to get the green light from the publisher. They loved what you did with the St Francis Home for Wayward Boys story, and how you managed to get close enough to the victims to earn their trust and uncover the gruesome details. That's the sort of story they want to see for your second book of the contract.'

This is exactly what I was afraid she would say.

'*Monsters* has been a bigger success than any of us predicted,' she continues, 'and there's an opportunity to locate similar cases and deliver the same kind of success as you did for Freddie Mitchell and the others. See what you can dig up and I'll book some time in for us to discuss it early next week.'

I thank Maddie for her time, as I always do, leave what remains in my plastic flute, grab my bag and head back out. I know I'm lucky to have an agent who only cares for my interests and I don't like feeling down about the fact she has dismissed the project I've set my heart on. Catching the lift back to the lobby, I can't stop thinking about the look of raw anguish in Fitzhume's eyes, and although I'm certain I did the right thing in turning him down, it weighs heavy on my heart.

Chapter Six

NOW

Blackfriars, London

The warm breeze smacks my cheeks as I emerge from the revolving doors and, with my head down, I allow my feet to take control. I don't respond to the gasp of someone recognising me and quickly snapping a photograph on his phone. I'm not sure what he plans to do with an image of a woman with far too much on her mind and I'm not even bothered that I probably look haggard and distressed. When did it become okay for strangers to just take photographs of others without asking permission? The advance of mobile-phone technology has turned everyone into a potential paparazzo.

Bestselling Author Spotted in London, is hardly the stuff of sensationalist headlines. Maybe that image will appear on the front cover of one of those airbrushed glossy gossip magazines in the weeks to come, and then a panel of people whose opinion means nothing to me will dissect the lack of colour in my cheeks, the dowdy cardigan that has seen better days, and the messy hair clearly in need of a good brush and trim. None of this is anywhere close to my mind as I continue to pound the pavement, replaying the meeting with Fitzhume in my memory.

I know it's guilt that's forcing me to relive every sentence, but why should I be feeling guilty? I hadn't even heard about his granddaughter's disappearance until he mentioned it. In fact, it's *his* fault that I remained oblivious to the news after he *paid to have it kept out of the public eye*. But even if he hadn't, and the story had made every front page across the country, it's not my fault that she was never found; yet the contrition remains.

I stop suddenly as my mind comes into alignment and the truth pokes me like a stick in the eye.

Looking around, I'm suddenly conscious of my surroundings. I've been so buried in my own thoughts that I have no idea where I am or even if I'm anywhere near where I should be. To my left and right, traffic chugs slowly in both directions, beyond which the python-like Thames stretches as far as the eye can see. Like used dishwater, it is the heartbeat of the city, growing more polluted with every passing second – a damning indictment of the capitalists looking to profit from the downfall of others.

Stepping to the side of Millennium Bridge, I grip the railing as my knees threaten to buckle under the exertion of the journey here. There is a man leaning a few feet away and the scent of his vape smoke threatens the contents of my stomach. I'm about to shuffle further down when he ends the call he's making and pulls away, giving me a secondary glance as he does. I can see that look of recognition in his eyes but at least he has the decency to simply gawp rather than framing the scene for eternity on Instagram.

'Whoa, Emma, are you okay?' a welcome voice pants from behind me.

Turning, I can't even bring myself to smile at Rachel whose face is mostly hidden behind a large pair of black designer frames.

'You're white as a sheet!' she exclaims, and despite the warmth of the weather, my face feels like ice.

'I just need a minute,' I tell her, turning back to stare out to the river which could tell a million tales about those who pass and cross it each day.

'You didn't look a hundred per cent when I left you in the lobby,' Rachel explains, 'so I came back to check on you. We must have just missed each other in the lifts because I saw you exiting and had to run to catch up. What did the old man have to say for himself?'

I'm surprised she hadn't recognised Lord Fitzhume but I don't share his name. 'He wanted to hire me to write a story,' I say instead.

'That's a good thing, surely? Why the long face?'

Why *am* I feeling so guilty about turning down a man who's asked me to help find his missing granddaughter? I can't tell Rachel. It's been too long. Too many bricks have been laid in creating our friendship-bridge to tear them all down with a wrecking ball.

'I told him he'd be better off hiring a private detective.'

Rachel frowns at me. 'What aren't you telling me?'

Her eyes are searching for answers my mouth isn't prepared to give, but my body language isn't so discreet.

'What's going on, Emma? Don't tell me you're okay

because right now you look as likely to jump from this bridge as you do to walk from it. What's put you so on edge? I'm a journalist for *The Telegraph*; you know I'll find out eventually. If there's something troubling you then I want – no, I *demand* – to know what it is.'

A flash of the day we first met suddenly appears before my eyes: me dressed in faded dungarees carrying my dad's old, battered brown suitcase; Rachel in a mini-dress, exuding confidence I could only dream of. She wasn't the sort of girl I was used to speaking to – no chess club on her résumé. But she had been eager to find out all about her new roommate, opening a bottle of cheap supermarket wine and a bag of Doritos, and refusing to let me collect the rest of my things until we'd finished both. I could have told her everything then; no, I *should* have told her everything then, but somewhere in the back of my head I'd allowed my paranoia to keep quiet about the reality of my history.

She'd accepted me for who I was – at least, the version of myself I'd shared – and on that uneven foundation we'd built a friendship: her the beautiful and sassy princess, me the lady-in-waiting dragged along for the ride. I wouldn't have had it any other way. So, as she continues to burrow that inquisitive stare into my temples, I'm fighting with all my willpower not to undo history.

'Does it have something to do with what the old man said to you?' Rachel tries again, her intuition set to spot any tell or facial tick my body might divulge against my will.

I don't respond, but she was there when he said his granddaughter had been abducted.

Suddenly, all I can see is Anna.

At the time, Mum said I wasn't to blame, but I'll never

forgive myself for the argument that led to my sister stomping away in a huff. I still remember the scene as if it was yesterday. I'm sure my imagination has filled some of the holes in the memory, re-painting the background of the day, but that scowl on her face, those tears threatening to spill, are permanently etched on my mind.

I nod involuntarily as Rachel continues to await my response.

'What did he say to you?' she tries again.

I close my eyes, willing Anna's tear-stained face to dissipate.

'Does this have anything to do with the vigil you hold on that missing people website every night?'

My eyes snap open despite the sting of tears threatening to reveal all my secrets.

'You think I didn't know what you were doing in the early hours when we were in halls of residence? I would sense you some nights, coming over to check I was asleep before logging on. At first I thought you were one of those *World of Warcraft* nerds, but when I checked your browser history all I saw was that site. I figured you were deleting your internet search history, covering something much worse, but you weren't, were you? What is it you don't want me to know, Emma? I mean… I know what it is to keep secrets from those closest to you, and something tells me I'm getting close.'

I have to blink away the tears but I'm already past the point of no return. 'Twenty years ago, my sister Anna was abducted and never found.'

The weight lifted from my shoulders makes me feel as though I might even take flight from this bridge and I have to grip the railing tighter just in case.

Rachel's eyes narrow as the cogs behind them turn. 'Oh my God, Emma, I'm so sorry.'

I was bracing myself for a verbal assault that I very much deserve, but Rachel's reaction brings the tears closer to the precipice.

'I don't really remember what the argument was about. We were in the front yard, and I was on the skateboard Dad had bought me in the charity shop. I think Anna was saying I was doing it wrong, but I thought I knew better. She kept trying to get me off the stupid contraption but I didn't want to listen. If only I had let her show me… then she wouldn't have become upset and shouted that she was going to Grandma's house. If I'd known that would be the last time I'd see her… I would have stopped her going, or I would have gone with her, or even told my parents that's where she was going. But as a selfish and naïve seven-year-old I did none of those things; I was just happy to have the skateboard and yard to myself, without her interfering.'

Rachel hasn't moved, I'm not even sure if she's blinked in the last two minutes. I have to close my eyes to continue, as I don't want to see the hurt and disappointment in her eyes.

'I learned later that eighteen minutes elapsed before Dad came out of the front door and asked me where Anna was. I told him she'd walked to our grandma's house, which was only four minutes away. It wasn't uncommon for us to walk to her house, though I wasn't allowed to do it on my own, but Anna was two years older than me, and she was trusted. There were no main roads to cross, and the alleyway between our road and my grandma's road was surprisingly well-lit at night-time.'

I can still hear the piercing scream Mum let out when the

police officer shook his head and said there was still no sign of her.

The tears are falling even though my eyes remain firmly clamped shut. 'Apparently, another five minutes passed before Dad told Mum that Anna had gone to Grandma's house, at which point Mum phoned Grandma to tell Anna to be home by five for dinner. That was the moment the alarm was raised, the moment both my parents lost years off their lifespans.'

I'm not even sure if Rachel is still here. I can't hear her breathing and I wouldn't blame her for hightailing it away. I'm not the person she thought I was and it feels somehow fitting that the only other sister I have in the world would abandon me here and now.

Only, she doesn't. Instead, my best friend for the last eight years does something I don't deserve: she wraps her arms around me and pulls me into the warmth of her embrace. 'I am so sorry you've had to live with this on your own for so long. I don't blame you for not telling me, but I wish you had so I could have been a better friend.'

My sister never made it to Grandma's house and, despite an intense police investigation that seemed to last for months, she was never found. Nobody witnessed her journey; not a single nosey neighbour happened to be looking out of their window as she walked by; not a single dog walker happened to be in that alleyway when she was. Actresses were hired to play the two of us in the televised reconstruction and I remember thinking at the time that the actress playing Anna looked nothing like her, but I must have watched that reconstruction hundreds of times down the years and I now see that facially they were very similar. I met the two actresses before filming started and I think it's my memory of that conversation that made me believe that she was nothing like Anna. The actress wanted to play with my doll's house and she had such a pretty smile.

She wasn't *my* Anna.

Things were never the same at home after that. My parents seemed to argue more. Mum gave up her job so she could continue searching for Anna and Dad spent more and more time at work. Then one day, when I was twelve, they sat me down and explained that they were going to get a divorce. I cried myself to sleep that night knowing that, had I just let Anna use my bloody skateboard, they would have stayed together. Dad moved out to a grubby flat not much bigger than our old living room but it was two bus rides away. Even though I was a trustworthy child, Mum never allowed me to travel there on my own. That was the other thing that changed after my sister's disappearance: Mum's paranoia spiked. She wouldn't let me go anywhere on my own. Even when I turned fifteen, and all my friends would go out to the shops at the weekend, I was forbidden from going. I wasn't allowed to date anyone and I nearly didn't make it to university because she was so scared she'd never see me again. I had to promise I would phone or send her a text message every day so she knew I was safe.

I've never felt safer than I do right now, pressed up against Rachel's T-shirt. 'Anna's case file remains open and unsolved with the police,' I tell her. 'I receive a phone call once a year when someone draws a short straw and is instructed to review the file for updates, and inevitably lets me know there are no fresh leads.'

I allow myself to look up as I feel a drop of water splash against my forehead, followed by another and another. The sun is still shining brightly in the distance, but a passing cloud has decided to drop its payload in this time and place. Neither Rachel nor I move from our position.

'No wonder that guy's story upset you so much,' Rachel says tenderly. 'You poor, poor thing. I'm amazed you managed to keep such a secret so quiet for so long.'

'This year marks the twentieth anniversary of her disappearance,' I say, staring back out at the murky river. 'Twenty years of not knowing where she is, nor what happened to her, nor whether she's still alive.'

'That's one hell of a burden to carry on your own.'

I meet her stare. 'I'm sorry I didn't tell you before.'

Her lips flatten into a thin and strained smile. 'I understand it's a precious part of you, and I don't blame you for not sharing.'

In that moment, I decide I'm not going to bow to Maddie's pressure. I've spent the last three years fighting for Freddie and now, having to set aside Anna's disappearance, enough is enough. To hell with what my publisher wants, what Maddie thinks will sell, and to hell with Fitzhume for thinking I'm for sale. I know where my future lies, and that's moving heaven and earth to find out where my sister is.

I wrap my arm around Rachel's waist, not wanting this moment of revelation to end, but aware that it is beyond my control. A small tugboat emerges from beneath our feet, the sound of its wake crashing against the shoreline, reminding me of the sound of Weymouth Bay and all the promise of home.

'What time does your train go?' Rachel asks.

'Soon,' I tell her, checking my watch, the sound of home calling me to Waterloo.

Chapter Seven

THEN

Chalfont St Giles, Buckinghamshire

The sound of an engine revving was followed by the groaning of the driver as the tinnitus slowly began to fade.

'They've taken Cassie!' Elizabeth Hilliard yelled, though it sounded muffled.

Her whole body ached and as she tried to take in her immediate surroundings, she could feel shards of broken window pressing into her right shoulder. The seat belt had her fully restrained but, fumbling with the catch, she was able to wrestle the strap away, and move herself into an upright position.

Hobbs, the driver, was still groggy, his head lolling from side to side as his brain tried to make sense of what had happened. He was no use to her in that condition. Pressing her heeled shoe into his headrest, she delicately gripped the edges of Cassie's broken window, jagged edges breaking her soft skin.

Driving her left foot into the middle headrest of the rear seat, she managed to poke her head through the window frame, and scanned the road for any sign of her daughter's abductors.

To her right she just caught sight of the dark van with blacked-out windows as it broke around the bend ahead in the road. There was no way of seeing the registration number and she screamed out in agony as a hundred thoughts raced across her battered mind.

Where are they taking her? Who has taken her? Will I ever see her again?

Screeching tyres to her left were followed by slammed doors as the two occupants, a black couple dressed in white polo shirts and colourful tracksuit bottoms, exited and rushed over to the car.

'Jesus Christ!' the man exclaimed. 'Are you all right? What happened?'

Elizabeth turned to face the two of them, her mind still a blur. She knew she needed to act fast but she wasn't sure how to.

'I'll call for an ambulance,' the woman said, putting a phone to her ear and moving away from them so she could relay what had happened.

Her partner, with a crisp white sweatband wrapped around his forehead, looked as though he had just stepped onto the courts at Wimbledon. He was tall enough that he didn't need to stretch to see her.

'Let me help you get out,' he suggested, moving closer to the car, but hesitantly, as if he couldn't quite determine whether it was safe to be so close to a potential fire hazard. 'Can you move okay? Are there any broken bones?'

She didn't respond. Shock had settled in, her mind little more than clouds as grey as those overhead.

'Whoa, whoa there,' the man said, taking her hand in his, warmth radiating from it. 'You nearly passed out there. Here, let me help you out; I think there's something leaking beneath the car, and it smells like diesel.'

She allowed him to put his warm hands beneath her arms and he began to lift her before stopping.

'Hold on, all this broken glass could cut you up. I have a picnic blanket in the boot. Give me a second.'

He released his grip, and she nearly crumpled back into the belly of the car as her knees threatened to give way, but she just about managed to hang on to the jagged frame, watching the stranger race to the back of his car, open the boot, and return carrying a tartan woollen blanket that he then pushed in through the window, using it to bash out more shards. Flattening the blanket so that it covered the lower half of the window, he placed his hands beneath her arms again and almost effortlessly pulled her through.

'An ambulance is on its way,' his partner said, joining them. He helped Elizabeth to the edge of the road, several metres away from the upturned Range Rover.

Elizabeth looked back at the wreck, only now seeing that the entire rear passenger-side wheel was missing… but not just the tyre; it was as if something had bitten a chunk out of that section of the car. A thin trail of smoke rose from where she'd emerged.

'How are you feeling?' the woman asked.

Elizabeth was about to respond when a roaring burn in the back of her throat forced her head between her legs and she retched painfully. The image of Cassie disappearing with the gloved hand fired back to the front of her mind.

'Police,' she said, looking from the man to the woman. 'They took my daughter. Phone the police.'

With the narrow road now cordoned off to prevent further traffic, a team of men and women dressed in protective overalls swarmed around the car. Still groggy, Hobbs had been cut from the vehicle and transported to hospital for further observation but Elizabeth remained at the scene. Wrapped in a protective foil blanket for warmth, and with her knees tucked beneath her chin, she tried her best to answer the questions being thrown at her by the woman in uniform who had identified herself as PS Zoe Parsons.

'It looks as if some kind of propelled rocket was used to disable your car,' the young officer said, reading from her notebook. 'The fact that they stopped to take Cassie on this particular stretch of road suggests that this was a targeted attack as opposed to a chance encounter.'

Elizabeth wiped her eyes which hadn't stopped running since she'd demanded the couple who'd stopped to aid her call the police.

'Where is my daughter?' she asked again.

PS Parsons stepped further into the ambulance, closing the door behind her. 'You did the right thing in calling us. We've put an alert out to our colleagues across London. They're searching for Cassie based on the picture you forwarded to me and for the van based on the description you provided. We also have a team of officers scouring for CCTV to track the van's movements. We will narrow the search and do our best to get her back.'

Elizabeth didn't share her optimism. 'What kind of sick bastards would do something like that?'

'Mrs Hilliard, given the equipment used by the perpetrators, and the speed with which they were able to get away, I believe we are dealing with professionals. Now, either these men were hired by someone to cripple the car and take Cassie, or they're acting under their own volition. Either way, these are not just a couple of crooks who acted on the spur of the moment; this operation took time and planning. You said you were travelling back from a children's birthday party? Who knew that you would be there?'

Elizabeth frowned at the question. 'You think the parents of that child did this?'

Parsons shook her head. 'Not necessarily, but we need to establish the identities of anyone who knew you would be on this particular stretch of road at this particular time. Is this a road you travel along often?'

Elizabeth winced as the pain in her head erupted from where she'd bashed it during the crash. 'My driver chose the route. I think it's the direct way from their house in Rickmansworth to our home in Chalfont St Giles. I don't know. I don't drive.'

A knock on the side of the van was followed by a male officer opening the rear door and Elizabeth's husband Richard jumped into the ambulance and joined his wife on the edge of the mattress. He didn't embrace her; he never embraced her anymore. Reaching for her hand, he squeezed it limply.

'I'll give you two a moment to talk,' Parsons said, excusing herself and closing the door.

The formality of their relationship was as painful now as it had been when he'd first told her he was gay. Their tragedy was a marriage neither of them could leave because of the lies that held their entire world together. But right now, she just wanted him to hold her and tell her that everything would be okay.

Richard spoke first. 'I phoned your father and he's going to catch the next flight back from Geneva. He should be here in a few hours.'

Elizabeth wiped her eyes again. 'Who took her?'

He didn't respond, staring at his feet as if the answer might be found on his handmade moccasins.

'Richard, I swear to God, if this has got anything to do with you, I'll—'

The ambulance shook as he leapt to his feet and glared at her. 'What do you take me for? How could you think I would…?' But his words trailed off as his eyes filled with tears.

Elizabeth swallowed down her own sob. 'I didn't mean that you had taken her, but I know your line of work attracts *enemies*, Richard. You may not tell me about the day-to-day running of things, but I'm not deaf and blind. Not taking an interest is not the same as being ignorant.'

He was still glaring at her but anger was swiftly turning into shock. 'Tell me what you saw. Did they say anything?'

'I saw a glove. That's it. A single gloved hand that reached in and took our daughter.' She paused, watching the muscles twisting in his face and the way his eyes darted left and right, searching for answers. 'Oh my God… You know who took her, don't you?'

His head snapped up and, despite its shaking, his eyes betrayed the truth.

Elizabeth jumped down from the trolley, swallowing the space between them until her face was almost touching his. 'Who are they? What do they want with Cassie?'

Richard stepped backwards, almost bumping into the door. 'I don't know who's taken her; I'm as dumbfounded by this unfolding situation as you.'

But she didn't buy it. 'Either you tell me the truth or I'm calling in that police officer and you can explain to her what you know. So help me, Richard, I don't care who I have to throw under the bus to get my child back!'

He took her hand and pulled her to the opposite end of the cabin. 'Shush. I swear to you, I don't know who took her,' he whispered. 'Do you really think I'd be standing here if I did? You're right that my work does attract enemies, and I will kick over every stone until I find who is responsible, but I really am in the dark here too. There must be something else you remember about what happened. Are you sure they didn't say anything? Anything at all?'

Elizabeth closed her eyes, replaying the moment in her memory again. 'No, I told you, no words were spoken. Or if they were, I didn't hear them over the ringing in my ears. All I saw was that…' She didn't finish the sentence. She couldn't finish the sentence as the image in her head sharpened and for the first time she realised exactly what she had seen, something she hadn't noticed until that moment.

'Four fingers. The hand I saw was missing a digit!'

Chapter Eight

NOW

Weymouth, Dorset

I'm somewhere between sleep and waking when a loud banging at the door cuts through the haze. Opening my eyes, I'm surprised to see the ceiling fan overhead… until the temporary amnesia wanes and I realise I must have fallen asleep at my desk last night. My laptop is still displaying the homepage of the site I created to further the search for Anna. Having arrived home late, I'd made a coffee and headed straight for the desk, desperate to see if anyone had messaged with any news since I'd posted the new images. I had paid a specialist company to mock up some images of what Anna might look like now. It wasn't cheap, but what's the point of sharing a picture of Anna from when she was taken? If she's still alive she will no longer look like that same clumsy nine-year-old who preferred football to dolls, and trains to unicorns.

Her eyes are the same, but I don't recognise the rest of the face staring back at me on the screen. I supplied the company with some digital copies of pictures of Anna, her face captured at as many different angles as possible, in order for them to create a 3D composite of her face, which they subsequently aged with skin tone manipulation and various hairstyles. The Anna on the screen now is a virtual stranger to me, and if I walked past her on the street, there would be no way of knowing she was my big sister. It drives me crazy to think I could have walked past her in the last twenty years and not realised. I can't imagine what type of clothes she would be wearing these days. Would her obsession with dungarees and parkas have evolved into jumpsuits and trench coats or would she have found a completely different style?

I showed Mum the older versions of Anna but she didn't think they were an accurate portrayal of the daughter she's been mourning for twenty years. We don't often talk about that time anymore. It's too painful for Mum and I don't want to make her relive the nightmare. I remember the media attention that followed the police appeal for information. I remember my parents both being accused of negligence. I remember the police investigating them both in case they were somehow involved. Despite my witness account that both my parents were in the house when Anna stomped away from our front garden, the police weren't prepared to take the word of a vulnerable seven-year-old who would naturally jump to the defence of her parents.

I dare myself to sip the half-drunk coffee and wince at the error as the cold liquid washes over my tongue. Beside the mug lies the battered, old edition of Elinor Wylie poems that Anna would never be without… until that day. It's face down at Anna's favourite poem, 'Full Moon'; back then it was all just garbled nonsense to me, but now I understand why she loved it so.

Sitting upright, curious to know who could be disturbing me so early, I wipe the damp from the corner of my mouth with the back of my hand, pull the glasses down from the top of my head, and make my way to the front door, stifling a yawn as I unfasten the chain and stare through the gap.

'Morning, sunshine,' Freddie Mitchell trills from just outside, grinning. He lifts two takeaway cups and a small paper bag. 'I brought you breakfast. Can I come in?'

My mind is still half asleep, but I pull the door open and the five-foot-tall Freddie enters my flat, the smell of fresh pastry wafting after him as he heads through to the kitchen and places his treasures on the table. He immediately opens the blind, allowing bright sunshine to flow in through the window, and I won't deny feeling guilty at the state of the kitchen. Half a dozen plates, bowls, and mugs – which I'd meant to wash-up yesterday – are lined up beside the sink, but my eyes have barely left the screen of my laptop since I returned from London.

I'll admit it: I'm a slob when I become enveloped by a story. It isn't something I'm proud of, and I certainly wouldn't choose to invite people to my flat when it's in this state, but in my defence, I didn't invite Freddie over. Besides, he's not just people. Not anymore.

He's watching me as I rub sleep from my eyes. 'Heavy night?' he asks, without judgement. 'God knows, I've had a few of those.'

'Not what you think,' I say, stifling another yawn. 'I was working.'

Freddie nods. 'Well, it's just as well your fairy godmother has come to your rescue. Sit down and I'll find you a plate.'

He's emphasising his naturally effeminate voice, which is something he does when he's nervous of his surroundings, a defence mechanism he's been employing since he was a child. Even though he's rapidly approaching his fortieth birthday, it's still his go-to setting. I know that if I ask him what's wrong he'll pretend everything is okay, but if I can keep him here and talking for long enough, he'll eventually settle and tell me whatever is on his mind. I do wonder in hindsight whether others would have listened to his story sooner had they realised this about his psychological makeup.

He's finished searching through my cupboards and places a clean plate in the only clear spot on the table. 'Sit yourself down,' he encourages and I obey, pulling out a chair.

Opening the lids of the two cups – I know that Freddie only drinks green tea these days – I extract the latte from the cardboard cup-holder and take a sip. 'Thanks for this, Freddie. You really are an angel sent from above!'

He's started filling the sink with soapy water and has rolled up the sleeves of his flannel shirt. I'm not in the habit of allowing people to come into my house and start cleaning up, but this is another of Freddie's ticks, and I know better than to interrupt. He's wearing the same sleeveless faded denim jacket he had on the first time I met him in the soup kitchen. Back then, his hair was longer, and the baldness stretching from his fringe line to the crown of his head was slightly less wide. Amazingly, he now looks ten years younger than he did three years ago; it's amazing the rejuvenating effects of consistency. A healthier diet, a warm bed, and a decent shower have given Freddie Mitchell a new lease of life.

Of course, I know it isn't just the roof over his head that has re-energised him.

'Are you going to join me for breakfast?' I ask casually, opening the white paper bag and inhaling the sweet scent of pastry.

'No, I've already scoffed a sandwich on my way over. They're both for you. Call it a thank-you present.'

In the three years since we met, Freddie has gone out of his way to shower me with presents, and no matter how many times I tell him that there really isn't any need, he still insists. After that first night at the soup kitchen where I just sat and talked to him, he returned the next night with a bunch of daisies he'd picked while he'd been out and about. They were half-dead and covered in soil and cigarette ash, but the gesture had warmed my heart.

You wouldn't know it to see Freddie now, but he was close to death when he arrived in that soup kitchen. I was volunteering there on a break from university during my final year and I'll never forget the feeling of hopelessness that would come home with me each night, not because of who we were helping but simply because it never felt like enough. I wanted to put a roof over all of our visitors' heads but was powerless to do much more than serve them soup and offer a friendly and encouraging smile.

Freddie was outrageously flirtatious, even though it soon became pretty evident that he had no interest in anyone not of his gender. No, correction: he had no interest in anyone – at least, not in that way, or so he had expressed to me in the past. There are still so many scars in Freddie's life that he has yet to share with me but each has carved him into the man he is today, and I love him all the more for them. He's told me about those dark nights when, desperate for food, he was embroiled in schemes outside of his control and how, during one cold winter in 2010, he lost four months of his life due to the volume of drugs he was consuming.

'The HIV diagnosis was inevitable,' he told me the first time I properly sat down to interview him at The Black Horse, along Weymouth's seafront, 'but it doesn't define me, nor diminish me.'

Freddie is many things, but bitter isn't one of them. He is warm, caring, and one of the funniest men I've ever met. In many ways, he feels like a distant brother or cousin, but I know there are more sides to him than he will ever share.

'You didn't make it to The Black Horse last night,' he says now, his back to me as he rinses one of the plates with water from the tap.

Something tells me this is the real reason he's stopped by this morning. 'Yeah, I know,' I say apologetically. 'I was going to come, but then…' I pause, trying to rack my brain for an acceptable excuse for not joining in the celebration of the court's verdict. He'll see through any reference to deadlines with my writing. Eventually I settle for honesty. 'I didn't want to intrude.'

His shoulders tense as he spins to face me, the soap suds dripping from his rough hands to the linoleum at his feet. 'You will always be welcome among us, you know that. If anything, you're more welcome than any of the others.'

I was anticipating he'd say that and I don't doubt that he means every word, but I'm merely the portal through which their story has now been told.

'I'm sorry I didn't come. I meant to send you a message but I got waylaid. Was it a good turnout?'

There is a sadness in his eyes before he turns back to the dishes. 'We were all there. The three of us who… what did they call us in court? The plaintiffs. It's odd seeing Mike and Steve together like that again. All of us have gone off at tangents to one another and, to look at us, you'd never know we all started off in *that* place.'

Two things to know about Freddie Mitchell: he will never refer to himself as a victim and he will never mention the St Francis Home for Wayward Boys by name.

'You've *all* come a long way, Freddie. Just look at *you*. How many days sober now?'

The tension eases a fraction in his shoulders. '1,283 days without so much as a cigarette or bottle of Babycham.'

He doesn't mention the crack pipes, heroin needles, and wrappers of cocaine for which he used to beg, steal, and borrow.

'And now you're helping out at the shelter too. You should be so proud of how far you've come in such a short time, Freddie.'

An uneasy cloud of tension falls as two plates collide beneath the soapy water and I see Freddie's shoulders gently rocking. Dropping the pastry to the plate, I stand and slowly move in behind him, placing my arms around his shoulders and I just hold him. A warm soapy hand shoots out of the water and rests on my forearm.

'I'm sorry,' he whimpers.

'You've nothing to be sorry for, Freddie,' I say quietly.

We remain standing there for several minutes until the crying subsides and he has composed himself once again.

'Fifteen years,' Freddie eventually sighs. 'They gave him fifteen years for what he did to us. They were all abusers, but he was the worst. He was the one who started it. He was the one who got the others involved, and changed them. Fifteen years and he'll probably be dead before he's served any of it.'

When the police first interviewed the three accused, both Geoffrey Arnsgill and Timothy MacDonald – the co-defendants – pointed the finger at Arthur Turgood; both accepted responsibility for their crimes but said it was Turgood who forced them to conspire. Both should have been stronger, both should have said no, should have spoken out, and both would regret their choices for the rest of their lives.

'He's what, eighty now?' Freddie continues. 'He's already lived the best part of his life. What punishment is fifteen years after the life he's led? Getting away with unthinkable crimes against vulnerable children who didn't know better?'

There is nothing I can say. Any attempt to suggest that justice has been served – albeit shockingly late – will sound trite. Too little, too late. And whilst there are those of us who have fought and battled to deliver justice for Freddie and the others, the sentencing passed down by the judge is not enough for their victims. Nothing ever will be.

Freddie sniffs loudly and shakes my arms from his shoulders. 'What a cry baby I'm being. I don't know how you put up with me!'

And there it is: Freddie only lowers his guard for the briefest of moments and then it's back to business. His mask is back in place now and there will be no more display of emotion from him. Not today anyway.

'I only let you in so you can clean up after me,' I joke, returning to the table and finishing off the pastry.

He laughs with just the slightest echo of the recent upset. 'And I only come in and clean up because you're such a slob.'

It's my turn to chuckle as the face he is pulling is possibly the sweetest, most innocent look I've ever seen from him. He even flutters his eyelashes for effect, as if butter wouldn't melt.

'What's with all the papers on the table then? You got your next big mystery to solve?'

I look at the aged picture of Anna on the screen, along with the information I printed about Lord Fitzhume last night. 'Not exactly. It's hard to know where to go next.'

Freddie dries his hands on the towel hanging from the radiator. 'If you ask me, Turgood was just the tip of the iceberg. I reckon if you looked hard enough you'd unfortunately find others like me who suffered at the hands of monsters charged with protecting them. I wish our story was unique but the world is a sadder place than that.'

'Maybe I should quit while I'm ahead,' I muse, reminded of Maddie's dismissive tone about my proposal to focus my next book on Anna.

Freddie is directly in front of me now, waving a finger of caution. 'Don't ever say that!'

I'm almost laughing as I look into his eyes until I realise they are suddenly very serious.

'All joking aside,' he begins, 'you don't realise just how fine a writer you are, Emma. I have read your book three times since it was released and every time I find nuance and detail that I missed the previous time. Even though it's my life being laid bare, it often feels like I'm reading about someone else, and for the first time in forever, I feel like I finally understand who I am. It's like therapy for the untreatable! There must be a million other stories out there – people who are in a similar or even worse position than I was – and you need to find them and bring them back from the edge, as you did me. That is *your* purpose in this world. Where Jessica Fletcher saved the souls of the people of Cabot Cove, so you will save the rest of the world.'

I narrow my eyes at his mention of my personal literary hero and a small grin breaks across his otherwise determined face.

Reaching out, I stretch my hand around his. 'Thank you, Freddie.'

He frowns. 'What for?'

'For being you. For not judging me for living like a slob. For being my shining light at the end of a tunnel. For not giving up.'

He raises my hand and kisses the back of it. 'Don't stop being you either. You have great instincts, Emma. You see through all the bullshit and you write from the heart. Whomever you choose to help next will be lucky to have you aboard.'

I can't help but smile at my very own motivational coach. There's more truth in what he's said than I'd care to admit and I already know there is no cure for the writing bug once it has hold of your soul.

He straightens but doesn't let go of my hand. 'You know, if you've got any free time this week, we could do with all the help we can get at the shelter. I know you're this big, important bestselling author now, but don't forget us little people in your climb to the top, eh?'

The truth is, I will never forget Freddie, Mike, or Steve. Their stories have helped shape my author's voice and without them I would still be a struggling journalist at a small, county newspaper. They have brought this success my way and I want to give them something back, but I know Freddie will never accept charity.

I take a moment to get the words clear in my head. 'Freddie, I've been thinking about something for a while, and…' Here goes. 'I want to share the profits from the book with you and the others. After all, I wouldn't have had a book if it wasn't for—'

'Please don't do that,' he interrupts, shaking his head. 'I appreciate the gesture is coming from your heart but you've done enough for all of us and you deserve every success your book brings you. It was a necessary tool to kickstart the police investigation but it's more than that. Any old Tom, Dick, or Harry could have written about our hell, but you did it in such a… an *honest* way. Nobody else could have told our story so elegantly and we can't take any of the credit for that.'

'But I feel like I'm profiting from… from what happened to you.'

Freddie's eyes glisten but his smile remains. 'That's what makes you so special, Emma Hunter. I'm proud to tell people that I'm friends with this bestselling author with the world at her feet. You are the one positive light to come out of the darkness in my life, and I want to live vicariously through your success. So don't ever think that you don't deserve to be on the ride of your life, and don't you dare stop riding it either. You won't just be stifling your dreams, but ours as well. So, you cling on with all your strength, and we just might hang on with you.'

Chapter Nine

NOW

Weymouth, Dorset

Maddie's call comes just after Freddie has left. I'd promised I'd make an effort to get down to the shelter and soup kitchen tonight. In fairness, I could do with a break from staring at my screen, plotting out Anna's final movements, and looking for new gaps that I haven't previously considered.

'I'm on my way down with some *exciting* news,' Maddie shouts, still yet to get to grips with the hands-free phone kit in her old VW Beetle. I've tried explaining that she doesn't need to shout with Bluetooth, but she perseveres.

I wanted to ask what news could be so exciting as to warrant her driving three hours to Weymouth to meet me in person but she cuts me off before I have the chance.

'Can we meet somewhere nice for lunch? Not that dingy place we met last time. Somewhere that's heard of haute cuisine preferably. Are there any five-star hotels in Weymouth? Pick one of those and text me the address.'

With that, the line disconnected. Maddie is nothing if not efficient in her business dealings.

After an internet search of hotels, I narrow it down to The Waterside Hotel and Spa which is a little way in from the sea front and not somewhere with which I'm particularly familiar. I can't pronounce half the items on the menu so hopefully it will be adequate for Maddie's tastes.

Closing the door to my flat, I stand on the step, listening to the waves crashing against the rocks. A shimmer of sea breeze coats my cheeks and lips, the fresh salt assailing my nostrils. There really is no place like it. So many of my classmates at school couldn't wait to shake the sand from their shoes, as Rachel puts it, always talking about moving closer to London because, "Nothing ever happens in Weymouth." They don't realise how wrong they are.

Admittedly, the streets quieten as autumn draws nearer but if anything, that's when nature comes alive and I don't think I've ever seen a more beautiful sunset than when I've walked along the shoreline.

Heading down the stairs to the main road, I notice there are more people on the beach than I'd anticipated. It's a warm Friday for late September, but the schools are all back now so this is usually the time of year when numbers dwindle, and yet there must be close to a hundred people out there, as well as some splashing about in the water.

I wave as I pass old Giuseppe, who is still advertising donkey walks along the beach, even though all three of his donkeys are tied up. He's been here for longer than I care to remember. He always had a soft spot for Mum and so, as a treat, she'd sometimes bring Anna and me down here for a ride; he never charged her. That all stopped after Anna disappeared. In fact, virtually all socialising stopped that day. Life became a monotonous stream of journeys from home to school and back again, and at the weekend, Mum would be out along the promenade of shops showing Anna's picture to anyone who'd stop and listen. Mirth and frivolity became distant memories and even supposedly joyous occasions such as Christmases and birthdays became days to mourn Anna's departure. I don't blame Mum for shutting down but when I look back on my childhood, I can't help thinking that I lost more than just a big sister that day.

Turning right as the shops come into view, I head up past the train station, past the retail park that was built in an effort to drum up visitors out of season, and on to the road that will eventually lead to Portland Bill. The same shudder that always greets me echoes along my spine when I spot the prison at the top of the hill. The same prison where my father hanged himself almost a decade ago.

'And I'll have the sea-bass risotto with the pomme frites,' Maddie says, handing the menu back to the immaculately dressed waitress whose long black hair has been slicked into a bun on top of her head.

The waitress reaches for Maddie's ribbon-folded serviette, shakes it out of shape, and gently lays it across her lap before repeating the exercise with mine. She can't be much older than twenty-one. I thank her and she bows eloquently before disappearing off towards the kitchen.

I don't think I've ever felt quite so out of my depth whereas Maddie looks to be in her element.

'Try the elderflower cordial,' she suggests, nodding at the fizzing flute she ordered for me.

I lift it and she clinks her glass against mine. The bubbles tickle my nose as I sip it. To her credit, it is delicious.

The room we're in is adorned with white Romanesque statues, with carefully placed stone petals to maintain the dignity of their subjects. The high-vaulted ceiling is made up of triangular-shaped glass panels which form a peak at the join and provide so much light. The room is air conditioned yet warm enough that I don't feel the need to pull my cardigan back on. I've chosen a blue cardigan today so Maddie won't worry about my lacklustre wardrobe again. I picked this one up from a charity shop in the town but it is still new to me and doesn't look worn. If I didn't know better, I'd almost be willing to believe we were staying in some foreign country. This isn't the Weymouth I call home.

'I suppose you're wondering why I've come all this way to speak to you,' she says, her eyes twinkling with excitement. She's clearly itching to tell me something as she hasn't stopped fidgeting since she arrived ten minutes after me.

'You mean it wasn't just for my sparkling company and repartee?' I tease.

She grins mischievously. 'Apart from that, I meant. Well, there are two reasons really, no, three, but we'll come to the last one in a minute. The first bit of news I received on the drive down here. I've been nodded the wink from a friendly source that *Monsters Under the Bed* will definitely be number one on the *Sunday Times* Bestseller list this weekend. It's rare for books to reclaim the number one spot after publication, but to do it three times in six months is almost unheard of. You should be so proud of yourself.'

Remembering Freddie's words earlier today, I don't challenge her.

'And,' she pauses for effect, and I'm half expecting her to begin tapping her fingers on the table to generate a drumroll, 'Reflex Media – who produced that serial-killer hit for Netflix last year – want to option *Monsters* for an eight-part television series!'

I don't think I've ever seen Maddie smile so widely, and for the first time I can see a small pocket of wrinkles where her lips join.

I should be as excited as Maddie is right now. I know the company she's referring to, and I know how hugely successful that serial-killer documentary was. It was a viral hit across the globe and it was a must-see even for someone as clueless as me. This is a big deal. No, correction, this is a *really* big deal.

'Wow,' I say, but I can feel the frown already forming. 'That's incredible news.'

'You bet your life it is!' Maddie replies, almost punching the air. 'Do you know how long I've waited to have this kind of a hit on my hands? They're sending over some numbers for the option later today but for once this is merely a formality. They're pretty confident that, given the book's success in the UK, and the trial verdict on Thursday, this will have TV executives bidding for the chance to distribute. I don't want to pre-empt their figures but we are talking *mega* bucks!'

I take a moment to compose my thoughts. 'What about Freddie, Mike, and Steve?'

Maddie's smile shrinks a fraction. 'What about them?'

'It's their story,' I tell her, not in an attempt to irk her but just stating a fact. 'They gave me permission to write *Monsters...* because they needed their story projected into the public eye, but we never discussed the prospect of their murky history being played out on the big screen for the world to witness in garish technicolour.'

She doesn't respond, studying my face carefully.

'Is it really my place to sell on their story to the highest bidder?' I try again.

'Darling, *Monsters Under the Bed* is *your* story now. The disclosure agreement they all signed included the rights for the story to be sold for feature production and they all signed up to it.'

I'm sure Maddie is probably right about the terms of the agreement they signed, as she's usually pretty switched on when it comes to contracts and erroneous clauses – that's what makes her such a good agent – but if I don't remember such a clause then I'd bet they don't either.

'It's great news,' I say, forcing a positive tone I'm not feeling, 'but can I talk to them about it before we agree to anything?'

Maddie looks like she wants to chastise me again but she closes her mouth and simply nods. 'If that would make you happier then so be it.' She raises her flute of elderflower cordial again. 'Mark my words, this sort of opportunity doesn't present itself very often and you'd be crazy not to take it.'

I thank her, and the flutter in my stomach reminds me that so many other writers would give their eyeteeth to be in my position.

'You said there was a third bit of news?' I ask, in a subtle attempt to change the subject.

Maddie almost spits out her drink as the memory comes

rushing back. 'Oh yes, of course, it's to do with your next project—'

'Oh great,' I say, pulling out the printed pages I brought with me and was hiding in my bag until after the meal. 'I've had some ideas on that too. I've put together an elevator pitch and rough outline of how to structure the story, starting with the moment Anna left the garden, but then flashing forwards to interviews with those who were involved in the early days of the investigation – the police, interviewed neighbours, and the like – and then…' I stop as I realise Maddie is shaking her head and clearly not listening.

'No, I've told you, your sister's disappearance isn't what the publisher is looking for. They want something new, something current, something to capture the nation's imagination in the same way *Monsters* did.'

'Yes, but you haven't heard how we can make Anna's disappearance more relevant,' I try again, but this time she holds up her hand to cut me off.

'I've got a story for you to work on. I've discussed it with the publisher and they think it's fab.'

I already have a sinking feeling as I ask, 'What idea?'

'It was your publishing editor who phoned me about it actually. Does the name Lord Fitzhume mean anything to you?'

I nod grimly, biting the inside of my cheek to keep myself from shouting.

'Well, it turns out he's some distant relative of the royal family. His granddaughter was abducted a year ago and although he's previously gagged every media outlet to keep the story off the front page, he's now prepared to relent. His only stipulation is that *you* tell the story for him. He's even used his influence to gain the support of the Metropolitan Police service, and a detective will be assigned to help you piece together the case history.'

'No,' I say calmly, but authoritatively. 'You told me I could choose my next project and I want to tell my sister's story.'

Maddie pulls a disappointed face. 'I know how important your sister's disappearance is to you, Emma, and if I could spend my remaining days helping you discover what really happened to her, I would. But – and don't take this the wrong way – nobody has been able to shed any fresh light on what happened to her in two decades, and the publisher isn't keen on the prospect of a story that doesn't provide an outcome to what happened to her. They *really* like the story Fitzhume has promised to tell, and you are contracted to deliver a manuscript that will get the publisher's sign-off. You signed a two-book contract with them, Emma, and they're within their rights to see that you deliver on it.'

My cheeks are burning, part in frustration but more because I feel like I've disappointed a parent. I know Maddie has my best interests at heart. If she says I have no choice but to hear what Fitzhume has to say then there is little point in wasting energy on protesting.

Lunch arrives but the conversation that follows is stilted as neither of us knows how to move past the unspoken spectre lingering ever at my shoulder.

Chapter Ten

THEN

Chalfont St Giles, Buckinghamshire

Detective Chief Superintendent Jagtar Rawani cut an unassuming figure as he moved between the rich crimson leather sofas, eyeing the large family portrait hanging above the unlit fireplace. He towered a good foot above Elizabeth Hilliard and, even though the doorways in the old manor were relatively high, the detective had felt the need to duck as he had been shown into the drawing room, declining Rosa's offer of tea. Elizabeth had also declined but not because she wasn't parched; she was already making light work of her father's single malt.

'It's a beautiful painting,' DCS Rawani commented, still transfixed by the enormous reminder of what had been taken from them only four hours earlier.

The detective was staring at Elizabeth as if expecting an answer. Had she missed his question?

'Sorry, what?' she said.

'I said, is it recent? The painting. I was just trying to work out how old Cassie would have been when it was painted.'

'It was completed five months ago,' Elizabeth replied, squashing herself further into the armchair where her father had often allowed her to sit upon his lap while he had studied the markets in one broadsheet or another.

'Will Mr Hilliard be joining us soon?' the detective asked, turning and fixing his impatient stare on her.

Some other detective had arrived at the scene shortly after Richard had turned up, and had begun coordinating efforts. It was she who had told them it was best to return home and await news. Neither she nor Richard had disagreed; what more could they have done at the scene to get Cassie back? Neither had the kind of connections required to track down child abductors.

Elizabeth shuddered at the thought of what the abductors might be doing to poor Cassie, nearly slopping the glass of single malt across her lap.

As soon as they'd got in, Richard had said he had business calls to make and had headed through to his office, locking the door. In a state of numbness, Elizabeth had gone up to the main bathroom, switched on the shower and emptied a bottle of antidepressants over the counter beside the basin, scattering them, trying to calculate how many would be necessary to take away the pain. In the end, she'd scooped them into her hand and returned them to the bottle. Her father wouldn't have been happy to see her so close to giving up.

He'd know what to do. He'd return and make sure the bad men faced justice for their crimes. He always knew what to do.

The door to the drawing room opened and Richard marched into the room, thrusting his hand out towards the detective, offering him a drink, and asking for the latest update in the case. Elizabeth didn't need to think too long about what had perked him up and, knowing Richard, the trace of white powder would still be clinging to the tip of his nostril for all to see exactly what he'd gone into his office to do.

Traditionally handsome, Richard still had a full head of thick brown hair thanks to his little trip to East Asia for a discreet transplant last year. He wasn't physically strong, yet he had a physique that most men his age would kill for. His secret wasn't to watch what he ate – in fact, Elizabeth couldn't recall the last time she'd actually seen him eat anything – but in the appetite-suppressing white powder. He didn't hide his drug use from her just as she didn't hide her ever-increasing reliance on alcohol and pills to encourage sleep.

'Have you tracked the van yet? My wife said it was navy blue, but the road we were on only goes to one place and they must have traffic cameras and the like you can view. Where did the van go after leaving the main road? Surely if you find the van you'll find Cassie.'

He didn't realise he was talking too fast and Elizabeth made no effort to point it out. If he was stupid enough to snort a line of cocaine while there was an on-duty police officer in the house then he could face those consequences alone.

The detective was clearly sizing Richard up, and for a moment Elizabeth thought he might arrest her husband there and then. Instead, he steered Richard to one of the sofas and sat down beside him.

'We are doing everything in our power to locate the vehicle used to take your daughter, Mr Hilliard. I have a team tracking down and viewing traffic and privately owned security camera feeds to monitor the van's movements. We don't have a registration number which makes the trace more challenging, but we are trained professionals and this is what we're good at. We will pursue every avenue until we learn what happened and who is responsible. The reason I'm here now is to try and establish exactly who would want to take Cassie and what their motivation might be.'

Richard clapped his hands together excitedly. 'Good. Good. Absolutely. Any way we can help, we're happy to.'

It was as if Elizabeth was no longer there, sitting in the corner, observing the drama playing out like a scene on the stage.

'Thank you, Mr Hilliard, and I appreciate my questions aren't going to be easy to hear but I can assure you they are a necessary evil. I need to look at every angle in order to narrow down and eliminate possibilities.'

'Just like Sherlock Holmes,' Richard said, before erupting into unconstrained laughter that was inappropriate for the situation.

'Tell me, Mr Hilliard, can you think of anyone – perhaps a business rival or an unhappy client – who may have wanted to cause you serious harm?'

Richard's laughter stopped in an instant. 'No. None at all.'

'What is it you do for a living, Mr Hilliard?'

'I run a company specialising in the tracing and purchase of rare antiquities on behalf of a very exclusive client list,' he replied, more composed now.

'Can you be more specific?'

'My clients – customers – come to us when they want a specific piece of art or an antique. We have contacts across the globe and so if, let's say for example, you could afford to, and wanted to, purchase a Monet, you would come to us and say what you're looking for and what price you'd be prepared to pay. We will then reach out to our contacts and see what's available in the market and place a bid on your behalf. If it's accepted, we then carefully ship and deliver the painting to you, taking a commission for our efforts.'

DCS Rawani's gaze took in the rest of the room: a Matisse, a Degas, and a Gauguin. 'It must be a lucrative business judging by some of the pieces you have hanging here.'

'This is my father's house,' Elizabeth spoke up, catching the pair of them off-guard.

'Yes,' Richard chimed in, 'as my wife says, this is my father-in-law's house. That said, most of our clients aren't shy about the cost of artwork and when someone really wants a specific piece they're often prepared to pay whatever it takes to get hold of it. It's not uncommon for fees in the millions to be exchanged.'

'And your commission is…?' the detective asked.

'Depends on the nature of the piece, but anywhere between ten and twenty per cent after delivery.'

The detective whistled through his teeth. 'You probably make more in one deal than I earn in a year.' He paused to let that sink in. 'That sort of money might make you a target for criminals. Have you noticed anyone suspicious hanging around either here or at your work premises?'

Richard shook his head.

'What about you, Mrs Hilliard? Have you noticed anyone or any suspicious vehicles hanging around? Maybe you've spotted a particular car or motorbike several times in different places at different times and thought it seemed a touch odd?'

Elizabeth shook her head too. 'No, nothing. I'm sorry.'

'Any threats received by either of you, even something so

small it didn't necessarily register as a threat? Maybe something on social media, or email, or in the street?'

'Nothing that immediately springs to mind,' Richard concluded. 'Are you sure I can't get you something to drink? I'm parched. Rosa! Rosa!'

The housekeeper entered the room, head bowed, shoulders stooped, awaiting instruction.

'Ah, there you are. Be a dear and fix me a gin and tonic, would you? Lemon, but no ice. Thank you.' He turned back to the detective. 'Are you sure you don't want a cup of tea? Glass of water?'

'No, I'm fine, thank you.'

Rosa nodded and shuffled off back out of the room.

'I would like to speak to your house staff tonight as well,' the detective said. 'Is Rosa your only member of staff?'

Elizabeth snorted but didn't follow it up with a comment, choosing to drain her glass instead.

'There's also Teddy,' Richard said. 'He's our gardener and general errand boy, but I don't see how speaking to either of them is going to help track down the men responsible for snatching Cassie.'

Elizabeth snorted again, imagining exactly what Teddy would reveal about her husband's proclivities if put under pressure.

The detective stood suddenly and moved back across to the fireplace, taking another long look at the canvas of the three of them. He kept his back to them as he spoke. 'It is my belief that your vehicle was deliberately targeted in this afternoon's attack. Whoever is behind it knew that the Range Rover would be on that section of road at that time, which is why they brought a rocket-propelled grenade launcher to disable the vehicle. They targeted it, but it's not clear to me yet whether they intended to snatch Cassie from the outset, or whether they were targeting one of you. Given that they left Mrs Hilliard in the car unscathed, it's likely she wasn't part of their plan, but that doesn't mean they weren't after you, Mr Hilliard.'

The detective spun round on his heel, but neither Richard nor Elizabeth reacted. 'Either way, these people *knew* the Range Rover would be there, which suggests they had insider information. Who's to say your housekeeper, driver, or gardener didn't slip that information to them, or to some intermediary, for a few quid extra in their pocket?'

Elizabeth could see her husband's mind whirring with the possibility that his biggest secrets could come tumbling out of the mouth of his young lover, who really did have an eye for garden landscaping.

'Then there's the royal connection,' the DCS said, turning his stare on Elizabeth. 'It's your father's side that's distantly related to the royal family. Is that correct, Mrs Hilliard?'

Elizabeth peeled herself out of the upright chair and stumbled towards the drinks trolley at the far end of the drawing room where Rosa had just filled Richard's glass before returning to the kitchen via the second door. Filling her own glass once again, Elizabeth was light-headed as she struggled to retrace her steps back to the armchair.

'Yes,' she slurred, once she was re-seated.

'If Cassie was the target, it could be a veiled attempt at striking out at the royals. It's been done before. I will be liaising with the Specialist Royal Constabulary to pursue that angle.' He turned back to Richard. 'I'd like you to supply a full client list for your business, along with the names of anyone who petitioned for your services and for whom you were unable to deliver the item they sought, anyone who could be disgruntled. I'll speak to your housekeeper now but would appreciate you giving me the gardener's contact information tonight.'

Richard's face paled but he nodded and excused himself from the room just as Rosa entered, handing him the gin and tonic as he passed. Elizabeth watched the detective ask her to sit and answer some questions, calculating whether to tell him the true nature of Richard's import company. If it meant getting Cassie back then it was a price she was prepared to pay, but if it had nothing to do with the business, she didn't want to call the wolves to their doors.

For now, she would wait.

Daddy would be home soon, and he'd know what to do.

Daddy always knew what to do.

Chapter Eleven

NOW

Weymouth, Dorset

Lunch with Maddie ended with me promising I would think hard about the option from Reflex Media with an emphasis that I'd be throwing away the opportunity of a lifetime if I declined it. She still doesn't understand that it isn't a choice I can make without consulting Freddie and the others.

There's less of a decision to be made with my next project. I signed a contract with my publisher to produce a book that will get their sign-off, but I did *not* say I would sell my soul to the first pariah to come along and wave wealth and royal relatives in my face. I am shocked – no, *outraged* – that having been turned down by me directly, Fitzhume thinks it's okay to strong-arm me via my publisher. I think my initial assessment of him in the lobby of Maddie's offices was spot on: he is a man used to getting his own way.

He's the sort of bully I've spent my life fighting against: the populars in secondary school making snide comments about anyone who even slightly diverged from the accepted norm; the drunk students in bars who thought it was fine to put their uninvited hands on me when dancing in a club; and the wardens at the St Francis Home for Wayward Boys. These are all people who think the usual rules and laws don't apply to them. Fitzhume appears to be exactly the same, and I so desperately want to take a stand against him but I know that Maddie is right, and that my options are somewhat limited. If I refuse to go along with the publisher's suggestion, they'd be within their rights to sue for breach of contract. I doubt very much they'd do that, given the publicity surrounding my name and the first book, but I don't want the hassle and stress that goes with all that.

What I need is advice, real advice from someone who knows me better than any of the friends and colleagues I've made along the way to this point. I just hope today is a good day for her.

The walk from the hotel restaurant took longer than I'd anticipated but I thought the air would help clear my head. Unfortunately, the brief downpour I've just stepped out of has left me with a head full of questions and a damp blazer and jeans. I'm sure rain wasn't forecast for today.

The wrought-iron gates are wide open as usual, and I'm grateful that I came on foot as the streets outside the home are tail-to-tail with cars of all shapes and sizes. I can't say for sure whether all these cars belong to guests visiting ailing relatives inside the home but given there are only thirty rooms inside the small purpose-built care home, I'd be surprised if all the residents had a visitor. I can't remember ever seeing the inside full of guests.

Heading in through the gates, I stop to stroke the

overweight ginger cat sitting on the stone steps up to the large painted door. Her name is Ginger by all accounts – no prizes for imagination to whoever named her. She snuggles her head into the palm of my hand as my fingers gently rub the soft fur between her ears. It must be three months since I've stopped by and, if I didn't know better, I'd say Ginger hasn't moved from this spot.

The front door is locked as always, and I'm about to press on the buzzer to signal my arrival when the door opens and a young woman in a purple tabard emerges. I recognise her as one of the nursing staff, though her name escapes me. She smiles in my direction as I step through the door and feelings of inferiority bubble to the surface once again. I do so admire those who follow a selfless vocation and give themselves to the service of others: doctors, nurses, police officers, teachers, firefighters. Their roles seem so much nobler than the profession of writer and occasional journalist.

I'm being hailed in almost every newspaper for uncovering the truth about what happened to Freddie and the others, when really they should be shouting praise for people like this nurse, a true lifeline to those inside who rely on her. Where are her awards for cleaning and tending and caring for those too mentally or physically infirm to look after themselves? Why aren't we all asking for *her* autograph?

Closing the door behind me, I allow my nostrils to adjust to the distinctive smell that clings to every molecule of air inside the place. I suppose it's something the nursing staff eventually get used to, but the only way I can get through it is to breathe through my mouth wherever possible.

Signing in at the reception window, I tell them I'm here to visit Mrs Bronwyn Hunter, known to the nurses as

Winnie. The woman behind the desk checks I know how to find her bedroom, and I confirm I do, then move further into the house nodding at a couple more of the nurses I recognise as they make a break for the front door. It must be shift-changeover time, which would suggest it's just after two o'clock. Patient feeding happens on a strict routine: eight, twelve, and six, with food served for one hour. Patients are free to request cups of tea and coffee, as well as fruit and biscuits throughout the day, but only when a member of staff is free to help. Mum's room is on the second floor, where the more physically able are homed. She isn't here because she can't get about on her own. She can dress and feed herself, and is capable of using the facilities unaided; her difficulty is in remembering when and how to perform those activities.

I arrive outside her room and press my ear to the door to see if she's moving about. If she's asleep, I really don't want to disturb her but I can just about make out the gentle rumble of applause coming from within, meaning she has the television on. Knocking sharply twice, I push down the door handle, and poke my head inside.

'Hi Mum, it's Emma,' I say brightly.

Her room is modest, with a small toilet and shower cubicle off to one side. She is seated in the only tall-backed chair, which has been dragged away from the small round table to a distance of only two metres from the television screen. She doesn't turn to face me as I speak.

'Mum? It's Emma,' I repeat as I enter the room and close the door behind me, but she still doesn't move. For a moment I think she must have fallen asleep in the chair when she suddenly looks at me.

'Ah good, there you are. There's something wrong with the television.'

The picture looks clear enough and I can hear every word the presenter is saying.

'What's the problem?' I ask, moving closer.

'It's supposed to be *Countdown* now, but this rubbish is on.'

I step back, studying the television screen. 'This is *Countdown*, Mum. Look, there's Rachel Riley by the board of letters. See?'

I look back at her and she's squinting through her large round glasses. 'Don't be silly, this isn't *Countdown*. Where's Carol Vorderman and Richard Whiteley?'

It would appear that today is not a good day.

'They don't present the show anymore, Mum. They were replaced many years ago. Do you remember?'

She continues to squint. 'This isn't *Countdown*!'

'It is, Mum. Look, there are the two players behind the desks with their mascots. See?'

She stands, tutting, and barges past me, grabbing the remote from in front of the set and switching it off. 'Well, I don't know why they have to mess about with the schedule and put on programmes that aren't what they've advertised! Why can't they get the easy things right?'

I don't argue and instead move across to the table. The window beyond it has a view of the sea, though I notice there are fewer surfers and paddlers out there now.

'How are you doing, Mum?' I ask absently. 'I brought you some new magazines to read,' I add, lifting up the carrier bag and lying it flat on the table. 'There's also a new ball of yarn. I thought you must be running out of the last lot I brought.'

She appears beside me and nudges the carrier bag. 'What's

all this then?'

I take a deep breath. 'They're the magazines I just told you I got, and some more wool.'

'Oh,' she says, moving back to the television. '*Countdown* should be on in a minute. Do you want to stay and watch it?'

Alzheimer's is one of the cruellest illnesses the human condition endures. It is cruel for those afflicted, but cruellest on the families who have to watch as their loved one slowly evaporates. It was also early onset and sporadic, coming seemingly out of nowhere in the years after Anna's disappearance when Mum was only in her forties. I know she's still in there somewhere, and even if her memory is misfiring today, I need to try and reach her.

Leaving the bag on the table, I walk towards her, take her hand in mine, and lead her to her bed, encouraging her to sit on the bedspread with me. Keeping her hand in mine, I look into the deep brown eyes we share.

'I need your help, Mum,' I say, unsure what she will make of what I want to talk about. 'It's about Anna. Do you remember Anna?'

'Of course I remember my own daughter,' she tuts.

'That's good, Mum,' I smile reassuringly. 'The thing is, I've spent the last seven years searching for the truth about what happened to her all those years ago and I feel like I've hit a wall. I've checked every witness statement, walked her final journey until my blisters developed blisters of their own, and I've failed to make a breakthrough. I've failed her and I've failed you and I'm sorry. I'm so sorry, Mum.' I pause to check I still have her undivided attention. 'I've been offered a job in London and I don't want to take it but I'm not being given much choice. I want to decline the offer and stay here and keep searching for Anna, but I could spend the next twenty years searching for her and still not make any progress. I don't know what to do.'

She blinks at me and opens her mouth to speak before closing it again.

'Yes, Mum?' I press, desperate for one moment of pure clarity where my old mum is back – the mum from before Anna vanished. 'What is it?'

She opens and closes her mouth again. 'What time is it?'

I check my watch and raise my arm so she can see for herself. 'Quarter past two, Mum.'

She flattens the pleats in her violet skirt as if brushing invisible crumbs from the material. 'Ah, well, we can't hang around here for too long. Anna will be home soon.'

The breath catches in my throat. 'What?'

'Well,' she says, still brushing the skirt, 'it's like you said. It's after two so I'll have to leave to collect Anna from nursery soon. I do hope she's had a fun day.'

A single tear escapes my eye and runs the length of my cheek, pooling on my chin line before gravity carries it away. This isn't the first time she's spoken to me of her toddler Anna, a child so full of life and energy with a brilliant future ahead of her.

'No, Mum,' I quietly correct her, my voice straining with sorrow. 'Anna went missing, remember? She went to Grandma's house but she never arrived. You do remember, Mum. Tell me you remember, Mum… please.'

My vision is misting up but she is oblivious to it. She stands and plonks herself back into the tall chair. 'Could you fetch me a cup of tea and a digestive biscuit, dear? *Countdown* will be starting in a minute.'

Chapter Twelve

NOW

Weymouth, Dorset

The house looks so different to how I remember it from my childhood. The short driveway is still separated from the pavement by a now very rusty gate and the single-pane window frames at the front of the house look as though they haven't been painted in years. Dad used to do it every spring and I have a vivid memory of him tottering on a ladder rubbing the panes of Anna's bedroom window. I remember thinking how brave he was to climb so high, risking falling off, just to make the house look nicer. The frames have now yellowed in the sun, and the paint is so dry it's peeling. He'd turn in his grave if he could see the state of his former castle.

There is another 'For Sale' sign jutting out of the lawn beside the short driveway. The place always seems to be on the market these days, as if prospective buyers snap it up for the bargain that it is, and then change their minds once they realise its tragic history. I wouldn't want to live here again, not after what happened, not now it stirs more bad memories than good.

We moved out during my parents' divorce. Mum couldn't afford to pay the mortgage on her own and Dad certainly didn't need a three-bedroom property keeping him trapped in Weymouth. He'd always had big dreams, wanting more out of life than the wife and two daughters he'd somehow picked up along the way. I couldn't blame him for feeling trapped and if anything, Anna's disappearance probably gave him the out he'd been looking for all those years. He used to tell me how he was born for big things, that if *I* followed my dreams, one day I too would realise what I was put here to do. He had always been a believer that every person was born to fulfil a purpose but most of us are too blind to realise what it is until it's too late. He never did tell me what it was that he believed he was born to do, but telesales certainly wasn't it.

I caught a bus from Mum's care home to the old neighbourhood, wanting a last look at the old place, wanting to walk Anna's final route one more time, hoping for that momentary glimpse of something that would make all the facts fit.

The metre-high brick wall enclosing the garden is exactly the same as when we lived here, the cement between the bricks still crumbling under the influence of Mother Nature. On that Sunday afternoon, I remember Anna and me leaning against the wall, sitting on the cool, fresh grass and staring up at the house. Anna was telling me a story about the giant dragon climbing up the side, trying to stand on the roof so he could find his lost mum. She was so imaginative, telling me how the dragon's huge claws were making the roof tiles cascade to the ground, and how we'd have to be careful not to get hit by one.

Her stories felt so real that even now, as I stare up at the roof, I can still picture the giant purple dragon with its oval-shaped pink belly and shock of spiky green hair between its ears.

Dad's car hadn't been on the driveway that day. In fact, it had been several months since he'd used it, bored of the daily chore of opening and closing the gate when it was easier to just park on the road directly in front of the house. That was why were able to play on the concrete strip, which is where I had been practising with that infernal skateboard.

'You're doing it wrong,' her voice echoes in my mind.

I was wobbling aboard it, just trying to get my balance while it was stationary, but she kept pulling on my arm, trying to get me off so she could show me how to do it. She was two years older than me, and always trying to bestow her wisdom and experience on me when all I wanted was to live those experiences for myself.

'I'm going to Grandma's,' she scowled – her final words to me.

Her ghostly image, eyes streaming, stomps through the gate, right past where I'm standing, not closing it properly as she tore off to the left and down the road. I follow her now, trying to put myself in her shoes, trying to understand whether she stuck with her plan to go to Grandma's house or whether she deviated from that journey for some reason unknown to any of us.

I'd lost sight of her after she passed the Jeffersons's place, four houses away. Passing their house now, it looks so different. The current owners have built a porch extension at the front and their once green lawn and concrete driveway have been replaced by a purple and orange brick patio. The windows are all double-glazed; in fact, as I pause and stare at the other properties in the immediate vicinity, they're all double-glazed now. It's only our old house that remains frozen in time, abandoned by all who've lived there.

The alleyway is a further ten properties along the road, dissecting Deane Road and Corsica Way, a natural divide, though why the original developers saw a need to call the long strip of road by two different names is beyond me. Arriving at the alleyway now, it is as dark as I remember it being back then, even in the late September sunshine. The alleyway is lined by the tall fences of the two properties that border it, but both have large trees and bushes overhanging the fences which seem to come together at the highest point of the path, creating a kind of leafy wooden arch and blocking out the light. It's the sort of tunnel I'd picture in an illustrated fairy-tale about princesses and monsters.

My enduring memory of this public footpath is of pictures of Anna's face taped to every fence panel, and to the lampposts at either end of the darkened passage. Mum printed loads of posters with Anna's face on after what happened and would stick them up wherever she found a pylon or lamppost without one on. She laminated some of them too so they wouldn't smudge in the rain. She even got in trouble at one point for the number of posters she was sticking up, but she didn't care; it only seemed to spur her on to put up more. She didn't want anyone to forget that her daughter had gone missing, and needed help to find her way home.

A shiver jolts through my shoulders and the air in my lungs is decidedly cold as I step into the alleyway, counting the three hundred and five steps of its length as I go. It was a habit I developed back then, a way to keep my mind off all the monsters I imagined were lurking, waiting to snatch me away as they had Anna.

I keep my head bowed as I move along it now, scanning the well-trodden paving slabs, searching for that crucial clue that has been missed for the last two decades, but is just waiting to be discovered. It doesn't matter that an entire team of crime scene investigators scoured every inch of the public footpath, nor that thousands of people and pets must have been up and down here in the last twenty years. A variety of weeds and grasses shoot out from beneath the rotting fences, creating a green trim along the walkway; it all adds to the sense of foreboding as I continue to count my steps. I stop at step one hundred and fifty-two, the midway point of the alley. In my childish mind, this was the place where Anna disappeared – equidistant from both entrances. When I was thirteen, I made a special trip here on the anniversary of her disappearance and stood in this exact spot. I waited an entire hour, willing the monsters to come for me, so I would know once and for all where she had gone.

They never did.

This point of the alley is where it is darkest. The overhanging trees and bushes let no light permeate and yet, as I look just beyond the last branch, I can see the upstairs bedroom windows of the first house on the road into which the footpath leads. I don't remember noticing the room before, and with net curtains hanging, it's impossible to see inside. From memory, that property belonged to the Napier family, who were away on a three-week trip to New Zealand when Anna disappeared, so were never considered suspects for understandable reasons. Such a pity that they hadn't been home as the view from that room would have looked straight into the alleyway and they would have been able to see if a monster – whether fanged and ferocious like in my mind's eye, or someone altogether more human – had grabbed my sister and dragged her away. Right now, I would sacrifice anything to be taken back to that day.

With a heavy sigh, I return my eyes to the ground and recommence my counting until I reach the end of the footpath which then opens out into Bletchley Street, where my Grandma used to live. I continue to walk until I reach what was her house. She died a year and a half after Anna's disappearance, and the house was bought by a developer. I've always believed she died of a broken heart, even if the doctors did blame it on cancer. The property developer knocked down her house and, owing to the large rear garden, erected two smaller properties on the site, which now make up 123A and 123B Bletchley Street. I wish she were here now. Even after Anna's disappearance she always gave the best hugs, the kind of embrace that told me the world would one day make sense again.

It is dark by the time I make it to the soup kitchen beside Weymouth's only shelter for those in need. It is a purpose-built dormitory which prioritises beds for victims of domestic abuse, though most soon become occupied by those who would otherwise find themselves on a park bench or the beach for any number of reasons. Whilst it has been a warm day – aside from the brief shower after lunch – it is much cooler now and I'm glad I nipped home to grab my anorak and scarf. Whilst the shelter and attached kitchen offer a warm and friendly atmosphere, the door is left open leaving a constant draught blowing at the volunteers behind the tables.

'Look what the cat dragged in,' Freddie Mitchell calls out for the benefit of the room as I enter. He knows such a formal announcement will have me cringing but I know he's only doing it to try and help me break free of the bashful shackles.

He's still wearing the same flannel shirt and sleeveless denim jacket he had on when he called round at mine this morning, though he's covered his balding head with a navy-blue beanie hat.

'How lucky we are to have a celebrity amongst us downtrodden folk this evening,' Freddie continues. 'Ladies and gentle friends, may I introduce you all to Weymouth's hottest new property, bestselling writer Emma Hunter.'

He begins a ripple of applause but most of the glum faces squashed in at the tables just look at me as if I'm not even there. I ignore their stares as I walk over to the table and embrace him.

'Sorry about that,' he whispers. 'Just trying to lighten the mood in here. How long can you stay for?'

'Probably until ten if that's okay? I've got an early train to catch in the morning.'

'Ooh, hark at you, Miss Big-time. Jetting off to somewhere exotic, I hope?'

If only, I don't say.

'If you can call West London exotic then I guess so,' I tell him. 'My agent, Maddie, wants me to meet with a man whose granddaughter was abducted last year; I think he hopes I can somehow piece together the clues in a way the police haven't managed to. I've told him it's unlikely, but he wants me to try.'

'Good for you! Given your own history, I'd have thought

you'd be chomping at the bit to help someone in a similar position.'

I hadn't thought about it like that. All this time I've been resenting Fitzhume and his bullying tactics, but underneath it all, he's just a worried grandparent, desperate to find out the truth about what happened to Cassie. Wouldn't I bully and fight to the end for Anna too?

'Grab a ladle and get the lid off that second pot, would you?' Freddie says, pointing at the large urn beside the one he's been working from. 'It's after seven, so we're expecting a rush any second. You couldn't have come at a better time.'

I do as instructed and the steam mists up my glasses as I raise the lid, but that's soon forgotten as the delicious fragrance of leeks and potatoes wafts up at me. I'm almost salivating as I dunk the ladle into the hot broth.

There is a momentary break in the queue and I use it to seize my chance. 'Freddie? There was something I was meaning to speak to you about… My agent, Maddie – you remember meeting her, right?'

He reaches for a knife and begins to slice portions of baguette, filling the straw basket beside the pile of napkins and clean spoons. 'Vaguely. She was the one who looked a bit like Sybil from *Fawlty Towers*, right?'

I chuckle at the comparison, picturing Maddie's face when I tell her about Freddie's first impression. 'That's her, yeah. She stopped by to visit me earlier today, and she said…' I take a deep breath. 'Apparently there's a television company interested in putting *Monsters Under the Bed* on screen.'

A huge smile stretches across his face. 'That's incredible news! Well done you!' The smile starts to fade as the implications of the news sink in. 'You mean they want to televise *our* story. Mine and Steve's and Mike's story… what they did to us… Turgood and…'

He doesn't finish the sentence and I nod grimly.

He drops the bread knife, stumbles back, and places his hands over his mouth as if he's about to retch.

'I haven't accepted their offer,' I say quickly, so he understands that I'm not here after the horse has bolted. 'And at the moment they only want to option the book for a series so there's a chance that they would later decide not to go ahead with it.'

A queue is once again starting to build so I reach for my ladle and begin to fill bowls. When the queue dies down again, I move across to Freddie but he shirks my attempt to hug him.

'Please, Freddie, if you tell me you don't want the story told through film, then I'll reject the option and we don't have to discuss it again.'

He lowers his hands and I can see now his eyes are shining in the dimly lit room. 'I don't know what to say,' he tells me. 'When I first told you my story, I never expected you to believe me. I was so used to people telling me I was mistaken or that there was nothing they could do, but you… you told me you wouldn't stop until you made people listen. And boy did you deliver! But I… I don't know how I feel about my life – those incidents – played out by actors for all to see.'

'I understand that, and that's exactly what I thought you'd say. That's why I wanted to ask you first.'

'What have the others said? Have you spoken to Mike and Steve yet?'

'Not yet; you're the first.'

He takes a deep breath and releases a sigh. 'Okay. Let me

speak to them and see what they say. When do you have to make a decision by?'

I shrug pathetically. 'I don't know, but Maddie suggested they'd be sending the paperwork over in the next week.'

He leans in and kisses my cheek to show there are no hard feelings. 'I appreciate you letting me know. I'll try and get hold of Mike and Steve tomorrow, and give you a call.'

We return to ladling soup and no more is said about the Reflex Media offer for the rest of the night. I'm exhausted when I make it home, but I do finally feel ready to start the next chapter of my life.

Chapter Thirteen

THEN

Chalfont St Giles, Buckinghamshire

Rummaging through the mirrored cabinet in her private bathroom, Elizabeth Hilliard's eyes finally fell on what she'd been searching for; the small brown bottle of pills the doctor had prescribed during those dark days following Cassie's birth. He'd referred to them as mood stabilisers back then, and she'd never been more in need of stabilising than right now.

Glancing at the label, the words merged in and out of focus as she searched for any kind of best-before date, as though examining a packet of meat in Waitrose. Finding no such date, she unscrewed the cap and tipped the bottle until two blue and red capsules dropped into the palm of her hand. She rolled them around with her thumb, in reverence at the power they possessed, before dropping a third capsule out of the bottle and thrusting her hand towards her mouth. Washing them down with a glass she'd filled up at the basin, she was about to return the plastic bottle to the safety of the cupboard before changing her mind and dropping it into the pocket of her pale pink satin gown.

Closing the cabinet door, she stared at the tired eyes, hung cheeks, and mess of hair of the old woman in the reflection. For the first time, it was as if she was staring into the face of her own mother, pictures of whom adorned every surface of her father's grand room in the east wing. Pinching the skin between her eye sockets and cheeks, she wouldn't accept the similarity. She'd never felt so close, and yet so far away, from the woman who had brought her into the world, one who had managed to slip away and avoid the heartache that was now permeating every cell of Elizabeth's almost lifeless corpse.

Returning to her bedroom, Elizabeth knew sleep wouldn't come, as it hadn't last night, despite drinking her father's single malt into the early hours. Some semblance of sleep must have caught up with her at some point, yet there were also large portions of the night spent staring at the red digits of the bedside clock, willing the time to pass quicker so she would be reunited with Cassie sooner.

The sound of doors slamming outside prompted her to turn towards the window and, gliding across to it, she found herself staring down through half-open blinds at an estate police car now parked directly in front of Richard's Jaguar. She couldn't see the faces of the two uniformed officers because of their flat caps, but she recognised the navy-blue turban of Detective Chief Superintendent Jagtar Rawani, towering above his colleagues. She hadn't expected him to return until they'd found Cassie, which could only mean he had news.

Hurrying from the room – pushing away all thoughts that the news could be anything but positive – she raced down the winding staircase, not in the slightest bit concerned that three virtual strangers would see her in her night clothes.

Rosa was just opening the main doors as Elizabeth reached the final step, and she paused momentarily to run a hand through her unruly hair and to take two quick breaths to settle her racing heart, and then joined Rosa at the door.

'Mrs Hilliard, good morning,' the detective said quietly, 'would you mind if we came in and spoke to you and your husband privately?'

Elizabeth stepped back and ushered Rosa to the kitchen to fix coffee, while showing the detective through to the drawing room, while his two colleagues – one of whom she now realised to be a woman – waited in the hallway.

'Is your husband available too?' the detective asked, as he ducked beneath the door frame once again.

'I don't know where he is,' Elizabeth replied, instantly regretting the level of honesty displayed. 'What I mean is, I've only just woken and I have yet to see him this morning.'

'It would be best if I spoke to you at the same time, if possible,' he said, offering the thinnest of smiles to show no offence was intended.

'I'll go and find him,' Elizabeth said, closing the door behind her and marching across the hallway, past the two officers who averted their eyes, and finally arriving at the closed door to Richard's office. Knocking twice, she didn't wait to be invited in but when she opened the door she found the room to be empty.

Frustrated, she left the room, ensuring the door was closed, conscious of the presence of the two officers who might just be tempted to snoop. Elizabeth smiled in their direction before turning and heading towards the kitchen. The smell of fresh bread hit her the moment she entered and her stomach growled with dissatisfaction.

'Rosa, have you seen Mr Hilliard this morning? Do you know where he is?'

The housekeeper immediately stopped filling the kettle with water. 'Si, Mrs Hilliard. He is tennis.'

Rosa's language skills had improved in the five years since she'd worked exclusively for the family but they were still far from perfect. 'You mean he's *playing* tennis, Rosa?'

'Si.'

Elizabeth didn't stop to question why her husband – experiencing the same heartache and remorse as she – felt the need to work on his backhand at such a dark moment in their lives. Heading out through the reinforced patio door, she pulled the satin robe closer as the morning's chill threatened to envelop her entire body. Bending left at the water fountain, she stuck to the patio slabs, moving further away from the house until she arrived at the wire-fenced court.

'Richard, that detective is here,' she called across the court. 'He wishes to speak to both of us.' She made no acknowledgement of Teddy dressed in a brilliant white polo shirt and the tightest of shorts that left little to the imagination.

Richard immediately stopped what he was doing. He dropped the racket to the painted floor, grabbed a small towel hanging from the corner of the net and wrapped it around his shoulders before joining her beyond the fence. 'What does he want?'

'He hasn't said…' She moved away before pulling up and leaning towards him so he would hear her whisper. 'Must you flaunt your floozy in front of me? Show some discretion, Richard. The world is watching us.'

She didn't wait for him to respond, marching purposefully back to the kitchen, grateful for the warmth emanating from the oven which filled the entire room. Rosa was just extracting the freshly baked loaf from the sandwich tin, and it was all Elizabeth could do not to cave in to her ravenous hunger. Holding her head high, she continued back into the hallway and entered the drawing room, surprised to find the detective seated in her father's upright armchair.

DCS Rawani stood as they both entered, remembering his public-school upbringing. 'Thank you both for seeing me at such an early hour,' he began.

Elizabeth had no idea what time it was, but the morning sky was certainly bright enough to suggest it had to be after nine o'clock at least.

'The reason for my call is to update you on our progress overnight. Ordinarily in situations such as this, we would engage a Family Liaison Officer – a trained member of the team – to be the conduit between us and you, but given your reticence to that offer last night, I thought you would prefer to hear any news from me directly.'

Richard used the towel to wipe the perspiration from his forehead as Elizabeth desperately tried to protect her nostrils from inhaling the stench that had followed him into the room.

'You have news then?' Richard said eagerly.

'Some,' the detective replied cautiously. 'Firstly, I want you to know that we have thrown everything at tracking down Cassie. Every available resource has been working non-stop since the incident yesterday afternoon and we are bearing fruit as a result of that hard labour. After an extensive search of traffic and security camera feeds, the team has managed to identify what we believe to be the van used to transport Cassie from the scene. We tracked the van to an area surrounded by farmland and, unfortunately, a distinct lack of cameras. However, we narrowed the search down to two particular farms with large barn areas where a van could be hidden from the view of the helicopters we've had in the sky searching. Raids were carried out on those two barns in the early hours of this morning by specialist tactical teams, and the van was located.'

Elizabeth gasped and reached for Richard's hand to keep her legs from failing her. 'You found her?'

'There were no persons discovered in the vicinity of the van or barn, unfortunately, and due to the lack of camera feeds in the area, we have no immediate way of knowing how or where they went from there.'

Elizabeth's heart sank.

'We now have a team of CSIs combing the area for forensic evidence that *will* tell us where they went next. We are checking for tyre prints, as it is unlikely they left the premises on foot. The important thing is that we discovered supplies in that barn: food, water, camping equipment, and clothes. I believe that we would have apprehended them there today had something not spooked them. That tells me that we are closing the net on these guys, and whilst I don't wish to give you false optimism, I believe we are getting closer to apprehending them.'

Elizabeth's hand shot up to her mouth as tears threatened to escape. Turning to Richard, she searched his face for confirmation that he too could see the light at the end of the tunnel but he remained stony-faced.

'How can you be certain they took Cassie with them?' he said, narrowing his eyes.

The question seemed to throw even the experienced detective. 'I… um… it's like I said, we are processing the evidence from the scene, and so far there is no reason for us to suspect they haven't taken Cassie along with them.'

'But you aren't certain?' Richard challenged again.

'With respect, Mr Hilliard, these things take time, and—'

'How do you know they haven't killed her and buried her somewhere on that farm?'

Elizabeth's legs gave way and she crashed to the floor, Richard making no effort to help her up.

The detective looked down at her sympathetically, but didn't budge under Richard's unyielding glare. 'We're not ruling anything out, but so far there are no signs of a struggle so we feel confident that they still have her, and that she is still alive—'

'But you don't *know* for sure. That's what you're saying, right?'

'Richard, just stop it!' Elizabeth cried.

DCS Rawani was about to speak again when the door to the drawing room opened and a much older man with a full head of the whitest hair entered, and immediately went to Elizabeth's aid, his cane echoing dully on the thick pile of the carpet.

'Darling, darling,' the old man declared, as he joined her on the floor. 'I came as quickly as I could.'

The detective saw Richard Hilliard roll his eyes and then stomp from the room without excusing himself.

'Daddy, they took her. They took our Cassie,' Elizabeth said to the older man, burying her tear-stained face in the shoulder of his thick sheepskin overcoat.

He kissed the top of her head before resting his cheek

against it. 'I know, my sweet child, I know, but I'm here now and I promise you we will not stop until we get her back.'

DCS Rawani had never met Templeton, Lord Fitzhume, but the Commissioner had been quick to remind him of the man's reputation and connection to the royal family. The man before him didn't look like the formidable, all-powerful peer of the realm who had been described. Instead, he was like any other parent, consoling a child in the most desperate of times. This room and this house, probably once full of love and a child's laughter, now bore the grief and heartache of a funeral parlour.

Chapter Fourteen

NOW

Ealing, London

Boarding the first train from Weymouth to London was not as easy as I'd first thought when I booked the ticket on Friday afternoon. At the time, 5:37am had seemed reasonable. Achievable. Yet when the alarm beckoned me at 4:45am, I instantly regretted having booked it at all.

I'll admit that I am not a morning person. I used to be. I can remember being up at the crack of dawn most days when I was a teenager, desperate to squeeze in a few extra minutes of the latest book I was reading before Mum would drive me to school. Somewhere in my fledgling twenties – and I'm blaming university life here – that all changed, my body self-adjusted, and suddenly, being awake before seven on any given day became a challenge.

The train carriage was empty when I boarded, a second warning that my decision to cave in to Maddie's demands might not have been the smartest choice. I say *choice* like I really had one, but I can't run the risk of being sued by the publisher for breach of contract. I've seen plenty of horror stories in the online writers' community, where a successful author made too many demands and was promptly dropped. That can often be the worst thing for a published writer. Being axed during a contract is almost like being marked out as unclean in medieval times; it doesn't matter how good your next manuscript is, your grave is already dug.

The empty carriage was definitely a silver lining this morning though. I was able to find my seat without having to ask some dangerous stranger to move, and with my headphones in and laptop open, I was soon deep in writing notes – questions that I'll pose to Fitzhume and Cassie's parents – ahead of the next few days of research. Unless you've been a writer, it's difficult to share what the process is like and I'm aware it can be different for everybody, but when I write, it's like the real world just melts away. Suddenly, nothing in my periphery exists, like an opaque bubble forms around me, shutting out all colour, noise and distractions, leaving just me and the voices in my head. Sounds mental, I know, yet it's the single most enjoyable experience in my otherwise arid life.

Before I know it, we're pulling in to Southampton Central, and that's when the train fills rapidly, to the point where I can no longer see the exit doors from my seat and I'm pressed up against the window because the giant beside me seems unable to keep within the confines of his own seat. I stopped writing at that point. For a carriage clearly sign-posted as a 'Quiet Coach', there is nothing serene about the atmosphere. Adults and children are standing in the aisle as the train bustles and bumps its way to the next station, where I disembark, and wait twenty minutes for my second train to Reading, where I change again and wait ten minutes for the final train to Ealing Broadway. Four hours of my life that would have been totally wasted had I driven. At least I managed to get my thoughts down, and over the next few hours my subconscious will continue to work through the angles of how to tackle a story I know nothing about.

Disembarking from the train with my laptop bag over one shoulder and the small holdall I crammed with jeans, shirts, and jumpers (even though temperatures are not due to dip below eighteen degrees in the next week), I'm almost sent tumbling by a man in a cheap-looking suit who pushes past me as if there is a race to be the first to the security barrier. He mutters an apology without turning back to see if I'm okay, and in that moment I'm reminded of why I could never live in London permanently. Everyone is always in such a rush, there is no courtesy, and as I climb the stairs at the station exit, the grey sky overhead is dull and threatening. It's only four hours since I left Weymouth and I'm already craving that fresh sea air and brilliantly blue sky. I miss the sound of seagulls squawking as they tell each other stories of chips and ice creams they've managed to pinch off unsuspecting visitors to our wonderful little seaside town.

It takes me a moment to get my bearings, and in that time, as I'm loading directions to Rachel's flat into my phone, I'm barged into three times by strangers who don't even have the decency to mutter an apology. The map app on my phone tells me to head left towards the main parade of shops that make up the thoroughfare of Ealing Broadway before turning left again and heading towards the signs indicating Acton. The buildings here, although not as tall as the skyscrapers in Central London, tower above me and are all so packed together that it feels as though they are slowly closing in, trapping me in their vice-like grip.

The few shop fronts either side of me represent bespoke cafés, fast-food restaurants, and temping agencies. Does one town really need three agencies offering temporary assignments within a fifty-metre radius of one another? Are there really that many employers looking for temporary staff in West London? What does that say about the state of our economy?

Traffic is heavy in both directions as I continue along the way; tall red buses edge slowly forwards, kamikaze cyclists dart in and out of lanes wherever they spot a gap, and traffic lights change sequence every ninety seconds. You would think that it was rush hour on a busy weekday morning, rather than half past nine on a Saturday. Again, everyone here seems to be in such a hurry to get to wherever they're heading, nobody stopping to take in their surroundings. That's probably why there are stray crisp packets, cigarette butts and chewing gum on virtually every paving slab; everyone is just too busy to look at the damage they're causing. Am I the only one looking?

It takes me fifteen minutes to reach Rachel's flat, one of three in a former townhouse, all sharing a communal entrance. Rachel once told me that her landlord owns the dozen townhouses on this part of the road, and had them all converted to flats, meaning he's raking in at least thirty-six thousand pounds per month just for this block. That's more than I earned in freelance articles and royalties last year (though Maddie has promised this year will be much more fruitful, even after her commission).

Rachel's flat is on the ground floor and the large window directly in front of me is her open-plan kitchen-lounge-diner.

The blind is still drawn, which strikes me as odd, as she definitely knew I was due to come and drop my things this morning. I don't want to wake her if she's having a lie-in, but I also don't want to drag my holdall to the midday meeting with Lord Fitzhume and Maddie.

Climbing the run of three steps up to the front door, I search for Rachel's name on the panel of door buzzers and tentatively press it. We haven't spoken since my revelation about Anna on the Millennium Bridge and I won't deny it's been playing on my mind all morning. What if she's changed her mind about me staying here now? I'd have to find a hotel somewhere and I'm not sure where to begin.

Two minutes pass and so I press again, now worried that either she's had to rush out or this is her way of saying that our relationship is over. I'm about to phone her when I hear a door inside open and then she is at the main door, her usually perfectly straight hair in a tangle of curls, the oversized T-shirt hanging down over one shoulder, and only knickers covering her lower half. My cheeks are burning before I can even say hello.

Rachel looks equally shocked by my appearance at her door. 'Emma, hi,' she says awkwardly, glancing back towards the door to her flat. 'I thought you weren't going to be here until ten. Wasn't that what we agreed?'

'Sorry,' I say quickly, regretting not sending her a message to say I'd arrived in London. 'I'm a few minutes early. I can go and come back at ten, if that's—'

'Don't be silly,' she cuts me off, grabbing my hand and pulling me into the most awkward embrace I think we've ever had. She glances at the watch on my wrist. 'Goodness, I hadn't realised how late it was. Sorry, come in, come in.'

Following her in through the door to her flat, my embarrassment deepens as I see the tell-tale signs of exactly why Rachel has lost track of time: a cerise-coloured bra draped over the back of the sofa; two pairs of shoes kicked off in the kitchen; and as I study Rachel's face, I now notice that both her lipstick and eyeliner are slightly smudged.

'Oh God, I'm so sorry,' I whisper, conscious of whomever else is lurking just inside the bedroom door. 'Listen, I'll go and get us a couple of takeaway coffees from the café up the road and come back. I didn't mean to disturb you in…' I don't know how to finish the sentence, as I'm instantly transported back to that first time Rachel brought a boy back to our student house and I inadvertently walked in on them in the throes of passion.

She is trying desperately not to laugh but then it escapes and she grins at me. 'I suppose you were going to find out eventually. Yes, there is someone here, who you should probably meet. It's still early days, which is why I haven't said anything sooner.'

Another thought hits me. 'Hey, listen, if it's not convenient for me to stay with you this week, I can have Maddie find me a hotel instead, it really isn't a prob—'

'It would be for me,' she almost shouts in feigned offence. 'We're not living together, they just happened to stay over last night. You're absolutely fine to crash here for as long as you need. I've got the blanket and spare pillows out of the closet and so long as you're happy with the sofa bed, then I want you here.'

'So long as you're sure.'

She takes my hands in hers and squeezes. 'I'm positive. Now, would you like to meet the person who has left me in this state?'

Obviously I can't say no so I nod with as much enthusiasm as I can muster, restraining my natural introvert.

Rachel releases my hand and moves to the bedroom door, pushing it open with her foot and looking in. 'Emma Hunter, I'd like you to meet Daniella Vitruvia.'

Chapter Fifteen

NOW

Ealing, London

The shock is a double-whammy. First the mention of a woman's name, and then the striking beauty kneeling on the edge of Rachel's bed. Her hair is as long and dark a mane as I've ever seen, her cheekbones high but not overpowering. She is gently nibbling on a fingertip, mirroring my own bashfulness. As Rachel reaches for her hand she accepts it and perfectly pivots to enable her long legs to extend until she is standing, several inches taller than us both. Before Rachel even tells me, I know she must be a model.

'I had meant to have her out of here before you arrived,' Rachel admits, but there is no shame or embarrassment in her face any longer. 'I guess we must have lost track of time. I know there's a lot we need to talk about, but for now it might be best if Daniella and I both get dressed and cleaned up.'

Exasperated, I nod, not knowing where to look or how to react. Eventually, I head into the small kitchen area, and begin to fill the kettle from the sink. I can hear Rachel and Daniella whispering behind me and in my periphery, Rachel fetches up the scattered clothes from the floor and then the two of them hurry into the bedroom, closing the door. I exhale for the first time since the door opened.

How did I not know that my best friend – someone I've shared my most intimate of secrets with for the last eight years – was into girls? As the water inside the kettle slowly starts to froth and bubble, I rack my brains for any clues or signs that I missed along the way. When we first met at our halls of residence we were sitting in a group, all sharing brief details about our backgrounds and where we'd come from before arriving at Bournemouth University. The conversation inevitably descended into talk of previous relationships and at no point did Rachel mention that she'd had girlfriends. In fact, I distinctly remember being slightly jealous of the number of boys she'd had chasing after her in her teenage years. I'd only dated two boys by that point and neither had been all that serious. It didn't bother me that I was still a virgin when I first joined university as I had always – maybe I was somewhat repressed, I think in hindsight – believed I would give my virginity to someone I loved and cared about. Alas, that all went out the window on a drunken night out three months into my university career. That said, I never saw Rachel showing any particular interest in girls. Even when we moved into a house together for two years while continuing our studies, she never once brought a girl back, nor showed any particular interest in the Bournemouth LGBTQ+ scene.

Has she been hiding it all this time?

I'm hardly one to judge after my own revelation on the Millennium Bridge.

The kettle reaches its crescendo and I drop tea bags into three mugs. I'm now replaying every conversation we've ever had in my head.

The bedroom door opens and the two of them emerge, hand-in-hand. Daniella is in a figure-hugging crimson dress, partially hidden behind Rachel, though significantly taller owing to the enormous heels of her satin shoes – probably some Italian designer brand at best guess; fashion has never been my strength.

'You made tea,' Rachel says brightly. 'Glad to see you're making yourself at home already. Daniella needs to go. She's got to get home before starting work, so… I'm just going to show her to the door and then you and I can chat. Okay?'

I nod, the words trapped in my throat and I watch as they bustle out. I can't hear what they whisper at the main door but then Rachel returns, not exactly avoiding my gaze, but not making an effort to meet it either. She now looks more like the Rachel I've always known, wearing slacks and a plaid shirt, radiant as ever.

She pushes the door to the flat closed with her bottom and takes a deep breath. 'Before you say anything, I want to apologise for dropping an unexpected bombshell on you like this. I wasn't deliberately keeping myself from you, but I didn't know how to tell you, and it just never seemed to be the right time. Anyway, I'm sorry you had to find out like this, and I really hope this doesn't change anything.'

She finally looks up and I can see she's finding the atmosphere just as charged as I am. I want to tell her that there is nothing that could ever destroy our friendship and how it's none of my business who she dates. The shock melts in an instant, and whilst I am ashamed that she even needed to come out to me at all, I just want to tell her how happy I am for her. If only I could write to her. I could always write what I couldn't say.

'Why would it change anything?' I eventually murmur, really uncertain how to put my thoughts into words. 'You've found someone who makes you happy.'

Her fear softens to relief. 'You're really okay?'

I frown. 'Of course, Rach. Why would I be anything else? You being gay is something you never should've even had to have told me. I should never have assumed otherwise… I'm sick to death of assumptions. They can go and get in the bin as far as I'm concerned.'

'I'm not gay,' she says, before adding, 'I'm into girls *and* guys and non-binary folk. I think. I don't know. It's still a recent thing in my head. I don't know what I am, but when I met Daniella I… fell head over heels for her in a heartbeat.'

We've never had this kind of awkwardness between us and I don't like that something has constructed this invisible barrier. Reaching for one of the mugs, I swallow the distance between us and hand it over, clinking it against the mug in my own hand.

'I'm so pleased for you,' I say, and I can feel my cheeks widening into a huge smile.

She tentatively smiles back. 'You mean it? You're not angry that I didn't tell you sooner?'

I shrug slightly. 'I wish I'd been the first person you told but I can understand why you may have found that difficult.'

'With everything that's been going on with you this last year and a bit – meeting Freddie, the investigation, the book, the success, then the trial – it's been tough to get enough time with you to properly catch up on everything that's been happening. I'm not saying that's anyone's fault – God knows I've been equally busy – and with the distance between where we live… I'm sorry I didn't speak to you sooner. When you messaged yesterday and asked for a place to crash for a few days, I was so excited and I'd planned to open some wine tonight or tomorrow and bowl out with it, but now you've saved me the time.'

I've never been comfortable with hugging people I've only just met and I've never understood the need for the French-inspired requirement to peck cheeks twice and feign excitement. In fact, in the world, I can think of only three people I would willingly embrace without it feeling awkward, and that's why I now wrap my arms around Rachel's shoulders and gently rub my hand over her back.

'Have you told your mum yet?' I ask. I can feel her head shaking as her chin bashes against my collarbone.

'God, no. You know what she can be like. As I said, it's still so new. I only met Daniella three months ago and last night was the first time I've seen her in a fortnight. She's been away in Milan and I wasn't expecting her to turn up on my doorstep last night, but as soon as she knocked we couldn't keep our hands off each other. Sorry, overshare?'

I pull us apart so she can see the honesty in my eyes. 'No more than that time you went into intimate details about how you seduced a traffic warden to get out of a parking ticket. This is a picnic after that.'

She smiles again, wider now and carries our mugs to the two-seater sofa which will become my bed for the next few nights. We sit, and drink our tea. Silence descends, but it isn't awkward, just the natural break in conversation between two friends who can almost read what the other is thinking. In some ways, it's as if the conversation continues in our heads, transmitted telepathically so that none of the rest of the world can hear.

'What do you fancy doing today?' Rachel eventually asks.

I check my watch. 'Maddie is coming here to collect me at eleven, before we head out to Chalfont St Giles to meet with Lord Fitzhume.'

Rachel clicks her fingers. 'That's who it was. The old guy from your agent's office the other day! I knew I recognised his face but I couldn't place it. Wow! What are you meeting him about?'

She's clearly forgotten what Fitzhume said about his missing granddaughter and I don't know how much I should tell her about what he shared with me on Thursday. If he really did spend significant money to keep the press away from the story, would he be angry if I told a journalist employed by *The Telegraph*? I know if I swore her to secrecy she would keep her word, but I don't know whether it's my place to say.

'He wants to hire me to write a memoir piece,' I settle for. 'You can't tell anyone because I haven't signed a contract to do it yet.'

Her face scrunches in puzzlement. 'A memoir? Sorry, but surely there are a hundred biographers or ghost-writers out there he could hire. Don't get me wrong, I believe you could write *anything* you put your mind to… which is why a memoir seems such an odd choice for your next book. I was picturing you as a Jessica Fletcher type, going after the untold stories, and unearthing the secrets buried within them.'

She knows how much I used to love watching reruns of *Murder She Wrote* on television between lectures, and would often join me with snacks and wine.

'I haven't said I'll definitely do it yet,' I say. It is a half-truth. 'That said, we've been summoned to meet him to hear what he has to say.'

'He's some distant cousin of the royal family or something, isn't he?'

I nod. 'Apparently. I tried to do some background checking on him the other day but there was very little online. Even Wikipedia was limited to his name, place of birth, and an old photograph.'

'Yeah, I can't really recall anything else about him either. Certainly nothing scandalous, but then it's not really my area of expertise, is it?'

Something triggers in the back of my mind. 'Could you do me a favour and just have a look into his name and his daughter's from the last year? Is there anyone at the paper who would generally cover peers of the realm, and would potentially know him?'

'Probably, why?'

I don't immediately respond but eventually I relent. 'Okay, what I'm about to say is strictly off the record. *Okay?* It doesn't go any further than this room.'

There is an excited shine to her eyes and she lowers her mug to give me her undivided attention; I can almost picture the tape recorder in her head being clicked on.

'Okay,' I say for the third time in as many seconds, lowering my voice as if there might be someone else able to overhear our conversation. 'When he came to see me on Thursday, he told me that his granddaughter was abducted a year ago and never returned home. That's why he wants to speak to me. He seems to think that I'll somehow be able to find out what really happened to her, even though there was a full police investigation.'

Her eyes are so wide that I'm half-convinced they may just pop out of her head. 'I don't remember hearing anything about that. Was she taken from this country?'

'I think so. He said he'd taken measures to keep the story from hitting the papers so I'm not surprised it's news to you. Can you ask around? Don't mention the abduction specifically, just see if anyone recalls any controversy or his name coming up in conversations around this time last year?'

She nods and immediately reaches for her phone. 'What are you thinking? You don't sound happy to be meeting with him.'

'He didn't really give me much of a choice, and I can't help thinking there's a lot more to this story than he's told me… and that's what worries me the most.'

Chapter Sixteen

THEN

Uxbridge, London

'You'll just have to drop us here,' Richard told their temporary driver. 'It doesn't seem as if they have a carpark.'

Elizabeth could barely bring herself to look out the window at the dreary brick monument which had probably once been the pinnacle of structural engineering but had never seemed so out of place, so out of time.

'Are you ready for this?' Richard asked, leaning towards her, his voice little more than a whisper.

She met his gaze and gave an affirmative nod, though still not totally sure why he'd insisted they visit the police station in person. She'd been quite content with the daily visits from the lead detective, but at breakfast Richard had said they shouldn't be sitting back and waiting for news. It wasn't that he didn't have faith in DCS Rawani's investigation, but he felt a little additional targeted pressure would do wonders to keep the detectives' minds focused on the task at hand. She hadn't wanted to argue, not in front of her father; best to keep up appearances when he was around.

'Here will do,' Richard said, when the car door was in line with the red-framed frontage which resembled the entrance of a shopping centre rather than a place criminals should fear. It was only the words 'Metropolitan Police' beside the entrance that told her they were in the right place.

The car lurched to a halt and Richard jumped out, offering his hand for Elizabeth to slide across the leather upholstery, and then he helped her down. The new 4x4 – something Korean, Richard had mentioned – would serve until a replacement for the Range Rover was delivered. The vehicle that had collected Elizabeth and Cassie that day at the Connors boy's birthday party was a write-off by all accounts, not that the police had released it from their forensic examination yet.

Elizabeth caught the face of Gerry Connors in the rearview mirror as he nodded at her before moving the 4x4 on. It didn't sit well with her that their new driver – while Hobbs recovered in hospital – was the reason she and Cassie had even been out on Saturday. Richard had said he'd performed all the usual checks on him and Connors had come up clean, but there was something about that large, unkempt beard of his that troubled her.

Richard released her hand as they reached the kerb. The building was three storeys high, in the centre of the town, and only a stone's throw from the Magistrates Court. What she couldn't get over was the number of windows the building had, none of which were barred. The front door automatically slid open as they approached and a cold blast struck from the air conditioning unit immediately inside the atrium. Having never been inside a police station before, she hadn't known what to expect and was relieved to find no obvious ne'er-do-wells shouting obscenities in the lobby.

'Be with you in a minute,' the young woman behind the front desk said as they approached. She finished typing whatever message she was writing and then looked up with a bright smile.

To Elizabeth's horror, the woman couldn't have been much older than eighteen.

'We're here to see DCS Rawani,' Richard said authoritatively, offering no smile in return.

Not put off, the woman in a white blouse and navy jumper maintained her cheery expression. 'And what is it you wish to see him about, please?'

Richard pressed himself over the counter. 'Just tell him it's Richard and Elizabeth Hilliard. He'll know what it's about.'

The woman's face changed as though in recognition of the names, replaced by a plain, emotionless expression. It was an improvement, but meant that news of Cassie's abduction was rife in the station.

'I'll see if he's free,' the woman said, picking up the phone from behind the desk. 'Take a seat, please.'

DCS Rawani appeared in the waiting area minutes later, his tight turban in keeping with his perfectly knotted neck tie, but his face one of confusion. 'Mr and Mrs Hilliard, good morning. I wasn't expecting to see you; is everything okay?'

It was a terrible opening question but Elizabeth remained quiet, allowing Richard his moment.

'No, everything is not okay,' Richard began, his words carefully chosen and rehearsed. 'Our daughter has now been missing for more than forty hours and you don't seem any closer to bringing her home.'

The detective didn't immediately respond, instead opening a secured door with the pass hanging around his neck and ushering them through. Whatever he wanted to say was clearly not fit for the young woman's ears. He led them down a narrow corridor of yet more glass walls, most with venetian blinds drawn closed, until they arrived at a closed fire door. He punched a code into a pad beside it and opened it for them to enter. The framed photograph of a woman in a sari with two children strapped into a pushchair suggested this was his personal office.

'I wish you'd phoned,' he said. 'I would have been happy to come to you and saved your journey into Uxbridge this morning. You want an update on the case, I take it?'

'The last we heard from you, you'd traced the van to a farm and you were closing the net, but that was this time yesterday. Where are the men who took Cassie, and where'—the lump in his throat grew—'where is our daughter?'

The detective lifted a cube box of tissues from the edge of his desk but Richard declined the offer. 'Finding Cassie is our number one priority, Mr Hilliard. I assure you that we are doing absolutely everything within our power to locate her and bring her home safely. I can understand you're distraught with the amount of time it is taking, and I know that if I were in your position I would be equally frustrated. I have a son and a daughter, and if either of them was ever... rest assured, nobody here is taking your situation lightly.'

In that moment, Elizabeth believed every word. When he'd first appeared at the house on Saturday night, and even when he'd stopped by yesterday morning, all she'd seen was a man –

a highly qualified man – doing his job. Now, though, she could see an empathetic father who got it.

'Would it help if I showed you what we've been doing since we last spoke?' the detective continued, turning the monitor so they could both see as he opened a window and typed in his credentials. 'I have three teams undertaking specific investigations as part of the wider piece. One team is working the scene at the farm, checking the tyre treads we discovered against known tyre treads we have in our database, to narrow down the field to the type of vehicle likely used to transport Cassie away from the barn before our raid. That takes time, but if they can pinpoint the type of vehicle it will help hone the CCTV search.

'I have a second team checking the whereabouts of the van prior to the attack to help us establish where it was in the minutes, hours, and days prior to being on that A-road with you. If we can trace it back to the source, then we'll be in a better position of uncovering who was behind it all.

'The third team is working day and night specifically on identifying the men who are likely responsible for the attack and the abduction. They're looking at known criminals with missing digits, as well as their associates, and also any leads on the rocket-propelled grenade that was fired at the rear of the vehicle. You must bear in mind that such launchers are expensive pieces of kit, and not something that just anyone can handle. Sure, anyone could fire one and create a mess, but whoever flipped your car on Saturday must have known what they were doing. A moving target is hard enough to hit, let alone taking out a rear wheel to disable a vehicle. I think that means the person who fired the weapon is either military, or has some kind of specific weapons training.'

He paused as he punched up another window. 'We have identified three men in the system who are known to be missing fingers. Interestingly, the most common type of missing finger in the criminal underworld is the little finger, as this is often the first targeted when criminals are trying to extract information, or sending a warning about an unpaid debt. Missing thumbs are the second most common, from accidents or assaults with blades and guns. Missing index fingers are less common, hence why we've managed to locate three men, all out on release, with this disability. I was planning on bringing these images over this afternoon, but as you're here, you may as well take a look now.' He left a second pause to ensure they had taken in his request. 'The faces I am about to show you may, *or may not*, be involved. My reason for showing you is to ascertain whether either of you recognise any of them. Maybe you've seen one of them hanging around recently, or you've come into contact with them at some historical point.'

He specifically looked at Richard as he said this last part before loading up the first image. The face that filled the screen looked like something straight out of an East-end gangster movie: the square, jowly face pocked with scars, the fair hair, and a scowl that made him look as if he wouldn't even spit on you if you were on fire in a desert. Elizabeth looked away as images of this fiend towering over Cassie filled her mind.

'Do either of you recognise this man?'

Elizabeth shook her head, feeling the warmth of tears on her eyelids.

'No,' Richard replied. 'Who is he?'

The detective pulled a face that told them he wouldn't be mentioning names or backgrounds until he knew for certain they'd found the right face. 'Please look again to be certain, before we move on to the next one. Mrs Hilliard, you don't recognise him from the attack?'

She forced her eyes to the screen again. 'He… the man who took Cassie was wearing a balaclava. I don't know.'

'Look at his eyes, Mrs Hilliard. Is there nothing you can recall about them? You haven't seen this man hanging around at Cassie's school? Or when you've been to the supermarket?'

'Do you really think that's the sort of person we would consort with?' she replied, before she could stop herself.

The detective didn't reply, instead loading up a second image. This one was a teenager, at best guess, with a shaved head, but a very narrow face and shoulders. The round spectacles made him look like the sort of person who hung out at science-fiction conventions dressed as a Vulcan, not some hardened lowlife who would disable the car and abduct their daughter.

'No,' Elizabeth said. 'It's not him.'

The detective watched her carefully. 'You're sure? You weren't so positive with the first one.'

'He's too skinny,' she clarified.

'And you, Mr Hilliard, have you ever seen this man before?'

'No,' Richard said, his frustration simmering below the surface.

The final face was of a much older man, his greasy, thin grey hair pulled back in a makeshift ponytail. Dressed in a vest and faded leather jacket, he looked like some ageing wannabe rock-star, and yet something about those eyes…

'It's him,' Elizabeth spat out.

DCS Rawani studied her reaction. 'You're sure?'

'You said to look at the eyes. Those eyes – the ice-cold greyness – that's what I remember. I think. Certainly more than the other two.'

The detective excused himself, leaving the image of the grey-haired man on the screen. Elizabeth couldn't keep her eyes off him as flickers of the balaclava-clad face and his merged.

What troubled her more was the fact that Richard was looking anywhere but at the screen.

Chapter Seventeen

NOW

Chalfont St Giles, Buckinghamshire

The cough and splutter of the engine stirs me from my daydream as Maddie floors the accelerator of the twenty-year-old classic white VW Beetle. The gearbox plays a tune that is hard to ignore and Maddie apologises for the slip in the transmission.

'When are you going to upgrade to something that doesn't argue with you when you have to travel on the A40?' I say, mimicking Maddie's ex-husband, who is always telling her how much of a death trap the old bug is.

'I can't replace Gertie,' she declares with faux indignation. 'A classic never dies.'

Maddie loves this car more than any other possession and I have no doubt that when it does eventually give up the ghost, she'll have it immortalised in some kind of garage or museum. Her argument is that it's cheap to run, has low mileage, and one very careful owner. Who am I to judge when I still have yet to own a car? I can drive, but it's been nearly a decade since I was last behind the wheel of a car. There's something endearing about the way Maddie stands by Gertie through thick and thin.

Passing through Denham, the bustle of London traffic dissipates as we leave the A40 and follow the A413 towards Amersham and the Chalfonts. A yellow sign at the side of the road warns us to take care due to a high crash-rate for the next two miles; it does little to settle the growing knot inside my gut. I've been dreading coming face-to-face with Lord Fitzhume again, worried that my usually patient demeanour will succumb to the frustration of dealing with a man for whom money seemingly buys everything. When Maddie collected me from Rachel's flat, I told her that I would hear him out, but that if I didn't sense there was a story, I would walk away and take my chances with the publisher. She didn't argue and has made no effort to try and persuade me otherwise, which is a relief.

The national speed limit signs are dotted along the side of the dual carriageway but Gertie struggles to get much over sixty-five as we pootle along in light traffic, eventually crawling through Gerrards Cross, Chalfont St Peter, and finally passing a sign welcoming us to Chalfont St Giles, twinned with Graft-De-Rijp in the Netherlands.

We've only been in the car for half an hour but London is now far behind us and the way of life here in Buckinghamshire feels more relaxed. Slowing at a pedestrian crossing, a man in a tweed coat, the collar upturned, crosses in front of us; a large huskie roaming free of a lead trots beside him. I watch as they cut through a gap in a hedge and on to a sprawling green landscape that stretches as far as the eye can see.

'It's nice here, isn't it?' Maddie comments, before pulling away again, much to Gertie's disagreement.

I don't respond, as I know what she is angling at, but it will take more than a few green trees to tear me from my little seaside town. Thankfully, it isn't long before we arrive at the gated entrance to a sprawling estate, where Maddie winds down Gertie's window and announces our arrival. The gates appear rusty and disused but they whir a moment later and open for us to drive through. The driveway must be a hundred metres long, surrounded by thick green conifers that carefully hide their secrets from the view of the casual observer. They're also tall enough to block out much of the midday sunshine, casting an almost permanent shadow over the gravel that crunches beneath the tyres.

My mouth drops open as the trees part and I see Fitzhume's mansion in its full glory. It really is a sight to behold and could comfortably house the entire homeless population of Weymouth, and yet Maddie has told me it is only Lord Fitzhume and a skeleton staff that live within the grounds.

A Hispanic woman in a black tabard answers the door and shows us through to a drawing room where we find Fitzhume sitting alone in a stiff-backed armchair. He doesn't stand as we enter but he beckons us to sit on the chaise longue opposite him. A fire crackles to our right, filling the room with the smell of burning wood.

He smiles at me, and although I recognise that slight twinkling of his eyes, he looks frailer than he did the other day. Dressed in dark brown trousers, matching slippers, and a pale yellow shirt with a cross pattern, he looks every inch the country gent.

'Rosa, would you make our guests some tea, please?' he says to the housekeeper who has remained waiting by the door.

'Si,' she almost shouts back, as she heads out of the room.

'Miss Hunter, I appreciate you coming all this way. I trust your journey here was without incident?'

I don't tell him about Gertie's sputtering. 'It was fine, thank you,' I say, determined to remain civil, remembering Freddie's words to me: *Given your own pain at what happened to your sister, I'd have thought you'd be chomping at the bit to help someone in a similar position.*

He turns to Maddie. 'I don't believe we've been properly introduced. Templeton Fitzhume.'

Maddie, so often the heart and soul of any party, responds quietly, 'Your Lordship.'

'Please, my friends call me Fitzhume, and I would encourage you both to address me in the same manner.'

The housekeeper returns, pushing a rattling trolley into the drawing room. This must have been prepared for our arrival as there is no way she could have made the tea and arranged all the cups in the little time she's been out of the room. It would appear that Fitzhume runs a tight ship, which begs the question of how his granddaughter was abducted in the first place. I'm also fascinated to understand why he's waited twelve months to launch this private investigation.

Rosa pours tea and passes a cup and saucer each to Maddie and me, leaving one on the small table beside Fitzhume before disappearing. It is only when the door to the drawing room is closed that Fitzhume folds up the broadsheet on his lap.

'I want to know what really happened to my granddaughter, Miss Hunter,' he begins without pomp or ceremony. 'One year ago, she was abducted on her return home from a birthday party by two masked figures and held against her will for a period of four days before the kidnappers contacted my daughter and demanded two million pounds in exchange for her safe return. Despite handing over that sum to the Metropolitan Police Senior Investigating Officer, Cassie was never returned to us. I believe that poor decision-making, careless operational management, and serious misjudgement are responsible for my heartbreak.

'When we met on Thursday, you asked me why I wanted your help to find her. Well, I read your book, and the detailed investigation you undertook into the ring that operated in that boys' home without impeachment for so many years, even when all doors were closed to you, and how you kept looking until you uncovered the full, grimy… Well, I need someone with that nose for a story, someone who won't give in until she proves her thesis.'

He pauses to wipe spittle from his chin with a yellow spotted handkerchief and I take my chance.

'With all due respect, Lord Fitzhume, I wasn't trying to prove a thesis. I listened to Freddie Mitchell and the other survivors, and I fought for them.'

'But you believed that they had been abused during their time at the home, did you not?'

'Yes, I did, but this isn't the same—'

'On the contrary, Miss Hunter, this is more similar than I think you realise. The detective who was running the investigation into Cassie's disappearance has closed every door to me since he botched the ransom exchange. Even with my friends in high places, I've been unable to get any of them to admit culpability for what happened. They had two million pounds in cash, ready to be handed over, and yet neither the money nor my granddaughter was returned.'

'Are you insinuating—?'

'I'm not *insinuating* anything, Miss Hunter. I'm telling you for a fact that they took my money and they botched Cassie's rescue. Someone knows exactly what happened and why they were so quick to close the case.'

It feels like he's leapt straight to the end of the story without intricately weaving the tricky middle plot, and I'm struggling to keep up.

'They are covering up their ineptitude and that speaks of the worst possible corruption. Your book went to the heart of bureaucrats turning a blind eye and covering their backs, which is why you are the perfect person to find Cassie.'

I look to Maddie for help but she is nodding along with Fitzhume.

He stands suddenly and, grabbing the gilt-edged cane leaning against the wall, he moves past us in the direction of the door. 'Come with me, please,' he eventually says when he reaches it.

Returning our cups to the trolley, we follow him out of the room, through the vast hallway with crystal chandeliers at either end, to a room with a closed door.

'This used to be Richard's – Cassie's father's – office,' he says, unlocking the door, and pushing it open for us to enter.

The room is so much darker than the hallway, with the curtains at the far side pulled firmly shut. We enter, unsure what to expect, but Fitzhume flicks a switch and the room erupts in a shower of light. It's impossible to know where to look first. The entire wall we are facing is covered in blown-up images of the same beautiful little girl; her blonde hair shimmers in each one, her small button nose, the most delicate of earlobes, and eyes as dark as tree bark.

The wall behind me is also covered floor-to-ceiling in printed images: Cassie on her first day of school; Cassie eating ice cream; Cassie splashing in a swimming pool; Cassie in full equestrian gear. The old man remains in the doorway, close to tears, not daring to step in, eyes darting from one image to the next. He is overwhelmed with grief and sadness and his earlier rant now makes so much more sense: he wants someone to blame for his loss. And why not level it at the men charged with bringing her home who failed in their task? To some this would simply be a room of cherished memories, but to me it resembles a shrine.

Taking his hand, all previous animosity leaves me, and the words that escape my mouth are not carefully chosen, but delivered on instinct. 'Okay, I will do whatever I can for you.'

For the first time since I met him, his shoulders relax, albeit only a fraction. 'You can have whatever you need. I have arranged for the police to open their casefile to you and one of their detectives will be assigned to take you step-by-step through the investigation. You'll also meet with Detective Chief Superintendent Rawani who led the case.'

If only it had been so easy with Freddie and the others, maybe it wouldn't have taken over two years to bring their complaints to court.

'I'll also need to speak to Cassie's parents. Is that possible?'

The first hint of relief peppers his face. 'Richard is primarily living out of the Kensington apartment. He's aware of what I'm doing but I'll need to make an appointment for him to see you. Perhaps Monday?'

'And your daughter? Will she be there too?'

Fresh sadness fills his eyes, and his face drops. 'Elizabeth is…' He sighs. 'Elizabeth is at the hospital currently receiving treatment. This whole mess, it… it took a toll.'

'I'm so sorry to hear that. I understand how much of an impact that would have had, probably better than anyone.'

'The specialist hospital is in Hampshire; I don't know how easy it will be to get you in to see her, but I will do my best and I will let you know when it's arranged.'

I don't ask why she's in a hospital so far away because there's only one specialist hospital in Hampshire that springs to mind: The Priory. Where the rich and famous go to get clean of their demons. I suppose I shouldn't be surprised how a woman in Elizabeth's position could develop a dependency on pain-inhibitors. Whether or not the problem existed prior to her daughter's abduction is neither here nor there.

For the first time since I met Fitzhume, I think I'm finally understanding why reading my book would make him think that I could somehow link together the clues that will bring him salvation, and even before I've said it, I can almost hear an augury in my words. 'I can't guarantee what I might uncover, nor whether you will be pleased with the outcome, but I won't stop until I've torn off every mask.'

Chapter Eighteen

NOW

Uxbridge, London

The room I have been asked to wait in is bright and airy, and the early afternoon sunshine pouring through the tall windows warms my cheeks. The slatted blinds and laminated furniture make it look as though I've stopped at one of those mocked-up rooms straight out of the Ikea catalogue. A smell of pine suggests a discreet air freshener is plugged in somewhere. They call this a soft interview room, made to look as welcoming and friendly as possible, primarily to speak to victims and the vulnerable. A small red dot in each of the top corners of the square ceiling remind me that activity in this room is permanently being recorded. I stop chewing on the cuff of my cardigan, as if that in itself is a crime.

Maddie suggested I head back to Rachel's and get settled before starting to investigate on Monday, but I don't want to spend any more time in central London than is necessary to complete preliminary investigations. Despite what Fitzhume seems to believe, this is not going to be a mystery that is solved in the space of a week. What most don't realise about the St Francis Home investigation is just how long it took. It was almost three years from the moment when Freddie and I first spoke in that homeless shelter, to the police finally taking the investigation seriously, and making their move on Arthur Turgood and his cohorts. Months of digging, of having doors closed in my face, of trying to locate all the boys who'd attended the home and who might have borne witness to what was going on. The toughest part was winning the trust of those who did eventually come forward: Freddie, Mike, and Steve.

Maddie reluctantly agreed but advised that she wouldn't be able to ferry me about today as she had a prior engagement. I asked her to drop me at the police station in Uxbridge. I should be able to make my way back to Ealing from here. I'm not great with the public transportation system in London, but I'll figure it out.

The door opens a moment later and a trouser-clad bottom pushes into the room, followed by a white shirt as the owner straightens and turns. Three large cardboard boxes in the person's arms cover everything else.

The boxes are lowered to the rectangular table and slid towards me, and only now do I take in the tanned face, dark brown hair, cropped beard, and charcoal eyes.

'Either you're Emma Hunter, or I've stumbled into the wrong room,' he says, his smile slightly crooked but not threatening.

'Yes, I am,' I reply brightly, 'and you're DC Jack Serrovitz?'

He pulls a face like a disappointed gameshow host. 'Ooh, close. It's pronounced Serra-vich, and I'm a police constable, rather than a detective. Otherwise, yes, we both appear to be in the correct room. Did anyone offer you a drink? I can't recommend the coffee from the vending machine, nor the tea, but I can vouch that the water is seventy per cent drinkable.'

He isn't what I was expecting. As we left the manor at Chalfont St Giles, Fitzhume said that the SIO had arranged for a former detective to talk me through the case notes. I was expecting some gruff recently retired has-been, but I'd swear PC Serrovitz is even younger than me.

He doesn't wait for me to answer the question about the drink before ducking out of the room, returning bum-first again a moment later carrying two transparent beakers of water and placing one on the laminated desk in front of me. A wet rim immediately forms around the bottom of the cup where some of the liquid has spilled out.

'What's in the boxes, PC Serrovitz?' I ask.

'The boxes represent everything we've got on the Cassie Hilliard case,' he says proudly. 'Had to carry them up from Records in the basement, which is no mean feat. Oh, and please call me Jack.'

'What about HOLMES2? I thought everything was digitised these days?'

HOLMES2 is the database tool the police use to record every lead and item of information that needs to be worked by a member of the investigative team. It's meant to keep everything organised and traceable, and also help identify links with any other cases, whether open or closed. He looks surprised that I know what HOLMES2 is.

'You're right,' he says after a moment, bemusement replaced with that slightly crooked smile, 'but I thought it would be easier to follow a paper trail, rather than jumping about in HOLMES2. Besides, it's a live system, and I'm not sure whether I'm supposed to show you that level of detail.'

The hairs on the back of my neck catch against the collar of my cardigan as I recall Fitzhume saying that he felt the SIO was covering his own back after the botched ransom exchange. 'You're supposed to be showing me *everything*.'

'And that's what this is,' he responds, slightly defensively. 'HOLMES2 contains non-leads; false-clues, whereas I was told you wanted to look at what we did actually piece together.'

I take a breath and regain my composure. 'Were you part of the original investigating team?'

He shakes his head. 'No. I was working in Camden this time last year, so this will be as fresh to me as it is to you.'

My blood begins to simmer again. 'So you have no idea what happened in this case?'

His brow furrows with confusion. 'Not totally, but I was under the impression that we were supposed to be looking at this with fresh eyes after the family petitioned to have a private independent review undertaken. I've been given a brief rundown by the DCS who was running as SIO at the time, and as far as we're concerned, the case is closed, but someone on high has agreed to have it looked at again.'

It certainly reminds me of the barriers I faced when trying to help Freddie and the others.

'Shall we just make a start?' I eventually say, lifting the lid off the first of the three boxes that he's stacked by the desk.

The box is full of plastic sleeves, each containing papers, some handwritten, some typed. Removing the documents from the first sleeve, I read through the preliminary witness statement taken from Elizabeth Hilliard, less than an hour after the abduction.

'Talk to me about the nine-fingered suspect,' I say after an hour of reading, when my tired eyes can take it no more.

He reaches into the third box and sifts through the plastic sleeves, until he locates the one he's looking for. 'What do you want to know?'

'Elizabeth Hilliard made a positive identification of one of the perpetrators, according to a note in the file made by the SIO. Who was he and why wasn't he charged?'

Jack removes a printed rap sheet from the sleeve, and slides the image across the table. 'Henry Amos, known to his friends as "Hank". Sixty-three-year-old petty burglar with a history of conning vulnerable pensioners into allowing him into their homes before making off with the family silverware. He most commonly posed as a utilities engineer, there to check meters and service boilers, that kind of thing. Very quick hands according to his profile and, ironically, light-fingered. He was brought in for questioning following Elizabeth Hilliard's believed identification and even managed to lift the interrogator's biro during the interview. Despite an intensive interrogation, he had an alibi for the time of the abduction and was released without charge.'

'But she said it was definitely him.'

I can see he's biting his tongue, desperate to say something, but he holds back.

'What?' I try. 'Please, just spit it out.'

'She said she recognised his eyes, but he'd been wearing a balaclava, so it would have been impossible to press charges on that alone.'

'But he was missing the index finger on his right hand, as she told officers at the scene of the crime.'

'Only after she'd spoken to her husband Richard.'

It's not immediately obvious what he's saying. 'What does that have to do with anything?'

He's holding back again and it's starting to irk. I stare at him expectantly until he cracks under the imposed silence.

'Put it this way, when she was initially interviewed, she couldn't tell us a thing about who had taken Cassie other than that they were wearing masks. Then her husband turns up, they have a private conversation, and suddenly she recalls that the suspect had four fingers. Two days later, when she's shown the faces of three ex-cons who only have four fingers, she points at Hank Amos and says she recognises his eyes, even though she hadn't been able to previously tell us what colour his eyes were.'

'You think she was lying?'

He holds his hands up defensively as if I've just accused him of murder. 'Whoa, whoa, whoa. I didn't say she was lying but I wouldn't place too much faith in the mouths of the parents. Often when a child goes missing, the parents are the first suspects to be ruled in or out of the investigation.'

He doesn't need to tell me this, as I experienced how my own parents suffered at the hands of the team put in charge of Anna's disappearance, and how the press subsequently twisted every poor decision my parents had ever made to fabricate their guilt for tabloid voyeurism. The fact that we'd been allowed to play within the confines of our front garden was suddenly called into question, even though both of us were mature enough to know not to go off with a stranger. Nor did it seem to matter that most of the children in the street would do exactly the same.

'You think her parents were involved?' I ask, watching him closely, uncertain whether he's really been assigned to help my review of the case notes, or whether he's some kind of stooge sent to persuade me that everything is all above board.

'I'm just keeping an open mind. I know that the DCS had his suspicions about there being some kind of insider involved, someone who knew when and where to strike for maximum impact.'

'You really think a parent could be complicit in their child being snatched?'

He shakes his head before shrugging. 'I don't know. I hope not. I know *I* could never be, but there are examples – recent examples – of parents colluding to cover up a more serious crime.'

'Witnesses saw Cassie get into that Range Rover after the party and you can't seriously be thinking that Elizabeth or Richard Hilliard fired the rocket-propelled grenade at the car themselves?'

He sighs. 'No, I don't think that, but when you take into consideration that Richard Hilliard's fine art and antiques dealership business was in financial difficulty, and that the nature of the work could bring him into contact with the sort of people who know other people, and—'

I slam my pages down on the desk. 'I want to see it.'

'See what?'

'I want you to take me to the abduction site.'

Chapter Nineteen

THEN

Chiswick, London

Gerry Connors slowly applied the brake. He was in the new 4x4, tucked behind a transit van, keeping the unmarked police car in sight, two cars in front. 'I'm pretty sure they haven't seen us yet, sir,' he said, his broad Belfast accent cutting through the silence.

'Good,' Richard grunted from the back, eyes glued to his phone. 'Keep it that way.'

They'd exchanged few words since the original meeting; it had been an informal interview of sorts during which Richard had grilled Gerry on his background, particularly his time in Northern Ireland before he'd moved to London. Gerry had spoken honestly – at least, the level of honesty he was prepared to offer anyone who asked. Not even Penny knew all the details of what he'd done before moving to less choppy waters.

'Are you sure they're going to pick him up now, sir?' Gerry

asked, glancing into the rearview mirror at the puppet-master he viewed with equal respect and disdain.

Richard Hilliard was a man for whom things always seemed to turn out for the best. Born with a silver spoon in his mouth, he'd been privately educated, fast-tracked to Oxbridge, and just as his father's business fell into administration, who should he meet but the daughter of a peer of the realm. Marriage had inevitably followed and the great Richard Hilliard once again landed on his feet. Some men had all the luck, Gerry surmised, though right now he wouldn't willingly swap places.

Despite the obvious envy, Richard had stepped up and offered Gerry a job when nobody else would. The hours wouldn't always be agreeable, and when Penny asked him later how his first day had gone, he wasn't quite sure how he would answer. Driving the Hilliards to the police station had been far from stimulating, but tailing the police as they made their way to the home of Hank Amos, the nine-fingered ex-con Elizabeth had identified, had certainly quickened the pulse.

'That's where they're headed,' Richard confirmed, meeting Gerry's stare in the mirror.

'Forgive me, sir, how can you be so sure?'

Richard's lips tightened. 'You'd be surprised what a bit of money can buy you in this town. Trust me, that's where they're going.' He looked away as a spattering of fresh raindrops caught on the window.

'And what is it we're planning to do when they do apprehend him, sir?'

Richard hadn't thought that far ahead, but something told him he had to see Hank Amos in the flesh, had to look into his eyes to know whether he had taken Cassie or not. That's all he'd been able to think about back at the station when Elizabeth had identified those icy eyes, plans for retribution coalescing in his mind until he couldn't see straight.

'I'll decide that when we get there,' Richard replied, uncertain what he would do if he recognised the guilt in Amos's expression.

There were people in the world without a moral compass for whom killing came easy; there were those who were employed and trained to do it under the guise of national security; then there were those who wore no guise at all. For them it was a bloodsport, plain and simple. But then there were those who felt each blow, each blade, each gunshot, as keenly as though it was their own flesh. Those operating outside of statehood, fuelled by their own deepest desires.

Richard didn't see himself in any of those categories. He was in the group of people for whom murder and execution were never a consideration. Yet when he had seen the picture of Hank Amos on the detective's screen, he'd felt a ball of tension growing in his gut, something that told him that if Amos had harmed Cassie, he would have to pay.

'I understand, you know,' Gerry said from the front, his focus still on Richard, with barely an occasional glance at the busy road ahead of them. 'If I was in your shoes, and my wee Sean had been taken, I would search the ends of the earth for the bastards responsible and kill every last one of them.'

Their eyes met again.

'Do you reckon you could then?' Richard asked. 'Kill those responsible, I mean?'

'Without a second's thought,' Gerry replied, before he could stop himself.

Richard's brow furrowed. 'It wouldn't bother you? Having someone else's blood on your hands?'

Gerry's stare intensified. 'Eye for an eye, sir. A father's only responsibility on this earth is to protect his family. To care for his offspring. If that honour was taken away by persons unknown then, yeah, I would have no issue with ending them.'

What Gerry didn't add was that he'd come to terms with the ghosts that haunted his own nightmares. There was no point living with regret.

Returning his gaze to the road, Gerry indicated as the unmarked police car had, but there would now only be one car's distance between them. It would help if he knew where they were headed so he could plan a detour, and avoid drawing unnecessary attention, but all Richard Hilliard's tipoff had said was that they would be sending a team of four plain-clothes officers to the address to make the arrest. Presumably they weren't concerned that Hank Amos might be armed, as otherwise they'd have sent some kind of specialist tactical team to take him.

At the next roundabout, the unmarked car took the second exit, while the car between them took the first. Gerry held back, waiting for another car to come around and take the second exit, inviting a cacophony of horns behind them, but a moment later, with two cars between them once again, Gerry pulled forward.

Five minutes later, the unmarked car pulled into a residential street and parked. Gerry had no idea which property they were looking at, so continued past to the end of the close before pulling into a space with barely a view of the unmarked car.

'What are you doing?' Richard asked. 'We're too far away.'

'Better that than them seeing us,' Gerry concluded, reaching into the glovebox and extracting a personalised set of binoculars he'd spotted at the Hilliards' house when he'd arrived that morning. He handed them back between the seats. 'Here you go.'

Richard pressed the binoculars to his eyes and watched as the four plain-clothes officers exited the car, two moving to the front of one of the townhouses, and the others heading down an alleyway that appeared to lead to the rear of the property.

The estate still looked new, the orange brickwork yet to be bleached by the sun and eroded by rain. A large, grassy island in the heart of the estate was bordered by an enclosed playground offering swings, a slide, a roundabout, and a climbing frame. Gerry wasn't familiar with Chiswick, but could imagine himself, Penny, and Sean settling somewhere like this estate, if only they could afford to move. Considering some of the much older properties they'd passed on their way to this large cul-de-sac, it was almost as if the developers had wiped the board clean and started again. That said, if Hank Amos could afford to live here, either Gerry had grossly overestimated the cost of a West London property, or crime really did pay.

'They're knocking on his door,' Richard commented, adjusting the focus of the binoculars. They had been a present from Elizabeth last Christmas, inscribed with his initials. At the time he hadn't understood why she'd chosen them as a gift, but now it felt almost as if fate had provided them for this very occasion.

The front door opened a moment later and a woman in a headscarf stood there and engaged with the officers, though Richard had no idea what she was saying to them. She turned away momentarily and then the face of Hank Amos appeared by her side. He looked much older than he had in the photograph on the detective's screen, but he seemed to be offering little resistance as he left the property, flanked by officers either side.

Richard opened his door and clambered out without even thinking, throwing the binoculars on the back seat and leaving the door ajar as he stalked away.

Gerry remained where he was, torn as to whether he should accompany his new boss or whether it was better to keep out of sight. If it was Sean in danger, Gerry would want as much support and muscle as he could get his hands on… but Richard wasn't like him, and Gerry sensed that it would be better to stay put.

Richard's focus never left his target as he swallowed up the space between them. It was only when one of the officers emerging from the alleyway intercepted him and told him to go home that Richard even realised how close he now was.

'Where's my daughter?' Richard shouted at the bewildered-looking Amos.

'Who's this muppet?' Amos fired at the officer closest to him.

The grey hair looked even greasier up close, straggled and hanging loose beyond the shoulders of the faded leather jacket and black Sex Pistols T-shirt. The skin around the man's eyes hung loose, as if he had dramatically lost weight recently.

'Mr Hilliard, please, go home,' Richard heard as a hand tugged at his arm.

He ignored the challenge and launched himself forwards, grabbing the lapels of the leather jacket and driving Amos backwards. The two officers struggled to maintain their hold and in the heat of the situation, all four tumbled to the ground, Richard landing on top of Amos.

'Where is my daughter, you scumbag?' he growled. 'Tell me what you've done with her, or I swear to God, I'll…'

'You'll what?' Amos fired back, shuffling to get free. 'There's nothing you can do to me that isn't already coming. Besides, I've no fucking idea what you're talking about.'

The two remaining officers dragged Richard off him before the other two helped Amos back to his feet.

'I know you took her,' Richard shouted with venom. 'You think I don't know people who can get to you? You think you're above the law? Screw you! If you've even touched a hair on her head, I will kill you.'

Amos glanced at the two officers who supported his arms. 'Can you believe this prick? Ooh, I'm quaking in my boots,' he laughed. 'Do me a favour, pal. I bet you can't even tie your own shoes. You posh twats are all the same.'

Richard reached into his trouser pocket, running his thumb over the point of the paring knife he'd grabbed from the block in the kitchen. Could he do it? Would that get Cassie back quicker?

'Come on, sir,' Gerry Connors said, placing a protective arm around Richard's shoulders and ushering him away, 'let's leave these officers to do their job.'

'Yeah, run along now,' Amos jeered. 'Oh, and while you're at it, have this on me,' he added, spitting a wad of phlegm.

Richard turned his face defensively, but couldn't stop the warmth flooding his cheeks. Gerry held firm, keeping him from retaliation as the two officers manhandled Amos towards a police van that had arrived in the road during the ruckus.

'You need to keep out of the way, Mr Hilliard,' one of the

other officers was now telling him. 'Let us do our job and we will find your daughter. If you continue to interfere, DCS Rawani will not be happy.'

Gerry led a reluctant Richard back to the waiting Range Rover and helped him in, using the sleeve of his suit jacket to wipe the spittle from his employer's face. 'I'll take you home, sir, and it's probably best if we don't mention any of this to Mrs Hilliard.'

Richard didn't respond, the blade of the paring knife heavy in his pocket. One thing was for sure: he definitely didn't have it in him to kill, but he was no longer so certain his new driver Gerry Connors fell into the same category.

Chapter Twenty

NOW

Chalfont St Giles, Buckinghamshire

'This was the point of impact,' Jack Serrovitz says, crouching down and indicating the scorched crack in the concrete. 'You can still see where the explosion damaged the road.'

The patrol car's blinking hazard warning lights cast an eerie intermittent orange glow over the scene. Studying the darkened patch, I can almost picture the ball of flame erupting when the rocket-propelled grenade made contact with the rear axle of the Range Rover.

'It's lucky the whole car didn't go up in flames,' I say aloud. 'Had they been off by a couple of inches, they'd have surely hit the fuel tank.'

Jack studies the findings report the crime scene investigators had produced at the time before marching further away from the patrol car. 'According to this, because of the speed the Range Rover was travelling at, it continued along the road for several more metres before it began to tip and roll, finally ending up on its side, right… about… here.' He freezes and waits for me to catch up. 'To all intents and purposes, this was the extraction point.'

I allow my eyes to lose focus, imagining how the day unfurled from that point, seeing the van screeching to a halt, the perpetrators leaping from it and clambering on top of the disabled Range Rover. It's the widest point of the road, where the density of the bordering hedges and trees lessens ahead of a gated track leading into the neighbouring farmer's field. Of the entire length of the road, it is the perfect point to attack. Could that be a coincidence?

'As you can see,' Jack continues, 'the road isn't particularly well-used on account of the inability for vehicles to pass both ways. On that particular day, it was several minutes until any other vehicle came along. Mr and Mrs Benjamin were the couple who stopped to assist Elizabeth Hilliard and the driver Hobbs. They were on their way home after a tennis tournament at a sports club in nearby Northwood. Neither could recall seeing a van on the road and their first thoughts were that the driver had simply lost control of the vehicle.'

I raise my hand to shield my eyes from the bright afternoon sun. 'Remind me, what were the Hilliards doing on this road on that Saturday?'

'Returning from a children's birthday party,' Jack says, without missing a beat. 'Gerry and Penny Connors were hosting a party for their seven-year-old son, Sean, who was in Cassie's class at school. Apparently they hired a bouncy castle, gave the kids some food, and then the party ended promptly at four. Wilfred Hobbs, the Hilliards' regular driver, drove Mrs Hilliard from her yoga class to the Connorses' home, and from there they proceeded from Rickmansworth, through Maple Cross, until they reached this road on the outskirts of the Chalfonts.'

Looking over the wide rolling hills of green to my right, and the close knot of trees to my left, it doesn't make any sense to me. 'Why on earth would anyone plan to strike here?'

Jack looks up from the file and considers the view. 'It's secluded, so less likely to be overseen by witnesses.'

I shake my head at the suggestion. 'Put yourself in the mind-set of the gang who took her: if you're planning to snatch Cassie Hilliard – regardless of the reason – you would want to do it with the minimum of fuss, right? You'd want to get in, grab the girl, and get out as quickly as possible.'

He nods. 'I guess.'

'So why wait until this moment on the journey home to attack? If you know – and presumably *they* did – that Cassie is being collected at 4pm, why not grab her there and then? Why follow the vehicle to this secluded road where you could get stuck in traffic, or meet a car coming the other way? I understand what you're saying about it being out of sight of witnesses, but it's the neck of the bottle in terms of the journey back to their house in Chalfont St Giles. It's the one moment where unforeseen traffic is likely to play a part.'

'What are you saying?'

It's the million-pound question, and I don't really know why it bothers me so much. 'I'm just trying to get into the mind-set of those responsible, that's all.'

Jack smiles, and I find myself mirroring his expression.

'Ah, but you're forgetting the first lesson they teach us on day one of police training,' he says coyly. 'Criminals are stupid.'

It's a fair shout, and certainly not the first time I've heard it. But there is a small proportion who *are* smart, and my instinct tells me that the people responsible for the abduction of Cassie Hilliard are in the latter category.

Jack moves across to the small grass verge before the gated path. 'With the Range Rover upturned, it wouldn't have been easy for the van to get past, and you can still just about see where it drove up and over the verge here, the fender getting scratched by the hedge. Scrapings taken from here were matched back to the van when it was discovered in the barn early the following morning.'

I squeeze the twigs of the hedge between my fingers, feeling their bite as they break the top layer of my skin. 'Was the owner of the van ever traced?'

He nods again. 'The van was stolen from a long-term airport carpark the day before the attack. The van's owner was away with family in Benidorm and not best pleased to arrive home and discover that his van was in the pound undergoing forensic examination. He eventually got it back but was never considered a suspect.'

'The team discovered the van in the barn of the farm in the early hours of Sunday morning but it took a further two days before they positively identified the vehicle used to transport Cassie from the farm to their next hideout, right?'

'Correct. In his notes, the DCS commented that he felt confident that they were closing the net, and that the gang had fled the farm in a hurry because of the supplies they'd left, but that was later ruled to be a misnomer.'

'What do you mean?'

'Well, when the team did identify the white Nissan Qashqai that left the farm – presumably with Cassie in the back – it turned out they had left barely half an hour after they'd arrived. By the time the team raided the barn on Sunday morning, they'd been gone for ten hours already. The family were fuming about that, from all accounts.'

'So, the clothing and food supplies were never going to be used?'

'It was later determined that it was a false lead, deliberately planted to throw the team off the scent. Either that or it was a contingency that they never had to use.'

I return to the scorched mark on the concrete, crouching to examine it again. 'What can you tell me about the weapon they used to disable the Range Rover?'

Jack consults the file again. 'Russian-manufactured, based on the ballistics, but readily available on the open market to anyone if you know where to look. It was a shoulder-fired anti-tank weapon system that releases a rocket equipped with an explosive warhead. The one in question was single use, meaning that had they missed, they wouldn't have had a second bite at the cherry.'

I raise my eyebrows, not au fait with where one would go to purchase such a weapon.

'The dark web,' he says, meeting my confused stare. 'This kind of tech isn't something you buy off a guy on a street corner. That's fine for handguns, and maybe semi-automatic pistols, but something like this – something with a real kick – you have to go online for that. Are you familiar with the dark web?'

I nod, having come across the term when I was delving into Freddie's story. 'It's the part of the internet that's hidden from the general public where criminals and perverts can buy anything from guns to drugs to child pornography.'

'That's the place. Did you know it was originally created to allow the armed services overseas to send encrypted messages home? Unfortunately, it's taken on quite a different purpose these days. The team located several sites on the dark web where such a weapon could be purchased, but were unable to secure a list of recent buyers; no surprise there.'

'So the perpetrators are familiar with using the dark web to aid their cause,' I concur.

'Not only that,' Jack says, waving the file in the air. 'The ballistics team also concluded that at least one member of the gang would have had some kind of specialist weapons training in order to fire the RPG. Maybe tactical training, or some branch of the military. Could be European, but just as easily a foreign combatant on home soil.'

'Richard Hilliard had dealings abroad, didn't he?'

Jack nods. 'Imported antiques from the Middle East, or so I read in the file.'

'Did the investigative team look into whether he'd attracted enemies abroad? Maybe his strong-arm tactics to secure valuable antiques for European clients put someone's nose out of joint.'

'I think enquiries were made, but he claimed there was nobody he could think of who would want revenge on him. And the DCS concluded that if the gang's motivation was revenge on Richard Hilliard, they would have targeted him directly, rather than his family.'

I'm not so easily convinced. 'Who knew that Richard Hilliard wouldn't be in the car that day? What if he *was* the target, but in their panic they snatched Cassie instead?'

He shakes his head dismissively. 'The ransom request for the return of Cassie would suggest that theory is unlikely.'

He has a point.

'Something else the ballistics team noted in the file,' Jack continues, 'was the difficulty of the shot. It's one thing to fire an RPG at a static target, but at a vehicle travelling at between thirty and forty miles an hour on a bendy road like this, would take one hell of a lot of luck, or a vast amount of skill and experience… which again lends itself to a military background.'

Another vehicle has now pulled up behind the patrol car and the driver is exiting, presumably to check whether the road is closed.

'Are we done here, or is there anything else you want to see?' Jack asks.

Taking one final look at the scene, I shake my head and follow him back to the car.

Jack speaks with the driver behind us before climbing in next to me in the front. 'Where to now? Back to the station?'

'No. I'd like to speak to Penny and Gerry Connors. Could you drive me to their home?'

His brow furrows. 'How come? Their statements are in the file we looked at. They confirmed the time Cassie was collected and that they didn't see a navy-blue van follow the Range Rover as it pulled away. A full background check was run on the two of them, with no reason to believe they were involved in what happened.'

Fixing him with an innocent face, I notice that his dark brown eyes have flecks of green in them, which I hadn't spotted earlier. 'I'm curious, that's all. In my experience, when researching a story, it's important to learn information for myself, rather than just relying on somebody else's interpretation of the facts. Humour me, will you?'

He doesn't argue. Instead, he starts the engine and follows the narrow road to its conclusion before choosing a wider road for our journey to Rickmansworth. Even though Penny and Gerry Connors were officially ruled out as persons of interest last year, Gerry's redundancy certainly would have given him motive to sell information about his new employer to the highest bidder, and that's enough to pique my interest.

Chapter Twenty-One

NOW

Rickmansworth, Hertfordshire

The home of Penny and Gerry Connors is unremarkable. It is a traditional semi-detached three-bedroom property with a virtually identical frontage to the rest of the properties in the long street. Odd numbers are on the left as we ascend the hill and evens are on the right. The Connors live at number 79, and presumably Gerry Connors is the man on the driveway, smearing soapy bubbles over the bonnet of the hatchback.

He looks round at us in stunned surprise as Jack pulls the patrol car onto the kerb, blocking any potential for exit from the driveway.

'Can I help you with something?' Gerry Connors asks, his thick hazelnut beard resembling something a family of birds might nest in.

'Mr Connors?' Jack asks, holding out his identification. 'My name's PC Jack Serrovitz, and this lady with me is—'

'You're the woman off the television,' Gerry says, cutting off Jack mid-flow and staring straight into my soul.

I do so dislike being recognised. The introvert always lurking like a shadow comes to the fore and I just want the ground to swallow me up.

Taking a deep breath, holding it for seven seconds, and then gradually releasing it – an old yoga trick – I thrust my hand towards Gerry Connors. 'That's right. I'm Emma Hunter.'

He wipes the suds from the back of his hand on his jeans and shakes it. 'What can I do for you?'

'We'd like to discuss the disappearance of Cassie Hilliard with you and Mrs Connors,' Jack says, regaining control.

Gerry sneers. 'It's been a year; we want nothing more to do with that family.'

It's an odd reaction. From what I'd read in the file, Gerry stepped into the lurch when the regular driver, Hobbs, was hospitalised. My story-sniffing nose is twitching, but I also sense that he doesn't want to say any more on the subject.

'I appreciate that, Mr Connors,' Jack says, 'but Miss Hunter and I are reviewing the events of twelve months ago, and she'd really like to ask you and your—'

'You're looking to do an exposé, like with that boys' home?' he asks, his gaze burrowing deep again.

'Not exactly,' I answer honestly. 'I'm just looking at the details.'

He reaches for the sponge in the bucket before slopping it onto the roof of the hatchback. 'Good luck getting them to spill their secrets. Hundreds of skeletons in their cupboards but they won't let you at any of them. Mark my words: when the shit hits the fan, that lot know how to close ranks.'

He turns his back to us and I get the impression that we won't get anything else out of Gerry so I try a fresh tactic. 'Is Mrs Connors inside? I could really do with using the toilet before we take off. Is that okay?'

'Penny will let you in,' he says, without turning back. 'Just ring the bell.'

Jack steps forward and leads me to the porch door which he opens then leans in and presses the doorbell.

A woman in a flour-dusted apron appears a moment later. She sees Jack first and pulls a confused face. 'Can I help you with something?'

'Mrs Connors?' he asks. 'I'm PC Jack Serrovitz and I was hoping to ask you some questions about your memories of the Cassie Hilliard disappearance. Would you mind if I come in?'

She's less resistant than her husband and steps aside, holding the door open for us. Although she takes a long look at me, she doesn't immediately recognise my face. I breathe a sigh of relief.

'You'll have to excuse me,' she says, pushing past us and heading along the narrow hallway into the kitchen at the end. The radio is blaring, almost covering the hum of the fan oven. 'I'm making cookies and I'll have to get them out in a moment. Would either of you like a cup of tea?'

The sweet smell of baking fills our nostrils and I'm momentarily transported back to my grandmother's kitchen in the days, weeks, and months before Anna disappeared. Every memory I have of being at my grandma's house is filled with the smell of cakes, biscuits, and pies. I'm not convinced she baked every time we were there, but they're the only memories I have.

'Tea would be lovely,' I answer for the both of us. If my

experience of interviewing historic witnesses has taught me anything, it's always to accept the offer of a drink. Tea means we will be in her home for at least twenty to thirty minutes: plenty of time to ask my questions and learn more about the family secrets Gerry hinted at outside.

Penny opens the oven door and drags out the tray of cookies, the sweet aroma intensifying in the room, and it's all I can do to keep from salivating. She makes us tea and invites us into the mid-sized dining room adjacent to the kitchen which has a large sliding patio door. Framed images of the parents with a young boy – presumably their son, Sean – are lined up on the sideboard behind where Penny and Jack sit, across the table from me.

She catches my eye as she passes me a mug of tea and there is a moment of recognition. 'Have we met before?' she asks. 'There's something so familiar about your face.'

If her husband has seen me interviewed on the television then there's every chance she has too. 'My name's Emma Hunter. You might have seen me talking about my book on the news.'

She snaps her fingers together, a rewarding smile breaking across her face. 'That's it! Oh wow, I didn't realise I had a celebrity in my house. I feel like I should have used the china cups and saucers now, rather than these grotty mugs.'

'Oh no,' I say quickly. 'I much prefer a mug, and there's really no need to go to any special lengths for me.'

I detest the word celebrity. It's hard enough to accept myself as a writer but I'm sure that within the year nobody will remember who I am or what I look like. God knows, I hope that's the case!

Jack opens a notebook and skims the list of questions he

prepared before we pulled into their road. 'Cassie Hilliard was here at this house on the day she disappeared, is that correct?'

Penny nods firmly. 'Yes, it was Sean's birthday and we threw a small party for him and his school friends.'

'How did Cassie seem to you at the party? Was there anything odd about her behaviour that you can now recall given everything that's happened since?'

'Only what I told the officers at the time. She was a nice girl, as far as I could tell. Fairly popular with her classmates too.'

'Specifically, Mrs Connors, I think you said something about her wandering off during the party?'

She takes a sip from her mug. 'Yeah, that was a bit odd. A car backfired and she mistook it for a gun and hid.'

I've read the interviews that were conducted with Penny and Gerry Connors in the aftermath of the abduction, but memory can be a funny thing, with additional details being recalled much later in some cases.

'She said it was her father who'd told her to hide if she ever heard a gun,' Penny continues, staring off into the distance, 'which was odd in itself. I tried to speak to Cassie's mother when she came to collect her, but she wasn't interested in talking to me, so I left it. Don't you think it's weird to tell your six-year-old daughter something like that?'

She's looking straight at me and I feel obliged to nod.

'Your husband had just started to work for the Hilliards, hadn't he?' Jack asks.

Penny nods but there is something bitter in her eyes – resentment maybe. 'He'd been made redundant from the factory six months earlier and we were on the last of our savings. He would have done anything. He'd already met with

Richard Hilliard prior to the party, though at the time his duties had yet to be explained to him. And then, after their other driver got injured, he was tasked with driving them around. I told him I didn't want him to become their glorified chauffeur, particularly in light of what had happened to the other driver, but they didn't give Gerry much of a choice. Thank God they weren't attacked again when Gerry was with them.'

'Gerry doesn't work for them anymore?' I enquire innocently.

The look of resentment deepens. 'No. Well, after what they said, it didn't seem right for him to be there any longer.'

There was no mention of any dispute between the Hilliards and the Connorses in the file. 'Forgive me, Mrs Connors, but can you elaborate on what happened?'

Her eyes are shining when she meets my gaze. 'After everything he did for them in the days after she was taken...' She shakes her head in disgust. 'Well, first there was the moment that Richard tried it on with him. He made a pass at Gerry, who of course rejected the advance. Who'd have known that Richard was gay? Even though it made things awkward, Gerry continued to work for them and he became a rock for Elizabeth. But then when the ransom went haywire and the money went up in flames, Richard had the gall to accuse Gerry of working with the men responsible.'

My head is spinning at the level of new information she's just dumped here. I have so many questions but it's Jack who speaks first. 'Richard Hilliard denied ever making a pass at your husband and claimed that Gerry invented the story in retaliation for the accusation Richard had made.'

'That's bullshit!' Penny says, her cheeks quickly reddening

as she covers her lips with her hand. 'Sorry, it's just that Gerry told me the day it happened. How Elizabeth had kicked Richard out and how it was just the two of them in the hotel room. Richard leaned in and tried to kiss him. That was the same day they were to pay the ransom, so how Richard can have the nerve to suggest Gerry invented the story is beyond me. Covering his own arse, if anything.'

'You said Gerry was there when the exchange happened?'

'They weren't supposed to be. Apparently, the lead detective had said he and his team would handle the money exchange, but Richard never was one who stuck to the rules. He had Gerry drive them to a hilltop overlooking the location and they watched it unfold. You're better speaking to him about it but from what he told me, Richard had binoculars. After the detective handed over the bag of money, the kidnapper went back to the van to collect Cassie and bring her out when suddenly all hell broke loose, and a shootout ended with a stray bullet striking the petrol tank of the van. The whole thing ignited in a ball of flames. From what Gerry said, there were flaming motes fluttering down from the sky like snowflakes.'

Jack's face has lost its colour and I can't be sure how much of this was briefed to him by the DCS before we met.

Penny stands, her mug now empty. 'If you want to know who's behind that little girl's death, I'd look no further than the Hilliards themselves. That's where you'll find your answers.'

Chapter Twenty-Two

THEN

Uxbridge, London

Elizabeth was disappointed that Richard hadn't come to the hospital with her. After their exploits at the police station, where they'd appeared united in the desperate search for their daughter, she had hoped he would maintain that front. Instead, he'd told her he had an important call to make with a third-party supplier in Egypt and had the new driver – Gerry Connors of all people – take them home.

It didn't feel right employing a parent of one of Cassie's classmates; it would create unnecessary tension should she ever run into either Gerry or his overly anxious wife Penny at school. It was Richard's decision to have Gerry drive them around while Hobbs recovered in hospital, but her father hadn't argued so she was stuck with him.

'They reckon there's rain due next week,' Gerry said now, in a too familiar tone, his thick accent not the easiest to understand.

That was the problem with new drivers: they never understand the correct protocol. They weren't employing him for his conversation. Hobbs knew to speak only when spoken to, whereas Gerry seemed to think he was driving a taxi cab.

Elizabeth didn't respond to his statement, choosing to look out of the window instead.

'Apparently storm Iris is going to bring torrential downpours across the whole of the UK in early October too.'

Elizabeth kept her eyes glued to the window as the car bumped along the road and was relieved when it pulled up at the carpark barrier.

'I'll drop you at the entrance and then find somewhere to park,' Gerry said, and the cellophane crunched as Elizabeth picked up the bunch of flowers she'd collected on their journey into Hillingdon.

The entrance to the hospital was a sight to behold: men and women in various states of dress – some in pyjamas, others in dressing gowns, a couple of nurse uniforms, and one woman in a rain mac – all inhaling cigarettes like it would be their last. Elizabeth waved her hand in front of her face as she passed through the low cloud of smoke, appalled that nobody had moved them further from the entrance.

She knew Hobbs was in the A&E Observation Unit but had no clue where to find it. Approaching the front desk, she asked the man in the brown jumper who looked like a store security guard. When he spoke, she couldn't understand a word of what he said and was about to give up when she felt a warm hand on her shoulder.

'It's this way.'

Turning, she was surprised to find Gerry beside her.

He offered a warm smile. 'I managed to get a space near the front and I figured you might need some help finding the ward.'

He was slightly out of breath and must have run the entire way. She had expected him to wait with the car but he seemed intent on helping her, and his accent wasn't as unintelligible as that of the man in the brown jumper who was now studying his phone screen.

Gerry ushered her to the left, along a narrow corridor where people of all ages and colours passed by, each lost in their own little world, none of them smiling.

'I spent a wee bit of time in the Observation Unit,' Gerry said, as she kept stride with him, 'so I know where it is.'

'Thank you,' she said, when they arrived at the heavy doors to the ward.

'You need to use the antibacterial gel before you go in,' he said, nodding at the wall and offering to take the flowers from her. 'It's to stop any germs getting onto the ward.'

She wasn't accustomed to being told what to do but she hadn't stepped inside a hospital since Cassie's birth and thus obliged him by squirting the ice cold gel into her palms.

'Now rub them together until the gel evaporates,' Gerry continued, miming the action.

Elizabeth rubbed her hands together, the smell of the alcohol in the gel making her nose twitch. Then thrusting out her hand for the bunch of flowers, she moved to the doors which whirred open when the sensor read her presence. Again, she expected Gerry to return to the car, but he followed her through.

'I don't require an escort,' she said under her breath.

'I'm sorry, but I promised your father I wouldn't leave your side,' he replied discreetly. 'He's worried about you, you know.'

Increasing her pace, she advanced to the front desk and was about to ask which room Hobbs was in when the Chinese nurse behind it spoke.

'No flowers.'

Taken aback, Elizabeth wanted to argue that she'd spent twenty minutes choosing the perfect bunch that showed both her concern for a dear family friend and her gratitude that he had managed to keep them both alive. Without looking at her, the nurse tapped a sign on the wall behind her that clearly indicated flowers were not to be brought onto the ward.

'Well, what should I do with them?' Elizabeth replied, flustered.

'Leave in box over there,' the nurse replied, pointing at a cardboard box propped against the wall behind them. 'You take when leave.'

Gerry snatched them from her and placed them in the box before she could argue.

'Could you tell us which room Wilfred Hobbs is in please?' Gerry then asked the woman.

She checked her computer screen and responded.

'Thank you,' he said. 'Come on, it's this way.'

Elizabeth made a mental note to speak to Richard about Gerry's overly familiar attitude and forcefulness when she saw him next. He either needed to buck up his ideas or find a new employer, as far as she was concerned.

To his credit, he located the room where Hobbs was one of six patients. He lay in bed, wrapped tightly by the white sheet over his legs. Elizabeth gasped when she saw the strapping around his chest, and the plaster cast running the length of his right arm.

'Mrs Hilliard,' he winced as she came closer, straining to smile, but clearly struggling.

A woman in a headscarf who was seated at his side lowered her magazine.

'This is my wife, Susan,' he said. 'Susan, this is Mrs Hilliard.'

The woman in the headscarf bowed her head in reverence, which Elizabeth thought quite unnecessary.

'It's a pleasure to meet you, Mrs Hobbs,' Elizabeth said. 'How are you feeling, Hobbs?'

'I'll pull through,' he said, wincing again with the strain of speech.

An awkward silence descended with Elizabeth uncertain of what she should say, conscious that it was her family that had indirectly caused his injuries.

'Mrs Hobbs?' Gerry eventually spoke up. 'You look like you could do with a nice cup of tea and a slice of cake. Why don't you show me where the hospital cafeteria is and I'll treat you? Mrs Hilliard, would you like us to bring you back a cup of tea?'

'No, but thank you,' she said, grateful for his intervention once again.

Susan Hobbs vacated the chair and followed Gerry back out of the room, leaving Elizabeth and her injured driver space to speak more freely. Elizabeth sat in the chair and took his hand in hers, surprised at how cold it felt.

'I am so sorry, Hobbs. What have they said about your injuries?'

'I'll be out of action for several months I'm afraid, Mrs

Hilliard. Punctured lung, fractured elbow, fractured knee cap, and two broken ribs.'

Elizabeth's hand shot up to her mouth. Having escaped with only bumps and bruises, she'd had no idea how big an impact the crash had had on her driver.

'I am so sorry, Hobbs.'

'It's not your fault, ma'am,' he reassured, giving her hand a gentle squeeze. 'I just wish I could have done more.'

Given his injuries, it was a wonder he'd survived. He was in his early sixties and he'd worked for her father for as long as she could remember. Whilst his grey hair and slight frame showed signs of his age, she still looked upon him as the tall man with fair hair who was always happy to play catch with her on the long, boring summer holidays when her father would be away in India or Malaysia.

'What do you remember of the accident?' she asked. 'I keep reliving the moment from the loud bang to the car rocking and then seemingly tipping onto its side. Did you see the van?'

He coughed, pulling his hand away to cover his mouth and taking a moment to regain his breath. 'I told the police everything I could remember. The van was dark – blue or black maybe, I think. I'd seen it in my mirror but it hadn't given me any reason to suspect it was dangerous in any way. I think I was looking at you and Cassie in the mirror when I heard the explosion. At first I thought I'd hit something, but there was nothing outside the front and then I must have blacked out as the next thing I remember is waking in the back of the ambulance in agony. They said I have concussion too, so I must have banged my head during the tumble.' He paused and his eyes were shining when he spoke again. 'When they told me what had happened… with Cassie, I mean… well, I just… I just…'

Elizabeth fought back her own emotions. 'It wasn't your fault, Hobbs. She was right there in front of me and I could do nothing to stop them taking her.'

A single tear rolled the length of his cheek, evaporating between the cracks in his dry skin. 'I've always thought of young Cassie as like a granddaughter of my own and although I would never wish to presume, I've always thought of you as I would a daughter. I'm absolutely devastated by what is happening to you both and if there's anything I can do, you've only to ask.'

It was all she could do not to burst into a sob, but she'd cried so much in the last two days that her tear ducts remained dry. 'Is there anything else you can remember? The registration plate of the van or when you first noticed it? Anything at all?'

'I'm sorry, ma'am, but I really can't recall anything further. The doctor said my head would be groggy for a few days but that it's possible other memories might return as the trauma eases. I promise you, if I remember anything, you and the police will be the first to know.'

Elizabeth's mobile erupted into life, a cacophony of noise that brought with it scowls from the two nurses changing the sheets of the bed closest to the window.

'Phones should be switched off,' one of them said, and Elizabeth was about to cancel the call when she saw Richard's name on the screen.

He knew she was visiting Hobbs so he wouldn't be phoning unless it was important. Pressing the phone to her ear, she answered the call.

'Elizabeth? You need to come home immediately. They've just messaged the house… the kidnappers. They told me they have Cassie and if we ever want to see her again, we're going to have to pay.'

Chapter Twenty-Three

NOW

Uxbridge, London

'Cassie died when the van exploded?' I ask, when Jack and I are back in the car and leaving the Connorses' home in Rickmansworth.

He keeps his eyes fixed on the road. 'I didn't know that's how it went down. The DCS didn't go into too much detail when briefing me. All he said was that the exchange went south and that they lost Cassie and the money.'

I feel sick to my stomach, and I'm sure if my stomach had anything more than this morning's croissant in it, my face would be even greener now.

'What else haven't you told me?'

I don't mean it to sound so bitter but I've almost started thinking of Jack as my partner in this thing – silly, I know – and now I see him for what he is: the guy who drew the short straw and got lumbered with me.

His eyes lock on mine. 'I told you: this is as fresh to me as it is to you.'

The statement sounds heartfelt and the look he's giving me makes me want to believe every word, but how can I trust someone I barely know?

I eventually settle for, 'Why you?'

'Why me, what?'

'Well, I'm assuming you didn't win a competition to get stuck with babysitting me while I look through the files?'

His stern cheeks break into a small smile and the atmosphere lightens. 'I volunteered, actually. The DCS was looking for someone with a bit of detective experience to go over things with you and I put my hand up. I read your book and I really enjoyed it. I mean, I know it doesn't paint my colleagues in the best light but I loved the tenacity of the language. It felt like I was reading a fantastical adventure, and I had to keep reminding myself that it was a true story.'

The heat rises in my cheeks and I have to look away. I remind myself that this is the moment when I need to stop telling myself that he's only saying these things to butter me up. Then another thought strikes: why do I care what he thinks? After I tell Fitzhume there's nothing more to investigate, I probably won't ever see him again.

'What's wrong?' he asks, as we pull up at some traffic lights.

'Nothing,' I reply, suddenly conscious that the sleeve of my cardigan is wet again.

'I was going to bring in my copy of the book and ask you to autograph it but I didn't want you to think I was just some sad fanboy; I really did enjoy it. Is that why you wanted to look into Cassie's disappearance? To right some other wrong?'

'It wasn't my choice,' I begin to say, but I stop myself. 'Did you really volunteer, or are you just saying that to make me feel better?'

He narrows his eyes. 'Honestly, no. I'm currently fulfilling a role where I look at historic cases anyway so I was the obvious choice, but if the DCS had asked for volunteers, I'd have been at the front of the queue.'

That makes more sense; he must be one of the Met's equivalents of the PC who reviews Anna's case each year for fresh clues.

'You said you have detective experience?'

He looks back to the road as the lights turn green but doesn't answer the question.

'Jack? What did you mean when you said you have detective experience?'

Again, his answer isn't forthcoming, but eventually he glances over and when he sees I won't let it drop, he responds. 'I *was* a detective constable for a bit but I stepped away from it.'

His tone is sullen, close to regret, and I want to ask what would have made him reach such a decision but it feels like trespassing.

'You hungry?' he says a moment later as a large golden 'M' comes into view up ahead. 'I just realised we never stopped for lunch and it's nearly five o'clock.'

Food is exactly what I need but I remember Rachel said that we'd go out for food when I got back. 'Thanks, but I've already got dinner plans.'

'Oh, I see, okay, well where do you want me to go next? Do you want to go back to the station and give the files another hour or so? Or should I drop you back at your hotel?'

My eyelids are suddenly really heavy and all I really want is a good book and the warmth of a soft pillow. 'I'm not in a hotel; I'm staying with a friend. Drop me back at the station and I'm sure I can make my way back to her flat on the tube. There's a direct train from Uxbridge to Ealing, right?'

'Oh, you're staying in Ealing?' he says, suddenly swinging the car to the left and exiting the roundabout at the first exit. 'You should have said. I'll drop you off there instead.'

'Oh no, there's really no need,' I try to stay, but we're already joining the A40.

'It's no bother,' he adds, as we leave the slip road.

When I first met Fitzhume, he was adamant that Cassie was still alive and that the police had bungled her return, but I don't understand why he could be so convinced when, if what Penny Connors said is right, she died when the van exploded in a ball of fire.

'What did you make of what the Connorses told us?' I say casually.

'Which part? The bit about Richard Hilliard making a pass at Gerry?'

'No, the bit about the shootout and the van exploding.'

'I don't know. It's her account of what her husband said he witnessed. All I know is that there was an explosion of some sort, resulting in the death of one of the kidnappers. There was an inquest at the time, but an independent hearing found no culpability on the DCS's part.'

Something stirs. 'Hold on. *One* of the kidnappers died? What happened to the other one?'

His brow furrows as he looks at me. 'He was arrested, of course. I thought you knew that?'

I don't remember Fitzhume mentioning that the abductors

had been caught but I'm not sure why my mind automatically assumed they were still out there somewhere. Maybe that says more about my cynicism than anything else.

'Where is he now?'

'Serving at Her Majesty's pleasure. I can find out which prison he's in if you want, but I doubt he'll be much use to your story.'

'Why not?'

'Let's just say, he wasn't the most cooperative of suspects. He gave "No Comment" interviews following his arrest, and even when charged, refused to tell us anything more about his partner. When the case went to trial he pleaded guilty and is due to spend the next thirty years behind bars.'

I don't know why but the thought of speaking to a witness to events who isn't biased by family loyalty has the creative cogs turning in my head.

'Can I meet him?' I ask.

'What for?'

'Everyone has a story they want to tell; just because he wouldn't speak to the police, doesn't mean he won't speak to me.'

'I don't know how that would work. I'm pretty sure the DCS wouldn't want me helping you to contact the prison to arrange such a visit. I'm happy to find out which establishment he's in but it would be up to you to reach out to the governor and request the chance to speak to him.'

'What's his name?'

'Leroy Denton. Career criminal. Been in and out of prison since he was fifteen. Nasty piece of work, from what I've heard. I'd be very surprised if he was willing to speak to you.'

I jot the name down in my phone and resolve to ask

Maddie about the angle when we next speak. 'Penny Connors also suggested that the Hilliards themselves could have been involved in Cassie being taken. Were they fully investigated at the time?'

A sign for Ealing appears overhead and Jack indicates for the exit. 'Whenever a child goes missing, the parents are the first to be challenged. A full examination of their histories and possible involvement was completed at the time but there was nothing to link them to her being taken other than the family's wealth and the indirect royal connection. When the ransom demand was made, it soon became clear that money was the motivation for the attack on the Range Rover and the abduction of Cassie.'

He pauses and takes a deep breath. 'I wouldn't pay too much attention to the suspicions of Penny Connors. After the exchange went wrong, there were a lot of heated words between the families and I believe Penny tried to sell the story to a tabloid, which only worsened matters.'

I wonder how much money Fitzhume had spent to quash that story.

'You should come back to the station on Monday,' Jack continues, 'and we can finish reading the case files. I'm pretty sure by the end you'll see that what happened last year was nothing but a set of unfortunate circumstances. A tragedy, certainly, but some big conspiracy theory? I don't think so.'

The conversation dries up as we head through Perivale, the traffic stop-start all the way to Ealing Broadway. The silence isn't my friend. As the sunlight begins to fade over our heads and the shutters are drawn on the high-street shops, I'm reminded that this isn't my home. Here, where the daytime life is closing, the nightlife is just stirring, with the neon lights of restaurants and bars flickering to life. In Weymouth, 5pm marks the end of the day and whilst there are restaurants and pubs in the town, they're more conservative in their attempts to attract business.

I miss home.

There, I've said it. I've been in London for fewer than twelve hours, and I already wish I was back in Weymouth, listening to the crashing of waves. I feel like I can't breathe in all this smog and vape smoke. In my opinion, the only thing London has going for it is the anonymity; anyone can get lost in a city of millions. People pass by the window totally oblivious to the fact that I am watching them, and probably not caring about it anyway. I'm convinced that if I were out on the pavement and suddenly dropped dead, it would be minutes, rather than seconds before anyone stopped to check on me.

What makes it worse is knowing that while I'm here and digging into the Hilliards' history, there's nobody out there searching for my sister. I am her last hope of getting home and this distraction isn't helping anyone, least of all her.

I tell Jack where to stop and he finds a space several doors down from Rachel's flat. I'm reaching for the handle when his fingers brush my trailing hand.

'I'm sorry if I made you feel awkward. Here I was, assuming that a bestselling author would realise how brilliant she is, but I never meant to make you feel uncomfortable. I'm not saying this because I'm trying to make you feel better, but *Monsters Under the Bed* really is a great story and you should be very proud of it.' He pauses and I can feel his stare burning into the side of my head as I fixate on the glove box. 'Anyway, I won't mention it again. Okay? And hey, if you change your mind about dinner, I know a great Mexican restaurant in Ealing. Do you like spicy food?'

Reaching for my satchel, I open the door and bail out. 'Sorry, but I must dash. Thanks for everything today. What time should I meet you at the police station on Monday?'

'I'll be there from eight, so any time after that is fine.'

Slamming the door, I hurry up the stairs, only now realising that Rachel didn't give me a spare key. Pressing the buzzer beside her name, I'm willing Jack to drive away... but he remains where he is. What is he waiting for? I'm back now; it's not like I'm going to get attacked by some pervert on the prowl. When Rachel finally opens the door, I push inside, grateful to finally be indoors.

'Good, you're back,' she says, grabbing my hand and dragging me in through the flat. 'So I did some digging like you asked and I heard a very interesting story about your Lord Fitzhume. Grab yourself a glass of wine and I'll tell you all about it.'

Chapter Twenty-Four

NOW

Ealing, London

Two sips of the sauvignon blanc and my head is already feeling woozy. Rachel is dressed in tight jogging pants, the T-shirt I found her in this morning, and a cotton hoodie zipped to the middle. She's straightened her dark brown hair and is glued to her laptop screen. How can she look so relaxed and yet so beautiful? It would take me an hour's worth of preening to get anywhere near that level and even then I'd still miss the mark. Clearly London life suits her.

'So, I did some digging,' she says, chewing one of the arms of her glasses as I take a seat on the sofa beside her. 'Turns out, you were right! There was a bit of a hoo-ha involving your friend, Lord Fitzhume, last year.'

'He isn't my friend,' I correct.

'Okay, well, whatever he is, I spoke to the chief political correspondent at my paper but he was next to useless. He said he was too busy and that there weren't any scandals featuring his friend Fitzhume.'

I frown at where her trail of thought has gone. 'Would a political journalist really hear about something so salacious? I would have thought you'd be better off speaking with whoever covers crime, or civil matters.'

She's smiling at me, an expression that says I've jumped in with both feet without understanding where I'm going to land. 'He gave me the answer I expected him to give. I knew he and Fitzhume were old university buddies and I just wanted to test the water. I wanted to see whether he'd pass a message on to his old friend. Sure enough, the very next call from his desk was to a private number, a landline, but one that's off-directory. Judging by the dialling code, however, I'd say it's not a million miles away from his neck of the woods.'

She raises her eyebrows like she's solved some great mystery, but so far she's not told me anything I couldn't have figured out for myself. I'm about to tell her as much when she puts her glasses back on and turns the laptop so I can see the screen better.

'Anyway, I reached out to a friend at one of the tabloids, someone I know would be chomping at the bit for a story like this. I won't tell you which paper she works for, but if I said most of their front-page exclusives involve celebrities falling off the wagon or shagging other celebrities, I'm sure you can hazard a guess. And before you tell me off for discussing your client with a tabloid hack, don't worry, I had a good cover story. I told her I'd been asked to do some background research on Fitzhume as he nears his seventy-fifth birthday as part of some schmaltzy weekend magazine feature, and just wanted to ask if she'd ever come across anything not on Wikipedia.'

Rachel points at the screen which is open on a bold headline declaring:

ROYAL ABDUCTION!

'Tessa sent me this,' Rachel explains. 'They were all set to go to press with the copy, a front-page exclusive, until a legal injunction was applied and they were ordered *not* to print the story. She said she'd held on to the image for posterity and it still rankles that the story never made it out.'

The columns of text beneath the headline are too blurry to read without zooming in but I recognise the picture of the upturned Range Rover as one from the file Jack and I reviewed earlier.

'How did she find out?' I ask naively.

'Tessa didn't want to reveal her source but she gave me enough hints that he was part of the scene-of-crime team, or whatever they call themselves. He supplied the photograph and details about where the accident had occurred and the immediate aftermath. What's most interesting is that the story was set to break on the Monday after the abduction, which means the story was written on the Sunday. How on earth he managed to get it quashed on a Sunday evening is anyone's guess.'

'You said this was an exclusive? So nobody else had wind of the story?'

Rachel removes her glasses and swaps them for her nearly empty wine glass. 'That I can't tell you without reaching out to other hacks. I didn't want to disturb the hornets' nest too much so I stopped with just her. I trust her enough to know she won't go mentioning our conversation to anyone else. God knows I've thrown plenty of bones her way in the past and I know she's looking to progress her career away from the red tops.'

'So she knew about the abduction, but was she able to tell you anything more about what happened after Cassie was taken?'

'Afraid not. She said that after the court injunction came through, she was told in no uncertain terms not to go anywhere near the family or the story.'

It's my turn to look surprised. 'And you're telling me that didn't make her even more eager to get to the bottom of it?'

Rachel laughs and a small wrinkle appears just below her left eye, but disappears almost immediately. 'That was my first thought too. Any journalist worth their salt would be staking out the country manor and watching the police coming and going to get any angle on the story. But it wasn't her editor who warned her off it. My friend Tessa didn't say so in as many words, but I got the impression that the warning was delivered by someone far more serious.'

Either I'm missing an obvious reference or Rachel isn't being clear enough, but I have no idea what she's suggesting.

'Security Services,' she clarifies, draining the rest of her glass.

I almost laugh out loud. 'You're saying James Bond warned her off?'

She shrugs. 'More likely MI5 than MI6, but essentially that's what Tessa suggested. Clearly your friend Fitzhume has friends in very high places. To get a High Court judge out of bed on a Sunday evening to pronounce the injunction, and then to have some kind of spy or civil servant deliver a personal warning to the journalist threatening to spill the beans takes some kind of power. What is it you said Fitzhume did in his younger days?'

'I didn't; *he* didn't.' I close my eyes, trying to recall what he said when we met in the lobby of Maddie's offices. 'He said he hadn't been as involved in his daughter's life as much as he would have liked because he was busy "chasing after one foreign adventure or another". You don't think…?'

The question is too ridiculous to finish. Fitzhume is a peer of the realm and a distant cousin of the royal family, not some covert operative from the 70s.

Rachel is raising her eyebrows so she clearly thinks that there could be more to his past than I'm giving him credit for. 'I'm not saying he was Secret Service, but he clearly has friends in high places. Makes you kind of curious, doesn't it?'

I don't like the suggestive look she's making and I take a long sip of my own drink.

'I want to help you write the story,' she says, a moment later. 'Think about it: your first story in a mainstream newspaper, aided by my experience and contacts. I'm sure if we spoke to my editor, he'd—'

'Absolutely not,' I say in no uncertain terms. 'Fitzhume didn't request my help to write a story about what happened. Whilst I know my publisher and agent think there's a book somewhere in all of this mess, something tells me that Fitzhume is going to be less willing to agree to it if I can't uncover something new about what happened.'

'What makes you think you won't?' she says eagerly, not yet prepared to drop the subject.

'Because his granddaughter died at the ransom exchange. That's the official verdict. I don't understand why he thinks differently as presumably they found her DNA or remains in order to close the case, so I think he's just an old man clinging to a dream. So far, from what I've read in the file, everything was done above board by the police. There's no story here other than a family's loss and a grandfather's heartbreak.'

Rachel picks up both our glasses and carries them to the small kitchen countertop before topping them up with a bottle from the fridge. She doesn't utter a word as she carries them back and reclaims her place beside me.

'I understand your reluctance,' she says, 'and it's okay, I didn't expect you to say yes when I asked. That's okay too. It's still early days but I believe there is a story here, and with careful persuasion Fitzhume will agree to us publishing it. You said yourself he doesn't look well and I'd say that's why he's reached out to you now: he *wants* the story told. All I'm asking is that you keep me in mind, as and when you decide to put pen to paper. I have contacts here in London that would otherwise be unavailable to you. It's good to have a friend on the inside sometimes.'

She passes my glass back to me and then clinks hers against mine. That's the great thing about our friendship: there's never any animosity. Even when we were at university together and we'd meet some guy we both fancied – who would inevitably end up with Rachel – any tension quickly evaporated; most of the time the guy in question would turn out to be a dick and we'd both realise I'd had a lucky escape.

'We should go out,' she says suddenly. 'Tonight. As in out-out. Daniella has had to fly to Paris for some last-minute photoshoot, so I'm at a loose end. Ealing doesn't have much to offer by way of clubs but we could catch a tube to Hammersmith. What do you think?'

I can't think of anything I'd rather do less than go clubbing in London. I know that, as a twenty-seven-year-old, society expects me to be making the most of my youth and freedom and burning the candle at both ends, but I've never been much for getting drunk and dancing recklessly. Besides, I need to check the missing people site for any new messages about Anna.

'Come on,' she says, standing and tugging me to my feet. 'We'll go through my wardrobe and find you something sparkly to wear. You never know, you might get lucky.'

I wrench my hand free. 'I don't need a boyfriend to be happy. I'm quite content being single.'

'Who said anything about a boyfriend? I just want you to get laid. How long's it been?'

My cheeks burn. 'It doesn't matter. Please, Rachel, let's just stay in. We could get a takeaway, see what's on Netflix—'

She has my hand again and is dragging me into her bedroom, plonking me on the bed, and opening her wardrobe. 'Let's see…' Hangers scrape against the rail as she peruses her outfits. 'You're a size twelve, right? I'm sure I must have something in here, which… oh, yes, *this* one.'

I don't want to look up, but I force my eyes towards the khaki-coloured knee-length dress.

She looks so pleased with herself. 'I reckon with sheer tights and a pair of matching heels… yes, this is the one! I'll straighten your hair, paint your nails, and even fix your makeup too if you like?'

She thinks she's helping, trying to distract me from my obvious need to focus on Anna, and I don't want to upset her. 'I'm not as sad a case as you think, you know,' I say with another sip of wine, hoping to curb my inhibitions. 'I was in fact asked out tonight by the police constable who's helping me with the case file.'

She raises her eyebrows. 'Is he hot?'

I was expecting her to assume I was making up Jack's offer of dinner, and her question throws me. 'Um, well, I mean I suppose he's cute in a nerdy sort of a way. I don't know really; I hadn't looked at him like that.'

Rachel is grinning. 'You're blushing! Ooh, you fancy him.' She bursts out laughing at her babyish voice, before collapsing on the bed beside me, almost spilling my wine. 'Seriously though, he must fancy you if he asked you out.'

'I don't think it was like that,' I say, with another sip of wine. 'I think he was just trying to be friendly, thinking I'd be on my own. I'm sure that's all it was.'

She playfully slaps my arm. 'I was just teasing. Come on, let's get you ready, and then I'm going to show you the side of London you've been missing. Trust me, by the end of the night you'll see why you should move here and leave sandy old Weymouth behind once and for all.'

I don't argue as she pulls me off the bed and in the direction of the bathroom, even though I know Weymouth is more to me than just home.

Chapter Twenty-Five

THEN

Chalfont St Giles, Buckinghamshire

The usually unassuming DCS Rawani wore an intense look that didn't sit comfortably on his face. 'What else did they say?'

Richard had been on the treadmill when his mobile had started ringing and he'd almost ignored it, until he'd looked at the display and seen the call originated in Cairo. He'd been awaiting a call from a collector in possession of a rare amulet, an item Richard had long been seeking for a particularly rich and well-connected client.

'They told me to check my email and await further instructions,' Richard now recited to the detective.

'Describe the voice to me.'

Richard had barely registered what the voice had said, let alone how it had sounded. In fact, it was only when he'd received the email with a photograph of Cassie that he'd connected the dots.

'I don't know,' he told the detective. 'He sounded… rough.'

'Rough how? English?'

'Yes, English. Southern rather than northern. Put it this way, when I hear the voice in my memory now, I'm picturing a builder with big tattooed arms and a sneer. The sort of person you wouldn't want to meet in a dark alley.'

'Low-pitched voice?'

'Yes, definitely deep, with poor annunciation. As I said: rough.'

'Did you recognise the voice? Have you heard it anywhere before?'

Richard shook his head. 'We don't move in the kind of circles that bring us in touch with criminal lowlifes. I've never heard that voice before.'

'Okay, Mr Hilliard, thank you. The team and I will set it up so that we can record the conversation when they next make contact.'

Elizabeth listened eagerly, hugging Richard's arm tightly as he sat pressed into the side of the chaise longue. To her, he was the closest link to her daughter and she would cling for as long as possible to the prospect that Richard was the key to getting her back. She'd raced from the hospital, apologising to Hobbs, and with Gerry Connors breaking every speed limit to get her home. The detective and a small team of men dressed in Kevlar vests had just arrived at the property, and then proceeded to place surveillance equipment into every corner of the drawing room. No matter how much it irked, every word in this room would now be recorded for posterity.

Gerry had made himself scarce when the police had said only necessary parties should remain in the room. Undoubtedly, he would be skulking in the kitchen with Rosa. Elizabeth hoped he would remain discreet when he left their home tonight, but she sensed his wife would revel in any kind of gossip and would probably interrogate him before he'd even killed the engine.

'How could they have got her to Egypt?' Elizabeth asked now, as the problem played on her mind. 'We have her passport and you said you'd put an alert on all ports and airports. How could she have slipped through the net?'

The detective's expression softened as he fixed her with a sincere look. 'I would be very surprised if Cassie was in Africa, Mrs Hilliard. It's more likely that they used a contact in Egypt to place the call, or that the call was made from here in the UK and bounced off multiple satellites to hide its origin. We're looking into that now but it will take time to trace back. As will the origin of the email. Unfortunately, as our technology advances, so does theirs. Now, you have confirmed that Cassie is still dressed in the same outfit she was wearing when you last saw her?'

The image of Cassie slipping through the window and out of her grasp filled her mind. 'Yes, in the photograph she's still wearing the Ariel costume but her red wig is missing.'

The detective looked at the tablet screen where the saved image of Cassie stared up at him. It was unmistakeably her, though the tears and fear in her eyes didn't fill him with any comfort about her safety.

'When they phone back, you need to ask for proof of life,' DCS Rawani said. 'Tell them you won't even consider paying any ransom until you've heard her voice.'

Elizabeth's spine straightened. 'But we have the photograph. That's definitely Cassie, which means she must be alive. Why else would they have they gagged her with that cloth?'

Rawani's eyes remained on the screen a moment longer, choosing his words carefully. 'We don't know when this picture was taken, Mrs Hilliard. I hope beyond all hope that it was today, but for all we know they could have snapped it the day they took her. From the look of the dark metallic surface in the background, I'd argue the picture was taken in a van of some sort, very possibly the van they dumped and which is now in our possession. In order to be sure she's safe, we need to hear her speak.'

He hadn't said it but she could read between the lines. 'You think she's already dead?'

'No, Mrs Hilliard and I have to assume she is alive until the very last minute. My aim is to bring her back safely to the two of you by any means necessary. Ordinarily, I would warn you against paying money to these men, however you have both told me independently that you're prepared to pay any amount to see her again and as that is your decision, I am here to facilitate that transaction.'

It sounded so methodical, as if Cassie was nothing more than a commodity, or one of Richard's precious antiques.

'We will continue to search for these men,' Rawani continued, 'regardless of any deal that you strike with them. They won't be allowed to get away with it. This ransom demand suggests that Cassie was probably the target all along. The last thing you want is to pay them and then they try the same thing again. Or maybe they target a different family and child next time.'

Elizabeth's eyes bulged under the strain of tears. 'I know

she's still alive. I don't care how much it costs me; even if I have to sell my soul to the devil himself, I'll do it.'

Richard's arm appeared around her shoulder and she felt his warm lips press against the top of her head. 'We both would. Just tell me what I have to say to get her back and I'll do it, detective.'

Rawani locked the tablet and rested it on the small table beside him. 'The good news is that they haven't said not to involve the police. That's a good sign and means that they're probably expecting to have us listening in. I believe that's why they sent the email, so that we could be in place for when they make their financial demand. As I've said before, this gang strikes me as the professional sort and that also plays to our advantage. For now, we will allow them to think that they are the ones in control.'

A woman in Kevlar appeared beside him. 'We're good to go, sir. As soon as the phone is answered, the trace will begin.'

'Good,' he replied, before looking back at Richard. 'When they call, just pretend like we're not here. If they ask if we are, answer honestly. We don't want them to think you're deceitful and the chances are they've probably been watching us unloading our gear. Stay calm and don't let your anger or frustration come out. Think of this group as a means to an end. Do you think you can do that?'

Richard nodded.

'Good. Think of it as any other business deal. They have a particular product that you're keen to acquire and they will name their price. This isn't a time for negotiation. Ask them for proof of life, and once they've provided it, agree to pay what you're comfortable with and then ask how they want the exchange to occur. Some kind of electronic transfer, I would hope, because then we can trace it back.' He paused and checked his watch before offering an empathetic smile. 'I'll give you two a moment but expect the phone to ring any min—'

He didn't get to finish speaking as the sound of the phone ringing cut through. Tense anticipation dropped over the room like a shroud. The woman in the Kevlar vest carried the phone to Richard and gave him a thumbs up.

Richard's entire body trembled beside his wife as he pressed the phone against his ear. 'H-h-hello?'

Elizabeth strained to hear any response but it was impossible with the phone against the other side of Richard's head. The detective and his small team were standing, heads bowed and headphones on, and in that moment, Elizabeth felt totally isolated – the only person unable to hear what was being said.

'Pr-pr-proof of life,' she heard Richard stammer, and the detective nodded approvingly, but Richard's fear turned to alarm instantly as he lowered the phone.

'They hung up,' he shouted at Rawani. 'You told me to ask for proof of life and their response was to hang up.'

The detective's face was ashen. 'They'll phone back,' he said, but couldn't even convince himself.

'And what if they don't?' Richard grizzled. 'What if that was our only chance?'

Elizabeth couldn't breathe. She hadn't felt any kind of control since Saturday afternoon, but now it was like her life was playing out in front of her, directed by puppet strings, and she with no way to wrestle it back.

Did hanging up the phone mean the detective's worst fears had been confirmed? She didn't dare ask the question aloud, terrified that hearing the words in her own voice would somehow make them prophetic: had they already killed Cassie?

Everyone jumped as the phone's ringtone cut through the silence once more. This time, Elizabeth didn't wait to be invited. Snatching the phone from Richard's hand, she answered the call and switched on the speaker.

'Daddy?' Cassie's terrified voice echoed and Elizabeth's legs gave way, the phone tumbling from her hand.

'Cassie? It's Mummy, darling. Tell me you're okay…'

'Mummy?' she said. 'I'm scared, and—' But the phone was yanked away from Cassie and her screams could be heard fading into the distance as the caller moved further away from her.

'You have proof of life. She is alive… for now. You will pay us a sum of two million pounds, in used bank notes. This will be delivered in four transparent sacks to an address we will give you tomorrow. When we phone at precisely 7pm you will have one hour to get to the address and leave the money. If you do not abide by our rules, you will never hear from Cassie again. We do not want to kill her but we will not hesitate and you will never find her body if you try any tricks. We are aware that the police are listening but their attempts to trace the calls and our email will fail.'

'Please, I want to speak to Cassie again,' Elizabeth tried.

'No,' the voice replied without emotion. 'You have your proof. Get the money ready for tomorrow. We will phone at seven.'

The line was disconnected and Elizabeth crumpled her face into the carpet and sobbed.

'Did we get the trace?' she heard the detective mutter to the woman in Kevlar.

'Not long enough. Somewhere in Afghanistan this time. They clearly know how to evade our communications tracker. Not surprising if they're military-trained.'

'Everyone out now,' Richard roared, standing and dragging the door open.

'Mr Hilliard, we need to—'

But Richard wasn't listening, just pointing at the door. The detective and his three colleagues obeyed and Richard closed the door behind him, helping Elizabeth back to her feet and holding her in his strong arms. 'I swear to you we'll get her back.'

She allowed herself to fold into his core and be held but his next sentence sent a chill through her entire body.

'I know how to get her back... and keep the money too.'

Chapter Twenty-Six

NOW

Kensington, London

The sunglasses I've borrowed from Rachel are doing nothing to stop the growing ache behind my eyes. It isn't even that sunny as I emerge from South Kensington tube station at 8am on Sunday morning. God knows what time we got home this morning, and I don't even want to think about the amount of cocktails Rachel bought for me as we traipsed from one bar to another, so she could introduce me to her new friends. They all seemed charming enough, from what I can remember, but if I were asked to pick any of them out of a line-up, I don't think I'd be able to.

My stomach rolls again as the sound of a departing tube echoes up through the pavement and I can feel every tremor throughout my body. I shouldn't have come. It would have been far better just to phone Fitzhume, tell him I'm sick, and ask him to reschedule. It's not as though he gave me a lot of notice about meeting his son-in-law, Cassie's father, Richard.

An answerphone message left shortly before nine last night, which I then didn't hear until an hour later, by which point it was too late to phone back and cancel.

I suppose it had been sheer luck that Rachel had still been sober enough to set an alarm on my phone and send me a message with the address of where I am to meet Fitzhume. I was tempted to drag her along with me this morning but I have a vague recollection of her being sick in the bathroom in the early hours so she'll undoubtedly be in an even worse condition than I am. Besides, I haven't mentioned her involvement to Fitzhume yet and I kind of feel I should ask his permission before outsourcing any work Rachel's way. So far she's only given me a bit of background on why the story of Cassie's violent abduction didn't make the front page, but something tells me I'm going to need her support again at some point.

I'm not a regular consumer of alcohol. I'm not tee-total, and don't mind the occasional glass of wine, but most nights I can take it or leave it. By the time we arrived at the second bar last night, all my inhibitions had been shed, and whilst I had sensed I would regret going along with Rachel's suggested combinations, it hadn't stopped me. What I wouldn't give to go back to last night and tell myself to slow down. I bought a croissant at the bakery at Ealing Broadway station before boarding the tube, but it's done little to settle my stomach. The last thing I want is more food, but ultimately it might be the best thing for me, so I buy a bottle of water and a banana from the only shop that doesn't have its shutters drawn in South Kensington.

I don't know this part of West London all that well and

despite the fact that it's even closer to the hub of the metropolis, it looks and smells cleaner, though I'm sure it can't actually be. There's no chewing gum ground into the pavement, no litter strewn in the gutters. Behind these dark-rimmed glasses, it almost feels like I've stepped out into a different city. The cars that line the street look expensive and they shimmer in the early morning light. I recognise the badges of Ferrari, Aston Martin, and McLaren, and know they aren't the kinds of cars you buy unless you want people to know you have money. As I continue to follow the directions on my phone, I find myself in a road full of tall, thin townhouses, all protected by freshly painted metal railings. Each must be at least three storeys high, though looking through the railings, I can see they all have basement rooms beneath the level of the road too. It must be odd having every room on a different floor, and I could imagine each property would be a bugger to keep clean. I struggle enough dragging the vacuum cleaner around one floor, let alone two or three flights of stairs. But then, thinking about it, if I could afford one of these properties, I could probably afford to employ someone to keep it clean, much as Fitzhume has with his housekeeper Rosa.

My destination is up on the left, apparently, and as I near number 43, I immediately spot the long Bentley parked a few doors up, from which an elderly-looking chauffeur now opens the door and helps Fitzhume emerge.

'Thank you, Hobbs. That will be all for now. Please wait in the car.'

The suited chauffeur taps a finger against his flat cap in a kind of salute before moving out of the way and returning to the driver's seat. Fitzhume is dressed in a three-piece suit with a large camel-coloured coat draped over his shoulders and the trusty cane between his fingers.

'Good morning, Miss Hunter. I trust you found the apartment without too much difficulty?'

'Just about. Sorry I'm a few minutes late; I'm still trying to get used to the tube and got off at the wrong stop to begin with.'

He wanted me to meet him at eight o'clock precisely, and I feel obliged to offer the apology, even though it's only four minutes after eight.

'That's quite all right, Miss Hunter. I'm pretty sure my son-in-law will have totally forgotten we're coming anyway. Still, we should get inside and out of this cold.'

I'm in a long-sleeved T-shirt and thin jeans and I'm sweating profusely (though some of that could be the alcohol working its way out of my system). He looks dressed for winter, so I don't understand why he would think it's so cold, but I don't challenge it. I'm keen to get this meeting over and done with so I can get back to Rachel's and sleep off the rest of this hangover.

Having finished the banana, I'm not sure where to dispose of the skin. There are no dustbins along the street and I don't remember passing any since emerging from the station, so in the end I drop it into my small satchel, making a mental note to throw it away at the earliest opportunity.

There are six steps leading up to the large black door and I want to offer Fitzhume some support as he struggles to mount them but he bats my hand away, relying solely on the cane. When he reaches the top, he ignores the doorbell and knocker, and thumps the end of the cane against the door three times.

'Before we go in,' he says, leaning closer so he can keep his voice low, 'I should warn you not to place too much reliance upon Richard's version of events. The truth is, we've never really seen eye-to-eye, and he – how can I put it? – he isn't one who readily accepts responsibility for his own misdemeanours.'

It's an odd comment for him to pass but my head is too foggy to digest why that might be. The door is thrust open a moment later and at first I assume that Richard has a girlfriend staying who he's sent to invite his guests in, but then I realise the elegant figure dressed in the red and yellow flowery kimono, eyes smudged with last night's eyeliner, is actually the man we're here to see.

'Come in,' he says, with a roll of those chestnut eyes and a flourish of his arm.

Fitzhume leads the way through to the kitchen that dominates this floor of the townhouse. As I enter, I see Richard with his back to us over by a coffee percolator that puffs away like a steam engine. A hardened glass ashtray on the breakfast island in the middle of the room is overflowing with hand-rolled cigarette butts and cigarillos. A cloud of fog hangs just beneath the thick brown beams that criss-cross the ceiling, and unless I'm very much mistaken, tobacco isn't the only thing that's been smoked in here in the last twenty-four hours.

'How are you, Richard?' Fitzhume asks, but there's no trace of concern in his tone.

Richard grunts a response. 'You want coffee?'

'Please,' I say, keen to show I don't carry the same level of hostility.

'No coffee for me, thank you,' Fitzhume says, as the cane wobbles beneath the pressure he's placing on it. The man looks like he needs to sit down but I sense he won't say so in order not to show any sign of weakness. I don't think he needed to give me that pep talk on the doorstep; it's clear these men do not get on.

Richard fills two cups and carries them across to the breakfast island. 'Cream and sugar?' The pungent smell of whisky on his breath wafts across the counter.

'Black is fine, thank you,' I say, taking the cup and sipping from the edge, burning the tip of my tongue in the process but forcing myself not to grimace.

I don't know what I expected of Richard Hilliard, certainly not someone who looks more hungover and ill than I do. The eyeliner and the fluorescent kimono were also not what I had imagined when Fitzhume first described him and then I recall what Penny told us about Richard making a pass at Gerry. Maybe the last twelve months have been Richard's way of embracing his true self.

'Should we go up to the sitting room?' Richard asks.

'Perhaps we could just stay here,' I reply, nodding at the stools that line the breakfast island, and conscious that I don't want Fitzhume to have to ascend more stairs.

Richard doesn't wait for the older man's confirmation, quickly scraping one of the stools against the hardened wooden floor. 'What do you want to talk to me about?'

Do I assume Fitzhume has told him what he has asked me to do? I feel off kilter, uncertain of whether I should offer some kind of introduction or just bowl out with my first question. Fitzhume is making no effort to speak but I think it's taking every ounce of his strength to remain upright.

'Would you like me to help you onto a stool?' I ask Fitzhume, in an effort to be friendly.

'I'm perfectly capable,' he snaps back, still glaring at his disinterested son-in-law, 'but I prefer to stand.'

I lift the stool closest to me, surprised by its weight, and then shuffle my bottom onto it. Fitzhume remains upright at my side, his shadow casting gloom over the other two of us. Extracting the phone from my pocket, I switch on the voice recorder and stand it on the counter between Richard and me.

'I'd like to hear your version of the events surrounding Cassie's abduction,' I say, as calmly and as matter-of-factly as my hangover will allow.

His hand reaches into the wide pocket of the kimono and withdraws a packet of cigarillos. He extracts one and puts it between his lips before striking a match and lighting the tip. The sulphur dioxide produced from the match plays distractingly on my nose as Richard inhales deeply.

'You want to know why my daughter was murdered?' Richard says, looking me straight in the eye. 'There's only one person to blame… and that's the stingy miser standing beside you.'

Chapter Twenty-Seven

NOW

Kensington, London

I'm expecting to hear the thump of Fitzhume's cane on the hardened floor and his outrage as he defends himself, but he doesn't speak.

'What has he told you so far?' Richard sneers, making no attempt to hold back his contempt. 'Did he blame the police for not getting her back? That's usually his opening gambit. Or did he tell you it was all my fault? The truth is, had he not done everything to keep the story under wraps, we would have had a better chance of catching the men who took her.'

'Hold on,' I say, trying to recall what Rachel told me yesterday afternoon, 'I thought the police *did* capture the men responsible. I heard that one died at the scene and the other is locked up now.'

'Too little too late,' Richard growls, squashing the barely smoked cigarillo into the glass ashtray, sending the other butts scattering across the table.

Sliding off the stool, he tightens the kimono and storms out of the room without another word, and it's only when I hear his footfalls on the staircase that I realise he's not coming back. I look up at Fitzhume who hasn't adjusted his stance since we came into the room.

'I'm sorry about that little outburst,' he says, shrugging. 'Richard always was hot-headed. I used to wonder if that was what first attracted Elizabeth to him; she always did like to take risks, always pushing the envelope to see what she could get away with.'

'Do you think he's coming back?'

Fitzhume fumbles for his handkerchief and he wipes the thick veil of sweat from his hairline. 'I honestly don't know. Perhaps it was a mistake my coming here with you. Why don't you go up after him and I'll wait for you down here? Perhaps he'll be more forthcoming without me there.'

I don't want to leave Fitzhume on his own as he looks as though he might keel over at any minute; he's clearly trying to mask whatever pain he's in so that I won't fuss over him. I lower myself from the stool and press my fingers into the sleeve of his coat. 'If you need anything, just shout. Okay?'

'You could fetch me a small glass of water before you go,' he says, the strain starting to show on his face.

Nodding, I go from cupboard to cupboard searching for a glass. I eventually find a tumbler which I fill from the tap. By the time I turn back around, Fitzhume has managed to sit on the stool I vacated and he looks more at peace. Placing the glass on the counter top, I leave him where he is and head back through the hallway which is bathed in fresh sunlight from the semi-circle window above the thick oak door. There are framed reproductions of well-known masterpieces along the walls here and all up the stairs. They're pictures I've seen hundreds of times before but I couldn't tell you any of the names.

The steep staircase has a central line of speckled carpet, held in place by brass buffers on each step. Treading lightly, I ascend, all thoughts of my hangover gone. How did I end up in the middle of this family drama? If my publisher could see how broken they all are, I'm not sure they'd be so keen for me to continue to dig.

There is a marked drop in the temperature as I reach the top step where I find two rooms. The one on the right is a large bathroom with a tub in one corner and a shower cubicle in the other, a toilet bowl, basin and bidet, and it's painted in an abhorrent lime-green shade. My stomach rolls with the colour and I force myself to look away. Inside the second room I can see net curtains blowing wildly, almost ghost-like as they catch on the breeze of the large open windows. Moving closer, I see there is a navy-blue futon against one wall and a leather corner sofa opposite the window, on which Richard is sitting hunched over. He straightens as I enter the room and now I see the traces of white powder on the surface of the glass coffee table that dominates the centre of the room.

He sniffs, wiping the tip of his nose, before lighting a fresh cigarillo and lounging back on the sofa. There is no shame in his eyes and he doesn't seem at all bothered that I have just caught him snorting what I presume is cocaine.

'Take a seat,' he says, his voice already sounding much more alert, and he waves his arm theatrically towards the opposite side of the sofa.

I oblige, placing my phone on the table top. 'Mr Hilliard, your father-in-law has asked me to look into your daughter's disappearance in an effort to understand what truly happened.

I have exclusive access to the police files and I've already interviewed the Connors family about the events leading up to the abduction. I wonder if you could tell me what you remember in the hours and days after she was taken?'

He smirked at the mention of the Connors but I don't want to press him on whether Penny's accusation is true or not – as I already sense it might be. It isn't relevant to their story.

He offers me the packet of cigarillos but I decline. 'The police detective – Detective Chief Superintendent Rawani – seemed obsessed with the possibility that Cassie had been taken because of the nature of the business I ran, but I never could understand why that was the only angle he was so focused on. Yes, I was running a high-net-value business, but most of my client base was made up of people with more money than sense, people like my esteemed father-in-law, not the kind of people who would ever dream about abducting a little girl.'

'So who do you think was behind it then?' I ask openly.

He sucks deeply on the cigarillo. 'All I know is that whoever it was, they stole the best part of me. Cassie wasn't the only one who died that night; something in me left along with her spirit. Well, it did for all of us. Elizabeth wasn't the same after it happened. She withdrew into herself, barely surfacing in the days that followed and when she did, she was so tired and raw from crying that all she wanted was medication to send her back under. That's why *he* had her committed to that hospital, but she isn't getting any better. It's the second time he's put her in there and she'll get cleaned up as she did last time but as soon as she's back in the real world, she'll sink back into herself. Despair isn't something you can cure with pills and counselling.'

Boy, don't I know it, I don't say, as the memory of Anna leaving the front yard fills my mind.

'Where is your wife, Mr Hilliard?'

'The... oh, what's it called...? The Priory, in Hampshire somewhere. She's been there for the last two months. He won't let me see her, of course, but then I'm not sure she wants to see me either. Are you married?'

I shake my head.

'Then you won't understand the impact the loss of a child has on a marriage. Even the strongest of couples can't usually survive. It tears through the binds you've joined together and it's only those who learn how to retie those binds who survive.'

He squashes out the cigarillo, before pulling out a small transparent bag of white powder and shaking it like icing sugar. Instinctively, I turn my face away, as if somehow not seeing him spilling the powder onto the table top and ordering it into a line with the dusty credit card will mean it isn't happening.

'You want some?' he asks, holding out the rolled twenty-pound note. 'It's good shit, not that crap they flog at clubs which is cut with fucking fertiliser and bleach. I get it from a guy in Chelsea and it's as close to pure as money can buy. I should know.'

I keep an eye on the door to the room, waiting for the moment the police are going to storm in and wrongly assume that I'm somehow complicit in this narcotic usage... but there is no sound beyond the distant hum of traffic along the main road.

'No, thank you,' I finally say, shuffling uncomfortably. I

look for anywhere I can fix my gaze while he sniffs up the mess.

Rubbing the end of his nose again, he leans his head back against the sofa cushion, allowing his eyes to close.

A thought stirs somewhere in my own cloudy mind. 'You said earlier that the detective was solely focused on the business you *ran*; does that mean you're no longer working in that line?'

His eyes remain closed but I can see his chest shaking with internal laughter. 'Didn't have any other choice, did I? That oaf downstairs forced me out.'

I don't know whether it's the drugs that are loosening his tongue or whether this is what Fitzhume warned me about on the doorstep.

'In what way?' I ask.

The eyes remain closed, his head sunk into the cushion. 'Well, when those bastards made their play, when they demanded two million pounds in exchange for the safe return of our Cassie, I turned to him for help. He reluctantly agreed to loan me the money, but on the condition that I use the company as collateral. He had his namby-pamby solicitor draw up the paperwork so it was all official. Can you believe that? His own granddaughter is missing and he had to consult a fucking lawyer! It beggars belief!'

His eyes snap open and his head lolls as he tries to focus on anything in the room. I've no idea how much product he's put up his nose this morning but I'm tempted to phone for an ambulance when he double-takes and eyes me suspiciously.

'When the money went up in smoke,' he continues, the venom dripping from every word, 'he came collecting. But the business was already in trouble – some of my debtors hadn't paid what they owed – and so he had the business liquidated to claim back his money. I went from running a luxury-goods company to being unemployed in the space of three days. Not that I cared at the time because I was too swallowed up with grief, but it was the final nail in the coffin for the two of us. I made my move from that creaking manor not long after and took up residence here. And now I spend every day trying to forget the fact that someone somewhere stole everything from me.'

Everything seems so exaggerated with Richard Hilliard but as he buries his head in his hands and his shoulders sag, I can hear he is crying, and I know it isn't forced. I've heard that level of vapid sobbing before – from my own father when Anna never came home.

Stopping the recording, I thank Richard for seeing me and make a swift exit to find Fitzhume waiting for me at the bottom of the stairs. I'm about to explain what his son-in-law has said but he raises his hand to cut me off.

'We'll talk in the car,' he says. 'I've managed to arrange a meeting for us with my daughter Elizabeth. Hobbs will drive us, and then return you to your home. Is that okay with you?'

The sofa bed in Rachel's living room is calling to me but when I see his desperation staring back at me, I don't argue. Opening the front door, I'm about to offer Fitzhume my hand when I hear my name being called by someone on the street. Turning, I see an unfamiliar face: a man whose chin is lacquered with a five-o-clock shadow, the hairiest moustache I've ever seen above his lips, and his bald head covered with a baseball cap. He's holding out a mobile phone in one hand while grasping a small notepad in the other.

'Emma, Emma,' he calls again with a thick Australian

twang. 'Ken Johnson, *Eye in the Sky News*. What brings you to London? Is this your next case? Can you tell me what you're working on?'

I have no idea why there is a reporter here nor how he knew that I would be.

'Lord Fitzhume, is this anything to do with what happened to your granddaughter? Her name was Cassie wasn't it? Lord Fitzhume? Lord Fitzhume?'

I'm grateful when Hobbs appears and grabs hold of the reporter's arm, dragging him out of our way.

'Oi, that's assault,' the other man shouts at Hobbs, but despite his age, one step forwards by the chauffeur is enough to have the journalist take two steps back.

I help Fitzhume to the car and, once inside, Hobbs speeds us away as the journalist keeps his phone trained on the window beside me, still shouting out his questions and suppositions.

'Sorry about that,' I say, breathlessly. 'I seem to get recognised more and more these days.'

Fitzhume seethes silently. 'It isn't your fault my dear. In this town nothing stays a secret for long, and I am quite certain it wasn't you who tipped him off. There are always spies among us.'

Chapter Twenty-Eight

THEN

Chalfont St Giles, Buckinghamshire

Fitzhume started as the door to the drawing room opened suddenly. From his place in the tall armchair, he saw Richard's eyes appear in the gap of the frame.

'Do you mind if I join you?' Richard asked.

The last thing Fitzhume wanted was to make small talk with his son-in-law but, given the circumstances, and assuming Richard would be feeling equally lost in such a murky situation, he relented, offering a simple and efficient nod.

The door opened wider and Richard entered carrying two glass tumblers rattling with ice. 'Thought you could do with a top-up,' he said, indicating the empty glass on the small table beside Fitzhume.

The older man didn't reply, merely watching as Richard stalked across the ornamental rug, stopping as he reached the drinks trolley. The crystal lid of the decanter clunked as it was removed. Fitzhume closed his eyes at the cacophony; it didn't seem to matter how many times he'd instructed Richard on how to gently twist the stopper as it was removed to avoid that friction.

Handing over the caramel-coloured liquid, Richard tipped his own glass towards Fitzhume, before taking a seat on the chaise longue. 'Cheers,' he offered, taking a sip of the drink.

'To getting Cassie home,' Fitzhume countered, before placing the glass beside the empty one on the table. That was another difference between the men; Fitzhume knew to allow the single malt to acclimatise to the ice, rather than diving straight in. Some lessons just couldn't be taught.

'Rosa's gone home for the evening,' Richard said, to break the eerie silence. 'She said it's her daughter's birthday, and that you'd agreed for her to finish by seven.'

Fitzhume could vaguely remember receiving a letter from Rosa several weeks earlier requesting the absence; he'd meant to get hold of a birthday card and send Rosa on her way with a token of his appreciation, but time had escaped him. He would have to make it up to her tomorrow instead. Whilst she had been in his service for more than twenty years, she felt more like family than a housekeeper; she probably knew more about his life and history than any of the other people he shared his home with... but then, he'd deliberately kept Elizabeth protected from his past.

'Yes, that's fine,' Fitzhume responded absently. 'Where is Elizabeth?'

Richard rolled his eyes out of sight of Fitzhume. He'd come in to check on how his father-in-law was dealing with the stress of the situation and, as always, his primary concern was the health of his spoilt daughter. So many times, Richard had wanted to speak up, to tell him that she was a grown woman capable of making her own mistakes without the ever-watchful eye of her father. But it was best not to get on the wrong side of Fitzhume, particularly in light of the request playing on his mind now.

'I put her to bed with a Valium, which should help her rest. She's not coping with things.'

Were any of them, Fitzhume thought, though he didn't say it aloud. That said, he didn't like how quick Richard was to palm off Elizabeth with medication when a talk and comforting arm would probably work better.

Suddenly standing, Richard moved across to the main window and stared out through the open curtains at the darkness slowly enveloping the gravel driveway and surrounding woodland. He hated how isolated the estate was from the rest of the world. It seemed to serve as a way for Fitzhume to keep the manor locked in the past, like he was clinging to a time before the technology boom of the 80s. Hell, even the housekeeper was dressed in apparel more befitting the nineteenth century.

However, Richard's attention wasn't on the driveway. Instead, it was focused on Fitzhume's reflection, trying to read how easily the conversation would flow. The old man looked paler than usual, and even though he was sitting back in the armchair, his shoulders were hunched and his left knee was twitching against that infernal cane that never left his side. If there was any other way, Richard wouldn't be psyching himself up, but two million pounds was not something he could easily lay his hands on, especially before the morning. He had no choice but to ask.

'I'm glad I've caught you on your own,' Richard began

with another sip of the whisky, grimacing at the burn in his throat. He'd rehearsed the speech several times in the bathroom mirror upstairs and had tried to think of every challenge Fitzhume would throw at him, but still he felt the hairs standing up on the back of his neck as he spoke. 'There was something I was meaning to ask.'

Richard paused, studying the reflection; the old man remained static, save for the jiggling knee.

'As you know,' Richard continued, 'the way my company works, a lot of our profit is reinvested in larger pieces, awaiting review by potential clients, and payment. Whilst two million pounds is barely a drop in the ocean against the annual turnover, releasing such a sum in this short a period of time isn't easy.'

Richard paused again, willing Fitzhume to interject and just offer to fund the ransom, but the older man remained silent, seemingly content to watch him squirm.

Richard took a long drink of the whisky, but it barely touched the sides of his anxiety. 'So, what I was wondering was whether you… what I mean to say is… I wondered if you could… I mean, if you had…' The words were deserting him. He'd had it so well-rehearsed but his mind was blanking faster than he could stop it.

Fitzhume's cane banged against the floor and despite the softening of the carpet pile, the noise still echoed around the room. 'Spit it out, Richard. I'm too old and tired for your usual nonsense.'

Drink drained, Richard left the window and returned to his seat, placing the glass on the carpet by his feet and forcing himself to look into Fitzhume's eyes. 'I need you to lend us the two million pounds for Cassie's ransom.' He released the breath he'd been holding since finishing the whisky.

Fitzhume's expression remained blank and Richard would have given anything in that moment to read the older man's thoughts.

'No,' Fitzhume finally said, reaching for his glass and swallowing a mouthful.

Richard blinked several times, certain he must have misheard. 'What do you mean, no?'

Fitzhume raised his eyebrows. 'Why should I *lend* you the money? You are her father and you should be able to scrape it together.'

The walls were spinning. 'It's two million pounds, for God's sake. It's not like I can just walk to a cashpoint and withdraw that amount of money. Everything I have is tied up in the business—'

'A business I financed from the beginning, not to mention the doors I opened for you to establish a network of potential clients. What return have I seen on my outlay? Diddly squat. And having spent the best part of ten years blowing profits on frivolous trips overseas and wining and dining clients, you now come to me, cap in hand, to ask for more.'

This couldn't be happening. 'Look, Fitzhume, I know we've not always seen eye-to-eye on some matters, and I'm not asking you to like me, but this is your granddaughter we're talking about here. Show some fucking emotion! You're her grandfather.'

Fitzhume's cane echoed off the walls. 'A *real* father would have already found the men responsible for this and strung them up. But what are you doing about it?'

'The police are doing their jobs, so—'

'What are *you* doing about things, Richard? How are *you* trying to get Cassie home safely?'

'There's nothing I can do other than pay what they've demanded.'

'That's the problem with you, Richard. It's always been your problem. You have no backbone. You're too emotional.'

Richard rose to his feet, shaking his head as he moved to the trolley and refilled his glass. 'At least I have a heart. I cannot believe you're willing to leave your granddaughter in the hands of monsters for the sake of money that I know you already have in that safe of yours in the basement.'

Fitzhume's temple furrowed and his eyes narrowed.

'Oh, you didn't know I knew about that,' Richard mocked, finally feeling as though he'd wrestled back some semblance of control. 'Elizabeth told me about it when I moved in. She said you kept it there for emergencies and that it would pass to her and Cassie upon your death. A little gift that HMRC wouldn't be aware of: no inheritance tax. So don't lecture me about being a good father. Had you been more present in Elizabeth's life when she was growing up, maybe you wouldn't have spent the last fifteen years pandering to her every whim out of guilt. I know you've never liked me, Fitzhume, but what is it about me that you find so appalling?'

Fitzhume didn't miss a beat. 'You've never been good enough for her. Elizabeth needs a man who can protect her but you've only ever been out for yourself. I had hoped that Cassie's arrival would see a change in you but if anything, it only drove a greater wedge between you and Elizabeth.'

'How dare you? I *love* my daughter more than anything else on this earth!'

'More than the men you do business with?'

'What is that supposed to mean?'

It was Fitzhume's turn to bask in the revelation of a secret. 'Do you think I don't know about the second business you run on the side? How antiques aren't the *only* thing you import from Asia? It can't be cheap for you to pay border control to turn a blind eye to every fourth crate you import. Maybe that's why you can't afford to do what's necessary to save the daughter you claim to love so much.'

Richard could feel the heat in his cheeks but he ignored it, instead throwing himself to the floor, crashing to his knees by Fitzhume's feet. 'I am begging you, Fitzhume. I don't care what you think of me, I just want Cassie home where she belongs. I'll do whatever you want. If you want me out of Elizabeth's life then I'll go but you *have* to lend me that money.'

'Pathetic,' Fitzhume sneered. 'This is the problem with so-called men these days. Pleading instead of fighting. You would have benefited from the intense training I received at Hereford – not that you could have survived there for more than an hour with the SAS. You aren't a real man, Richard.'

Warm tears splashed against Richard's cheeks as the last of the fight left his bones. 'Please, Fitzhume. I wouldn't ask if I wasn't desperate.'

Fitzhume shook his head in disbelief. 'What would Cassie think if she could see you now?' He sighed. 'It's lucky for her that she has one real parent in her life.' He sighed again in resignation. 'Very well, Richard, I *will* lend you the money for my granddaughter's ransom, but on the condition that you put up your alleged company as collateral. I don't trust you, Richard, pure and simple. I will give you that money, but I will expect every penny returned within the next two years, or I will shut down your little business and see you driven out of my daughter's and granddaughter's lives forever. Do you understand?'

In truth, Richard had stopped listening as soon as Fitzhume had said he would front the ransom. To hell with the company. If everything went to plan, Cassie would be home by tomorrow night, without a single penny exchanged.

Chapter Twenty-Nine

NOW

Kensington, London

Had the reporter chased us from South Kensington, he would have easily caught up with the Bentley because we meet temporary traffic lights and roadworks not far from Earl's Court tube station. Thankfully, he must have stopped his chase at the door of Richard Hilliard's townhouse. Fitzhume hasn't spoken another word since we turned out of Richard's road and his earlier reference to spies among us has me recalling what Rachel learned about how easily he quashed the story of Cassie's abduction and death last year. The thought that the British Security Services are somehow monitoring our meetings and conversations sends a shiver down the length of my spine.

I dismiss the thought. This is the real world, not some cloak and dagger mystery. But what's the alternative? Fitzhume looked just as shocked as I did when the reporter appeared, so I have no reason to think he would have leaked the news. Plus, that would totally contradict his previous stance on sharing information with the press. Who else knew we would be meeting Richard Hilliard today? Fitzhume appears to trust his driver, Hobbs, but is that faith misplaced? Or maybe Fitzhume let it slip to another member of his staff? Was Rosa the housekeeper's name?

I hadn't told anyone where I'd be this morning. The only people who even know I'm in London with Fitzhume are Maddie and Rachel, and neither would know what address I'd be at…

The thought trails into feelings of anger.

Rachel was with me when I listened to Fitzhume's message last night and she was the one who messaged me the address.

The memory of her words is like a battering ram against my already fragile mind: *your first story in a mainstream newspaper, aided by my experience and contacts.*

Surely my best friend of eight years wouldn't betray me so easily, regardless of how keen she is to be a part of the story. Or am I being naïve? She always says things in the capital are not like they are in smaller regions. I hate to think of her leaking the story so that I feel compelled to reach out to her for support and in an effort to make sure the story is told in the right way. It's all such a mess.

What did he say his name was? Ken Johnson, and I can only presume that *Eye in the Sky News* is some kind of online journal or blog because I've never heard of it. Pulling out my phone, I search both names, immediately seeing the Australian journalist's image on the screen – though he looks much smarter than the sweaty man in T-shirt and shorts we just met. Clearly the image associated with the online newspaper has been professionally shot, but there's no escaping that huge brown moustache curling down the sides of his mouth. He appears to be the only reporter associated with *Eye in the Sky News* and I'm in no doubt that this is obviously a personal project of his, as most of the stories he's written about are almost lifted and shifted from the mainstream newspapers, with the addition of his own byline and thoughts. Topics covered in the last week include post-Brexit Britain, why shows like *Britain's Got Talent* should be banned, and the growing strain on the NHS.

I don't spend too much time reading his opinionated drivel as it isn't to my taste, and the page-visits counter at the bottom of the homepage suggests he is far from making any kind of splash in the real world. According to the counter, I'm only the eight hundred and seventh visitor. Hardly mainstream, but breaking the story of Cassie's abduction could send him and the site stratospheric. There is a 'Contact Us' email address beside the page-visits counter but I cannot see that Rachel would even know Ken Johnson, let alone use him to put me under pressure.

'What did Richard tell you?' Fitzhume eventually asks, as we near the M3 exit off the M25.

Pocketing my phone, I think back to the conversation. I have no idea whether Fitzhume is aware of his son-in-law's heavy use of cocaine but it doesn't feel like my place to say.

'He said he misses Cassie a lot,' I reply, 'and that he hasn't been the same person since she went missing.'

Fitzhume silently considers me for a moment. 'He didn't tell you how I drove him out of business?'

Heat rises to my cheeks. 'He did say something about you making him sign a contract or something.'

Fitzhume's lips flicker into something close to a smile

before he wipes the edges with his handkerchief. 'Richard Hilliard is a leech; he always has been. He's always reaching out for the next rung, trying to get further up the social ladder. That doesn't make him a bad person. I've known lots of people – men *and* women – who do the same. Nevertheless, that's how he operates. I am certain that is why he latched on to Elizabeth and once he got his claws into her, she was never the same. I had hoped she'd see him for what he is before it was too late, but they married without my knowledge and she soon fell pregnant. By then it was too late. The only silver lining was sweet, sweet Cassie.'

He pauses to press the handkerchief to the corner of his eye. 'Time and again, Elizabeth would come to me to ask for money on his behalf. She'd never admit it was for him, but she would say she needed money for new clothes, or there was some charitable benefit she wanted to support. I would always oblige, not wishing to upset her, but deep down I knew she was giving some, if not all of it, to him. So, when he then approached me directly to ask for the ransom money, I knew I had to act. He claimed his own money was tied up in acquisitions in the business, yet when I asked to see the books and evidence of this investment he was cagey. He didn't know that I suspected his so-called business was merely a front for other villains to ply their trade.'

This is news to me, but I remain silent, allowing Fitzhume to wax lyrical and justify why he wasn't more willing to pay the ransom for Cassie.

'One of my friends – whom I'd naively introduced to Richard some time before – approached me to express her concern about something she'd discovered inside a priceless vase he'd secured for her. A bag of white powder, she told me.

I thanked her for her discretion and had it disposed of. Then I watched and waited. Within a few weeks, his stress and anxiety doubled, but whenever Elizabeth would ask if he was okay, he'd make up some story about visa issues or whatnot. It was enough to spur me to hire a private investigator to dig a little deeper. I was disappointed to learn just how deep Richard had become involved with one particular family with known connections to the Albanian criminal underworld. I had to do whatever I could to keep Elizabeth and Cassie away from the dangers of being affiliated to that kind of world, which meant getting Richard free of it. I had an official contract drawn up by a solicitor so that after the ransom had been paid, I would be in a position to have the business wound up and my family finally free.'

He pauses and fixes me with a sincere look. 'I know it sounds cruel and underhand but I believed Cassie would be returned safely and then we could all move on as a family. Despite my reservations about Richard, I knew he would never stop that side of his business unless his hand was forced.'

'Why didn't you tell the police what he was doing? If you were so keen to have him out of Elizabeth and Cassie's lives, why not have him arrested?'

'I'm a stubborn animal, Miss Hunter, but I'm not cruel. A daughter needs a father figure in her life – God knows I learnt that the hard way with Elizabeth. For all of his faults – and there are so many – Richard was a good father to Cassie, and she would have been devastated to have him torn from her grasp. I made the most of the opportunity, but it was for everyone's benefit, not delivered out of spite. Alas, had I kept more of an eye on Richard, then maybe Cassie would be here with me now.'

'I know he went to observe the handover,' I say. 'I learned that from Penny Connors. But she also said something went badly wrong at the exchange.'

He nods. 'Richard's doing, I believe, not that he ever admitted as much. From what I understand, the police and the kidnappers weren't the only people on that bank that night. A gang of Albanians opened fire and that was how the van holding my granddaughter went up in flames. One of the gang died in the crossfire and was later identified as an Albanian who was affiliated with the family with which Richard had been doing business. It would have been typical of Richard to send in his own people and fail to take control of the situation.'

'Were any arrests made? Did the police question Richard about his involvement?'

'Yes, yes, but you're missing the point, Miss Hunter. The only witness to Cassie even being in that van when it exploded was that Leroy Denton – the kidnapper that the police managed to apprehend at the scene. All forensic examination uncovered was a few bone fragments but the heat of the blast made amplification of genetic markers impossible. Not even micro CT imaging picked anything up. Those remains were unidentifiable so they could have belonged to anyone: another gang member hiding in the van as back-up, a driver who stayed behind the wheel in case they needed a quick getaway…

'These are not the deluded pipe dreams of a distraught grandfather, Miss Hunter. As long as there is doubt, there is hope. *That* is why I firmly believe my granddaughter did not die at the exchange.'

My head is spinning and I can't tell if it's the hangover taking hold or the speed at which the car is travelling. 'Putting to one side the police investigation for just a moment, even if you were right, where on earth do you think Cassie has been for the last year?'

His lips curl up at the edges. 'That is why I've hired you, Miss Hunter. You're going to find her for me.'

Chapter Thirty

NOW

New Forest, Hampshire

The moment we leave the M27, I already feel one step closer to home. The air here is fresher, less clogged with smog and irate drivers. Hampshire's New Forest was always a favourite destination of my parents; they used to bring Anna and me here for picnics at any opportunity. Back then, Dad was so keen for us to learn about nature and wildlife, and here ponies and cows roam freely, waiting to be inspected and petted by visiting tourists.

The road here is lined with trees, shedding their yellow and brown leaves and creating the perfect autumnal picture. I don't have an eye for photography but even I can tell that this would make quite the scenic muse for budding artists. The forest is rich with colour and hints at the secrets that lie beyond the trees. A brown road sign warns that we are nearing The Priory, as if it is some kind of dangerous port of call.

According to the internet search I performed to kill the hundred-minute journey time, The Priory Hospital in Hampshire is one of the country's leading centres for the treatment of a wide range of mental health conditions, including depression, anxiety, and stress. I wonder which of those Elizabeth Hilliard is being treated for. Fitzhume hasn't been too forthcoming about the reason he had his daughter sent here, but given the loss she suffered a year ago, I can only imagine the impact on her mental health.

Hobbs slows the car and waits for a gap in traffic before pulling in through the open gates of the entrance. The Grade II listed building is like a fortress from here, overshadowing the 1.5 acres of green lawn and flower beds. It is all enclosed by the foreboding trees, as if somehow Mother Nature herself holds the grounds within her grasp. The cream-coloured walls mean it almost blends into the overcast pale sky. As the car pulls into a marked space in the carpark in front of the building, I can't get over how quiet the surroundings are. In the two days I've spent in London, I think I've already grown accustomed to the constant hum of traffic, tubes and overcrowding. Stepping out of the Bentley, I can't even hear the road we have not long left behind. It truly is as if we've entered a vacuum.

Fitzhume leaves Hobbs with instructions to wait with the car before pointing his cane towards the pillared entrance of the grand building. From here, it is more reminiscent of the sort of hospital you'd see in films from the 60s. There is no accumulation of smokers at the entrance, no sign of automated doors, or multi-floored eyesore structures. This building is more like an elongated house – not as large as Fitzhume's manor – with just two floors, though there is a large glass-roofed extension jutting out to one side, and I can't escape the feeling that we've been driven to some luxurious hotel rather than a centre for health and wellbeing.

I've heard stories of celebrities being sent to The Priory to deal with addiction to alcohol and narcotics, but I'd always imagined some kind of prison-like setup, not this. I instantly feel underdressed in my jeans and long sleeved T-shirt, unlike Fitzhume in his tweed jacket and beige trousers.

I'm surprised when the doors to the building don't open but he points at a sign to the right of the door.

'All visitors must be announced,' he says, like I should be familiar with the protocol of such a place.

He presses a buzzer and an angled camera above us whirs as it focuses on our faces.

'Lord Fitzhume to see my daughter, Elizabeth,' he proclaims towards the microphone built into the wall.

There is a moment's pause, before an incessant buzzing sound confirms the door's lock-release mechanism has been engaged. Fitzhume pulls the door open with ease and nods for me to go through. The reception is bright and airy with a striking sense of cleanliness; the fragrance of lemon and lavender hangs in the air and the oak-panelled desk looks new and untarnished. A woman and a man in the brightest of white uniforms each offer a warm and welcoming smile.

Fitzhume signs the guestbook and hands me a pen to do the same. Scanning the page, I recognise the names of a couple of the patients who have been visited in the last week but I try to cover my shock.

'We will have Elizabeth brought down to the Pennington Room,' the red-headed woman behind the desk says, 'but before you see her, Dr Navillius has asked if he can speak to you first. If you both take a seat, I will notify Dr Navillius that you have arrived.'

We are ushered towards two lightweight white plastic chairs in keeping with the feel that we have walked into a spa, rather than a hospital. There is a small glass-fronted fridge on the floor between us containing bottles of mineral water. On top of the fridge stand leaflets advertising some of the hospital's available treatments. I reach for one to pass the time, learning that 92 per cent of patients stated that they would recommend the centre to friends, while 97 per cent said that they felt safe and secure during their stay.

'I should warn you,' Fitzhume whispers beside me, 'before we go in… Elizabeth is in a delicate condition. I want you to meet with her so you can understand the impact that the last year's events have had on my family, and to give you the opportunity to ask her any burning questions you may have. However, she may not behave as you would expect. She is vulnerable, and there is a chance she will come across as uncommunicative or even sullen. Please don't confuse that with her not wanting to be of assistance.'

Richard Hilliard's conclusion resonates in my memory: *despair isn't something you can cure with pills and counselling.*

I'm about to ask Fitzhume if perhaps we shouldn't have come when an olive-skinned man approaches. He has the darkest hair I think I've ever seen. He is wearing an identical white top to that of the man and woman behind the counter; it is short-sleeved and his arms are thin but covered in charcoal-coloured hairs, which do little to obscure his tanned skin. A small blue and white flag adjacent to his name badge suggests that he is of Greek descent, or certainly capable of mastering the language.

'Lord Fitzhume,' he says brightly in unaccented English, 'a pleasure to see you again.' He stops and looks at me.

'I'm Emma Hunter,' I say quickly, though I'm not sure he needed telling.

His eyes widen in recognition and I can feel the heat rising to my face.

'A pleasure,' he says, extending his hand for me to shake. His eyes return to Fitzhume. 'Thank you for agreeing to see me first. I wanted to discuss Elizabeth's treatment as I think we may need to try something more advanced to make a breakthrough this time. We can step into my office for privacy.'

Fitzhume nods and follows the doctor along the corridor to our left. I'm about to retake my seat when he gestures for me to follow. The last thing I want to do is intrude but I'm not prepared to argue with him either.

Dr Navillius's office is like something out of the Argos catalogue. Open-plan, and as bright as the reception area we have just left, it has a small desk and bright yellow chair that are angled away from the wall; in front of the desk are two hard-backed chairs and a small round table. The walls are bright white and the dark laminate floor is in stark contrast. It wouldn't surprise me to learn that a feng-shui specialist had carefully designed the office to encourage better mental health.

Dr Navillius invites us to sit in the two chairs, while pulling the yellow swivel chair around the desk to join us. Interlocking his fingers, he rests them beneath his chin, his face donning an expression of concern. 'Elizabeth is not responding to treatment, Lord Fitzhume. As you know, our therapeutic treatment programmes are recovery-focused, attempting to support the patient on her journey to better mental health and ensuring that she has the tools to avoid reverting to old habits upon reintegration into the real world. Each treatment programme is tailored to the specific needs of each patient and the level of support and care is determined by our dedicated team of professional counsellors, psychiatrists and mental health professionals.

'Since her arrival here in late July, Elizabeth has refused to engage in any of the treatment plans we have devised for her. I understand the significance of the events that led to you bringing her here, but I want to be upfront and honest with you and say that what we have tried so far has failed to get through to her. The first step in overcoming addictions and improving health is acceptance of the problem but in your daughter's case, I feel like her addictions are not born out of a need; rather, they are a choice.'

Fitzhume's eyes narrow. 'What are you saying, Dr Navillius?'

Navillius eyes me cautiously before continuing. 'It is my belief that Elizabeth is choosing to use alcohol and drugs to keep herself in a vegetative state. For obvious reasons, we don't allow patients to indulge their addictions here, but we do use mild prescription medicines to help break addictions to certain substances. Elizabeth has refused all options for alternative medicines. She shuts herself away in her room, refusing offers of fitness training, classes on relaxation techniques, and art therapy. The only time she emerges from her room is to eat and attend her mandated counselling sessions, though from what I understand she spends those in silence. It is as if…' Dr Navillius doesn't finish the sentence, as though he has caught himself before he oversteps the mark.

'As if… *what?*' Fitzhume pleads.

Navillius glances at me again, his eyes urging me to leave the room so he can speak more easily, but as I begin to stand and make my excuses, Fitzhume raises his hand above my leg; he wants me to hear everything.

'I don't believe Elizabeth wants our help, Lord Fitzhume,' Navillius finally says. 'She is sober, and has been since her first week of arrival. We pride ourselves on offering bespoke treatment plans, but if the patient won't engage – as Elizabeth refuses to – there is little we can do. We have seen all kinds of patients here over the years but I've never come across someone who simply refuses to get well.' He pauses and reaches for a pad of paper from the desk behind him. 'You checked her in because you wanted to clean her of her addictions. I can tell you that she hasn't had any kind of medication or alcohol in over seven weeks and has expressed none of the symptoms of a patient desperate for her next fix. To all intents and purposes she is clean, but I know that if I were to sign her release papers it would only be a matter of time before she found some new way of shutting herself off. It is my opinion that Elizabeth does not want to get better.'

Fitzhume's eyes are glassy and I can see he is fighting to keep the tears at bay. For the first time, I think I really see just how broken he is. For all his bravado, cane-banging, and pragmatism, he is just as fragile as his daughter. Though he has managed to paper over the cracks for appearances' sake, the pain inside is eating him alive.

Reaching for his weathered hand, I clasp it with sincerity.

'Why don't we go and see her? Maybe seeing you will be the spark she needs to step away from the abyss.'

A single tear escapes as he nods, squeezing my fingers in return. I can't help picturing my own mother as I think of how Dr Navillius has described Elizabeth's condition. Maybe the Alzheimer's has been a blessing to her rather than a curse. At least now she doesn't have to remember the despair of her loss.

Chapter Thirty-One

THEN

Chalfont St Giles, Buckinghamshire

The knock at the door startled Elizabeth Hilliard, and was enough to drag her mind back to reality and the task laid out before her on Cassie's bed. The bedroom remained exactly as it had been left before the incident on Saturday afternoon, and even though Elizabeth had given her daughter instructions to tidy away her soft toys, they remained strewn across the carpet. Looking over to the door, she saw the thick beard of Gerry Connors in the gap and nodded for him to push the door wider.

'I'm sorry to disturb you, Mrs Hilliard,' he said through that heavy Belfast accent of his. 'I made you a cup of tea,' he added, raising the mug towards her. 'Sorry, I didn't know if you took sugar or not.'

Leaving the bundled pile of clothes on the bed, she moved across to accept the drink. 'Thank you,' she said. 'That's kind of you.'

'To be fair, I was making myself one and I figured you'd probably benefit from one too, on today of all days. How are you holding up?'

Elizabeth wasn't used to her father's hired help taking such an interest in her but she wasn't put out by the intrusion.

'I was just folding some of Cassie's laundry,' she said, indicating the overflowing pile. 'Rosa usually does it, but I thought… it doesn't matter.'

'No, please,' Gerry said gently. 'It can be good to talk. Please, tell me what you thought.'

Elizabeth placed the mug on the dressing table just inside the door and looked back at him. He certainly wasn't the usual help that Richard or her father hired; he was more rugged and less polished than the likes of Rosa and Hobbs. He struck her as someone not used to being submissive to others and yet there was a softness when he spoke. When he asked how she was holding up, it had sounded like he really wanted to know. She couldn't recall the last time Richard had sounded so interested, if ever.

She bit her lip. 'I thought it would somehow bring me closer to her… her scent representing her aura somehow. I don't know… It's silly.'

'Not at all,' he replied without missing a beat. 'I read once that just thinking about a person – someone you miss, or someone you love – can be enough to trigger the thought of you in their mind too – like a psychic bridge, particularly between parent and child. I know it sounds far-fetched and whimsical, but I like to think that whenever I think about my son Sean, it's because he's thinking of me.'

She considered him for a moment. The dark blazer barely fitted across his broad chest and the neck tie looked as though it was choking him; he was definitely not someone accustomed to such formal attire. But was he mocking her? Would he and his wife have a good laugh at her expense later?

'Do you really believe that?' she asked, desperately hoping his answer would convince her.

He took a step closer. 'Do I believe it actually happens? I honestly don't know. But do I believe it brings me comfort? Absolutely. I used to have to work away a bit – in my previous job – and whenever I was away, I'd always take a framed photograph of my son and wife with me. Every night I would look at that photograph and try to picture what they would be doing at that moment. Most of the time, I wouldn't look at it until last thing at night so I'd always assume that wee Sean was asleep, but then I'd imagine what he was dreaming about.'

A broad smile broke out across his face at the memory. 'He's obsessed with football so I always liked to imagine him dreaming about scoring for United at Wembley in some cup final. Then I'd think about Penny, and a couple of times, I swear to you, she'd send me a text message at the exact moment I was thinking of her. Has that ever happened to you? You know, like, you think about someone – maybe a friend – who you haven't seen in, like, forever, and the next thing you know they're phoning and asking if you want to meet up?'

She nodded, though she couldn't recall any such incident. She'd certainly not thought about Richard, and then received a call or message, and she was sure he'd never taken a photograph of the three of them away with him on one of his business trips. Did that mean their marriage wasn't as strong as the Connorses'? Did she even care anymore?

'In fact,' Gerry continued, lifting Elizabeth's mug and securing a coaster beneath it, 'the very last time I was away on business, when I got back, Sean told me he'd had a dream about me while I'd been away. He said that in it he was playing football with a host of players from the Premier League, and even though he was much smaller than them, nobody could get the ball off him, and he scored the winning goal. Apparently, when they handed him the trophy, he saw me in the crowd cheering and he said it was the best dream he'd ever had. Depending on how much of a cynic you are, you could argue that it was mere coincidence, but I prefer to consider the prospect that the two of us have this unbreakable bond that allows such moments of magic.'

Returning to the pile of washing, she picked up a T-shirt and shook it to get rid of the creases. 'How long have you and your wife been married?'

She heard him suck in a breath through his teeth while he pondered the question. Frankly, he could have told her any answer as she had no way of checking, nor the desire.

'Must be twelve years almost. Time flies, especially when you have a little one to occupy every waking moment. What about you and Mr Hilliard?'

Elizabeth was about to answer when she decided to wait a moment as he had. 'Seven years. We conceived Cassie on our honeymoon.'

Then, for no reason she could fathom, her eyes filled instantly and a sob escaped her throat. Gerry moved closer and took her in his arms and, despite the invasion of space, she found herself burying her head in his shoulder, allowing him to just hold her while she took breaths to compose herself. Public displays of emotion in front of the hired help were not acceptable and she felt embarrassed and awkward as she peeled herself away from his grasp.

'Forgive me,' she offered.

'You should never apologise for missing your wee daughter. Please don't feel embarrassed; I won't mention it to a living soul, I promise.'

It didn't make it any easier for her and she returned to shaking out the T-shirt.

'You know,' Gerry said, stepping forward and taking the shirt from her hands, 'there's a much better way of folding shirts… like this. Do you mind?'

The laundry was usually one of Rosa's duties, and although Elizabeth had insisted on doing it today, in hindsight she had no idea how Rosa usually did it, nor whether there was some new technique with which she was unfamiliar. Allowing him to move closer to the bed, she watched as he laid the shirt on the made bed, and began to fold the T-shirt at odd angles, before presenting her with the perfectly squared apparel. It took a couple of seconds at most, and she genuinely couldn't believe how easy he'd made it look.

'Do that again,' she said, eager to study the technique closer.

Reaching for a second T-shirt, he repeated the process, but even on second viewing she couldn't work out exactly how he had achieved it.

'Where did you learn how to do that?' she asked.

He smiled at her. 'Having a son who's mad on football and climbing trees, you can imagine the number of muddy shirts and trousers he gets through in the space of a week. I saw the trick on the internet and I've been doing it ever since. It's not as difficult as it looks, but it gets perfect results every time. Let me show you.'

Taking her hands in his, she shuddered at the rough feeling

of his skin on hers, but allowed him to guide her outstretched fingers to the final T-shirt in the pile. They grasped it and laid it out flat on the sheet.

'Fold it here,' he said, moving her hands like those of a puppet, 'and here, and then pull these two sections, and… voila.'

Her version wasn't quite as square or professional as his two earlier examples but it was certainly a step in the right direction. She couldn't escape the slight smile splitting her own face.

'Impressive. Tea *and* laundry. I'd better warn Rosa… you'll be after her job next.'

He chuckled at the suggestion. 'I'm not sure about that. You haven't even tasted the tea yet. It could taste like pish. Besides, I'm not sure I'd fit into those tabards of hers.' He paused, studying the doorway. 'Is there anything else I can do for you, Mrs Hilliard?'

Elizabeth shook her head, feeling the weight on her shoulders temporarily lessened. 'No, that will be all, Gerry. Thank you.'

He bowed his head slightly and headed back through the door, leaving it ajar. She didn't take her eyes from him until he'd disappeared from sight down the stairs. Silently chastising herself for the onrushing thoughts in her head, she looked at the three folded T-shirts, unfurled her version, and tried again. But no matter how many times she tried to get it right, the corners were never quite as straight and right-angled as his. In the end, she gave up trying, and placed the items of clothing in the chest of drawers on the other side of the bed.

She was about to head out of the room when she remembered what Gerry had said about the photograph of his wife and son. Locating the framed picture of Cassie, taken on her first day of school last year, Elizabeth cradled it to her heart and lay down on the small mattress. Surrounded by her daughter's scent and the image of Cassie in her mind's eye, she allowed her eyelids to close. She focused on trying to build that psychic connection with her daughter, trying to read if she was okay, and in need of her mother's love.

It was probably all poppycock and Gerry had probably only said it in an effort to cheer her up, but rather than giving up, she pressed the frame harder into her chest, willing her soul to send out the message of undying love. And in that moment, beyond all scientific and rational thought, she felt her daughter answering the call. Elizabeth didn't know how, but in that fleeting moment she knew in the deepest recesses of her soul that Cassie was still alive, and the feeling filled her heart and mind with hope.

Chapter Thirty-Two

NOW

New Forest, Hampshire

To look at her, you wouldn't know Elizabeth Hilliard is only seven years older than me. The gaunt woman before me, whose dark, straggly hair looks as though it hasn't been washed and brushed in a decade, is like a ghost in some horror movie set in the nineteenth century. Her appearance isn't aided by the long yellowing nightgown that bunches at the wrists and hangs just above her ankles. I can actually imagine her disappearing through one of the walls when our backs are turned.

Dr Navillius has shown Fitzhume and me into one of the treatment rooms. It's in keeping with the rest of the centre in that it feels more like a spa in a hotel than a room designed to encourage the treatment of mental health conditions. Maybe that's just my own ignorance on how modern mental illness is treated, though Freddie Mitchell has never described any of his counselling sessions in such a fond light. I must remember to phone Freddie and check how he's getting on. I don't like how things were left between us at the shelter on Friday night, and I hate that Maddie put me in the position where I felt compelled to ask him for permission for *Monsters Under the Bed* to be optioned for a series.

Elizabeth Hilliard hasn't spoken a word since she was escorted into the room. Fitzhume went over to embrace her but it was a one-way interaction; even as he tried to kiss her cheek, she showed little affection towards him. From the pictures I saw in the police file of Elizabeth, this is not whom I had expected to meet. In those photos, she is carefully made-up, not a hair out of place; this Elizabeth is a walking zombie. Her skin is a sickening grey and hangs from her cheeks, her hollow eyes lost in their sockets just above, and cold sores pool at the corners of her mouth. Richard said his wife was a woman in despair and I don't think I've ever seen a picture of despair more accurately illuminated.

That's not quite true though, is it? Sitting and staring at this shell of a woman, I'm instantly reminded of my own mother on those nights immediately following Anna's disappearance. No matter how much I tried to love her doubly hard, it was never enough… *could* never be enough. My mother went into total shutdown overnight and although she was able to find the motivation to hang all those missing posters, she was never the same. Elizabeth is wearing the same defeatist look I see in Mum's eyes every time I visit her at the home, even on her good days.

Fitzhume introduces me but doesn't explain who I am nor what I'm doing here, which feels more than a little awkward.

Of course, no more awkward than the fact that I'm trespassing in their lives, and digging into their most heart-wrenching recent history. I remember feeling the same way when I first started asking questions about the St Francis Home for Wayward Boys; at the time I was driven by the notion of seeking justice for Freddie – and later Mike and Steve – but those first sessions felt very much like I was trampling on their lives. At least I was able to find some kind of positive resolution to their tragedies; I wish I could do the same for the father and daughter before me.

I once asked my English professor what he enjoyed so much about writing, and his response was: it's like reading a story in which you become deeply immersed, whose characters you know intimately, but you get to choose from an infinite number of endings. Maybe that's the difference between writing fiction where you control the puppet strings and detailing the true events of a situation. I am merely a conduit for projecting other people's words, rather than a master storyteller. If I could control the ending of this story, I'd have Cassie miraculously appear to reunite this family, but real life doesn't work like that. Something tells me that reaching the same conclusion as DCS Rawani and his investigation team won't bring the closure that Fitzhume and Elizabeth are craving.

'Miss Hunter would like to ask you some questions about your recollection of events last year,' Fitzhume says once the three of us are seated on faux-leather upright chairs placed in a makeshift circle.

Elizabeth grunts without making eye contact. Her attention is focused on a space on the wall between Fitzhume and me, though when I turn to look I can't see anything of interest there.

Fitzhume leans closer to me, his voice little more than a whisper, but Elizabeth must be able to hear every word. 'You'll have to forgive my daughter, Miss Hunter. She has good days and bad days, and alas this appears to be the latter. Go ahead and ask your questions.'

I again picture my own mother, trapped in a room in a nursing home she didn't choose. Is it as much of a prison as this hospital is for Elizabeth?

Clearing my throat, I unlock my phone and switch on the recorder before skimming the questions I jotted down on the journey over. 'Mrs Hilliard, I'd like to know what you remember of the day when… the day of the exchange.'

Elizabeth doesn't respond, her eyes still fixed on the patch on the wall.

I don't repeat the question, nor do I move on to my next question. I've become very patient in my adult life and I know that the best way to encourage someone else to speak isn't to pester and badger, rather just to remain quiet and allow them to fill the awkward silence.

I watch Elizabeth, trying to determine how much of this sullen and lost aspect is genuine, and how much of it is an act for her father's benefit. I don't mean that to sound as cruel as it does, but from Penny Connors's account of Elizabeth, she would certainly be capable of exaggerating her feelings of loss and despair.

'Come on darling, answer Miss Hunter's question,' Fitzhume sputters, lines forming in his forehead.

Still I remain quiet.

Elizabeth's gaze finally turns towards me and there is the briefest moment of scorn in her glare, but it passes in the blink of an eye. Yet in that moment I learn all I need to about Elizabeth: here is a woman who has been dictated to all her life – what clothes to wear, what school to attend, which friends to choose, what to say, how to think, and maybe this is finally her opportunity to choose how to mourn the passing of her daughter.

Call me naïve, but I think she *wants* to speak to me. She looks like she is bottling up years of repressed anger and disappointment, and if I can tap into that frustration, maybe there's a way to break through.

I turn to Fitzhume on my left. 'Would you mind leaving us to talk alone for a few minutes? I don't wish to be rude, Lord Fitzhume, but perhaps she'll be more open woman to woman.'

Spittle forms at the side of his lips. He wipes it away with his handkerchief before hoisting himself up and heading back out of the room. With the door closing, I move my chair closer to Elizabeth. I lock my phone, knowing I won't be getting answers to those questions. I'm not great at sharing my feelings and thoughts with others. When you grow up with two parents who are more interested in other matters than listening to you, you learn to bottle it up.

Resting my open hands on my knees in a non-threatening manner, I take a deep breath. 'I know what it is to lose someone you hold so dear,' I start, not sure whether she's listening; her gaze is back on that patch on the wall. 'Twenty years ago, my sister – my best friend – disappeared. I know it can't possibly be the same as losing your own child, but you need to understand that Anna was my link to the real world. She was two years older than me and in my early life I learned more from her than I ever did at school. She was the one who showed me how to fib to my parents and get away with it. She taught me how to swear, even at that young age. She explained that no matter how hard you work, there will always be someone who seems to be doing better than you. And she also taught me that appearances can be deceptive.'

I pause, studying her face, looking for any kind of twitch or reaction to my words but there is no movement. It seems I'm going to have to dig deeper to break through the foundations.

'We were playing in the garden when she decided she was going to visit our grandma's house. That was the last time I saw her. Not a single day has passed when I don't regret not begging her to stay, or going with her. Hindsight truly is the harshest gift we were blessed with, don't you think? But we're human, aren't we? We try and move on, we try to come to terms with our regret and not let it dictate the rest of our lives.

'If only my parents had allowed themselves to accept they had no control over what happened to Anna… They blamed themselves, they blamed me, and they blamed Anna. But sometimes things happen that are beyond our control, and as much as I am trying to move on and live with my inaction that day, it isn't easy.

'I'm not judging you, Mrs Hilliard; I know better than most how long it can take to come to terms with losing one so close to you.'

Her head twists slowly to meet my eyes. 'I remember the *feeling*. You asked what I remember of that day – the day we *lost* Cassie – well, all I can remember is the feeling of *her* deep inside my soul. It's never left me but now I know it is just a callous trick my mind plays on me.'

I have no idea what she's talking about but this is the closest to a real answer she's delivered.

'Tell me about it, this feeling… what was it?' I push.

There is a shine to her sunken eyes but it looks as though any tear splashing onto her cheeks would cause the dry and coarse skin to dissolve like mummified rags.

'I could *feel* her that morning. It sounds stupid – God knows I know how ridiculous it sounds, particularly given everything that unfolded – but I *felt* her, I swear it. Every sinew of my body and soul told me that she was alive and that we would be reunited that evening. I think it was the happiest I'd ever felt, happier than even before she'd been taken from us. I had a spring in my step, foreseeing the second chance I would have to be a better mother to Cassie, to be the mother she deserved. Our driver had spoken to me about this kind of psychic bridge or bond he felt with his son and as I lay in Cassie's bed, I could feel her with me. The feeling remained with me the entire day and even when the detective arrived at the house and broke the news that Cassie had… died in the explosion, I didn't believe it. I told him he had to be mistaken, that I could still feel that bridge to her. They thought I was crazy, that it was just a symptom of whatever pills I'd taken, but I was adamant. And then… the police and coroner found the bone fragments in the carcass of the van, and that was the moment I realised how foolish I'd been. This feeling – this psychic bond – was nothing more than wishful thinking.'

'Why do you say that?'

I know the feeling she's talking about, because I feel the same thing with Anna. It's not as strong as it once was, but I have this constant feeling that she *is* alive out there somewhere, waiting to be discovered. I need to believe it's more than my overactive imagination.

'Because my daughter is dead,' she snaps. 'Multiple people

saw her in the van before it exploded, and her bone fragments were found amongst the remains.'

'Your father believes Cassie is still alive. He believes that the police made a mistake.'

She smirks. 'My father is not a well man, Miss Hunter. He needs some positivity to cling to in his final days, and he will do everything in his power to convince others that he's right. But how else do you explain the bone fragments?'

Fitzhume hasn't looked well since I met him on Thursday, but Elizabeth is the first to acknowledge there could be more wrong with him than old age.

'Cancer,' she says, as if reading my mind. 'He thinks I don't know but he is hardly quiet when speaking to the oncologist on the phone and not exactly discreet with his mail. I don't know exactly how long he has left, but it won't be long.'

'So, in your opinion, Cassie definitely died?'

'We buried the bone fragments in a coffin at the cemetery,' she fires back. 'My father can hope all he wants, but nothing is bringing her back. It's the hope that kills you. Why else do you think I do *all* this? It isn't grief I'm running from. I'm just desperate to mask this sodding feeling.'

'It won't always be this painful,' I say, unable to maintain eye contact without my own eyes misting. 'I know it feels like it always will, but people are resilient. The pain never goes away, but with time it can become more manageable. You need to give yourself a break and acknowledge that it's only been twelve months. Maybe in another year or two—'

'You don't understand what I'm going through,' she interrupts with a rage I've witnessed in Fitzhume before. 'There is no place for me in this world anymore. I know what it is to bury a child, and no parent should ever have to go through that. That's why I continue to play out this charade for my father's sake. But once he passes…' She pauses to compose herself. 'You wanted to know the truth, Miss Hunter, and now you do. Pack up your things and go home. Don't string my father along anymore. For all our sakes.'

Chapter Thirty-Three

NOW

Ealing, London

The return to London is quiet, and for most of it Fitzhume's eyes are closed. It isn't clear if he's sleeping, or merely processing the day's events. If he is as ill as Elizabeth suggested, then I can only imagine what a toll the last year of grief has taken on his health. Elizabeth's final words have remained on repeat in my head since I left her in that clean and efficient room: *don't string my father along anymore.*

I must have dozed along the way too because, before I know it, we are exiting the A40 at the Perivale junction and all the road signs point to Greenford, Ealing, and Acton. Remnants of this morning's hangover remain nearby, though I'm no longer feeling nauseous, just tired and with a dull ache behind my eyes.

I have nothing but sympathy for the Hilliards. Both are clearly struggling with their grief though they attack it in different ways, but neither is able to move past what happened. I wonder how I would react in their situation. Would I manage to rise from the ashes or would I allow my life to drift away? Had Anna gone from my life at a later age, maybe I would still be in a darker place now. As it was, losing her at age seven was confusing and heart-breaking, and whilst I've made little progress in tracking her down, at least I'm trying.

Pulling up outside Rachel's flat, the dark sky is already starting to take shape above the corners of the neighbouring flats. Lights shine out from windows in a haphazard pattern, and in some ways the run of blocks resembles a half-opened advent calendar.

'Will I see you tomorrow?' I hear Fitzhume say, as I reach for the door handle.

I lower my hand and turn back to face him. 'Can I be totally honest with you, Lord Fitzhume?'

'Please,' he says, the hint of a smile just out of reach.

I take a deep breath. 'I've met your son-in-law and I've met your daughter. I've spoken to them both and neither has given me any reason to believe that your granddaughter could still be alive and out there.'

He opens his mouth to speak, but I raise my finger so he will allow me to finish.

'I have reviewed about two-thirds of the police file, and so far there isn't anything untoward about the investigation that I can see. The witness statements, the detectives' logic, and the investigative steps followed are all by the book. I understand why you are so desperate to believe there was some kind of conspiracy in what happened, but I would be doing you a disservice if I continued to encourage those thoughts. I appreciate you trusting me with the knowledge of what happened, and you have been nothing but hospitable in arranging for me to speak to Richard and Elizabeth. You clearly have some sway with local law enforcement to get me access to their files too, but not every situation is a miscarriage of justice.'

His face drops and it kills me that I'm upsetting this gentle, dying man.

'When I started investigating the St Francis Home for Wayward Boys, I knew there was truth in what Freddie Mitchell and the others had told me of the abuse they suffered. I can't describe exactly what it was, but it was almost as if I could smell the story and the cover-up. That's why I worked day and night to battle to get the truth out there. I wanted to see Arthur Turgood and his cronies brought to justice for what they did. If I'm honest, I've had no sense that things with your situation are anything but above board. I don't smell a story or any kind of wrongdoing, other than the tragedy you've all suffered. Unfortunately, sometimes bad things happen to good people, and there is no rhyme or reason for it. You, Richard, and Elizabeth are as much victims in all this as poor Cassie, and I genuinely wish there was some way I could bring you all the closure you so desperately deserve, but I just don't think it's going to happen. I'm sorry.'

I wait for him to shout and have Hobbs drag me from the car but he is silent for a long time. I'm starting to think he's sending me to Coventry when he dabs his eyes with the handkerchief that's been in his hand since we got into the car.

'When we met on Thursday you mentioned your missing sister to me. How long has it been since she was taken?'

I don't recall specifically telling him that Anna was missing, let alone that she may have been taken but I let it pass as I can't be certain with the dull ache remaining in my head. 'Twenty years.'

'I'm sorry,' he says, fixing me with a hard stare. 'Cassie's only been missing for a year; I can't imagine what it must be like to carry that pain for two decades. Alas, I don't think time will be a problem for me.' He takes a breath. 'I'm dying, Miss Hunter. The prognosis is that I may not see in the New Year. I feel responsible for what happened last year. I was the one who insisted we keep it out of the newspapers as I was terrified of the intrusion journalists would make in our lives. I've always been quite old-fashioned, believing it is better to wash one's dirty laundry out of the public eye. I couldn't see how sharing our tragedy with the wider world would help but as I see the end of the line rapidly approaching, I'm starting to question *every* decision I've ever made. I suppose that's par for the course. I can't help thinking that had I acted differently last year, the outcome would have been better.'

My heart goes out to him. 'For what it's worth, I don't think it would have made a difference, and I can understand why you didn't want journalists on your doorstep. If my past year has taught me anything, it's that fame and public recognition aren't what they're cracked up to be. At least in my case it served a greater purpose and ensured Freddie, Mike, and Steve got the justice they deserved.'

He tries to smile, but the pain remains in his dark and weary eyes. 'That's kind of you to say. Nevertheless, I see the effect it has had on Elizabeth and it kills me to think there's nothing I can do to fix her before I pass on. When I'm gone, there will be nobody there to keep her on the straight and narrow, and boy does she need that kind of support.'

I should probably tell him what she said about giving up

when that happens but I don't have it in me to add to his pain and terror. I should probably tell somebody, but it isn't my place to interfere and I don't know who I could tell other than her husband… and I'm not sure there's a lot he could do to prevent it in any case.

'Please, Miss Hunter, don't abandon us just yet. Finish reading the casefile, and if you still don't believe there is anything untoward, then I will release you from this duty and wish you on your way. As an incentive for finishing your work with me, I'd like to set up a charitable trust in your sister's name. I read recently that more than a hundred thousand children are reported missing every year in the United Kingdom. That statistic appals me, but when it happens to you – when it's one of your offspring taken – it feels like it is only you it is happening to. I'd like in some way to help those families who have experienced, or will experience, something like we've faced, after I'm gone. I will have my solicitor draw up the necessary paperwork, but I would like to have you appointed as one of the trustees, if you would do me the honour.'

The cynical part of my brain reminds me that this offer comes with the demand that I continue to look into Cassie's disappearance, but given all the good such a trust could do to suffering families, how can I not accept?

'I don't know what to say,' I murmur, my throat suddenly dry. 'That's very generous.'

'It's the least I can do. I want the riches I've accumulated to be put to better use once I'm gone. I've already promised Hobbs that he will be able to retire with an ample pension once I'm gone, as can Rosa. They've been with me for as long as I can remember and anyone able to put up with my mood swings deserves a happy retirement.'

I glance towards Hobbs in the front of the car but his shoulders remain straight, his eyes fixed on the road ahead.

'Okay,' I finally say. 'I am happy to accept your offer and I will return to the police station in the morning and continue to look through the file, but I can't make you any promises.'

He pats my hand, and the chill radiating off his fingers makes me shiver. 'I don't expect you to. Even concluding that everything was above board will bring some level of closure. Thank you, Miss Hunter.'

I take my cue to leave and exit the car, hurrying up the stairs to Rachel's flat without looking back. Using the spare key, I'm in through both doors within seconds and am surprised to find Maddie seated on the sofa bed, glass of wine in hand, while Rachel's face is glued to her tablet.

'Here she is,' Maddie declares with a sip of the wine, before tottering over to me. 'I was starting to worry you'd been kidnapped or something.' She laughs, but it lacks humour.

Rachel is next over, thrusting the tablet towards my face. 'Have you seen this? You're trending on Twitter.'

Her tone is bitter so I accept the tablet and scroll through the trending titles. I'm no social media expert; my profiles on Facebook, Twitter, and Instagram were created by Maddie in order to generate interest in the book, but I do understand how Twitter trends work. I can see my name listed alongside "Cassie", "Fitzhume", and "abducted".

'What on earth is all this?' I say, looking into Rachel's eyes for any kind of clue.

'Some Australian journalist called Ken Johnson has told the world that you've been hired to investigate the abduction of

Cassie Hilliard. After all you said to me about keeping quiet, I can't understand why you would tell some second-rate hack about it.'

I can't believe she thinks I have anything to do with this. Is this just her way of deflecting the blame? 'You think I told him? I thought *you'd* let something slip. He was waiting for me and Fitzhume when we left Richard Hilliard's townhouse.'

The hurt on her face tells me I've overstepped the mark.

'I'm sorry,' I say quickly, angry with myself for doubting my best friend. Fitzhume's assumption that it was Richard who leaked the news is probably more accurate.

Maddie clears her throat and as I turn to look at her, I see she's raised her arms as if she's preparing to restrain me. 'Don't be cross.'

My eyes widen as my aching brain connects the dots.

'I thought it would help generate a bit more publicity for *Monsters*. I've got my next call with Reflex Media about optioning the series on Tuesday and I thought it would strengthen our side of the negotiation.'

The red mist is descending. 'I can't believe you would do something like this, Maddie! I gave my word to Fitzhume that I would keep everything under wraps until some kind of progress had been made.'

'I'm sorry I didn't warn you first, but you hired me to manage the business end of your writing and that's what I'm doing. It's a bit of harmless publicity that will have your publisher *and* the public salivating for more. It's part of the long-term strategy for your career and in a year or so you'll see that I was right.'

I know there's probably some truth in what she's saying but it doesn't ease the sting. 'I haven't confirmed to you that I want you to have that meeting with Reflex Media yet. I haven't heard back from Freddie or the others about whether they're comfortable with their stories being played out on screen.'

'Relax, will you? I personally met with Mike, Steve, *and* Freddie this morning. I paid for them to come up to my office where we sat and discussed the proposal like grown-ups, and they all agreed to what's on the table. I offered them a cut of the sale of the rights to sweeten the deal and they have all signed to agree it.'

I can usually tell when Maddie is fibbing to flatter my ego or convince me she's right, but this time I can't trace any hint of deceit. I'm surprised Freddie agreed to meet with her without me present, but then he doesn't owe me anything so maybe I shouldn't be so surprised. If he, Mike, and Steve are happy for the series to be optioned, then I really don't have any recourse to disagree, though I'm not happy with the lack of control I seem to have over my life right now.

What I wouldn't give to be back in Weymouth, walking barefoot along the shore by the light of the autumnal moon.

Chapter Thirty-Four

THEN

Chalfont St Giles, Buckinghamshire

With the wind rustling the leaves in the thick branches over her head, Elizabeth Hilliard ploughed on through the forest, her boots squelching with every step along the uneven terrain. As a child, the woodland surrounding the country manor estate had terrified her. So dense, and stretching on for what had appeared an eternity, she had avoided it at all costs, particularly when night came and the darkness provided a thick veil over all of the forest's secrets.

What she'd never appreciated until now was just how picturesque it looked, the soggy leaves underfoot a beautiful palette of yellows, oranges, and browns. There was a real sense of the beckoning autumn whilst overhead a few leaves near the top clung to the last days of bright sunshine, retaining their green shade for as long as possible. The life of a leaf seemed so much easier: sprouting, growing, reaching maturity, and finally dying and falling to become mulch to encourage future trees and leaves. Why couldn't humanity adopt a similar approach? Why did life have to be so much more complicated? Whatever happened to people pulling together to make a better future?

It had been like that once; she was sure she could remember reading about it in history books. Yet somewhere down the line something had changed. Selfishness had crept in until this moment where everybody only seemed interested in what they could get for themselves. After all, that had to be the reason some heartless thugs had chosen to attack her car and snatch the most precious of jewels from her life.

Stopping, she took several deep breaths, determined to clear her mind of any ill will towards whomever was responsible for abducting Cassie; focusing on negativity and hatred would not help her. Besides, once she was reunited with Cassie only a few hours from now, the world would once more make sense. She resolutely believed that she would see her daughter again and the butterflies in her gut were desperately trying to burst free. Even now, just thinking about that photograph she'd clutched so tightly in Cassie's room, she could feel that unbreakable bond with her daughter.

'We're coming for you,' Elizabeth whispered, inhaling deeply before blowing the promise into the air, waiting for it to catch on the wind, to be carried all the way to wherever Cassie was waiting to hear it.

Her footing on the uneven ground slipped slightly and, looking down, she spotted the spiky husk of a conker. It was cracked open but the brown gem inside was still waiting for extraction. Carefully picking it up with gloved fingers, she cracked the shell wider and deposited the brown seed into her palm, running her thumb over the cool, smooth surface. Instantly she was transported back to a memory from her childhood, of conker picking with Hobbs. She couldn't have been much older than six or seven, and she'd been adamant she didn't want to set foot in the forest, but Hobbs had told her that she had nothing to be scared of, that he had been charged with protecting her, and would do so until his dying day. He'd extended his hand and she'd taken it, his bravery gripping her arms as he led her through the stumps.

He'd encouraged her to forage for conkers but had told her the key was to find those with a flat edge – cheese cutters he'd called them – as they made the deadliest of weapons in a conker battle. She'd gathered maybe a dozen conkers and he'd sifted through them, discarding most of them until he came across what he was looking for. Holding it up to the little light that had managed to penetrate the overhead cage of branches, he'd shown her just how sharp that flat edge was, and how with the right amount of force, it could break through even the toughest of opponents. He'd scooped the discarded conkers into a carrier bag and led her back to the main house. He'd used a gimlet to poke a hole into their chosen weapon and fed an old shoelace through, securing it with a knot at either side.

'This one is yours,' he'd said warmly, before lacing the remaining ten or so conkers, and lifting them up, one at a time. 'I want you to swing yours in an arc to crash into mine as hard and as quickly as possible. Go ahead, don't worry, it won't hurt.'

She'd followed his instruction, missing three times until he'd shown her a better technique. The flat-edged blade had torn through the first conker like a warm knife through butter, and she could now recall the thrill of excitement it had given her. She'd been bouncing around, eager to try again.

'Always remember, Elizabeth,' he'd told her when only

cracked fragments remained, 'you don't have to be the biggest or bravest to cut through your enemies, just the sharpest and most efficient. Never be afraid to be who you are. Promise me that.'

She had made a pinkie-promise, but in hindsight had never lived up to it. That would all change now. Today was her rebirth. Today was her chance to be the mother her daughter craved, and the daughter her father had wished for.

Her lungs bursting with fresh air, her soul rejuvenated, and the butterflies still fluttering, she marched purposefully back towards the house, the creative part of her brain seeing the large estate as less of a ball and chain around her neck and instead as somewhere she could turn into a proper family home. It was such an old-fashioned building, trapped in an era long forgotten, yet it had such potential to be so much more. Just like her. Just like that conker.

Richard was leaning against one of the pillars that framed the front door, one leg tucked beneath him, but standing proud on the other. A cloud of light grey smoke escaped his mouth as he exhaled the cigarette fumes. She'd known he had started smoking again – the smell on his clothes and breath was impossible to miss – but this was the first time she'd caught him in the act. She half-expected him to squash it under foot, but he didn't seem to care that she'd caught him; at least it would be one less secret between them.

'Where've you been?' he asked as she approached.

'I went for a walk,' she responded, not breaking her stride. 'I wanted to clear my head.'

He looked as though he could do with a clearer head, particularly with what was coming up, but then maybe it was easier for him to cope with the stress with alcohol in his system. Who was she to judge? God only knows how many times she'd sought solace in pills and alcohol that kept her mind shielded from harsh realities.

Not anymore, she thought, taking another deep lungful of air.

'The detective and his team are inside,' Richard said, instantly cutting through the positive energy she was trying to project. 'They reckon the kidnappers will phone imminently, and they want to hear everything that's said and attempt to run another trace on the call. They're probably wasting their time, but who am I to argue. At least they're trying.'

'And the money?'

He took one more drag on the cigarette before flicking it away into the distance, creating a small trail of sparks as it danced across the gravel pathway. 'All bagged up and ready to go. I never realised just how heavy that amount of money would be. It'll take at least two of them to carry it.'

The weight and value of the money didn't bother her at all; every penny would be well-spent to bring Cassie back safely. Right now, that was the only priority and she would have willingly given up everything – the house, the cars, the staff – just to hold her daughter again and breathe in her scent.

She stopped when she was no more than a foot away from him. 'What you said the other night, about having a plan to save Cassie *and* the money… I want you to forget about it. Okay? I don't want you doing anything to jeopardise her return.'

He glanced around nervously, as if the detectives inside were listening to every word. 'Keep your voice down, will you?'

You don't have to be the biggest or bravest to cut through your enemies, just the sharpest.

Fixing him with a hard stare, she shook her head. 'I am asking – no, I'm *telling* you – don't do anything to put Cassie's life at risk. I don't care about the money. I'd pay double to have her back. Do you hear me? Money can be replaced; our daughter can't be. So, whatever foolhardy idea you've been working on, I want your word that you will forget all about it.'

She pictured her conker smashing the others over and over again.

'I don't care about anything else you've done up until now, Richard. I'm prepared to put all of that behind us and start over, but I swear to God, if you do anything that threatens Cassie, I will…'

She didn't need to finish the sentence as he closed the gap between them, pulling her into his embrace and squashing her face against the rough woollen lapel of his overcoat. 'Okay, okay, I'll call them off. Okay? Just stop talking about it where people can hear.'

She wrestled her face free and looked up into his soft brown eyes. 'Promise me.'

He met her stare. 'I swear to you.'

Separating, she led the way back into the house, just as the phone began to ring in the drawing room.

Chapter Thirty-Five

NOW

Uxbridge, London

I'm not in the best of moods when I finally arrive at Uxbridge police station and I'm frustrated that it's almost half past eight. I hate being late for meetings. It literally makes my skin crawl. In my defence, it isn't my fault that the tube I was on broke down just outside of Sudbury Town and had to be moved before they could put us on an alternative one. And then, as the rain threw itself down, my phone's screen was blurry with water and it took me twice as long to get my bearings and follow the route to the station. Soaked to the bone – this supposedly waterproof jacket has not stood up to the challenge – I head into the station with a sense that today is not going to be my day.

Every passing minute is another chance to turn it all around, my dad would tell Anna and me whenever we were upset about something not going to plan. Peeling off the jacket, straightening my fringe in the reflection of the front door, I take a deep breath, clear my mind of negativity and approach the front desk.

'Hi,' I say, presenting my warmest and most self-assured smile at the officer behind the counter. 'I'm here to see PC Jack Serrovitz. I'm—'

'Oh, I know who you are, Emma,' the girl replies, her brace making her jaw look as though it's been mechanically wired. 'I loved your book,' she gushes. Her hair as red as fire.

'Thank you,' I reply, willing the impostor-syndrome voice in my head into submission. 'That's kind of you to say.'

She leans closer to the window. The lanyard she's wearing identifies her as Constable Denier. 'I probably shouldn't tell you this, but when I read about how those boys' allegations were ignored, and essentially covered up… well, let's just say it's not the first time I've heard of things like that happening in the force.'

She can't be any older than me and it worries me that in her relative inexperience she's already witnessed similar scenarios.

'It's why I wanted to become a police officer,' she adds, straightening. 'I figured it would be better to change attitudes from the inside. You know what I mean?'

Her outlook is refreshing and my frustration at a poor night's sleep is quickly forgotten.

'I know I probably shouldn't ask this,' she adds, 'but I've got my copy of your book in my locker; do you think you could sign it for me?'

I take a deep breath. 'I'd be happy to. I should be here most of the day so just stop by and I'll sign it for you.'

'Great! Who did you say you were here to see again?'

'Jack Serrovitz.'

Her smile is replaced by a heavy frown. 'Oh, I don't think I've seen him yet this morning. Give me a second and I'll phone downstairs and see if he came in the back way.'

She picks up the phone and places the call, leaving my gaze to wander around the small reception area. I take in the variety of coloured posters with warnings about pickpockets in the town centre, cyber bullying, and fraudulent telephone calls. Where are the warnings about keeping your children safe from predators who will look to destroy family bonds?

'Emma? It seems Jack hasn't arrived yet,' Constable Denier tells me, hanging up the phone. 'He should have been in at eight but no sign so far, I'm afraid. I guess he might be off sick. Did you have a meeting arranged with him?'

I grind my teeth at the possibility that I've just traipsed across West London and through driving rain for no reason.

Taking another deep breath, I am determined to keep my frustration in check. 'He told me to meet him here at eight. We're reviewing an old case, you see. Is there anyone else I can speak to? It's really important that I crack on with the review as I have deadlines and things.'

I don't want to mislead her, but the thought of being stuck in London for any longer than necessary is filling me with dread.

'I can see if anyone else is available. Is Jack the only person you've been working with or do you have any other contacts I can reach out to?'

The only other name I have is DCS Rawani, and I'm sure he has better things to do than babysit me, but perhaps he can at least grant permission for me to work alone in that room with the file. Ultimately, I'm not expecting to learn anything I don't already know, and as far as I'm concerned, this is a tick-box exercise.

'Can you check if DCS Rawani can sign me in? I'm sorry, he's the only other person I'm aware of connected with this particular case.'

Her face pales at the prospect of having to place the call to someone so senior. 'Give me a second,' she says, disappearing through the door behind her. Through the frosted glass, I can see her consulting a man in a crisp white shirt who's sitting behind a desk. I can't hear a word of what's being said, but I'm guessing she's checking with her colleague whether she will get in trouble for disturbing Rawani.

Denier and her colleague return to the counter a few moments later. The three stripes on the man's lapel tell me he is a sergeant of some kind. He has a thick silver moustache, which contrasts with his red cheeks. He asks me to repeat the purpose of my visit and so I tell him about the Cassie Hilliard case, Fitzhume's request, and Jack's support. He considers what I've said before telling Denier to escort me to one of the interview rooms and arrange for the papers to be brought down to me.

I'm relieved they haven't turfed me out. The sergeant returns to his desk while Denier leaves her room and buzzes me through the secured door, out into the corridor, and along to the room where Jack and I spent Saturday afternoon. She brings me a beaker of coffee from the vending machine and it's not long before I have the boxes in front of me once again. I sift through to find the file I stopped at.

There is a transcript of an interview with Gerry Connors,

undertaken in the hours after the failed exchange. The notes in the preamble to the transcript highlight that Connors has a criminal record as a result of a conviction for larceny when he was eighteen. It seems he was spotted fleeing the scene of the botched exchange and the investigative team were checking his story against the one fed to them by Richard Hilliard who was picked up at the same time. I locate a copy of the transcript of Richard's interview and compare the pages. Whilst both interviewers ask what the two men were doing so close to the scene despite being ordered to stay away, there is a noticeable difference in the tone of the questions. Richard's interview focuses on whether he'd had any involvement in the firefight that ensued between the kidnappers and the Albanian gangsters who arrived on the scene unannounced. Connors's interview, by contrast, focuses on his time in Northern Ireland, and whether he had any affiliation with the two kidnappers identified at the scene.

Both men protest their innocence and when pushed about what they were doing at the exchange, their accounts are almost word-for-word identical. Richard said he was there to watch that nothing happened to the bags of money prior to Cassie's return, and Connors confirmed that was why he was asked to drive Richard there. A cynic would argue collusion between the men, but two honest accounts of the same event would also bear trademark similarities. Regardless, this isn't news to me; Penny has already said that Gerry was asked to drive Richard to oversee the exchange.

Voices outside the door catch my attention and I'm sure I can hear Jack. Standing, I move closer, opening the door a crack to check.

'Nice of you to join us, PC Serrovitz,' I hear the silvermoustachioed sergeant saying sarcastically. 'Hope we didn't drag you away from anything too important?'

'Sorry, Sarge,' Jack says, just out of sight. 'I won't let it happen again.'

'What was it then? A heavy night?'

'You know me better than that, Sarge,' Jack replies jovially. 'I'm always in bed by ten on a school night.'

'Yeah, yeah, and the rest, Jack. I still remember what it was like to be young, free, and single, and in my twenties. I won't ask whose bed you were in last night.'

'Seriously, Sarge, it wasn't like that. The alarm didn't go off, and then it was a nightmare getting a certain someone out of bed, that's all.'

'Oh I see...' came the knowing reply. 'Blonde or brunette?'

I close the door, having heard enough. Returning to my seat, I pick up the interview notes but even though my eyes dance across the words on the page, I'm not taking them in.

I start as the door opens and Jack ploughs in, apologising for his late arrival and promising me he won't allow it to happen again.

'Good, I can see you've made a start with the files,' he says. 'How was the rest of your weekend?'

'Fine,' I reply through gritted teeth, keeping my eyes on the page I'm pretending to read.

'Good, good,' he says, failing to stifle a yawn. 'I'll just grab a drink and then I'll join you. You want anything from the machine?'

I tap the top of the beaker and shake my head. I don't look up until I hear the door close. This just won't do. What's wrong with me? I'm being childish, and for no reason whatsoever. I think of my father's words again and it is enough to rebalance my mind-set.

Maddie's name appears in the display of my phone and I answer.

'Morning, Emma. How is my favourite client this morning? Not still cross about yesterday, I hope?'

After much consideration during my tempestuous night's sleep, I can understand why Maddie leaked the story to Ken Johnson, but I do wish she'd asked me first. That way I could have told her that the story is dead in the water and there is every chance this will not become book two in the publishing contract. It feels like her actions have brought unnecessary attention.

'I'm fine, Maddie. What can I do for you?'

'Well, I thought I should phone and let you know straight away.'

I check my watch but it isn't even nine o'clock yet, so she can't have already had her meeting with Reflex Media about the optioning of *Monsters Under the Bed*.

'You'll never guess who I've just spoken to,' she continues.

'Unless you're about to tell me that Ryan Gosling wants to meet me, I'm not sure I want to know.'

'Ryan Gosling's too old for you, Emma. No, better than that anyway. I received a call from the prison governor at HMP Portland, and one of the inmates has asked you to come and visit him.'

HMP Portland stands on Portland Bill, overlooking Weymouth, and serves as a constant reminder that despite the idyllic scenery, there is a darker world out there.

'I don't know anyone in there,' I reply, shifting uncomfortably, my voice too bright.

'Maybe not, but someone knows you. It seems my work with Ken Johnson may yet bear fruit. A Mr Leroy Denton has told the governor that he has more information about the case and is finally ready to share it but will only speak to *you*. There's a chance he's about to reveal exactly who was behind the plot to abduct Cassie Hilliard.'

Chapter Thirty-Six

NOW

Uxbridge, London

'No way, absolutely not!'

DCS Rawani hasn't stopped pacing his tiny office since Jack and I knocked five minutes earlier and informed him that Leroy Denton wants to meet.

'You know what it'll be,' Rawani continues, no let-up in his pace. 'He'll have seen the stories in the press about you reviewing this case and he'll be thinking, *here's my chance for fifteen minutes of fame*, or some kind of cash pay-out. That'll be his motivation for suddenly coming forward. You're aware of that, aren't you?'

At first, I'm not sure which of us he's addressing. I look to Jack for support but he's hunched over, his gaze fixed on the almost bare carpet between his loafers.

'That's as may be,' I finally respond, when Rawani turns his attention to me, 'but I've not made any new progress just reading through the file. So far, your investigation turned over every stone looking for the truth, but you drew a blank when it came to discovering why Cassie was taken. What harm can it do to go and listen to what Denton has to say?'

'You mean apart from wasting time and generating unnecessary false hope?'

I'm not surprised there are so many threadbare patches in this carpet if pacing is Rawani's response to stress triggers. I can't really understand why Jack thought it necessary for us to come up here and ask for Rawani's permission. As far as I'm concerned – and based on what Maddie told me – the prison governor has agreed for Denton to see me. As Denton has already been convicted, I'm free to speak to him without police intervention. I could have not told Jack about the call and simply headed to HMP Portland alone tomorrow; part of me wishes I had done that instead. Out of professional courtesy, I thought it only right to tell Jack, but I didn't know this is where we would end up.

'He had ample opportunity to speak during the investigation,' Rawani continues. 'He was cautioned, offered legal representation, and asked open questions at interview. We asked him how he'd become embroiled in the kidnapping and ransom exchange, but he refused to say a dicky bird. The only two words he said throughout the process were "no comment"… and he said them *a lot*. Have you read through the transcripts of the interviews with him? We even suggested he might want to engage his solicitor to prepare a statement on his behalf but he refused even that. I don't think waterboarding would have got him to speak!'

It's always amazed me how common a 'no comment' interview is in the British justice system. I've always thought that if I was facing charges for something I hadn't done, I'd be fighting my way to prove my innocence rather than clamming up and allowing them to believe my silence represented guilt. What had happened to people being open and honest?

'At trial, his barrister mooted the possibility of Denton going on the stand to answer questions, but he flat-out refused that too! The only time he spoke in court was to confirm his identity. That man showed no remorse for his actions and even when sentence was passed, he didn't utter a word. Now, having been inside for the best part of a year, he suddenly grows a conscience and wants to come forward? It smells fishy to me.'

I don't disagree that the timing is suspicious and I'm almost certain contact wouldn't have been made with Maddie had she not leaked the story to Ken Johnson, but there's no point in worrying about any of that now. I understand why Maddie did what she did and whilst I don't agree with her choice of actions, her heart was in the right place… sort of. But if her decision leads to Denton shedding light on who was really responsible for the operation to abduct Cassie, then some good might yet come of it.

'What can you tell me about Denton?' I say. I've read the interview transcript and based on some of the questions that were asked, I have learned that Denton was a serving soldier in the army. But I still don't know how he ended up in the criminal justice system prior to the botched exchange; that detail wasn't included in the file.

Rawani considers me and the question, maybe trying to work out what angle I'm coming from, or maybe assuming that I'm just after background detail for a book.

'I just want to try and understand his motivation better,' I say in an effort to reassure him.

Rawani halts his pacing and drops into his chair across the desk from us. I'm relieved as I was starting to feel a bit nauseous watching him going backwards and forwards.

'Leroy Denton was dishonourably discharged from service in early 2016, allegedly for knocking out the front teeth of his superior officer. The victim decided not to press criminal charges but Denton suddenly found himself out in the cold. With no real qualifications, he struggled to secure employment. As can be the way in such cases, he turned to crime to pay the bills, and the rest is history.'

I'm certain there's more to Denton's backstory than the abridged version Rawani has offered, but he doesn't seem willing to offer any more, instead interlinking his fingers and resting them on the desk.

'How come Denton is in HMP Portland anyway? I thought the prison service tried to keep prisoners local to family, or at least close to wherever the crime occurred?

'He's from your neck of the woods,' Jack speaks up. 'Well, from Somerset somewhere. That's your sort of area, isn't it?'

My focus remains on Rawani. 'What about the man who was at the ransom with him… the guy who died… his partner?'

Rawani narrows his eyes. 'Oscar Gjoni? Also former military, though he wasn't dishonourably discharged like Denton. Not sure how the two came to meet. They didn't serve in the same unit, but perhaps they met overseas, as both completed tours in Afghanistan around the same time. It was hard to get hold of their records; military intelligence is not quite so willing to share their secrets. Gjoni was definitely the brains of the operation though.'

It's quite a bold statement to make, particularly given that Denton refused to cooperate with the investigation.

'And that is based on…?'

Rawani fires a disbelieving look at Jack who is no longer hunched over. Why do I feel like the new girl in class who's just asked a question with an answer obvious to everyone else?

'Denton left school at sixteen with barely a handful of GCSEs to his name. He was an army brat, so he naturally followed in his father's footsteps and joined up. He's not the sharpest tool in the box, if you follow my meaning. The level of planning that went into the attack… someone like Denton wouldn't be capable of that level of ingenuity, even if he'd spent his entire military career in specialist tactical training. There had to be someone else pulling the strings, and Gjoni fits that mould: educated at Cambridge, his military career was fast-tracked, and most of his time *was* spent in specialist tactical training. It was his job to plan and lead incursions into enemy territory with the littlest fuss in order to achieve an objective as efficiently as possible. Sound familiar?'

Jack spoke at length about the planning and precision that must have gone into the attack on the Hilliards' car on that tight stretch of road we viewed on Saturday. It's not unreasonable to assume that Gjoni's experience would make him a key player in how it went down.

'When you take into account that the barn full of supplies we located the morning after the abduction, which made us think we were hot on their trail, turned out to be a smokescreen sending us in a different direction, you can't conclude anything but Gjoni being the ringleader.'

I accept their conclusion but it still leaves an open question in my head. 'Why did he do it though?'

Rawani looks puzzled. 'What do you mean?'

'Well, you said Denton was down on his luck, struggling for money and so turned to a life of crime. It's not unreasonable to assume that a job like this probably would have paid well. At the very least, a share of a two-million-pound pot of gold would be enticing. But where's Gjoni's motivation? Just the money again? It strikes me that someone who could afford to be educated at Cambridge mustn't be short of a bob or two. So why did he risk it all to abduct Cassie and then demand that ransom? If his military career was as decorated as you suggest, it doesn't fit together logically in my head.'

I catch Jack nodding beside me.

Something flickers past in Rawani's expression but I can't tell if he's impressed or irritated. It disappears in the blink of an eye. 'Gjoni died at the scene so we weren't able to ask him that and, as I've said, Denton was less than forthcoming. What does it matter? We know he was involved. He was the one who took hold of the money at the exchange; his fingerprints were recovered from the van used to abduct Cassie to begin with. I have no doubt in my mind that he was responsible. Who am I to guess what motivates a criminal to break the law? Criminals are stupid and do stupid things. That's enough for me. What happened to Cassie Hilliard and her family was horrific, a genuine tragedy that I wouldn't wish upon my worst enemy. The people responsible were caught and the appropriate action taken, and whilst we failed to successfully bring Cassie home, I feel we did our job to the best of our ability. And that goes for me and my entire investigative team.'

His eyes apologise for the raised voice.

I take a moment to gather my thoughts, determined to get

the words straight before I speak them. 'With all due respect, detective, that isn't enough for Lord Fitzhume and the Hilliards. None of them have been able to move on from what happened last year, and whilst there should be some comfort in knowing that Gjoni is dead and Denton behind bars, they deserve more. Why was Cassie abducted that day? Why was *she* targeted? Sure, Fitzhume is rich, but there are richer men in the UK. Yes, he's loosely related to royalty, but there are other families with closer connections to the royals, and besides, this doesn't feel like a politically motivated attack. So why them, and why Cassie? We know the who, the what, the how, and the when, but the most important question in any mystery is the *why,* and that's what I'm determined to discover for that family.'

It's only when I look down that I see how tightly my hands are gripped around the arms of my chair; my knuckles are white.

'Very well,' Rawani finally says, 'go and meet Denton, but keep in mind that his motivation for speaking now isn't out of goodwill. He'll be playing an angle of some kind.'

Again, I recall not needing his permission, but in a way I'm glad I've managed to argue my point.

'I'll send Jack down there with you.'

Jack sputters to life. 'Wh-wh-what?'

'That really isn't necessary,' I say at the same time. 'I don't think it was an open invitation; Denton is only expecting me to show up.'

Rawani is smiling wryly now. 'If he's about to share information relevant to the investigation, then I want to know what it is. If he wants his fifteen minutes of fame, then this is the price he'll have to pay.'

I'm not convinced Denton will see it that way and I can imagine him refusing to speak to either of us with Jack there, but I'm not prepared to throw away my chance of getting home sooner.

'I'll be heading back there this afternoon,' I say forthrightly, facing Jack, who is still squirming awkwardly. 'I can give you the names of some hotels that won't rip you off.'

'I have plans for tonight, sir, that I can't break,' Jack finally says. 'If you're happy for me to do so, then I'll drive down first thing in the morning.'

'Agreed,' Rawani concludes, as if I'm no longer in the room. 'We don't have a budget for hotels anyway.'

'If you give me your address, I can pick you up on the way,' Jack offers.

It's like I'm suddenly ten years old again and I'm due to have a friend visit my home for the first time; feelings of panic tear through my mind at the prospect of Jack seeing where I live and judging me as a result.

'It's okay, I'll meet you at the prison,' I reply quickly, hoping he doesn't insist.

'Sure, okay, whatever.'

'Then it's settled,' Rawani declares, looking unusually pleased with himself. 'But mark my words: the only reason Leroy Denton has decided to sing at last is because there's something in it for him. I bet his first question will be how much you'll be willing to pay for his song.'

Chapter Thirty-Seven

THEN

Chalfont St Giles, Buckinghamshire

Elizabeth didn't recognise the old drawing room where she'd often sat playing at her father's feet, while he read one periodical or another. In one corner, nearest the bay window, DCS Rawani was hunched over a laptop, headphones stretched over his turban, with two men clad in black beside him, equally focused on whatever was on the screen. In the other corner, a large speaker system had been tentatively balanced on one of the smaller coffee tables and the piercing ringtone it was emitting echoed off the old walls. Everyone here had a purpose, save for Elizabeth and Richard; they were merely bystanders as the suffocating scene played out around them.

Elizabeth hurried over to her father, dropping to the floor and pressing her head into his knees, grateful to feel his big, warm hand stroking the top of her head just as he had done the day he'd had to tell her she would never see her mother again. She just wanted it all to be over so she could have Cassie back and prove herself to be the mother she knew she could be. The ringtone sounded again, startling her, but she kept her head where it was, not wanting to be within touching distance of the speaker.

'Should I…?' Richard began, his face as pale as a sheet.

Rawani removed his headphones and nodded. 'Remember, we need them to give us the location of the exchange as soon as possible so we can start gathering intelligence. Try and stay calm. Think of this as any standard business transaction. Cassie is the antique, and you've already agreed the price. Just get your daughter home.'

Richard's wide-eyed stare at his wife sent a shiver through her but she did her best to offer a reassuring smile.

'It'll be okay,' a gruff-sounding voice came from behind Fitzhume.

Adjusting her head, Elizabeth looked on in awe as Hobbs wheeled himself out of the shadows. The large plaster cast dominated his arm, making it poke out at an odd angle, but there was no sign of the chest bandages she'd witnessed in the hospital; these were probably covered by his pristine white shirt and purple cravat.

'Hobbs! What are you doing here?' she asked, but as soon as she saw his shining eyes in the crackling firelight, she knew all she needed to know: he was family, and in times of strife, families stick together.

The ringtone sounded again but this time was interrupted by the click of the connection as Richard accepted the call. 'H-h-hello?' he stammered, his throat dry.

'You are to bring the two million pounds to the Fernbush abattoir, off Woodlands Avenue in Reading. We know you've involved the police so we will be checking the bags for surveillance tracking devices and paint bombs. If you ever want to see your daughter again, make sure we don't find anything that shouldn't be there. You have one hour.'

'W-w-wait,' Richard stammered. 'Wait, I want to speak to Cassie.'

There was a pause on the line. 'No.'

'I want to hear her voice again, or there will be no money.'

Elizabeth stared wide-eyed at her husband and even Rawani was eyeing him suspiciously.

'You've had proof of life. You will see her at the exchange.'

'No,' Richard said staunchly, closing his eyes so he wouldn't have to see his wife's glare, though he could feel it burning through his eyelids. 'For all I know, you've already killed her. You put her on the phone now or there will be no money.'

Rawani cut through the room in an instant, reaching to snatch the handset from Richard.

'Wait,' the voice on the speaker said, before the sound of ruffling echoed around the room.

'D-D-Daddy?'

Elizabeth groaned in anguish, her eyes filling instantly. 'We're coming for you, baby,' she tried to say, but only her lips moved.

'Angel? It's Daddy. Listen to me, we're coming to get you, okay? Do you remember what I told you to do when you're scared? We're coming for you, princess.'

'Enough,' the kidnapper's voice cut off. 'You want the girl; we want the money. You bring the money to the abattoir in one car. You hear me? *One car.* If we see any more than that, the deal is off, and you'll never see your daughter again.

If we see any other vehicles hanging around the area, the deal is off. You fuck with us and your little girl is gone forever.'

The speaker banged as the phone at the other end was slammed down. Rawani turned back to his colleagues who offered glum shakes of the head.

'They scrambled the line again,' Rawani confirmed.

Elizabeth couldn't control her anger any longer, striding to where Richard was still holding the speaker's handset. 'How could you?' she screeched, slapping his arms.

He remained statuesque, accepting each blow, tottering as each venomous strike was delivered. 'I had to know,' he said resolutely.

It was enough for her to stop, accepting that she too had been relieved to hear Cassie's sweet, angelic voice. Richard had taken a chance – a reckless chance – delivering an ultimatum, but they'd conceded and agreed. Did that mean something? The fact that they'd obliged his request… did that mean that they really had no foul intentions towards Cassie? Were all their threats to harm her just bluffs?

'I want to take the money there,' Richard declared, as if he had any say in the matter.

'No,' Rawani answered dispassionately. 'One of my men will drive the money to the site and complete the exchange. It's too dangerous for you to be involved, Mr Hilliard. I couldn't vouch for your safety if anything went wrong. Leave this to the professionals; it's what we're trained to handle.'

'Why would anything go wrong?' Hobbs said croakily from his wheelchair beside Fitzhume. 'They said any funny business and they will kill Cassie.'

Elizabeth and Richard stared Rawani down, suddenly

questioning whether his actions could put Cassie's life in danger.

'There won't be any funny business,' he replied. 'We'll remove the tracking devices and dye packs from the bags as instructed and we will focus our surveillance efforts on long-range equipment. We'll use overhead drone footage to monitor their vehicle, or vehicles, as they leave the site. We have a helicopter and armed response units on standby for when the exchange has occurred. They won't see us until Cassie is safely in our custody. Okay?'

Elizabeth didn't know if that was okay or not. The gang had shown they were tactically aware, so didn't that mean they might pre-empt such a response? What if they had someone on the inside who could tip them off about the helicopter and waiting response cars? Or did that only happen in the movies? Her head was abuzz with questions, and pain, all her judgements clouded by the prospect that none of what was about to unfold was within her control.

She looked to Richard for support, but his vision was fixed on some distant spot, the motors turning behind those dark eyes. She couldn't read what he was thinking. She'd been forthright with him on the doorstep and he'd promised he wouldn't do anything to jeopardise Cassie's safe return, but had he changed his mind again?

'Scooter, come and meet Mr and Mrs Hilliard,' Rawani said, beckoning one of his colleagues over.

The young black officer stood to attention beside his boss. The skin around his eyes was taught and his manner was like a coiled spring.

'DC Scooter Ingleby will be the officer who delivers the money and collects Cassie for you. He is an expert weapons-trained officer, and the best driver we have in the Met. As soon as he has Cassie, he will hightail it out of there and get her medical treatment. I would trust this man with my life and the lives of my children. You can put the same level of faith in him.'

The officer nodded at them both. Words were not required. He would risk his life to save their daughter's, and in the next sixty minutes he would be the most important person in their futures. He wore the burden with pride and resoluteness.

'We've got aerial footage of the abattoir,' the remaining officer called out, Scooter leading Rawani back to the laptop. 'It's from Google, so could be out of date, but we'll get a helicopter to do a fly-by as soon as possible. So we have faster intelligence we can rely on while the drone comes into range.'

'That needs to happen ASAP,' Rawani confirmed. 'For all we know, they're already at the abattoir monitoring the site for unusual activity.'

'The abattoir is fifty minutes from here, sir, so we'd better get moving,' Scooter confirmed.

Rawani checked his watch and nodded. He turned back to Richard and Elizabeth, taking their hands in his. 'We will get Cassie back, I swear. She is my number one priority. Once she's safe, we'll go after the money and the men responsible for this.'

Elizabeth felt reassured but Richard made no acknowledgement of the statement. They watched on as the four large transparent sacks were carried out of the room by Rawani's colleagues, with him following closely behind.

'We'd better go too,' Richard said quietly to Gerry who had been standing at the back of the room.

'No, Richard,' Elizabeth chided. 'You promised.'

He rested his hands on her upper arms and stared deeply

into her eyes. 'I'm not going to do anything, I swear, but I need to be there when it happens. I want to make sure that Rawani and his team don't screw things up. All I want is Cassie back safely. I no longer give a stuff about the money. Like you said, we can always make more money.'

'What if they see you though?'

'We'll park out of sight. Trust me, Elizabeth. Nothing is going to go wrong. I will bring Cassie back home. You have my word.'

Kissing her cheek, Richard peeled away, with Gerry trotting behind, and both men disappeared through the door.

Deathly silence fell across the room.

Elizabeth had never wanted time to pass as rapidly as she did right now, but something told her the next hour would be the longest of her life.

Chapter Thirty-Eight

NOW

Weymouth, Dorset

Dorothy in *The Wizard of Oz* was right: there is no place like home. The velvety feel of the duvet as it brushes against the skin of my legs, the way the mattress effortlessly curves around my torso, like we were made for each other, and the sound of seagulls just beyond the window sharing the latest gossip is all tempered by the crashing waves.

I could stay where I am all day, if it wasn't for the 9am appointment at HMP Portland, which is a short taxi ride away. I realise now that Jack was just trying to be kind when he offered to pick me up this morning, and I had just panicked as soon as he suggested it. It had reminded me of being a child and having a friend from school come round for the first time. I wasn't ashamed of where I lived, but there was always anxiety about whether my home and family would appear *normal* to other people. That feeling has never really left me, even though

Maddie and Rachel have both visited my small flat, and neither has expressed any distaste.

Why should I care what Jack thinks about my town and home anyway? It's a question that troubles me, and one I can't immediately answer, nor dismiss. He's not a friend, or anyone I need to impress. When I look back on my life, he'll probably be barely more than a footnote, and once I'm finished with the Cassie Hilliard case, I'll probably never see him again. He must think I'm aloof, having twice rejected his offers of friendship.

Pushing back the duvet, I arch my back as I stretch the last of the fatigue from my aching muscles. It was after ten by the time I got home last night, after train delays disrupted the journey. I'd felt immediately ready to crash out in bed, but the second I stepped in through the door and caught sight of the photograph of Anna that hangs in the hallway and serves as a reminder of my life's mission, there was only one thing I wanted to do. Logging in to the missingpeople.org site, I had to rub my eyes when I saw the message box indicator flashing. Having not been on the site during my time in London, the overwhelming guilt that I had managed to miss a potential clue was almost paralysing. With the cursor hovering over the message button, I'd held my breath as I opened it, only to discover it was an invoice for webhosting from the parent site.

Part-relieved, part-frustrated, I spent the next two hours reviewing the published case history, tightening the words, rearranging the key facts so the most salient detail would be read first. With all the attention my book's success has brought, I'd hoped the knock-on effect would see more visitors to Anna's page, with someone – *anyone* – able to shed a fraction more light on what really happened, or where she might be now.

Seven hours in my perfect bed, and I feel refreshed and ready for a new day. I'm rejuvenated after the past few days in London, and whether this meeting with Leroy Denton pans out, or ends up a waste of our time, I'm home, and I could happily never return to London. Rachel's disappointed face flickers into my mind's eye. She wasn't happy when I broke the news that I'd be heading back here so soon. Despite my previous protestations, I think she was starting to believe that I really could leave all of this behind and start a new life in London as she has done. I love her to bits, but we're quite different in our approaches to life, and I think it's those differences that allow us to integrate so well together. I am the yin to her yang.

Washing and dressing, I'm ready to leave by eight, when the doorbell sounds. I'm not expecting visitors, but I did drop Freddie a message that I was back and asking if he fancied meeting for a proper catch-up one evening this week. Of course, it would be typical of Freddie to take that as an invitation to bring coffee and pastries around for breakfast. Despite Maddie assuring me that he and the others are on board with the optioning of *Monsters Under the Bed,* I can't help but feel he's been pressured into it by both Maddie and me. I know I wouldn't want to see *my* life being played out on the screen. Not again.

Opening the front door, the breath catches in my throat when I see Jack Serrovitz in his navy uniform, mid-yawn.

'Oh, thank God I found the right place,' he says, covering his mouth to catch the last of the yawn. 'Not very well numbered, the flats and houses in this street, are they?'

I don't know what to say first. The feelings of anxiety rush to my head, covering the concern that he has somehow managed to track me down despite my explicit instruction not to come.

'You never said you lived so close to the beach,' he adds, turning to look out towards the shoreline. 'It's nice here, isn't it?'

'I thought we were meeting at the prison,' I say as casually as I can manage with heat in my cheeks.

'Yeah, I know,' he says, his gaze returning to my face, 'but I made good time on the way down here and figured as I was early it was just as easy for us to go together. That *is* all right, isn't it? Sorry, I didn't mean to intrude. Your boyfriend or husband isn't about to come out here and lump me for whisking you away, is he?'

Grabbing my bag, I close the front door so he can't get a better look inside and so he won't be tempted to invite himself in for a coffee. 'Not much chance of that.'

'Oh, good,' he says, before quickly adding, 'it would be embarrassing to have to arrest your boyfriend for assault. Is the prison far from here?'

'It's about ten minutes to the island and then another five to the prison, I think. We have loads of time.'

He opens the front passenger door of the patrol car he's travelled down in and holds it open for me to get in before joining me inside. 'Have you got some kind of identification on you? Driving licence? Passport? You'll need it to get into the prison.'

Reaching into my bag, I pull out my passport and show it to him. 'The prison governor told my agent about all the requirements. Apparently, normal visiting hours aren't until after lunch, but morning sessions are reserved for legal visits and that's why he's organised for us to go in this morning.'

'Good to know. DCS Rawani has squared it with the governor for me to be there, though I don't know if Denton's been informed yet.' He starts the engine and pulls out into the road, following the signs for Portland. 'I wanted to apologise about yesterday,' he says after a few minutes. 'About my late arrival at work, and then not taking you up on your offer of hotels for last night. The thing is...' He takes a deep breath; I don't think I've exhaled since he arrived. 'My daughter won a poetry competition at school and we'd already arranged to go out for a meal together to celebrate. I didn't want to disappoint her.'

My heart sinks. 'Oh, I see. Well that's okay. I wouldn't expect you to disrupt your plans with your daughter.'

'We're not together, by the way,' he says suddenly. 'Her mother and I, I mean. Chrissie and I were high-school sweethearts. We thought we were in love when Mila was conceived, but we were both too young really. We tried to make it work, but not everything goes to plan, does it? That's why I was late to work yesterday morning. Mila stayed at mine on Sunday night but she refused to get out of bed until I promised she could have pancakes for breakfast.'

The overheard conversation plays in my mind: *it was a nightmare getting a certain someone out of bed.*

'How old is Mila?'

'Six; she'll be seven on Christmas Eve.'

'Same age as Cassie Hilliard then.'

'Yeah, so I can imagine how hard it must have been for her parents to cope with losing her. I don't know what I'd do if anyone ever...' He pauses again. 'Her mum and I are still friends, which is great, and we take it in turns to have Mila. You hear of so many separated couples that can't stand to be in the same room as one another, but we made a pact to keep things as normal for Mila as possible. It's not always easy, but she's my number one priority. You know?'

Jack doesn't look old enough to have a six-year-old daughter, but this new side to him is not unexpected. Maybe there have been clues in things he's said over the last couple of days that my subconscious has picked up on.

'You've gone all quiet,' he says. 'Sorry, I wasn't going to mention Mila to you yet, but I didn't want you to think I wasn't taking you or this case review seriously. Mila is everything to me, but when she's at school or at her mum's, this job is everything else. Mila is the reason I stepped down from being a detective; I didn't want a job that would keep me out at odd hours and potentially disrupt my ability to be a reliable dad. When I spoke to the DCS about it, he put me forward for this cold-case review role, and the rest is history. It's great as it allows me to still use my detective's logic, but lets me maintain a more regimented shift pattern.'

I'm not sure why he's suddenly so keen to pour his soul out to me, but I appreciate him trusting me enough to be honest.

'It sounds complicated,' I empathise.

He smiles that goofy grin. 'Life wouldn't be so much fun if everything was easy now, would it?'

The rest of the journey passes in comfortable silence and the car buffets in the wind as we cross the long, narrow bridge to the island of Portland. The small town centre, which always resembles something straight out of the history books, is littered with weathered shop fronts and not the usual high street names you would find in larger towns or cities. We turn before reaching the town, however, climbing the steep and twisty hill, detached and terraced houses either side of us. If it weren't for the signs, you'd never guess all this normality led to a Class-B prison.

Finally, we arrive at the top of the peak where the signs warn that only authorised personnel are to pass through the narrow tunnel up ahead. The high prison wall dominates the skyline, keeping those inside trapped, and those outside protected. It's been years since I've been up here… not since Dad was found hanging inside.

I'm grateful that Jack is with me to explain to the prison guards why we're here and that the governor is expecting us. Once our identification has been verified, we're escorted in through the secured doors, with each slammed shut behind us. The sound reverberates off every wall, reminding me that we're now trapped inside too. My pulse is racing by the time we're escorted into a square room with three chairs and a table in the middle. I don't know what I was expecting, but I thought there would be some kind of barrier between us and Denton. It seems we will all be in the same room, breathing the same air.

It's only now that I'm acutely aware of just how out of my depth I am here. What if Denton takes issue with something I say and reacts violently? It's too late to change my mind, however, as a moment later, the door at the opposite side of the room is unlocked and the large figure enters in grey jogging bottoms and a sweatshirt. He smirks as our eyes meet but grimaces when he spots Jack beside me. I'm expecting him to kick off but instead, he waits patiently for his handcuffs to be removed, before pulling out the chair across the table from us.

The table shakes as he lands on the chair. He rests his elbows on the surface, revealing tattoos on his thick, chapped knuckles. 'Thanks for coming,' he grunts. 'I'm a big fan of yours, Emma.'

I've never hated the sound of my own name as much as I do hearing it come out of his mouth. 'M-m-my agent said you had some additional information about Cassie Hilliard that you wanted to share,' I stutter, my throat suddenly dry.

'That's right,' he sneers. 'I heard you're writing a book about her abduction and I can offer you something that nobody else can: the truth about why she was taken.'

My anxiety evaporates as my interest is piqued. 'Go ahead, Mr Denton. I'm listening.'

He scowls in Jack's direction again. 'The first thing you need to know is that it wasn't my operation. I wasn't in charge, right? I was hired to help out Gjoni, but it was his gig. He was the one pulling all the strings.'

'Why did he want to take Cassie?'

'All I know is that he was paid to snatch her. We was introduced by an associate, and Gjoni knew I could handle myself, so he said he'd pay me to help him. Times was tough. A man's gotta do what a man's gotta do, you know? So I agreed. I didn't know the shit that was going to go down at that abattoir. He wasn't expecting it neither, but at least I lived to tell the tale.'

Reaching into my bag, I pull out my notepad and pen. 'Do you know who hired Gjoni for the job?'

Denton fixes me with a broad smile. 'We'll come to that, but before we do, you should know… I wasn't the only ex-con Gjoni hired to pull off this job.'

Chapter Thirty-Nine

NOW

Portland, Dorset

The private room has taken on a sudden chill, and I can feel goosebumps rapidly gathering on my arms. Denton doesn't seem to notice the drop in temperature, so maybe I'm just imagining it.

'I never did understand that about you lot,' Denton now sneers at Jack. 'You arrested me, but you didn't realise what was going on right in front of you. You seemed so willing to accept that it was just me and Gjoni involved.'

Jack tenses in my periphery. 'I wasn't involved in the original investigation,' he fires back, 'but from what I've read you weren't exactly chatty when it came to interview. Why now? What's made you change your tune? Do you really expect us to believe a single word of what you're going to tell us a year later? Why should we?'

'Believe it, or don't believe it,' Denton snarls, 'makes no odds to me; I'm just doing what's right.'

Jack starts to chuckle. 'Oh, I hadn't realised you'd suddenly grown a conscience inside. Why didn't you say? Oh, of course, now we'll pay attention to this so-called accomplice who you've been dreaming up for the last twelve months.'

Jack's attitude is starting to irritate me and I want to tell him to ease up or we're going to lose Denton's testimony. Clearly he's trying to push Denton's buttons – maybe in an effort to get him to say more than he'd intended – but at the moment he's in danger of causing Denton to clam up and dismiss us altogether.

Denton turns his attention back to me. 'The story I read online said you'd been hired to find out the truth about what happened to that little girl.'

'To Cassie, yes,' I reply, ready to take on the 'good cop' cliché if that's how Jack wants to play this.

Denton's face contorts momentarily at the mention of her name. Despite Jack's reservations, I'm starting to believe there may be an element of conscience and regret there.

'Her family want to know why she was taken and why things went so horribly wrong at the exchange,' I continue. 'The police were ready to hand over the money; Cassie's family thought they would see her again. What went wrong?'

'The abattoir was Gjoni's idea. Said he'd been there before. It was an army training camp or something. The place had been out of business for years but nobody seemed to want to buy the land. Maybe they were spooked by the possibility of dead pig ghosts haunting the site or something. I don't know. Anyway, he said it would be the ideal location to do the exchange as it had good links in and out of Reading. Close to the motorway, and, more importantly, a network of caves beneath the ground.'

'Caves?'

'Tunnels essentially. There's loads of them exist beneath the hills of Berkshire, from Tudor times when the Catholics had to worship in secret. They would use the tunnels to come together and pray before sneaking back to towns and hamlets under the cover of the ground. A lot of the tunnels are gone now of course. Land gets bought and redeveloped, but every now and again a bit of land is discovered with a full working network still intact. The abattoir had that.' He looks pointedly at Jack. 'And your lot had no bloody clue! I saw them searching inside the buildings but they totally missed the secret entrance leading underground.'

Jack has quietened and is now leaning slightly further forwards, eager to listen.

'Who was the other person in the gang?' I ask, returning to Denton's earlier statement.

'A nine-fingered fella called Hank Amos.'

My eyes widen at mention of Amos's name. 'The man Elizabeth Hilliard identified from a mugshot?'

Denton rubs the fuzz of hair covering his jawline. 'Yeah, we had a good laugh about that at the time. He was there when we disabled that car of theirs and grabbed the girl. He was supposed to wait in the van with Gjoni while I collected her, but the twat got carried away and raced me to the car. And of course she – the mother – was able to tell the police that a nine-fingered man had taken Cassie. As soon as Gjoni learned that news, he cut Amos free. Secured him an alibi in return for his silence. But then Gjoni got spooked the day before the exchange and invited Amos back into the fold.'

'Spooked in what way?'

'I don't know what happened really. Gjoni played his cards

close to his chest most of the time. He was the one in control and we were just his well-paid lackeys. In fairness, he did seem to know his shit. But on the morning of the exchange, something changed. He'd been coolness personified but then he received a phone call and he looked panicked. I asked him if it had been from the person who'd hired him but he never liked to talk about any of that. Next thing I knows, Amos is back at the site where we was holding the girl, and the plan changed.'

'Why come forward now, Leroy?' I ask, hoping that using his first name will convince him that I'm not a threat. 'Had you told the police about Amos's involvement when you were arrested, your sentence might have been reduced.'

'I'm no grass. Gjoni made it clear what would happen to us and our families if we came clean, and believe me when I say I had no doubt he would follow through on his threats.'

'Oscar Gjoni was caught in the crossfire and died at the scene. Why did you still stay silent?'

'Men like Gjoni are methodical planners. He was military intelligence for pity's sake! I had no idea who he was working for, nor what they might do if I started chirping, so I kept myself to myself, trusting that he would take care of my missus and my kids, as he'd said he would. Then Amos turns up here a couple of weeks after I was sentenced. He tells me he managed to get away and he'll make sure my missus is taken care of. He promised to send her monthly subs in exchange for my silence. It wasn't a request… I knew I would be doing time and if I gave him up, the reduction in my sentence wouldn't be huge so I agreed to keep quiet on the promise that he would live up to his end of the bargain. But that shitbag has done a runner and my missus ain't had a penny for two months. I was weighing up whether to reach out to the police when I heard about your involvement and decided you were my best shot at getting things sorted.'

I'm reminded of what DCS Rawani said in his office yesterday afternoon: *the only reason Leroy Denton has decided to sing at last is because there's something in it for him.*

'I don't know what it is you think I can do for you, Leroy. I don't have any sway or influence over probationary hearings or retrials.'

'I read your book,' he says. 'Got no time for nonces who do those sorts of things to kids. Parasites, the lot of them. But you managed to track them down and get justice for their victims. I've got a lot of respect for you, Emma. You see beyond what most can. To anyone else, that Freddie Mitchell was just some tramp who'd fallen on hard times, but you saw the human being. When this guy here looks at me, he sees a criminal who was fairly kicked out of the army, but I'm more than just my poor choices. In some ways, I'm a victim too. It was desperation that put me on a collision course with Gjoni, and once I was involved, he wouldn't let me out alive. I had no fucking idea we was going to abduct that girl until it was too late; and I certainly had no idea he'd hire a load of Albanians to come and deliberately mess up the exchange to confuse the police.'

Jack chokes on some saliva as he erupts into a coughing fit. 'Gjoni hired the Albanians?' he asks hoarsely when he's composed himself again.

'That's what I said, wasn't it?'

'So you knew they were going to come and open fire?' Jack questions. 'We believed they were there because of Richard Hilliard, Cassie's father.'

'I had no fucking clue that they would have guns and start shooting at us. All Gjoni had said was he'd planned to use a decoy to aid our escape into the tunnels, so that the police would be chasing their tails.

'The four of us arrived at the abattoir in the van: me up front with the driver, Amos and Gjoni in the back keeping the girl quiet. We waited there for twenty minutes before we saw the unmarked police car pull into the site. I'd never been more scared my whole life, despite two tours of Afghanistan. The exchange should have been simple. The plan was to show the girl to the police, him to show us the bags of money, and then for Gjoni to lead her to the midway point and swap over. The Albanians weren't supposed to turn up until the money was in the van, at which point we'd drop out of the back of the van into the brick building where the tunnel entrance was, out of sight of any helicopters the police might have had waiting.

'Gjoni got the girl out so the officer could see her and then he put her back in the van, telling me to go and check the money hadn't been tampered with. You ever seen that much money? It made me dizzy. I was terrified the black copper would cuff me there and then, but I also knew that if I deviated from the plan, Gjoni would go after my family, so I did as I was told. I helped the copper carry the four bags to the midway point between the vehicles, and had just started to walk back to the van, when the two cars screeched into the site, bullets whizzing left, right and centre. I dived out of the way, but Gjoni got struck, and dropped like a lead balloon.'

He pauses, his eyes misting as he stares out of the window behind us. 'Next thing I know, the van explodes in this ball of fire. One of the bullets must have struck the petrol tank or something. The Albanians hightailed it out of there and I didn't know what to do – not that I had much time to worry about it, as some copper landed on my back a moment later and cuffed me. To this day, I honestly don't know what happened, or why.'

Reaching into my bag, I hand Denton a tissue from a packet. 'Do you think it was Amos who betrayed you? Maybe he got to the Albanians and changed the plan?'

'No. The only reason that weasel survived is his natural instinct to run and hide when the shit hits the fan. When he came to see me here that first time, he told me how he'd made it out of the van seconds before it exploded and managed to get away through the tunnels. Lucky bastard.'

He pauses again and fixes me with a hard stare. 'The thing is, he wasn't the only one to escape the van before it went up. The only reason he left his post was because the girl got free. He charged after her into that building.'

Chapter Forty

THEN

Chalfont St Giles, Buckinghamshire

'Sir? We're here.'

Gerry's voice was distant, almost as if he was sitting in a totally different room. They couldn't be back already. It was only a blink ago when the scene before them had been lit up with blue flashing lights, swarms of black insect-like people scurrying to and from the burning hulk of what had been a van only minutes earlier. No, not *a* van, *the* van. From their lofty viewpoint at the summit of a hill, they'd been looking directly at the front of the van, not that it had been possible to make out any of the characters behind the glass. They'd watched the entire scene unfold, like some sick drive-thru movie without the benefit of sound. They'd watched the unmarked police car – driven by DC Scooter Ingleby – pull up twenty or so metres in front of the parked van with blacked out windows.

Richard had shouted in anguish as he'd seen Cassie – his sweet, innocent Cassie – dragged from the van and held out like some prize trophy before she'd disappeared from view back into the vehicle. Richard had ordered Gerry to get him down to the abattoir as quickly as humanly possible but they were half a mile away and the ground between them was not practical for a vehicle, even one designed to go off-road.

'Sir?' Gerry tried again. 'I really think we ought to go in.'

Richard couldn't move. His mind was still trapped back on the hillside, watching as the two rust buckets had screeched onto the scene, one at either end. Four men leapt out, assault rifles raised, as they targeted both Scooter and the masked men at the front of the vehicle.

It couldn't have been the Albanians. Despite their previous conversation, Richard had phoned them and told them the deal was off. He'd left countless messages after Elizabeth had warned him not to interfere and yet there they were, interfering.

It had been like some nightmare unfolding – Richard knowing what was coming, but powerless to stop the inevitable – and as the feeling of dread had grown, he'd prayed that it was just a bad dream. He would relive a thousand bad dreams if it meant the reality was having Cassie back in his arms.

Even Gerry had jumped at the sound of the first bullet. Despite their distance, they'd heard it, and watched the scattering of the main players as the two masked men had responded with gunfire of their own.

Run and hide, Richard had willed, hoping that the message would telepathically traverse the distance between them, and Cassie would hear her father's final words. *Run and hide, my sweet child.*

But even as he'd finished the thought, the van had

erupted in a ball of flame, ammunition from within whizzing into the sky like a firework display gone haywire. It couldn't have been real. No harm was supposed to have befallen Cassie. That had been the original agreement with the Albanians. Get Cassie out safely and then deal with the kidnappers. What the hell had gone wrong? He'd given them plenty of notice, so why had they chosen to ignore his messages?

'Mr Hilliard? Richard?' Gerry said, resting a warm hand on his. 'I know you're in shock, but your family needs you. You need them. I'll bring your stuff, but you really ought to go in.'

Their eyes met for the briefest of seconds, but Richard knew he was right.

A marked police car had stopped them as they'd left the hillside view, demanding to know what they were doing there and taking witness statements from both Richard and Gerry before releasing them pending further questions. They'd done nothing wrong; it wasn't a crime to watch. More like torture.

Elizabeth would know by now. Rawani had said he would send one of his team to the house to relay details of events as they unfolded.

Opening the car door, Richard remained where he was. His legs were like jelly and he was desperate to cling onto an alternative reality where the last two hours were just a nightmare from which he couldn't seem to wake. His legs did eventually move, his feet landing on the bed of gravel, each step crunching as if to announce the arrival of a dead man walking. By the time he reached the door, he couldn't see straight, his vision blurred by tears.

He found Elizabeth at Fitzhume's feet in the drawing room, her face smeared in mascara. He couldn't move beyond the door. Was this really what they'd become? Pawns in someone else's twisted game?

Richard opened his mouth to speak but no words would come. His mind was blank. Elizabeth nursed a glass of her father's finest single malt, while the old man himself looked on with the iciest of stares.

'What did you do?' Fitzhume bellowed.

Richard's head dropped.

'You couldn't just let the police do their job, could you?' Fitzhume yelled again, spittle landing on the rug between them. 'You always think you know best. You always want to be the big man.'

Richard glanced up at his wife, hoping she would interrupt and offer some kind of defence. They'd loved each other once, hadn't they? A child as perfect as Cassie could only have been born out of love, couldn't she? But as Elizabeth remained statuesque, clinging to her father's tweed legs, it was clear the final brick had been set in the wall between them. She couldn't even bring her eyes to meet his.

'I-I-I'm sorry,' Richard whispered, his throat drier than it had ever felt.

Elizabeth was on her feet in seconds, running towards him. The single malt had tipped over on the rug where she'd been coiled, but the spring had now finally been released. Swinging her arms at him, she charged, a guttural roar escaping her tear-stained face. As each blow hammered down on him, he remained motionless, barely able to shield himself.

'Get out!' she screamed. 'Get out of our house! Get out of my life! I never want to see you again! Get out, get out, get *out*.'

She burrowed the blows into him until her energy was

spent and she dropped to her knees, mouthing the mantra over and over, glaring at him with pure hatred.

Richard didn't speak at first, feeling the wetness on his own cheeks, but finally he nodded. 'I'll go.'

Fitzhume didn't need to say another word.

Gerry had just closed the front door when Richard emerged from the drawing room. The driver opened his mouth to speak, but Richard wiped his face with the sleeve of his shirt and marched purposefully past him towards the stairs.

'I need you to drive me to a hotel,' Richard dictated. 'I'm going to pack some things and then you will drive me.'

If Gerry was unhappy, he didn't say as much, waiting patiently at the foot of the stairs until Richard reappeared, a small carry-on case stuffed with shirts, trousers, pants, and socks. If he needed anything else, he would just have to go and buy it in the morning. He didn't want to spend another second inside the old country manor. It wasn't his home anymore, if it ever had been. He'd always felt out of his depth under the ever-watchful eye of Fitzhume and his spies. How many times had Hobbs and Rosa reported back on his activities? Well, not anymore. A clean break would be best for all concerned. With Cassie gone, there was nothing to keep him here any longer.

Gerry loaded the case into the back of the car then joined Richard in the front.

'Sir?' Gerry began, 'I just want to—'

'Drive,' Richard replied dismissively, before jolting as Gerry's hand brushed his knee.

Looking round, he wasn't sure what to expect, but a yearning had begun to sprout in the pit of his stomach. He instantly quelled it as he saw Gerry opening the glovebox.

'I thought you might need this,' Gerry said, removing the

unopened bottle of single malt and handing it over before slamming the compartment closed again.

Richard accepted it gratefully. He unscrewed the cap and threw it into the back before pressing the bottle to his lips and taking a long drink. He welcomed the burn as it washed over his tonsils. The engine started and the Range Rover pulled out through the gates, leaving the crumbling manor as nothing more than a shrinking reflection in Richard's side mirror.

By the time they arrived at the Savoy, more than half the bottle was gone and Richard was already beginning to believe that the scene at the hillside was in fact nothing but a horrible nightmare. Leaving Richard in the car, Gerry headed inside the hotel to make arrangements before returning to collect Richard. The uniformed valet at the rotating doors nodded when Gerry said he would return momentarily to move the car. The nod said it was okay; Richard Hilliard was known here and no fuss would be made about his state or condition.

Richard felt his arm being pulled around Gerry's shoulder and was grateful to have someone leading him through the overly bright lobby, towards the bank of lifts, and up to the third floor.

'It's along here,' Gerry offered reassuringly, Richard on one arm, the carry-on in his other hand.

Fumbling with the key card, Gerry drew Richard inside, half-carrying him over to the king-size bed and depositing him on top. He lifted the case onto the mattress, opened it, and hung the shirts and trousers in the mirrored closet. Richard didn't move an inch, already seemingly passed out in a drunken stupor.

'I'll have the reception desk wake you in the morning, sir,'

Gerry said, as he made his way towards the door, 'and I'll be here to collect you from 9am.'

He was about to open the door when a shadow fell across it.

'Don't go,' Richard said.

Turning, Gerry held out his arms, ready to escort Richard back to where he'd come from when Richard leaned in and kissed him on the lips.

'Stay with me,' Richard said breathlessly.

Rather than reciprocating as he had expected, Gerry pushed him away forcefully, sending him stumbling backwards and onto the floor.

'With all due respect, sir, you're drunk, and I'm not interested. Now, let's say no more about this. You're in shock and I'm prepared to overlook your misunderstanding.'

Richard wasn't used to men playing hard to get. Teddy never had; their first kiss in the garden shed had ended with the pair pulling each other's clothes off and climaxing on top of a stack of compost bags.

'I'll pay you,' Richard slurred, unbuttoning his trousers. 'It'll be our little secret.'

Gerry didn't respond, opening the door, and extracting himself from the situation, leaving Richard crumpled on the carpet, where he remained for the rest of the night, alone.

Chapter Forty-One

NOW

Portland, Dorset

I need a moment to compose my thoughts. 'You're telling us that Cassie Hilliard is still alive?'

Denton is grinning, revelling in the novelty of being the most informed one in the room. 'God knows what happened to her afterwards, but yes, she didn't die when that van went up in flames.'

My head snaps around to Jack but he doesn't look like he's buying the story.

'Oh yeah, sure, Cassie Hilliard didn't die at the exchange,' Jack says, contempt dripping from every syllable. 'Come off it, Denton, you must take us for fools.'

Denton's grin drops instantly as he raises three fingers into the air in reticence. 'Scout's honour.'

'You weren't in the Scouts,' Jack fires back.

'All right, soldier's honour then. I'm not lying to you. That girl did not die in that van. I swear.'

'Bone fragments were found amongst the remains of the van,' Jack replies. 'What do you hope to gain from spinning this bullshit? You think Emma here will print your lies to sell more books? She's got more integrity than that. If anything, you'll be no more than a footnote in the story. Come on, Emma, I've heard enough of this fairy-tale.'

'I've got no reason to lie,' Denton almost shouts, clearly affronted by the questioning of his scruples.

I can't blame Jack for not being willing to buy into the story; I have more than a few doubts myself. Even if the words had been delivered by someone with a less dubious reputation than a convicted criminal, I wouldn't be leaping to believe it.

That said, I'm quite touched that Jack has such a high opinion of my writing, even if it isn't one I share. If only he knew how much of a struggle it had been to complete *Monsters Under the Bed*. Every full stop was greeted with self-doubt and the reinforcement that I really don't know what I'm doing. I know how to structure a sentence and to avoid split infinitives, how to use prepositions and modifiers – my degree gave me grounding in that – but whether or not the content of the writing and overall voice is any good, I'm at a loss. Maddie says she loves my style of writing, but that could just be her way of making me more compliant with what she sees as marketable material.

'What was Gjoni's connection to the Albanians?' Jack questions.

'I don't know who they were. Some family with organised crime links is all he said. I didn't trust them, but he told me it was part of a bigger picture, that they would help shine the light away from us. When they actually turned up, I'd completely forgotten they were part of the script and wrongly assumed they were police, there to arrest us all. That was until the first bullet was fired. It struck the ground between Gjoni and me and that's when I dived for cover. I didn't even see most of the firefight because I was just doing whatever I could not to get shot.'

'Gjoni did get shot though,' Jack counters. 'If he had arranged for the Albanians to be there, how come they killed him?'

Denton fixes us both with an impassive stare before shrugging. 'I don't know. So much went pear-shaped that day and I still can't fathom exactly why.'

'But you can see how it looks from our point of view though, can't you?' Jack asks calmly. 'We know Richard Hilliard had indirect links to a family of Albanians, though we weren't able to prove he had anything to do with them turning up. It was generally accepted that he'd probably had a word with his contact and the message had filtered down through the ranks to get Cassie back at all costs. You telling us that their presence there was in fact as a result of you lot just doesn't ring true in my mind.'

Denton sits forward, wagging a finger. 'Hey, hey, they were nothing to do with me. I told you before that I'm just as much a victim of circumstance as anyone else who was there that day, save for Gjoni himself. He was a shady character who thought he knew better than everyone. It was his idea to attack the car on *that* Saturday on *that* stretch of road, and his idea to go to and abandon the barn full of supplies before retracing our steps to the other farm where we hid out. You know, we actually drove past several of your paddy wagons as they were on their way to the first farm. We were in an SUV at that point, with the girl gagged under blankets in the boot. Had we been stopped, we'd have been caught red-handed. But that's what Gjoni was like, don't you see? He liked to push the boundaries, and that's why he had those Albanians rock up.'

He sits back and takes a deep breath to settle himself. 'You want to know why Gjoni got shot? You'd have to ask the Albanians. Maybe it was an accident. Maybe he got caught in the crossfire. Or maybe he stiffed them on their fee and they retaliated. I have no idea, but they managed to get away scot-free, didn't they?'

'One of them also died at the scene.'

'Yeah, but I bet you couldn't formally tie him back to the family he worked for, nor to Gjoni.'

Jack nods.

Watching the two of them going back and forth isn't helping answer the burning question at the forefront of my mind, so I clear my throat. 'If Cassie didn't die in that van, where is she now? Where has she been for the last twelve months?'

'To be honest, I can't tell you that. Not because I don't want to, but because I genuinely don't know. When Amos came to see me, he told me the canary had reached the mines.'

'What does that mean?' I press, uncertain if I really want to know the answer.

Denton shrugs again. 'It was code to say he'd used the tunnels to get the girl away. Canary was the word he liked to use to describe her.'

'You mean Cassie?'

He nods with heavy eyes. 'Amos was reckless in coming here, but smart enough to know the screws wouldn't be too far from earshot. He loved the whole clandestine, secret-agent nature of the operation. He was into code words and being one of the lads. I didn't want no part of it. The last thing I need is more charges on my rap sheet, more time stuck in here. As I said to you at the start, I never would have signed up to Gjoni's plan if I'd known what he intended. I've got kids of my own and I'd kill any man who tried to take them from me. It sickens me that I could've allowed myself to wind up in such a mess but once I was in, there was nothing I could do to get out. As far as I was concerned, the sooner we got the girl back to her parents the better.'

'Where is Amos now?' I ask, aimed at both of them.

'That's what I was trying to tell you,' Denton answers first. 'He's gone AWOL, and left my missus without two pennies to rub together. She's got bills to pay and Christmas presents to buy.'

'I can have a check run on Amos's last-known movements,' Jack offers. 'See if he's been in trouble for anything recently. It could be that he's been pulled in for something and is also going to spend the next few months at Her Majesty's pleasure.'

'I doubt you'll find him,' Denton interrupts. 'Before we arrived at the abattoir, Gjoni told us that if anything went tits up, we would find a bag of money at the end of the tunnels. It wasn't everything he owed us – I think he was paranoid about either of us double-crossing him – but I know for a fact that Amos got his hands on that bag. There was supposed to be a cool hundred grand inside it – more than enough for a lowlife like Amos to live off for a year undetected as well as to support my family. He wouldn't have promised to if he hadn't found it and I don't think he'd have been stupid enough to get mixed up in something else with that kind of funding in his back pocket. You want my opinion? The reason he's gone AWOL is because someone else is on his tail.'

Jack stands and excuses himself, promising to phone the station and follow up on Amos's last-known whereabouts. I remain where I am, studying Denton's face. The yellow bruising around his eye makes him look almost jaundiced and the scab protruding vertically from his top lip looks fresh. I don't ask what led to those injuries.

'What's the real reason you're coming forward now, Leroy?' I ask innocently. 'I know you said it's because he's cut the support to your wife and children, but telling us about Cassie surviving the explosion, and Amos on the run with a bagful of money, isn't going to reconnect that supply chain. When we first stepped in here, you declared you weren't a grass, and yet that's exactly what you're doing to Amos now. Is it revenge?'

'You're a smart girl,' he says condescendingly, looking me up and down, with more than a glint of excitement in his expression.

I'm suddenly conscious that I'm alone in here with him, and whilst I've read up on his case history, it's hardly a full biography. I don't know what lurks behind those eyes, nor whether he's ever been violent or abusive with the women in his life. I cross my arms involuntarily, mentally counting the steps back to the door through which Jack has just left. I remind myself that if he does try anything, the prison guards watching and listening to every word will burst in within seconds. I try to relax my shoulders so he won't read my fear.

'Having Amos arrested won't get your wife the money she needs, so why tell us now?'

As he rubs a hand over the lower half of his face, I see the black eye and cut lip are not his only scars. 'Prison can be a dangerous place,' he comments. 'Being locked up in here makes you a sitting duck. If someone on the outside wants someone in here taken care of – made an example of – it's easy enough to arrange. There are plenty of men who know they'll never see the outside world who are willing to do anything for the right sum – even kill. I always knew Gjoni had a benefactor out there – someone who hired him to pull off the job – and I never had any idea who it was. As far as I was concerned, we'd failed them, and if he – or she – wanted me dead, it wouldn't be too hard to arrange… I spent days in here always keeping one of the screws within earshot or sight of me in case I got jumped. I was terrified in those first few weeks until Amos rocked up and said he would sort things on the outside and all I needed to do was keep my mouth shut. I wasn't sure if I could trust him at first, but after a month or so had passed and I was still alive, I began to believe what he said.

'But now he's disappeared – either done a runner, or someone's come for him – and I want the record set straight. I've done some stupid things in my life, none more so than what happened last year, but it was never my intention to hurt that girl.'

'Say her name,' I challenge, the breath instantly catching in my throat.

His eyes narrow and his face takes on new definition, more sinister than before.

'Say her name!' I shout this time, reflecting his newfound aggression as my own anger erupts. 'You abducted and imprisoned this innocent girl. The least you can do is admit what you did.'

His lips remain locked but his shoulders slump and he can no longer look at me. He waves his arm in the direction of the prison guard behind the one-way mirror.

Our meeting is over.

Chapter Forty-Two

NOW

Portland, Dorset

Jack is waiting for me in the visitors' centre reception bay, and his smile as I approach reminds me that not all men are as rotten to the core as Leroy Denton.

'You okay?' he asks, maybe spotting the tight lines around my eyes.

'Fine,' I say, but not even I'm convinced by the sound of my voice. I take a deep breath and try again. 'I'll never understand how people like that can reconcile their actions with their conscience. If I'd caused so much hurt and pain, I wouldn't be able to live with myself.'

Jack rubs my arm softly in an act of support but I twitch at his touch. 'I think he genuinely believes he isn't to blame for any of what happened. Unfortunately, I see that kind of thing on a regular basis amongst the criminal fraternity. By blaming their actions on others, they don't have to confront their own complicity.'

I'm suddenly conscious of the prison guard standing behind us at the reception desk and I nod at Jack to head back to the car. The moment we step outside, a huge gust of wind nearly sends me flying, and we both have to battle back to the safety and warmth of the car.

'How did you get on?' I ask once we're inside and I've endeavoured to straighten my fringe and windswept hair in the vanity mirror.

'I relayed to DCS Rawani what Denton told us and he was able to check Amos's record. No arrests in the last year since he was released following Elizabeth's identification, and not linked to any open enquiries since the Hilliard abduction. As far as the HOLMES2 system is concerned, he's either dropped off the planet or turned over a new leaf.'

I consider this statement, my brow furrowing. 'I suppose it's not unreasonable to think that he might have turned his back on a life of crime. I'm sure some must do so.'

I'm annoyed when I see him roll his eyes.

'I'm not naïve, Jack. I've met plenty of former offenders who have gone straight.'

He raises his hands in apology. 'You're right. I'm sorry. It's just… given Amos's track record, and how Denton described him, you can understand why I'd be surprised if he'd renounced his sins and joined a monastery.'

'I think your opinion of monasteries is too high if recent stories are anything to go by,' I say darkly. 'You don't believe Cassie is still alive, do you?'

He stares out the window for a moment before finally turning to meet my gaze. 'I *want* to believe that she is and that we'll find her, but the realist inside me refuses to hold on to unfounded hope. Why are you so keen to accept his fiction as fact?'

It's a fair question, and I don't know how to answer it. I want to tell him it's because I'm a good judge of character and that I felt there was honesty in Denton's eyes, and yet I know there were also moments of dishonesty mixed in there. 'The thing is,' I say, with a heavy sigh to mirror the ache in my heart, 'I *have* to believe she's out there waiting to be found. It's purely selfish, but that belief must be strong enough to fight for until the truth is proved beyond all doubt.'

I watch my fingers entangling as I struggle to find the words to explain what I mean.

'My sister, Anna, was abducted when I was seven years old. She left our house one afternoon and was supposed to arrive at my grandma's house a few minutes later, but she never did, and I never saw her again.'

Jack remains silent.

'She was only nine, but I've never stopped believing that one day we'll be reunited. I've spoken to counsellors about closure, and the police officer responsible for reviewing her case notes each year, and I accept that there is a far greater chance I'll never know what really happened than of actually finding her… but it's what keeps me going. *She* is my reason for waking every day; *she* is why I agreed to help Fitzhume. I love my sister, Jack, and you'll notice my use of present tense. There is *nothing* you can say to make me stop believing she's still out there… And if *she's* out there, then there's a chance Cassie is too… Before this morning, we believed Cassie died in that explosion because forensics found human remains. But now we have a witness telling us there was a driver waiting behind the wheel and that Amos was concealed in the back. Don't you see? The bone fragments could have belonged to the *driver*. And *if* Amos really was there, *if* he survived, *if* he escaped, maybe Cassie did as well. It wouldn't be difficult to check Denton's claim about tunnels beneath that disused abattoir, nor would it be difficult to check the visitors' log for last year to see whether Amos visited him and if the transcripts record him mentioning the canary. At the very least you could check whether Amos is still living in Chiswick.'

I'm breathless when I finish and he gives me a moment to compose myself. 'The DCS is sending a unit to Amos's home as we speak. I'm waiting for him to call me back and let me know whether he's there.'

My cheeks warm. 'Well, good. And if he *is* there... if, God willing, Cassie is too, will you accept that as long as there's doubt, there's hope?'

'We'll see,' he responds plainly, but his smile tells me I've won. He'd be a terrible poker player. 'Why didn't you mention your sister before?'

I honestly don't know why. 'I didn't want you to think I was crazy.'

'Can *I* be honest with you now?' he says, his voice quivering. 'I would like nothing more than to see Cassie reunited with her parents. I'm a father myself, so how could I not want to see this play out with them all back together? I don't want you getting ahead of yourself though. For all we know, Denton has just spun us a web of lies, and when Amos is discovered at home, he'll deny any knowledge of her survival or this mystery maze of tunnels beneath the Berkshire hills or the fact he was even there at all. We can't allow our hopes to cloud the truth. Okay?'

I'm sure he doesn't mean to sound so condescending. 'Agreed.'

Ten minutes pass in virtual silence while we remain in the prison carpark. We easily could have gone somewhere for a drink, or back to my flat to wait, but it would feel wrong to relax when Cassie's life could still be on the line. Jack's phone chimes and he makes no effort to shield me from the conversation as he speaks into it. I strain to hear what's being said but Jack ends the call within a matter of seconds and turns to face me. I can see it's bad news from the sadness that draws over his eyes.

'They've been to Amos's place and he wasn't there. When they arrived, they discovered the front door had been kicked open and so they entered, expecting the worst. Apparently the place was deserted, but it looks like someone has given it a good going over. *Ransacked* is how the scene was described. Could just be a simple burglary, but professional burglars tend to know where to look for the most valuable items. The way the scene was described suggests someone broke in to deliberately cause damage, or search for something.'

A flash of Leroy Denton's battered face instantly fills my mind.

'There's something else,' Jack says to divert my attention back to him. 'They discovered a bolted door in the kitchen leading to a basement or cellar of sorts. A child's bed, some pens and paper, as well as drawings were discovered inside. First assumptions are that a child was being held there.'

I suddenly feel like I might throw up and I have to choke back the urge as my face drains of blood. 'Cassie?'

'No sign of anyone there now, nor can they say when she

was there, if at all. They'll check the scene for DNA and forensics, but that's going to take a few days.'

What if Denton is right and Amos has been holding her there all this time? If he had come forward sooner, might she have already been found?

'As far as the DCS is concerned, they do not believe that Cassie was being held there. A death certificate was signed for Cassie Hilliard last year based on the remains discovered in the van, and aside from Denton's claim today, there is nothing to suggest that she has ever been inside Amos's home. It could just as easily be a totally different child who was staying in that cellar. An APB has been put out for Amos though, and his image will be shared with forces across the country. Right now, we need to wait and see what happens.'

'No!' I practically shout. 'Cassie Hilliard has had to wait a year to be found. We can't give up now.'

'Nobody's giving up, Emma, least of all me, but we don't know whether she was *ever* with Amos, let alone if she still is. And even if Denton was telling the truth, we don't know that Amos didn't keep her for a few days, before…' His words trail off.

'Before *what*, Jack?' I growl, my eyes stinging.

'We don't know that he wouldn't have killed her and buried her somewhere. As crass as it sounds, it would be far easier than holding on to her all this time.'

I ignore the twisting of my gut as nausea rushes up. 'What else do you know about Amos? Does he have any family or known associates he might call upon if he was in trouble?'

His brow furrows with confusion. 'What makes you think he's in trouble?'

I picture Denton's bruises again. 'You said yourself that

there was something suspicious about why Denton would come clean now. What if he's right? What if someone else is after Amos?'

Jack's frown deepens.

'You saw Denton's bashed-up face, and he told me that when people on the outside want something on the inside, anything and everything can be done for a price. What if someone wanted to know where Amos was and threatened Denton for the information? And what if Denton told them what he told us? His conscience would be killing him unless he found a way to share the responsibility. If something happens to Amos, Denton will feel justified in blaming us because now he's told us the truth. It's not his fault if we don't respond quickly enough.'

Jack tilts his head a fraction. 'So you think Amos somehow caught wind of the fact that someone was after him and he's done a runner?'

'It would certainly explain why he stopped paying subsidies to Denton's wife.' I allow the thought to fester in Jack's mind. 'So who would Amos turn to in his hour of need?'

Jack looks at his watch as if trying to decide whether to stick or twist. 'He has a stepsister in Honiton, according to his file.'

'That's just over an hour away,' I say eagerly, pulling the seatbelt around me. 'Can we go and see her? For Cassie's sake?'

He starts the engine without another word and we're soon haring back through Portland. Fate has thrown us together and I have to believe there is a reason for that.

Chapter Forty-Three

NOW

Honiton, Devon

It's nearly two by the time we reach the bungalow on a small estate not far from Honiton town centre. The drive along the coastal road has filled my mind with more memories of trips away with my parents. And Anna.

Is it wrong that I don't want to think of her right now? I feel guilty for turning my back but I can only concentrate on one crisis at a time. The more I think about what Leroy Denton told us, as well as that feeling Elizabeth has been trying to escape, the more certain I am that Cassie is still alive. It may be naïve, but I've quizzed Jack about Hank Amos's criminal record and there's no history of violence, nor murder. In my mind, as much as he might have wanted to see the end of Cassie Hilliard, I don't believe he would have been able to kill her. Despite how things play out in books and films, it really isn't that easy to deliberately take another human life – especially that of an innocent child. Sure, accidents happen all the time, but to intentionally murder a child takes a whole new level of inhumanity.

A woman emerges from the front door of the bungalow dressed in a smart, mustard-coloured woollen coat, a navy and butter-colour headscarf, and dark tights. She is about to open the door to the Mercedes on the driveway when she catches sight of Jack emerging from our parked car.

'Mrs Belvedere?' Jack says, swiftly moving around the front of the car, and offering her a smile of genuine warmth that would put even the most terrified of people at ease. 'Could you spare us a few minutes of your time, please?'

As she shields her eyes from the sun peeking over the low-rise homes across the road, I surmise she must be in her late sixties.

'I was just on my way out,' she says, an edge to her prim and proper Home Counties voice. 'It's Bridge Club on Tuesday afternoons, you see.'

'This won't take up too much of your time but it really is vital that we speak to you now,' Jack continues, heading up the incline of the driveway. 'It's about your brother, Hank.'

'Henry? Is he okay? Oh God, please tell me something hasn't happened to him?'

Jack shows her his identification which she spends an inordinate amount of time studying, as though she doubts its validity. 'I'm from the Metropolitan Police,' he says softly. 'It would be better if we could discuss matters inside. I appreciate you were on your way to an appointment, but I think ultimately it would be better if you cried off, if that's okay?'

She mutters something I can't hear from the car before turning on her heel and heading back to the large coal-black door. Jack ushers me to come and join him and I don't wait for a second invitation. I hurry up the driveway and Violet Belvedere starts at my sudden appearance. There's a moment of recognition in her eyes and the frosty demeanour is instantly replaced by a wide smile, like we've known each other for years. 'You're that... oh, what's your name...? I have a memory like a sieve sometimes. Emma? Emma Hunter, isn't it?'

I don't think I'll ever get used to this recognition thing. 'Yes, I am,' I say, with my own non-threatening smile.

'Come in, come in,' she gestures as the heavy door opens. 'Wait till the Bridge girls hear about this! We're all huge fans of yours. We read your book as part of Book Club over the summer, and – I'm not just saying this – it was one of my favourite books this year, in spite of the subject matter.'

She removes the headscarf and a mop of straw-like hair flops down over her ears, reminiscent of Worzel Gummidge. The hallway smells strongly of vanilla and I see now that the obsession with the colour yellow isn't restricted to her appearance. What little sunlight remains in the sky makes the walls positively glow with warmth and luminescence. It feels like we've stepped into a holiday home. The carpet bears the tell-tale signs of recent hoovering. A dish of beige potpourri sits alongside a cradled telephone set and a pad of paper and biro on a knee-high table are just inside the door. A three-tiered shoe rack to my left is full of freshly polished shoes and boots, save for a space into which she now places her strappy navy shoes. Everything appears to have a place in this carefully appointed home, and as she leads us through the hallway and into the large lounge-diner at the end, the warm glow of the walls and French vanilla scent follow us.

'You have a lovely home,' I say, as she beckons us to sit on the softly furnished two-seater sofa.

Recent experience of interviewing strangers has taught me that lowering defensive barriers as quickly as possible leads to a smoother conversation. Experience also tells me that complimenting a home is a quick way to achieve this.

'Thank you,' she says, offering us tea.

I hadn't realised how dry my throat is and nod quickly. Jack opts for a glass of water.

'Still or sparkling?' she enquires without batting an eyelid.

'Tap is fine,' Jack confirms.

Violet Belvedere disappears back out towards the kitchen we passed on our way in and I hear the kettle being filled a moment later.

'You'd never know these two were related,' I whisper, pointing at a framed picture of Violet and Amos, both dressed in festive jumpers, a fully decorated Christmas tree in the background of the shot.

'She's showing no nerves so far,' Jack replies, standing and circuiting the room. He glances at photographs on the mantelpiece, thumbs through a small stack of papers on the large dining table at the far side of the room and a pile of glossy magazines beside the small box television, which is covered in a thick layer of dust. 'I don't reckon Amos is staying here.'

She enters the room silently, placing a tall glass of water on a coaster on the coffee table beside the sofa. 'I'll be back with your tea in a moment,' she says, beaming at me again. 'Would you like Earl Grey, morning breakfast, or something fruity?'

'Morning breakfast is fine,' I reply, watching as she hurries back out of the room.

It's clear to see that Violet Belvedere takes great pride in her home and I'm struggling to picture her stepbrother abiding by her strict house rules. Jack is right: if Amos has been here, he isn't now.

'What is it you wanted to talk about?' Violet says when she's handed me a china cup and saucer, and has settled onto the three-seater sofa across from us. The question is addressed to me but it is Jack who responds.

'Can you tell us when you last saw Hank?'

She looks off to the right, her brow heavy. 'Now, let me see… it's been some time since he was here… I'm trying to recall if it was last Christmas, or the one before that.' Her gaze returns to me and her face lights up again. 'At my age, it can be difficult to recall what happened when.'

'So you haven't seen him in the last two to three months?' Jack presses.

'Oh, good heavens, no,' she says, returning the cup to the saucer. 'I'm sorry, but Henry and I aren't particularly close.'

'You're step-siblings, right?' I ask, sipping from my own cup. 'Was it your mum who married his dad, or your dad and his mum?'

It isn't particularly relevant to the conversation but I don't believe Jack's direct approach is going to secure us the level of detail we're seeking. I sense that she wants to speak and we need to probe gently or risk her shutting us out.

'My mother passed in the summer of 1966; I was only thirteen. Two years later, Dad wed Henry's mum. Henry is six years my junior. He was only eight when his dad was struck down by cancer. I think his mum couldn't afford to look after him on her own. She was working as a secretary at Dad's office. Their romance developed into thirty years of marriage until he passed away twenty-odd years ago; she died of a broken heart six months later.'

'I'm so sorry,' I offer sincerely. 'It must have been strange inheriting a younger brother at that age?'

'Because of the age difference, we didn't see that much of each other growing up. I went to teacher-training college at eighteen, and would then only see Henry when I returned for summer and Christmas holidays. I met and married my late husband when I was twenty-two, and Henry and I continued to drift apart. After Mum and Dad died, there wasn't a lot keeping us together. We would send birthday and Christmas cards, talk twice a year on the phone, but visits were very few and far between.' She pauses for another sip of her tea. 'Forgive my bluntness, but why exactly do you have an interest in my brother? He was never in care, if that's what you think. I'm not aware of any abuse he suffered growing up. He certainly never attended that boys' home.'

I look to Jack for guidance, uncertain how much we can or can't say.

'We're investigating a crime from last year,' Jack confirms, 'and we believe Hank – sorry, *Henry* – might be a key witness to what happened. It is really important we get hold of him as a matter of urgency. Would you have an address or telephone number for where he might be?'

'He was living in Chiswick, the last I heard,' she says, looking off to check her facts again. 'I'm sure I have his address, if that would help? And you can have his landline number. Alas, I don't own a mobile phone, so I don't know what his mobile number would be.' She stands and disappears, returning a moment later with a small address book with a flowery cover. She opens the book to a specific page and hands it to Jack.

'Thank you, but we've been to that address and he wasn't there. Do you have any idea where else he might be?'

There is a flicker in her eyes before she quickly shakes her head, disappearing out to return the address book to its proper place.

'Why don't you go and wait in the car?' I whisper to Jack. 'I'm sure she knows more than she's letting on and maybe she'll open up if it's just the two of us.'

He considers me for a moment before nodding and standing. 'If you'll excuse me, Mrs Belvedere,' he says, as she reappears in the doorway, 'I have to go and make a phone call.'

She shows him to the door, looking slightly flustered when she returns, and I can't immediately tell if it's because I've remained in her house or because she's holding something back. I want to ask her outright but some things can't be hurried.

'You wanted to know why we're interested in your brother,' I say, placing my cup and saucer on a vacant coaster, noticing the sides of her mouth rising slightly as I do. 'Last year, a young girl was abducted from her parents and we have reason to believe that Henry may know where she is.'

Okay, so much for softly-softly, but Cassie's life is at risk here.

'How old was she?' Violet asks quietly, dropping back onto the sofa, the crow's feet tightening with concern.

The sweat is cool along my hairline, but my heart is racing so fast that I'm sure Violet must be able to hear it too. 'She was six when she was taken and would be seven now.'

'A-a-and what would she look like?'

Has the temperature in the room suddenly dropped? The walls don't have quite the same glow to them. Violet's face is certainly a lot paler than when we first met, as if a cloud has now formed above our heads.

I reach into my handbag and withdraw a copy of the photograph of Cassie from the police file. I hand it over. 'Her name is Cassie Hilliard and her parents are distraught with worry. Have you seen her?'

Violet's hand shoots up to her mouth the moment her eyes meet the image.

'Where is she, Violet?' I push.

'H-h-he said she was his *stepdaughter*… He said they were in trouble… I-I-I was trying to help…' A single tear rolls the length of her cheek, leaving a smear.

'When was this, Violet?'

Her eyes meet mine and I can see they are filled with remorse and anguish. 'Three weeks ago. I gave him some money. A few hundred pounds. I didn't know.'

My pulse has quickened though I haven't taken a breath in what feels like forever. This is the first positive identification of Cassie Hilliard in a year.

'Where would he go, Violet? We think he's on the run from someone else and we need to find him before they do.'

Her eyes widen. 'Some men… they came here last week and asked questions about him. I told them I hadn't seen him. When you arrived today, I thought you were with them.'

'Who were these men, Violet? What did they look like?'

'I don't know. They were foreign-sounding, dark skin. African, maybe? I don't know.'

'Where did he go when he left here, Violent?'

'I-I-I don't know. He didn't say.'

'Have you got any way of contacting him? Did he leave an address or phone number?'

She's sobbing now, shaking her head. Tears are splashing down on the beige skirt covering her knees.

'Please, Violet. Cassie is only seven years old. She needs to be reunited with her parents. Please.'

Violet is still shaking but then she stops, her head rising. 'After he'd gone… I couldn't find the keys for my caravan. I usually leave them in the utility drawer in the kitchen.'

'Where is this caravan, Violet? Would he know how to find it?'

She wipes her face with the back of her hand but this time she nods. 'It's a static caravan in Torquay. It was the only thing Dad left me in his will. He wanted me to take my own children there on summer holidays, but I never… I never had any children.'

Standing, I thrust a pen and paper towards her. 'What's the address?'

Chapter Forty-Four

NOW

Torquay, Devon

It's dusk by the time we locate the holiday park and Violet Belvedere's static mobile home. Jack phoned ahead and there are two marked squad cars awaiting our arrival but I immediately notice they don't have anyone in custody.

'Place was empty when we arrived,' one of the officers says to Jack as they shake hands and introduce themselves. He fires me an awkward glance.

'She's civilian liaison,' Jack explains dismissively so as not to draw attention to my celebrity status.

The officer turns to face the caravan and I can now see that there are lights on inside. 'Because there was nobody home when we got here, we spoke to the site manager and she let us inside to look around.'

Jack climbs the steps, pulling on a pair of bright blue latex gloves, but not offering me any. I move to fall in behind him but he puts out a hand to stop me.

'Probably best if you remain outside,' he warns. 'If Amos has been here recently, or if any harm has come to Cassie, this may need to be treated as a crime scene.'

I'm a little annoyed but I know he's right, and so I move around to the front of the caravan, standing on my toes to look inside the main window. I see Jack being taken to the rear of the caravan, towards the bedrooms presumably. Just inside the window, I can see a faux-leather booth of sorts, a small square table in front of it and an open box of cereal on top of the table.

The brunette officer standing guard outside the static home offers a reassuring nod. 'What's he wanted for?' she asks. 'The perp?'

'Abduction and imprisonment,' I say, moving closer to her. 'Did you arrive with the other guy?'

She nods. 'A couple of minutes after. I was the one who went and fetched the site manager.'

'Did she say whether anybody had been staying on this pitch?'

'Not exactly. All the homes in this part are privately owned, hence their proximity to the main reception building and swimming pool. The residents here are free to come and go as they see fit and, from what she said, the owner of this particular home doesn't subscribe to their rental or housekeeping services so she was neither able to confirm nor deny whether anybody has been inside recently.'

Presumably Violet didn't rent the property out to others then. 'And the manager didn't say she'd seen anyone hanging around here in passing?' I ask.

She shakes her head. 'I got the impression that she doesn't spend too much time on site. She was hurrying off to a second site to cash-up for the day, so I think there's reliance on the rest of the staffing team. I can introduce you if you want to ask them any questions?'

'That would be good, thank you. I should probably check with Jack before wandering off anywhere though.'

'No worries. Is this anything to do with that Cassie Hilliard girl?'

I don't respond.

'I follow you on Twitter,' she adds, forcing eye contact. 'You were tagged in a couple of articles about her disappearance on Sunday.'

I don't think I'll ever feel comfortable with strangers knowing more about my life than me, thanks to the wonders of social media. I know it's a necessary evil – particularly in light of my chosen profession – but it can be quite disarming at times.

'I had a look inside,' she adds, leaning closer conspiratorially. 'I'd say somebody has been staying here. There was a pan with tomato soup residue around the rim sitting in the sink. The residue was still wet in places. I'd say someone was inside this home earlier today and that we weren't far from finding them here.'

The sky is even darker now and I can't resist the urge to wrap my arms around my front as a bitter chill whips against us. Spinning, I take in the immediate surroundings. Although I can hear the sea crashing gently in the distance, it's too dark to separate the horizon from the evening sky. There are no street lights in our immediate vicinity, and none of the ten static homes in my viewpoint have lights on. There's a ghostly feel to the whole place.

'We're almost out of season,' the young PC says. 'A place like this is heaving in the warmer summer months, but apart from a small spike in visitors in autumn half-term, business will be pretty quiet until the New Year.'

It reminds me of home, but it lacks the charm of Weymouth. Violet didn't say how often she comes to stay in this park, but the lack of forced entry at her caravan door would suggest whoever has been living here had use of a key. Was Violet lying when she said she had no way of contacting Amos? Had she waited until Jack and I left before phoning her brother to tip him off we were coming? I don't want to believe she would do that, given how remorseful she seemed when telling me about this place. Maybe whoever else is after Amos traced him here and they took him, or he scarpered before they could?

Jack reappears in the doorway and snaps off his gloves. 'If he was here, he's gone now,' he says. 'There are no bags of clothes, but it looks like both beds have been slept in recently. Looks like we just missed them.'

'We'll circulate both their faces to all units here and in the neighbouring counties,' the young PC offers. 'If he's nearby, we might still pick him – sorry, *them* – up.'

'We'll also ask our crime scene team to have a look for forensics,' the other officer adds. 'I'll need the DCI's agreement first. I'll call him now and let you know.'

Jack shakes both their hands and thanks them before leading me back to the car. 'There's not a lot more we can do now,' he says once we're back inside. 'I think we should find a place to crash for tonight and wait to hear back from the others. That okay with you?'

I nod, my eyes not leaving the only glowing caravan in the row.

The first hotel we locate only has one twin room available, and although Jack offers to go looking for somewhere else, I tell him I don't mind sharing. We're both adults and I'm pretty sure I'll be able to resist any overtures he's unlikely to send my way. I'm exhausted when we sit down to eat in the hotel restaurant.

'I feel I owe you an apology,' he says when the waiter has brought over our drinks.

'What for?'

'Well, you said Cassie was still alive and you were right. We found a child's sleeping bag and some toys in one of the bedrooms. There was also a crude lock fitted to the outside of the door, suggesting he was sealing her in there each night.'

I don't want to consider the prospect of what Hank Amos has been doing to Cassie for the last twelve months. I can only pray that she hasn't suffered, but I know that may be too much to wish for. Whatever happens, I'm more determined than ever to catch up with them, even if it takes me years.

'One thing I don't understand is why he's held on to her all this time,' I say, gently broaching the subject. 'Once the exchange went wrong and he'd secured Gjoni's bag of money, why not cut her loose? It must have been a real dampener having to keep her hidden, always looking over his shoulder.'

Jack takes a sip of his water. 'I don't have an answer. Maybe the hundred grand wasn't enough for him, and he hoped to extract more money from the parents.'

'That was my first thought too but if that was his intention, why hasn't he done that? Twelve months is plenty of time to contact them and confirm she's still alive and make the demand. In this day and age, he wouldn't even have to be present at an exchange. He could tell them she's alive, let them speak to her for proof of life and then give them an offshore bank account number to transfer the money into. Once the transfer was complete, he could leave her at an address and give it to them. It wouldn't take a trained tactical expert to organise such a plan.'

Jack is smiling at me and I hate that I'm not able to stop myself mirroring his expression. 'You love this kind of thing, don't you?' he says, the grin widening. 'You're like a modern Jessica Fletcher, using your research and writing experience to get inside the chief suspect's psyche.'

It isn't the first time such a comparison has been made, and in truth I'm flattered by it. I'm unable to stop myself smirking. 'If that's what you think, then you'd better watch your back. All her friends and family either ended up dead or accused of murder.'

He raises his eyebrows. 'We're friends now then, are we? I got the impression you wanted to keep things strictly professional.'

My face straightens and I can't help but feel foolish for misreading the situation.

'After you gave me the brush-off the other night,' he adds, 'I assumed you didn't do friendships with guys. It's okay, I get it. Some women don't think they can be friends with men.'

'I see. Any other outdated or altogether deluded prejudices you care to share, Jack?'

'No, that's not what I meant,' he says, quickly backtracking, and I'm pleased to see him looking flustered. 'I think it's only too right that a man and a woman can be platonic friends. I'm not looking for anything else from you. There's only room in my heart for one girl, and that's Mila. I'm sorry, I didn't mean any offence.'

Wow… the atmosphere has turned decidedly frosty all of a sudden and I'm not so sure us sharing a room was such a good idea.

'Forget I said anything,' he says. 'Please? I'm sorry. I do want to be your friend, Emma, and I hope – despite my ability to insert my entire foot into my mouth at times – you want to be friends with me too.'

I hesitate before nodding. 'Very well then. Let's put the misunderstanding behind us.'

'Good. Tell me more about your sister's disappearance.'

It's obvious he's deliberately steered the conversation to a new topic but at least it's one I'm prepared to discuss. 'What do you want to know?'

'I was going to say that I'll take a look at your sister's casefile if you're happy for me to do so? Fresh eyes can make a difference, but if you'd rather I didn't—'

'Can we focus on finding Cassie first? Then, by all means, let me know how you would have investigated things in the Met. I've looked and checked every angle I can think of but I'm always open to new possibilities.'

'Then it's settled.' He dabs the edges of his mouth with his napkin, dropping it on the table and standing. 'I'm going to check in with the officers at the campsite to see if they've got the all-clear to have the place tested for forensics. If the waiter comes by, can you order me cod and chips?'

Chapter Forty-Five

NOW

Torquay, Devon

'What exactly do you think you'll find there?' Jack asks, as we pull up on the spot of grass reserved for parking.

'I don't know, but if Amos rushed off in a hurry, it's possible he may have inadvertently left a clue that might tell us where he's headed. I've heard you say yourself that criminals are not the smartest, even more so when they're in a hurry.'

The blue and white cordon flutters in the gentle morning breeze but there's no sign of anyone standing guard beside the scene.

'I still can't believe the local DCI refused to authorise forensic processing of the scene last night,' Jack comments staring out at the caravan. 'The DCS wasn't pleased, I can tell you.'

'Does it really matter in the grand scheme of things? It's

pretty obvious someone's been here. Our best guess is that it's Amos, but regardless, he's not here now, and neither is Cassie.' I pause, summoning the courage to ask my next question. 'If I could just take a look inside, then maybe—'

'No. No way. Absolutely not,' Jack interrupts. 'It's more than my job's worth to allow a civilian to poke around inside. The DCS may still send someone down to look for prints and DNA and we can't risk contaminating the scene. I'm sorry, Emma, but no.'

I was hoping he wouldn't be so stringent but I know how much trouble can come from not following the rules. The clichéd renegade copper prepared to break all the rules to uncover the truth is the stuff of poorly plotted novels.

'You've already been inside though, haven't you,' I try again. 'So, there's no harm in *you* going in again and relaying to me what you see.'

It's my final card but at least he's considering the request.

'I can already tell you exactly what's inside. I can see it in my mind as clear as day: an open box of cornflakes on the table, a third gone. Three unopened tins of tomato soup in the cupboard above the stove along with a half-eaten loaf of bread. A two-pint carton of in-date milk and some processed cheese in the fridge. Do you want me to go on?'

I don't respond, instead opening my door and trudging across to the perimeter of the cordon.

'Whoa, whoa, whoa,' Jack stammers, as he rushes after me. 'If you step inside that cordon, I'll be obliged to arrest you. Please don't put me in that position.'

I still don't respond, stalking the perimeter, looking at the ground just inside. The grass is threadbare with thick, stodgy mud dominating the landscape – a result of a recent downpour.

'What are you looking for?' Jack asks, sticking nearby in case I make a break under the tape and disobey his command.

'Tyre tracks,' I reply. 'We know he travelled from Chiswick to Honiton to visit his stepsister but I'd be very surprised if he used public transport – too much CCTV, too many opportunities to be spotted. We also know he then travelled from Honiton to here. Again, I'd be shocked if he relied on public transport or taxis. But if he did drive here, where did he park? Because this space just inside the tape is the allotted parking for this static home and, as far as I can see, there hasn't been any kind of vehicle here in some time. Look, you can see what grass remains is standing tall rather than squashed flat. The mud is so thick but it doesn't have tyre tracks in it.'

Intrigued, Jack crouches beside me and looks at where I'm pointing. 'Okay, Sherlock,' he concedes, 'so what you're saying is that whatever vehicle he's driving, it wasn't parked here. What's your point?'

I straighten. 'For starters, where is it now? And secondly, where was it while he *was* here, assuming it was in fact Amos?'

Jack looks around the neighbouring properties almost as if he's expecting to be able to pick the vehicle out of thin air. 'Okay, I give up. Where is it?'

I frown. 'I have no idea; that's not the point. Maybe Amos is a bit smarter than we're giving him credit for. After all, he's managed to keep Cassie hidden for the last twelve months. If he knows people are onto him – the Albanians or whoever – and this is the only place available to him to hang out, he wouldn't want to draw unnecessary attention to the fact he's staying here. Had we not spoken to Violet Belvedere yesterday and had she not mentioned her missing keys, how long would it have taken you to run a background search on her and discover she held the deeds to this place?'

Jack considers the question. 'A few days maybe.'

'Exactly! It wouldn't have been so soon, but you would have got there eventually. And then the first thing you would have done is head here to search.'

He's looking at me blankly.

'So, he would want his car nearby for a quick getaway,' I conclude.

I can almost see the cogs slowly turning in Jack's head. 'You think he's still here somewhere.'

I snap my fingers as a smile breaks across my face. 'Yes, I do. The fact that the soup residue was still fresh on the pan suggests he left shortly before your Torquay colleagues arrived here, but where did he go? If he's panicking, he won't be thinking straight. He'd just want to find somewhere to lie low, somewhere he felt comfortable but wouldn't be seen.' Leaving the perimeter, I begin to head along the narrow road, jumping up to look through the windows of each static home in turn. There are no vehicles parked in the adjacent spaces, nor is there a single sign of life in any of them.

'What are you doing?' Jack asks, clearly bemused by my jack-in-the-box routine.

'My money says he never left this campsite yesterday,' I reply, as I leap up again. 'Maybe he was tipped off, or maybe he was lucky enough to be out when the police arrived but spotted them on his return and had to act fast. Both versions explain why all the bedding and food was left.'

Jack is now jumping to try and see into any of the other

properties, but most have the curtains drawn thus rendering his efforts fruitless.

'I would put money on him being inside one of these properties,' I continue. 'You've seen the locks are pretty flimsy. I'm sure it wouldn't be too difficult for an experienced burglar to get inside.'

'We could see what security footage the site has?' Jack suggests. 'Maybe we can trace him to a specific property.'

I shake my head. 'That'll take too long. Let's split up and try all the doors, looking for any sight or sound of movement inside. If you do find a resident, show them Amos's photograph and ask if they've seen him.' I stop. 'Can you find out what cars are registered to him? Maybe we'll spot that too?'

Jack places the call while I continue along the road, trying the doors but finding the first six all locked and seemingly empty. If only we had a team of searchers, this would be so much quicker. There must be at least a couple of hundred static homes on the site and there's no guarantee he'll still be in whichever one he targeted last night.

Jack hurries after me. 'He has an old pickup truck registered in his name. Dark grey with an "07" licence plate. You keep going this way and I'll head to the next row. Let's work row by row, checking-in with one another when we get to the end of each before moving on.'

I nod my agreement, the adrenalin prickling my arms.

'Be careful, Emma. We don't know if he's armed, nor what he might do to Cassie if pressured. Okay? *Any* sign and you call me over. *Okay?* I've put in a call to the local force for some support but I don't know when they'll get here. In the meantime, we can make a start.'

Butterflies are playing havoc with my insides and I can't help picturing Anna as I move from one home to another. Was she held somewhere like this? It's almost the perfect place to hide out with an abducted child. Coming to a site like this, you make the choice to live amongst strangers. It's a place where unfamiliar children are not out of place. There must be at least a dozen such parks in and around Weymouth, but they were never included in the search for my sister. Maybe they should have been. Making a mental note to follow up on that with Anna's case officer, I move on to the final home in the row before jogging over to Jack.

'Any luck?'

He shakes his head. 'Not so far. Managed to find one couple and showed them photos of both Amos and Cassie, but they said they only arrived this morning so couldn't help.' He looks towards the next row. 'We should get a map of the site so we can mark off which properties we've checked, otherwise it's going to turn into a maze. Can you see if the reception desk has any?'

'Okay, I'll see what I can find,' I agree, heading back the way I've come in the direction of the large leisure centre.

Jack jogs on to the next row of homes and soon disappears from view. As we now know what vehicle Amos owns, it wouldn't hurt to check the site's security footage for similar vehicles. Perhaps I could ask whoever's on reception to check the camera feed from the security barrier for the last couple of days. If it's as quiet as the empty homes would suggest, there can't have been too many coming and going.

The building looms into view and as I turn the corner towards it, my eyes drift across the area immediately in front of me. Steam billows from the chimneys above the enclosed swimming pool area, and just beyond it, a child is squealing with delight as she descends the climbing frame slide in the small fenced playground. I freeze, straining my eyes to focus on that area but the girl disappears from sight.

Was that blonde hair?

Breaking into a run, I move closer to the fenced-off playground but I stay out of sight, scanning all the equipment for any further glimpse of that blonde hair. I'm sure I didn't imagine it…

A hundred yards from the fence, I see her again and quickly duck behind the corner of the building before peering out an inch.

There's a grey-haired figure in a faded leather jacket and jeans sitting on a bench just inside the fence. There's the girl again, this time thrusting herself onto the hanging swing, pushing off, and gliding through the air without a care in the world.

From where I'm crouching, it's impossible to know for sure, but my heart is racing quicker than I've ever felt it.

I *have* to know.

I don't stop to call out for Jack. Instead, lurching forwards, I charge at the playground, eyes darting from the figure in black to the giddy child and back again, trying desperately to confirm it's her. It's so hard to see through the thick wire fence and climbing equipment.

'Cassie!' I yell, and in that moment the little girl's head snaps round and she looks straight at me.

And then I know.

Chapter Forty-Six

NOW

Torquay, Devon

She looks at me, then back to the figure on the bench. He hasn't moved but he looks poised to run at any second. Arriving at the gate to the playground, my eyes race over the immediate area, ensuring that this is the only way in and out. He could scale the fence, but not with Cassie in tow. To all intents and purposes, he's trapped.

This is where it ends, one way or another.

The gate's hinges squawk as I push it open and then it clatters against the wire fence. The girl has stopped pumping her legs but is still perched on the swing's seat. She looks so different to the picture I've seen countless times in the last week. Her hair is Rapunzel-like, as if it hasn't been cut in the last twelve months and her skin is less golden than I recall, presumably from months spent locked in a cellar. But as I look into her eyes, I'm positive I'm staring into the face of Cassie

Hilliard. Her mother had a similar haunted look when we met at The Priory.

'Everything's going to be okay,' I say, but my attempt at reassurance is barely more than a whisper. I need her to know that she can trust me, that the nightmare is over.

I could call out to Jack, but I doubt he'd hear me, and I'm certain that if I take my eyes off Amos he's sure to bolt. My phone is in my zipped coat pocket, but I'll need to take off my gloves to unlock it and dial Jack's number.

Stepping into the playground, I hold my hands out passively towards the girl and the man on the bench just beyond her. I don't want either to react suddenly to my presence here, but I'm totally out of my depth. If Amos makes a move on the girl, I have no way of stopping him as he's closer to her than I am to either of them.

'Cassie?' I try again, and she looks back to me at the mention of her name. 'My name is Emma. I've come to take you home. Okay?'

The terror in her eyes is unexpected. I've pictured the joy and relief she would show at being rescued but there is disappointment there too. It's the face of a child at a party whose parents have come to collect her from her friend's house. God only knows what he's told her to ensure her compliance. I think of what Freddie Mitchell and the others had to endure from their abusers – years of lies and threats until the will to fight back had diminished.

The man in the leather jacket stands and I freeze. 'Wait, no,' I say, the words evaporating in the condensation that plumes from my mouth. 'Stay where you are, Hank. We know all about what's gone on in the last year. Don't make things any worse for yourself. The police are here so there's no point in you trying to escape. Stay where you are.'

His hand drops to his side and then reaches into his pocket. My eyes widen as I wait for what he's about to pull out... a knife? A gun? Why didn't I fetch Jack before coming in so unprepared?

Amos's hand emerges and I choke on my own breath. And then I feel relief when he removes a cigarette from the packet and lights it, the end glowing orange as he inhales deeply. He isn't running. He isn't fighting. He's just standing there.

Cassie looks as though she might cry and slips off the edge of the seat. Keeping her eyes on mine, she sidesteps towards her captor.

'No, Cassie,' I say, willing my legs not to fail me as anxiety floods my body. 'Come to me, not him.'

She shakes her head. Her pout is heart-breaking but still she moves closer to him.

I stumble forwards, my feet moving as though they're trapped in treacle. She's maybe three metres from me, but only one from him. My hands are extended as far as possible but I'm not within touching distance. And then I stop dead as Cassie intertwines her fingers with Amos's and stands by his side.

I've read about Stockholm Syndrome, where victims of abuse bond positively with their abuser. The look of disdain gripping Cassie's features suggests that I am the threat to her, rather than the man to whom she's clinging now.

The gate clatters into the fence as Jack tears into the playground, skidding to a halt beside me. 'Don't move, Amos,' he snaps, scanning the scene, assessing the risk.

Amos stays stock still, save for the hand applying the cigarette to his lips.

'Are you okay, Cassie? My name is Jack and I'm a police officer. I've come to take you home.'

She cowers behind the arm she's hanging from. I can't blame her for being so wary of the two of us. If Amos is all she's known for a year, why would she trust two total strangers claiming to be her saviours?

It's a stalemate unless we can get closer to Cassie. But just as I'm starting to edge my feet forwards, Amos flicks away what remains of his cigarette and lowers himself to his knees. He turns Cassie to face him as Jack and I watch on. She is totally compliant.

'We spoke about this day, didn't we, my little canary?' he says tenderly, no malice in his gravelly voice.

The phrase triggers an alarm in my head. Denton said Amos's code word for Cassie was *canary*.

She nods glumly, before wiping her eyes with the back of her hand as the tears threaten to spill.

'We said there would be a day when you would have to spread your wings and leave me behind. It's the best thing for you, I promise.'

She shakes her head, and when she speaks her voice is barely audible. 'I don't want you to go, Uncle Hank.'

He wipes the tear from her cheek with his thumb, offering her an empathetic smile as he does. 'I wish I didn't have to go, but it's time. You need a proper life, rather than being on the run all the time. You need school, and friends, and parties, and fun.'

'Why can't you come with me?'

'I'm not allowed. I've… I've done some bad things in my

time and I need to pay the penalty for those things. I know it's hard for you to understand, but it's right.' He pauses and looks at the two of us. 'This nice man and woman will take you back to your mum and dad and you'll soon forget all about me and the fun adventure we've had. It'll be better for you this way. You'll always be my little canary.'

She throws her arms around his neck, resting her head on his shoulder.

Jack begins to move forward but I throw out my arm, holding him back. 'Give them a second,' I say, realising that Hank is no threat to her. Whatever has happened between these two over the last year, both will benefit from proper closure. Looking at the way he's handling her emotions, I'm tempted to hope their relationship has been nothing more than child and paternal guardian.

Oh God, please make it so.

'There's a good girl,' Amos says, as he attempts to break the embrace. 'It has been my honour to know you, Cassie. You have brought more laughter than I ever found in my life before and I will never forget you.'

She is sobbing as he peels her away and nods for Jack and me to come forward and take her from him.

I drop to Cassie's level and offer my most welcoming and open smile. 'My name is Emma,' I whisper again, uncertain what else to say. It feels false to tell her everything will be okay now. Her future will mean countless hours in therapy, additional school tutoring to catch her up on what she's missed, plus countless questions and emotional checks. This poor child has been through more than any of us will ever know or truly understand but there is so much more still ahead for her.

'I'll come quietly,' Amos says, looking up at Jack. 'It's time to stop running. I'm too old and you're certainly in better shape than me. Wouldn't be a fair race.'

'I'll caution you back at the car,' Jack says quietly, 'but you'd be best keeping shtum until then. Okay? Let's not make this any harder on her than necessary.'

Jack helps Hank back to his feet, but rather than applying handcuffs he walks him to the police car with a hand on his shoulder, as if they are just old friends going for a chat. I know Jack has done this for Cassie's benefit, as he doesn't want her enduring impression of the police to be of people who spoil adventures.

Cassie and I follow close behind, my hand draped around her shoulders, offering false assurances about the future. Jack calls for a van to collect the prisoner, as well as paramedics to check Cassie over. They arrive in a flurry of activity but I remain at Cassie's side throughout. When she's not crying, she's silent and despondent. When the paramedics ask her questions about whether she's in any pain, her response is to ask what is happening to 'Uncle Hank'. She is confused and bewildered by all these new faces, faces belonging to people she doesn't know, but who seem to know her. It must be so overwhelming and I desperately want to take her away from it all and get her back to Elizabeth and Fitzhume as quickly as I can, but she needs to be checked over. Her treatment will last years but it needs to start now.

Jack joins us when Amos has been handed over and escorted to the local police station where he will be held until a decision is taken over who will interview him, as well as where. The paramedics tell us that they want to take Cassie into hospital for a thorough examination, but at this point they are not concerned about her physical health. Although there is little colour in her cheeks, she isn't gaunt or malnourished.

I insist on travelling in the ambulance with her and ask Jack to make contact with Fitzhume and share the news. They need to know that Cassie is safe and well, but she is my priority until she's ready to be released back into their care.

She's been through so much. I will not add to her pain.

Chapter Forty-Seven

NOW

Torquay, Devon

Hours have passed since we discovered Cassie and Hank Amos at the park. I haven't let her out of my sight since. Although she is not my responsibility, I feel it's my place to protect her until Fitzhume and her parents arrive. She hasn't said much, and it's clear from her small outbursts of tears and stuttered breathing that she's somewhat overwhelmed by all the attention.

I almost cried myself when the specialist doctor and nurse told us there was no evidence of any physical abuse. Although she is under the national BMI for her height and age, there doesn't appear to be any lasting physical damage. But it still isn't right that he took and held on to her for so long, keeping her prisoner when he knew her family were out there waiting and hoping for news. That's the part I don't think I'll ever understand: why keep her for so long? If it was in an effort to extract money from the family, why didn't he? And if that wasn't the reason, what other possible explanation was there? My mind is blank.

'Here,' Jack says, as I meet him at the door to Cassie's private room, 'I thought you could do with some caffeine and sustenance.' He hands me a steaming paper cup of coffee and a Twix. 'Sorry,' he adds, 'it was the best I could find at the vending machine.'

I gratefully accept and turn to take another look at Cassie who is finally sleeping peacefully. Stepping out of the room, I close the door behind me so our talk won't wake her.

'Any news on her family?' I ask, opening the wrapper and offering one of the sticks to Jack.

He shakes his head gently. 'Thanks, but I had one on my way back here. In terms of news, Lord Fitzhume is being driven here by his chauffeur as we speak. I don't think he quite believed me when I said we'd found her. Correction, *you'd* found her.'

I frown at him. 'It was a team effort. It was only by chance that I was headed to the reception block. It could just as easily have been you.'

'But if you hadn't insisted I drive you back to the site—'

I hold my hand up to interrupt him. The last thing I need is anyone else blowing smoke up my arse. 'We found her together, Jack, and I won't hear anything more on the subject. That's what the book will say, so you'd better start getting used to strangers stopping *you* in the street and asking for your autograph.'

'So you're definitely going to write it then?'

I think back to the original meeting with Maddie at the hotel in Weymouth. 'My agent said the publisher was already keen on the idea and now, with this result, I can't see them changing their minds. I'm not sure how good it'll be without an ending.'

'What do you mean? The missing child saved from her abductor is the perfect ending, no?'

I shake my head. 'We still don't know who was behind the abduction to begin with. Gjoni might have been the ringleader, but Denton told us that Gjoni was hired by someone to target Cassie and her family in the first place. We still don't know who that figure in the shadows is. Nor do we know who attacked Denton in prison.'

'It could have been bluster on Denton's part. A sinister figure lurking in the background gives him an excuse for not coming clean sooner. I wouldn't place too much faith in such a story. Gjoni or Denton could easily have come up with the plan. Everyone knows the family is worth a bob or two; Fitzhume appears in the Forbes rich list on an annual basis. It wouldn't have been too difficult for one of them to see his name and face on the list, learn he has a granddaughter of school age, and go from there. It's not the most outlandish of theories. There doesn't always have to be a big conspiracy.'

'What about the gang of men Violet Belvedere mentioned?'

'Maybe that was the Albanians again, or maybe they're totally unrelated to Cassie Hilliard. It wouldn't surprise me if there's a long line of people Hank Amos has pissed off down the years.'

Jack looks over my shoulder and stares at Cassie for a long moment. I see a shadow fall across his face. I forget he has a daughter of his own and how emotionally invested he must have become in finding Cassie once we started.

'Are you okay?' I ask.

He forces a smile as he focuses back on my face. 'Yeah, fine. Tired, but fine.'

'When are you next due to see Mila again?'

'Not until Friday,' he replies sadly.

I rub his arm. 'I'm sure her mum wouldn't mind if you called in on your way home just to give her a cuddle. Would she?'

His eyes are watering. 'I was hoping the same thing.' He pauses. 'I'd like to introduce you to her one day. Would that be weird?'

My instant reaction is *yes, it would be very weird to introduce a total stranger to your daughter*. I bite my tongue instead.

'I think it's important she has strong role models in her life,' Jack continues, 'and if she develops even half the resilience, determination, and integrity that you display every waking minute, then I know she'll be okay to look after herself in this world when I'm no longer around.'

The heat rushes to my face. 'I'm really not that strong a role model for children. I live on my own. Some days I stay in my PJs all day because I'm too focused on writing to get dressed. I've been known to eat cereal straight from the box with a glass of milk on standby to wash it down. I average fewer than seven fruit and vegetables in a week, let alone a day, and sometimes I cry myself to sleep when I think of my sister out in the world with no way of reaching her. Is that really the sort of person you want your daughter growing into?'

He chortles at this. 'If she does then she'll have inherited more of her father's traits than I realised.' He pauses again. 'Why do you do that? Why do you constantly put yourself down?'

The heat isn't leaving my cheeks any time soon. 'I'm just a realist,' I say.

'No, it's more than that; I've only known you a few days, Emma, but I'd say you have absolutely no idea just how brilliant you are. What you think of as flaws, I see as endearing nuance. I don't know *any* adult who hasn't spent a whole day in their PJs. And, quite frankly, if anyone hasn't eaten cereal straight from the box at least once, there's something not right about them. You don't give yourself enough credit. You're a number one bestselling author. How many other people can say that?'

'There have been thousands of bestselling authors down the years. It really isn't—'

'There you go again,' he interrupts. 'I don't know a single other person who's written a bestselling book that exposed historic abuse at a children's home *and* who singlehandedly located a vulnerable child who the world believed was dead.'

His stare lingers for longer than I'm comfortable with but breaks at the sound of a cane thumping on the floor tiles nearby. Moments later, Fitzhume emerges, rushing as quickly as his ageing body will allow. He pauses momentarily to nod graciously at the two of us, his eyes already tearing up, before he bursts into the room and smothers his granddaughter in tearful kisses.

I well up too, but close the door to allow them the privacy they deserve. The driver, Hobbs, joins Jack and me at the door, and I can see he's trying to keep the emotion out of his face.

'Thank you,' he mouths at the two of us.

Jack puts an arm on his shoulders. 'Are you okay? You look like you could do with a seat.'

Hobbs nods and allows Jack to escort him to a row of three

plastic chairs just along the wall. I join the two of them, satisfied that my role as Cassie's guardian is complete.

'You arrested the man behind the abduction?' Hobbs asks, when he's composed himself again.

Jack nods. 'Red-handed, though he didn't make any attempt to escape when we found them together. An initial interview has been undertaken by the local police, and from what I understand, he's not hiding behind a solicitor or "No comment" interview. He reckons he didn't know what the job was that he was hired to do until they struck the Range Rover and grabbed her. He says he wasn't happy, and argued with Gjoni – the ringleader – about returning her, but Gjoni wouldn't listen, paid Amos off and sent him on his way. It was only days later that Gjoni then reached out again and said he needed help exchanging Cassie, and so Amos was at the abattoir when the van exploded.

'He caught up with Cassie in the maze of tunnels and told her she could either come with him or die alone in the dark. She had little choice. He used some of the money from Gjoni's stash to buy a second-hand mobile home and they lived in that for six weeks until he felt the pressure was off, and then he took her back to his house where she lived in a locked basement for three months until she knew no better. He told her she was in danger and that her parents couldn't keep her safe, which is why he'd been entrusted with her safety. Like most victims of abuse, she learned to fall in line. He's adamant he never struck or interfered with her sexually, but has acknowledged he used threatening behaviour to keep her subdued. Eventually he came to look upon her as a favourite niece and she took to calling him Uncle Hank.'

I wince as the hot coffee scalds my lips. 'Where are Cassie's parents?' I ask Hobbs.

'His Lordship has spoken with Elizabeth and she was overcome with relief, but he thought it best if she takes a day or so to get herself back into a fit state before she comes out of the hospital. She's going to need all her strength to resume maternal duties but we have no doubt she will come back better and stronger.'

'And Richard?' I ask, blowing on the surface of the hot drink.

'I don't know if he's been informed. His Lordship and Mr Hilliard aren't on speaking terms so I don't think he is in any hurry to alleviate Mr Hilliard's guilt at what unfolded at that abattoir.'

This feels unnecessarily harsh, particularly given Denton's admission that the Albanians' interference was instigated by Gjoni, and not by Richard as everyone had assumed.

'But he is *going* to tell him at some point, right?' I question.

Hobbs shrugs. 'It isn't my place to comment, Miss Hunter. His Lordship knows what he's doing and for now I think he'd rather keep matters private with just Elizabeth and Cassie. The family has been through so much and don't need outside influences clouding matters.'

I'm not so willing to let this go. I saw how upset Richard was when talking about Cassie's disappearance. Whether they're on speaking terms or not, Cassie's father deserves to know his daughter is alive and well, and Cassie deserves the chance to be reunited with her father. To rob her of that is criminal.

'I'll phone him myself,' I say.

Hobbs fixes me with a disappointed look. 'With all due

respect, Miss Hunter, you don't know the family as well as I do. I beg you not to interfere. Things are not always as they seem at first glance.'

'He *deserves* to know.'

Hobbs glares at me. 'It's none of your business, *Miss Hunter*. You've done your job in bringing little Cassie home to us. If you ask me, extracting Richard from Elizabeth's life was the best two million pounds his Lordship ever spent.'

'That will do, Hobbs,' Fitzhume says from the door to Cassie's room. 'Would you both leave us, so I may talk to Miss Hunter alone?'

Jack and Hobbs stand and move away as if they are being remote controlled. Fitzhume struggles to make it to the chair beside me, almost falling into it.

'I don't think I'll ever be able to put into words just how grateful I am to you, Miss Hunter. When we first met a week ago, I wasn't convinced you believed me when I told you Cassie hadn't died in that appalling explosion, but you are a woman of your word, and you have delivered what I knew you capable of. I will be forever in your debt.'

He stops to cough and when he pulls the handkerchief from his mouth, I see a patch of red.

'How are *you* doing, Lord Fitzhume?'

He pats my leg reassuringly. 'I am the luckiest man alive. I have had a long and interesting life, and now I get to spend my remaining days watching my daughter and granddaughter rebuild their lives. And I have you to thank for that.' He coughs again and this time keeps the bloody handkerchief out of my view. 'I too am a man of my word. My solicitor has drawn up the paperwork for the charitable trust to support the families of missing children. The Anna Hunter Foundation will be in place as soon as you and the other appointed trustee sign the paperwork.'

'Other trustee?' I enquire.

'Charitable foundations typically require at least two trustees who oversee the management and administration of matters. I thought the other should be someone with a similarly vested interest in seeing justice for such families. I reached out to your friend Rachel Leeming and she wholeheartedly agreed. I hope that's okay?'

'Thank you,' I say, choking back my urge to hug him.

'You are very welcome. I am sure you will do an admirable job in supporting families in a similar position to ours.' He glances back over his shoulder at Cassie's room. 'If you'll excuse me, Miss Hunter, I can't bear to spend another second away from my granddaughter.'

Chapter Forty-Eight

NOW

Chalfont St Giles

The old manor looks livelier than the last time I was here. The long expanse of gravel outside the property can hardly be seen, such is the number of cars and media vans abandoned there. Inside, a string orchestra is playing uplifting songs from West End stage shows to welcome guests as they arrive on the red carpet that stretches from just outside the door to the grand entrance and beyond. Additional staff have been brought in for this most special of occasions. A woman dressed head-to-toe in regency attire offers me a silver tray piled with tall flutes of fizz and I accept one, grimacing as I taste the bitter brut.

'There you are,' Maddie coos from just over my shoulder as she emerges from the grand bathroom suite which is clearly signposted for guests. 'When your next movie deal comes in you ought to think about buying somewhere like this,' she adds, eyes wide. 'It almost feels like we've stepped back in time. Incredible isn't it?'

No expense has been spared for this grand event. For someone who was so adamant about not courting the media's attention when Cassie was abducted, Fitzhume has clearly had a change of heart. There are representatives from all the major news outlets, including the BBC, Sky, and I'm pretty sure I saw someone wearing an 'Al-Jazeera News' identity badge.

A large 'Welcome Home' banner has been hung from one side of the grand entrance to the other in aid of Cassie and Elizabeth. They were officially reunited on Thursday, from what I've been told, but the media relations professional that the family hired to coordinate events recommended a grand moment to be captured by all the television cameras of the world.

'It's a story of triumph over adversity, of a family reunited, and an enduring message that sometimes good can overcome evil.'

Those were her words when I was introduced to the media relations person on Tuesday. She thinks I'm the perfect person to tell such a story, and I have now been formally commissioned to share the details of the case. My publisher couldn't be happier. Maddie reckons this book could have even greater success than *Monsters Under the Bed,* and for once that is music to my ears – not the success part, but the fact that people will finally start associating my name with a happier story. It will be nice to be introduced as the woman who reunited a family, rather than the one who outed the historic abuse at the St Francis Home for Wayward Boys.

'It really is quite the home,' I respond to Maddie's earlier question. 'Must be a nightmare to keep clean though. I much prefer my poky studio flat in Weymouth.'

She thinks I don't see her eyes roll but it's okay because I've come to accept that we won't always be on the same page about everything. Maddie's role in my life is to look after the best interests of my career, and that means I don't have to worry about those kinds of details. I don't know where I'd be without her now.

'They probably have a team of hired help; people who can afford places like this always do.'

I almost laugh as I picture Rosa the housekeeper and Hobbs the driver undertaking their cavalcade of duties. Not exactly a crack team, but I don't correct Maddie's hyperbole.

'What are you two on about?' Rachel asks, passing me a second flute of champagne and clinking her own glass against it.

'We were talking about Emma buying a new place closer to London,' Maddie responds, before excusing herself and hurrying after some actor she's interested in representing.

'Seriously?' Rachel asks, her eyes widening in excited anticipation.

This is all I need. I'm sure Maddie and Rachel have hatched a plan to keep nagging me about moving to London in the hope that one day I cave in and agree. They don't realise how stubborn I can be about my home though.

'No,' I say, trying to let her down gently, 'she's just stirring again.'

'It wouldn't be a bad idea though, would it? I don't mean uprooting from Weymouth for good, but surely your own flat in London where you can crash when you have to come to the city for meetings and promotional work... You know how much you hate staying in hotels because the beds and sheets are never as comfortable as home. If you had your own flat, with all the home comforts you've personally chosen, wouldn't that be better? Like a home from home.'

I can't deny there is some merit in that idea, though it would feel like I'm wasting money renting two homes and funding two landlords' mortgages.

'I'll think about it,' I say, and although she looks glum with this response, I really will consider the idea.

'I'm glad you invited me today,' she continues, deliberately changing the subject. 'It was nice to finally meet the benefactor of your sister's charitable foundation. I was flattered when he asked me to be co-trustee with you. I know it'll be a fair amount of work, and I don't mind doing my share, but I'll have to balance it with the day job.'

'I'm pleased he asked you too. I don't even know where to begin with it all, so at least we're going into it blind together.'

'We'll figure it out. It might be best to hold off on an official launch until this new book is ready. We could tie in the foundation's launch with all the publicity Maddie will line up for publication day. Kill two birds with one stone. What do you think?'

I nod, grateful that she agreed to come as my guest. I was certain Fitzhume was planning some grand gesture to make me the centre of attention and I didn't want to face that alone. He hasn't done anything yet but he has a speech planned for 2pm, shortly after Cassie and Elizabeth are due to arrive in a horse-drawn glass carriage. Very OTT, but the media outlets will lap it up.

'What's all that commotion?' Rachel asks, looking over my shoulder at the main entrance where I can hear raised voices.

Turning, it's impossible to see through the throng of people now gathering at the door and nearby windows.

'Come on,' Rachel says, grabbing my arm and tugging me away, the champagne almost spilling from the two flutes.

'Hold on, hold on,' I reply, wrenching my arm free and placing the flutes on the staircase she's now haring up. We turn left at the top and follow the long bend around to the front of the house where we can look down on whatever scuffle has unfolded below.

Richard Hilliard, dressed in a black suit and tie with a white shirt, is barely able to walk in a straight line as he slurs insults at the house and all inside.

'Jush wanna shee my daughter,' he shouts. 'Cassie? Cassie? Itsh Daddy.'

I haven't seen nor heard from Richard since meeting him that day in Kensington almost two weeks ago when I was hungover and he was snorting lines of coke from his table top. He told me at the time that his life had spiralled after what happened at the abattoir, and I would have thought that hearing she is alive and well would have seen an improvement in him, but if anything he looks worse off than before.

Fitzhume and Hobbs have now appeared in front of Richard and although I can't hear what's being said, Richard doesn't respond well to it, shouting even louder.

'You bashtard. You can't keep me from my daughter. I want to shee her.'

I remember what Hobbs said at the hospital about how Fitzhume would personally oversee any reunions between Cassie and her parents and I hate that it doesn't surprise me that he has deliberately kept Richard from seeing Cassie.

'Jeez, look at the state of him,' Rachel comments. 'With

everything his daughter has been through you'd have thought he'd have shown some decorum on today of all days.'

I don't reply, picturing Richard Hilliard slowly going out of his mind on whatever substances he's been consuming to deal with his inability to see Cassie. If ever there was a cry for help, this is it.

I freeze as Richard suddenly looks up and our eyes meet. I've seen that haunted look before… in the eyes of my father the day he was found hanging in Portland. My impulse is to shy away from the window but it's too late; he knows I'm here. Everyone else has been falling over themselves to praise and thank me for locating Cassie, but Richard is the first person who almost looks disappointed that she has found her way back to this monolithic house.

He waves his arm dismissively in our general direction before turning and stumbling away from the house. Hobbs hurries after him, taking his weight and leading him to Fitzhume's Bentley.

Fitzhume is wearing a churlish grin when he turns back to face the gathered throng. 'Obviously got started early. He'll be fine in a few hours. Come on, we best head inside before the special guests arrive.'

Opening his arms, he encourages them back into the building and I hear his voice boom from downstairs, demanding more champagne. I remain where I am, watching the Bentley pulling down the drive, Richard Hilliard's haunted expression still at the forefront of my mind.

'We'd better go and take our places,' Rachel comments, pointing at her watch. 'They'll be here in a minute.'

'You go,' I say, still staring out of the window as a hundred dots begin to join in my mind.

'Are you all right?' she asks, concern growing on her face.

'I'll be fine,' I reply, not quite believing the direction my imagination is taking me in, but clinging on to see how it plays out.

I don't know how long I remain alone at the window, but I gasp at a deep cough from behind me.

'The upstairs is out of bounds to… oh, it's you, Miss Hunter,' Fitzhume says, leaning precariously on his cane. 'I'm sure we can make an exception for you. Are you enjoying the party?'

I slowly turn to face him, nausea not far from my throat. 'Why isn't Richard welcome here?'

He frowns at the question before moving off in the direction of a set of hand-carved oak doors. 'Cassie needs people around her that she can rely on right now. She's been through a very traumatic experience.'

'I'd have thought any girl would benefit from *more* loving parents than fewer.'

He pauses, but keeps his back to me. 'That's a rather simplistic attitude in my opinion, and I'll ask you not to interfere in matters you don't fully understand.' He continues shuffling towards the doors.

'An operation so carefully planned… to threaten the sanctity of their marriage, and result in the safe return of your granddaughter and the expulsion of Richard from her and Elizabeth's lives… You must be very proud of yourself.'

He stops again but his head dips slightly, and I can sense the anger growing as his voice deepens. 'I don't know what you're implying, Miss Hunter, but you will have to excuse me while I take my medication. Please return to the party, and we can talk about the finer points of the charitable foundation in a few days.'

Was that a threat? I'm not so easily intimidated. Standing up to Arthur Turgood, Geoffrey Arnsgill, and Timothy MacDonald – Freddie Mitchell's abusers from St Francis's – taught me that bullies are at their weakest when you threaten their view of the world.

'Where did you meet Gjoni?' I challenge. 'He was ex-military, and from what Rachel told me, you had a stint in the army before taking on more secretive operations for Queen and country. Did you work with him directly, or were you introduced by a friend of a friend?'

He hasn't moved.

'And then Leroy Denton told me that Gjoni had a rich backer who was providing inside information, finances, and threats to ensure the mission was undertaken successfully… For a time, I wondered whether it might have been Hobbs – jealous of your relationship with the woman he sees as his own daughter – but I couldn't work out how he would connect to Gjoni. See, the thing that's disturbed me most since you first told me about your granddaughter's disappearance is the *why*. Why was she targeted? And why would they demand the ransom in cash? In this day and age, most kidnappers would prefer an electronic deposit of funds, transferred overseas to run the trail cold. The only reason I can see that the gang would demand cash would be to expose themselves to law enforcement. With all his tactical proficiency, Gjoni never would have planned it that way… unless someone else was pulling the strings. So what was the plan? The gang escapes with the money, but the Albanians lead the police to Richard's door, and when he fails to pay back the loan, you cripple his business, and send him packing?'

I've now caught up with Fitzhume and I can see he's struggling to contain his fury. His breathing is laboured, and his face has taken on an unhealthy red hue. I'm expecting him to yell for security at any moment, to scoff in denial.

I'm not expecting his next words.

'You will never prove any of that.'

Richard's haunted look and the terror in Cassie's eyes when I told her I had come to bring her home... Why didn't I see it before?

'So you admit you were the one who set all this up? You put your granddaughter's life at risk in order to force Richard out of your family?'

His head rolls so that his glare burns into me. 'Her life should never have been in any danger. They were paid enough to take good care of her. How dare you look at me like that! Do you know how hard I've worked to provide a life for my daughter and granddaughter? You have no idea the things I've done in the name of this country to keep people like you safe in your beds at night. This world is a wicked and evil place, and it is only by squashing out cockroaches like Richard Hilliard that good, decent people can go on with their lives.'

I silently curse myself for not setting my phone to record.

'Elizabeth was always such a poor judge of character. She took after her mother in that way. I forbade her from marrying Richard but she ignored me and sired his offspring. If it wasn't for my love for Cassie, I'd have had Richard taken out of the picture for good but I couldn't bear to see her grieve for him. Better that she looks at him with disdain than grieve him as some kind of martyr. That fool Amos hid her from me for months, but I knew you could unravel the knot, Miss Hunter. Now he'll rot in jail with Denton and the rest is silence.'

He straightens and takes a tentative step towards the oak doors.

'You dare print a word of this and I will have you brought up on charges of libellous defamation. You will be ruined, and for what? All's well that ends well. Cassie is back home where she belongs, and she will be the enduring light that keeps Elizabeth on the road to recovery. I will be in the grave in a matter of months, so I will never see the inside of a prison. Don't waste your time, nor your sister's legacy, over an honest effort at providing a safe future for my family.'

He opens and closes the doors on me and I'm left at a loss for what to do. There are reams of journalists gathered only yards away, but I can't make a statement without further evidence. I also can't just sit on this news. I have to tell someone. Right now.

Spinning on my heel, I run towards the staircase, searching for Maddie or Rachel. As I arrive at the bottom, my eyes fall on Jack.

'Jack, thank God, I need to speak to you,' I say, hurrying over to him and putting my arms around his shoulders.

He remains still.

'What's wrong?' I ask, sensing he's bearing a greater weight than my news.

'Can we go outside for a minute?' he asks quietly, barely able to meet my concerned stare.

I allow him to lead me out and he takes me along the driveway to where his squad car is waiting, away from all the other parked cars.

'Jack? What's going on?' I ask when he finally stops.

He's staring down at his feet when he speaks. 'Do you remember I said I would take a look at your sister's case history?'

My pulse quickens. 'Yes.'

'We have all kinds of new software – facial recognition, and… that sort of thing. So I ran Anna's face through one of those pieces and I got a hit. Another case where her face appeared and was logged.'

All thoughts of Fitzhume's confession vanish from my mind. 'Where, Jack? What are you saying? Have you *found* her?'

He shakes his head solemnly. 'No, not exactly. Her face – or at least a face that is a ninety-two per cent match – appeared in footage recovered from a hard drive in another case.'

I can't bear to think of where this is headed, but I also can't stop myself asking, 'Which case?'

He looks away, summoning the courage to tell me what I already fear. 'They were on the hard drive confiscated at the home of Arthur Turgood. I'm so sorry, Emma. I haven't watched the video – I couldn't bring myself to – but from what I understand, it isn't easy viewing.'

My knees give way and I drop to the hard gravel, not even noticing as the sharp stones rake at my legs.

Jack joins me on the ground rather than helping me back up. 'I've just come from HMP Stafford, the sex-offenders-only facility. I met Turgood to demand what he knows about your sister. He said he didn't recognise her name and that the videos on his hard drive were shared by men with similar proclivities to his own. He said he wouldn't be surprised to see the faces of a whole host of missing children appear in those clips. He said there's an entire network operating along the south coast. Your sister might just be the tip of an iceberg that stretches back decades.'

I swallow hard as my mind floods with images from my oldest, darkest nightmares, and for the first time in twenty years, I wish she'd died that day.

'I want to see Turgood,' I whisper.

Jack nods. 'I thought you'd say that. I've made an appointment and I won't rest until we find her.'

THE END

Emma Hunter will return in *Isolated*...

Acknowledgments

This is often the most challenging part of writing a book (after the dreaded synopsis, of course). That's because so many people contribute to a writer's work, whether directly or indirectly. When I think back to how this series developed, my first memory is of being camped in a hotel corridor at Disneyland, Paris in August 2019, while my wife, Hannah, was putting our children to sleep in our room. Sitting on an uncomfortably hard floor, with a plastic beaker of cheap white wine beside me, I started to think about all the things I'd discussed with my editors when we'd mooted the idea of developing a new series three months before. The key was to find a character who could develop over a series of books that would see her pursuing cases involving missing children, but without her being a police officer.

In those minutes in the corridor while I waited for my wife to join me, I would play out scenarios and ideas in my head, scribbling notes on a draft email in my phone, and trying to pre-empt the opportunities to add unexpected twists and turns to the plots. Over the course of that week of nights in the corridor, I scratched and scribbled until I'd shaped the outline of an 8-book series based heavily on themes that terrified me, but I felt would resonate with my readers. Had my wife not been so patient and understanding when she emerged from the room and found me guzzling wine and staring at my phone, who knows whether the series would have developed at all.

A month later, and my brilliant editorial team (here's looking at you Bethan Morgan, Kimberley Young, and Charlotte Ledger) had reviewed the pitches for all eight books, and provided valuable insight into how the series could be tightened, and the cast of characters fine-tuned to make them more realistic and relatable. The series was reduced to six books, focusing on two story arcs, and one overriding arc that would see our main protagonist Emma finally uncover the truth about her missing sister (you have so much more still to look forward to!).

And then I started writing the first book, getting to know Emma, Rachel, and Jack, finding out what makes them tick and how their lives were going to change over the course of the series. I know that probably sounds a bit cliché but I have to credit them too, as their voices have spoken to me (usually at the most inopportune moments when I should be doing other things), and encouraged me to tell their stories in the right way. Thanks should again come here to my wife, Hannah, who has continued to home school our two children while my free hours away from the day job have been spent hunched over our laptop reading and writing.

The feedback from my editors was so thrilling and encouraged the words of the remaining books to flow so easily.

The brilliant cover designer, Lucy Bennett, is next up for thanks and praise for conceptualising the entire series of covers based on those notes from that hotel corridor. As the series is released you'll see the brand concept developing and I hope you'll be as thrilled as I am with the output.

Thanks also to Lydia Mason, whose copy edit was relatively painless, and to Simon Fox, who kindly completed the proofread to pull out those all-embarrassing spelling mistakes. Finally, no book release is complete without the fervent effort of the marketing and publicity team, so big thanks to Melanie Price and Claire Fenby for all they've done to raise awareness of the series and encourage new readers to pick up the books.

So, in answer to that age-old question of 'How many people does it take to write a book?' there's your answer. Yes, *I* wrote the thing but couldn't have achieved such a well-rounded story without the back-up cast hidden in the wings. Of course there are those who indirectly contributed too, and I feel it only right to give them their minute in the spotlight as well:

Dr Parashar Ramanuj – my oldest and dearest friend, and the person I text in the middle of the night when I've thought of a plot twist that involves some gruesome method that only a medical expert could advise on.

Alex Shaw and Paul Grzegorzek – authors and dear friends who are happy to listen to me moan and whinge about the pitfalls of the publishing industry, offering words of encouragement along the way.

Mary Anne Yarde, who publicised an interview we did back in August to announce the arrival of this series.

Karen King, who has allowed me to pimp my books on her Tuesday Thriller Blog.

Rachel Gilbey, who organised the seven-day Blog Tour on my behalf, selling the merits of the concept to all who would listen and ensuring everything ran smoothly.

And final thanks must go to all my Facebook and Twitter followers, who regularly send me messages of encouragement and tell me how much they've enjoyed my books. There is no finer gift a reader can bestow than to tell the author how much they enjoyed a story, and the world (via a book review) to encourage others to give that book a chance.

I feel truly honoured to be able to call myself a writer, and it thrills me to know that other people are being entertained by the weird and wonderful visions my imagination creates. I love getting immersed in my imagination and the more people who read and enjoy my stories, the more I can do it, so thank YOU for reading *Ransomed*. Don't be afraid to reach out and let me know because YOUR message could be the one that brightens my day next.

Stephen

One More Chapter is an
award-winning global
division of HarperCollins.

Sign up to our newsletter to get our
latest eBook deals and stay up to date
with our weekly Book Club!
Subscribe here.

Meet the team at
www.onemorechapter.com

Follow us!

@OneMoreChapter_

@OneMoreChapter

@onemorechapterhc

Do you write unputdownable fiction?
We love to hear from new voices.
Find out how to submit your novel at
www.onemorechapter.com/submissions